Up Close

Henriette Gyland

W F HOWES LTD

This large print edition published in 2013 by
W F Howes Ltd
Unit 4, Rearsby Business Park, Gaddesby Lane,
Rearsby, Leicester LE7 4YH

1 3 5 7 9 10 8 6 4 2

First published in the United Kingdom in 2012
by Choc Lit Limited

A CIP catalogue record for this book is available
from the British Library

ISBN 978 1 47122 767 7

Typeset by Palimpsest Book Production Limited,
Falkirk, Stirlingshire
Printed and bound in Great Britain
by MPG Books Ltd, Bodmin, Cornwall

*Dedicated to British service men and women,
in conflicts everywhere, who selflessly put
their lives on the line.*

PROLOGUE

Through a pair of binoculars, the watcher saw the old lady's bedroom light come on. Her curtains were drawn, but when she stumbled out on to the landing, her white night-gown flapping around her like a ghostly shroud, she was clearly visible for a moment. Another light appeared, this time in the bathroom, and it stayed lit for ages.

Die, thought the watcher. *Why don't you just die?*

At last the woman fumbled her way back on to the landing, and a short sharp bark showed that the little Jack Russell she'd bought only a few weeks before was anxious about his mistress. She seemed not to notice and headed for the top of the stairs, swaying from side to side as if she were the worse for drink. As she disappeared from sight, the watcher ventured closer, leaving the binoculars to dangle from the branch of a tree.

Next, the light came on in the kitchen where the old lady doubled over, clutching her stomach as though being attacked by excruciating cramps.

Another grim smile. *I hope you suffer.*

The pain must have been severe, for her face

was twisted with the effort of staying on her feet, until she finally had to give in. Her cry of alarm could be heard through the single-glazed window, and she fell to her knees on the stone floor. Bemused, the watcher saw her retch violently. She was bringing nothing up, which meant she was clearly dehydrated.

Burn in Hell.

The old lady forced herself to get up again, but it was only temporary; a final, futile effort. She made it as far as the scullery, where she poured herself a glass of water direct from the tap.

The water never reached her lips. It sloshed down the front of her nightgown as her eyes met those of the watcher through the window. Her evident shock registered, and for one long moment they simply stared at each other, spellbound and frozen in time, as memories of their unwilling bond flashed through both minds.

Then shock gave way to determination, and as the dog barked and jumped up and down to gain attention, the woman steadied herself against the wall and made her way back to the main kitchen area, staggering, out of control. By the dresser she stopped, presumably to catch her breath, then suddenly brought her hands to her chest. Her mouth opened on a gasp, then she fell, almost in slow motion, knocking papers and a telephone directory off the dresser and hitting her head on the sharp corner. There was a moment's silence, then the little dog began to howl – a horrible, long drawn-out sound which sent shivers up the listener's spine.

The watcher's glee, so long in coming, was tinged with regret.

CHAPTER 1

Shadowy creatures from the deep swirl and eddy around her, clawing at her with their dead men's fingers and pulling her under. She wants to scream, but knows that if she opens her mouth, she will drown.

Panic seizes her as the water closes over her head. She makes one last-ditch attempt at reaching the surface, but she's miles under, and the pull is too strong.

Then, she's outside her body, seeing it all. The small legs thrashing wildly, kicking water everywhere, the scream muffled by water, the dark eyes – always so trusting – now wide, pleading, disbelieving. A lifetime passes.

Finally there is silence. Dead silence.

Her sleeves are wet. She stares at them because she can't remember how that happened. As she does so, she watches with mounting horror how the water from her clothes turns to mist and rises. It curls into liquid snakes that force their way down her throat and into her lungs, making her forget everything else.

Fighting the unspeakable pressure in her chest, she grasps for reality, but is sucked further below.

5

Air.
She must have air . . .

Lia Thompson woke, coughing and spluttering. The bedroom was dark and still, and for a moment she was completely disorientated. Then she remembered. Her grandmother's house and the unwanted legacy. She fumbled for her travel alarm clock with its luminous dials and knocked a bottle of pills down from the bedside cabinet.

'Oh, shit,' she muttered as the contents rained on to the wooden floor. The screw cap hadn't been put back on properly.

Five thirty in the morning. With a sigh she fell back on to the pillow, shivering. The tablets helped her sleep but there were side effects, the night sweats being the worst. Her pyjamas became soaked, and she woke up feeling cold. She shrugged out of her PJs, tugged at her dressing gown, which lay across the foot end of the double bed, and wrapped it around her. Then she huddled back under the covers.

Out of the blue she felt a rush of hysteria. She hated waking up to find herself alone. The world was so silent before the birds started to sing, as if everyone had decided to move to another planet and forgotten to wake her.

She stayed in bed for a while, letting the warmth creep back into her bones, then rose slowly and pottered over to the window. Flinging back the curtains, she stared out into the darkness. North

Norfolk was a far cry from Philadelphia, where she'd made her home for the past few years. There it was never really dark, and that was what had attracted her to the city in the first place.

That, and the fact it was a million miles from here.

In this isolated part of Norfolk the elements ruled unchallenged, and in the dead of winter it was still pitch black at this hour in the morning. Through the single glazing she could hear the North Sea, a continuous, distant roar, and she thought of the fishermen who would be out there, in an hour or so, eking out a living. She pictured them struggling to haul in their nets, gripping chains and tackles with their frozen fingers, while water sprayed over the side of the boat and made the deck slippery and treacherous.

And beneath the plunging waves Hell was waiting.

Closing her eyes, she blocked out the image. It was too much like her dreams.

What am I doing here? she thought for the umpteenth time, but the answer was simple.

When her grandmother had died, the task had fallen on Lia to sort out legal matters. Her mother, Connie, refused to have anything to do with it and even declared that she didn't want a penny from the estate.

It puzzled Lia. Connie earned very little and the money would enable her to retire in comfort when that day came, but grief made people do and say the strangest things. She'd hoped it was just talk, but after two weeks her mother remained immovable.

Sighing, she rubbed her eyes. When she'd stumbled into bed last night she'd been no closer to finding a solution to her problem. It didn't help that she was still jet-lagged from her flight two days ago.

I don't want any of it either!

She picked up as many of the tablets as she could find and headed for the bathroom across the landing. As she reached for her toothbrush, she caught a glimpse of herself in the mirror. A dark shadow rose from the bath behind her. With a scream Lia swung around, her heart thumping wildly in her chest.

There was nothing there.

Relief was followed by an overwhelming urge to cry. This was where . . . no, she wouldn't think about that now. Resolutely she turned her back on the bath and brushed her teeth so hard she drew blood.

'Coffee,' she said to her reflection when she dared face the mirror again. 'That's what you need.'

Putting on a pair of woollen socks, she went downstairs. The stair carpet was frayed, and she picked her way carefully to avoid catching her toes in the weave.

Everywhere was evidence of disuse. Dusty surfaces, yellowing paperbacks, long-dead thunderflies trapped inside picture frames. Only two

8

weeks since Ivy Barrington's death, yet the house looked as if it hadn't been lived in for months, apart from the kitchen and main bedroom. If her grandmother found it difficult to manage her home as she got older, why didn't she just say so?

Because Ivy was too proud. Guilt stole over Lia; she should have recognised the signs and done something to help the old lady without embarrassing her.

She made a pot of coffee, then sat down at the kitchen table next to an untidy heap of legal documents. Once again, Lia wished she didn't have to deal with all of this by herself.

Outside a dog barked. Lia glanced at the wall clock. Nearly six. A bit early for dog walking, she thought, but then again what did she know about this part of the world? She hadn't lived here in years.

She wrapped her hands around the mug for warmth. On her first day here her grandmother's Rayburn had played up, and because it was connected to the entire central heating system, the house was like a morgue. It was ironic, really, that she could understand the intricacies of a piece of high-tech medical equipment, yet she couldn't figure out how to work a simple oven.

The thought of work set her thinking of Brett and Philadelphia. Another world, another life. Bright lights, glass and polished steel; efficiency and progress. By now her fiancé would be on his way to bed, maybe watching the late news with a

9

brandy in his hand. She thought of the penthouse with its view of the Delaware River and longed to be there, right now, instead of in this cold and creaky old house with its dust and its memories.

The dog barked again, closer this time. Going to the scullery door to investigate, Lia found it locked. She slipped her hand behind her grandmother's Barbour jacket, which hung on a peg on the door, and lifted out an old-fashioned key. The door stuck, and she yanked it open. The sudden draught caused another to slam at the top of the house. Her heart gave a jolt.

Sodding house! Nothing bloody works, everything's falling to bits, and it gives me the creeps.

Outside, an old woman and a dog suddenly materialised from the darkness like a witch with her familiar. Lia recognised her as Mrs Larwood, her grandmother's closest neighbour, who lived in the flint cottage down the road.

'Good morning,' Lia said, wondering if it was normal to go visiting at six a.m.

'I've brought your dog,' said Mrs Larwood without preamble. 'His name is Jack.'

'What?' Lia stared at her.

Her eyes travelled from the woman's wizened face to the dog with something close to horror. He was a short-legged Jack Russell with a smooth coat and tan markings around his eyes. The dog stared back almost as if he knew something she didn't. A chill ran down her back.

'Ivy never said anything about a *dog*,' she

continued, aghast. 'She'd have told me if she'd bought one.'

'Well, she did, and you've inherited him.'

Mrs Larwood handed her the lead and brushed past her into the kitchen, where she deposited a plastic bag on the table, then fetched a mug and poured herself a coffee. Lia had to remind herself that around here people did things differently.

She tried to pull the dog into the house, but he remained stubbornly on the doorstep. 'Come *on*, you're letting all the heat out.'

Shivering, the dog put one tiny white paw in front of the other and crossed the threshold. Lia unhooked his lead, and he clattered past and over to the Rayburn, where he settled down on the jute rug in front of it.

If Mrs Larwood noticed Lia's irritation, she ignored it. Instead she stirred three spoonfuls of sugar into her coffee and said in her broad Norfolk burr, 'I found her, you know. Knocked her head, she had, on the corner of the dresser.' Tutting, she shook her head and grabbed Lia's arm with an age-spotted hand, forced from arthritis into the shape of a claw. It was remarkably strong despite its scrawniness. 'In a frightful mess, she was. Blood everywhere.'

'That's a bit too much information, actually,' Lia said, more to stop Mrs Larwood from going on than because she was squeamish. She saw blood every day in her job, after all. Freeing herself, she sat down and reached for her own coffee. As for blood everywhere, Lia took that with a pinch of salt. Ivy had died from a heart attack, so the coroner's report had said. True, she had hit her head as she fell, and head wounds bled, but you were more likely to bleed internally, into the brain. Anyway, the death certificate was unequivocal: it was the heart attack which killed her.

'So sad,' Mrs Larwood said. 'A woman in her prime.'

Lia hid a smile behind her mug. Ivy had been in her late seventies, but she supposed when you were as old as Mrs Larwood, who was ninety if she was a day, it was a matter of perspective.

Lia was used to sudden death, but it happened in other people's lives, not hers. Ivy had been a rock, a force to be reckoned with. For her to die like that had been almost an insult.

They hadn't been particularly close, but Ivy had always shown an interest in her, and had supported Lia when she decided to become a doctor.

'Go where the excitement is,' had been her advice; so Lia had dutifully uprooted herself and gone to the States, where she'd trained in Trauma, dealing with gunshot wounds and stabbing injuries. There she'd met an energetic young lawyer. Brett Melrose was pure-bred and Ivy League, with the right background and the right connections, and a rosy future lay mapped out in front of her, ready for her to seize it with both hands.

But the perfect life had sprung a leak in the form of uncertainty. Lia spent her time patching up the kind of people who received their injuries from the type Brett spent his time keeping out of prison. It seemed to Lia they were both engaged in a never-ending repair job from opposite sides of the fence without ever getting to the root of the problem.

Also, at the back of her mind was a nagging feeling that she'd left an important piece of herself behind in England. Something kept calling her back to North Norfolk, but she'd dithered, because sometimes it was easier to stick your head in the sand than to make decisions.

Then the dreams had started up again. Dreams of water and long pale fingers, dreams of death . . .

Mrs Larwood cleared her throat. 'Fit as a fiddle, she was, your gran. Always seen about the village, doing this and that. Then she got Jack here, to keep her busy. Was never without him.' She sighed and finished her coffee. 'Didn't think I'd outlive Ivy, not for a minute. Doesn't seem right, somehow.'

Lia merely nodded. If only the woman would leave, so she could collect her thoughts.

'And so upsetting for you to miss the funeral. Everyone was there, you know, at the church, and here afterwards.' She regarded Lia with a shrewd expression. 'Pressures of work, was it?'

Lia squirmed inside. 'We were short-staffed, I couldn't get away. I had to wait until I could take extended leave.' In fact, she'd persuaded herself there was no point in going through the ridiculous ritual of saying goodbye as society dictated. She wasn't going to feel any closer to her grandmother from sitting on a hard wooden bench and staring at a coffin, while everyone around her talked in hushed voices and cast her knowing glances when they thought she wasn't looking.

Mrs Larwood didn't appear convinced. With a last calculating glance at Lia she bent down to pat Jack's head. 'He's not so bad, you know. Has his little ways, but is very well behaved. Good guard dog, too. Grows on you.'

Lia looked at the pitiful creature on the jute rug. Not if I can help it, she thought. 'So, er, what does he eat, then? And when does he need to go for walks?'

Mrs Larwood straightened with difficulty. 'He'll tell you himself. I've left you a couple of tins of dog food and a packet of doggie treats, his bowls and some toys. Everything's in the bag.'

Lia had a quick rummage in the bag, then looked around her. 'There's no dog basket. Where does he sleep?'

'Ivy had him on her bed, I believe.'

Oh, no, thought Lia. *No way.* She was *not* sharing a bed with a dog.

'Looks like rain,' said Mrs Larwood. Pulling up the collar of her overcoat, she slipped outside and disappeared into the dim morning light.

Lia glared after her. When heavy droplets of rain began to fall, she had to laugh. 'I don't believe it!' she muttered. She prided herself on being quite capable of reading other people, yet somehow this crafty old woman had managed to outwit her. She returned to the kitchen, where Jack assessed her nervously. Cocking his head to one side, he raised his tan eyebrows.

There was that knowing look again.

Lia fast-forwarded through her dream earlier and its disturbing manifestations. She thought she'd put them behind her for good, but they'd returned with increased intensity after Ivy's death. She rarely shared them with anyone, yet this dog with his peculiar markings seemed to know exactly how she was feeling. Silly, of course, but his expression was so earnest she softened a little.

She fetched the dog food Mrs Larwood had brought and put some in a bowl with his name on it, then watched him munch contentedly.

Her grandmother hadn't been much for animals, barely tolerating other people's love for their pets. She'd never volunteered to dog-sit or feed someone else's rabbit during the holidays, and no animal had ever set foot in her house.

So what on earth had possessed her to buy a dog?

CHAPTER 2

Aidan Morrell parked his mud-splattered Honda four-wheel drive and killed the engine. He always left it behind a dense cluster of fir trees on the opposite side of a footpath which led to Holkham Beach, away from prying eyes. He took a moment or two to check today's tidal chart, then got out of the car and opened the boot.

When he was satisfied that his diving gear was all in order, he leaned against the tailgate and pulled his jumper over his head, stripped down to his boxer shorts, and dug a fleecy undersuit out of his bag. Frozen pine needles crunched under his bare feet, and a fresh breeze ruffled his thick brown hair, but he barely noticed. The cold never bothered him much.

Heavy, lead-coloured clouds held the promise of rain later on; the sea droned in the distance, and there was a sharp taste of brine in the air.

Perfect, he thought.

With an optimal tide and an on-shore wind, the conditions for winter diving were as good as they got. He felt a grin of pure joy spread across his features.

But his happiness was short-lived. As he pulled on the undersuit, the material caught on the puckered skin on his left thigh, and he winced. Against his will, his eyes were drawn to the livid scar, like a bystander part-revelling in and part-sickened by the carnage from a car accident. It always took him by surprise just how ugly it was. The scar, which covered the area from the top of his thigh to the knee, was several shades of pink. Crisscrossed with welts, he thought it resembled a fleshy version of an alien landscape.

Revulsion made him look away, but memories of how he got the scar continued to play in his mind like a series of stills. A warship in the Gulf, a stupid accident down in the ship's galley, where he wouldn't normally have gone. A storm blowing, creating high seas, the ship giving a lurch and then a tsunami of hot cooking oil from the deep fat fryer, which hadn't been properly secured. His leg, on fire, both literally and in terms of pain. He remembered the screams, which he later realised were his own, then passing out.

If only his mind could remain that blank, instead of reminding him every time he looked at himself. Reaching for his drysuit, he let the feel of the thick neoprene ground him in the present.

No, I refuse to think about it. It's over, done with.

His hands shook from suppressed emotion as he donned the suit and zipped it up, and he took a deep breath to force himself to return to the calm he'd enjoyed earlier, before the scar had reminded

17

him of the past. Diving in a heightened state of agitation was never a good idea. It affected a person's pulse and breathing, as well as judgement.

Besides, it was a long time ago.

Picking up his diving kit, snorkel, hood, and mask as well as a towel, he closed the boot, locked the car with his key fob and dropped the keys in a small waterproof container which hung from his weight belt. Then he headed to the beach.

The question of why Ivy had bought a dog came back to Lia as she nursed an unappetising bowl of cereal. For someone with no interest in animals it seemed irrational, not a word Lia would ever have used to describe her grandmother. Overbearing, yes. Perhaps a little eccentric, too, but not irrational.

She pushed her half-eaten cereal aside just as the dog polished off his own breakfast. In his eagerness to get to the last bit of food he pushed the bowl across the floor with his nose, scraping it against the tiles. Taking pity on him, Lia stuck her foot out to stop the bowl from wandering any further, and he hoovered up the remaining morsel in one big mouthful. He then licked his face with a floppy pink tongue, which was too impossibly long for a dog his size, and eyed her expectantly.

'What do you want now? Caviar?'

He gave a little whine and cocked his head.

'Sorry, but I don't speak dog language.' Lia carried her bowl through to the scullery and rinsed it in the sink.

Jack followed her, stuck his nose to the back door, sniffed, then whined again.

Lia glanced at the wall clock. It was gone seven. She longed for a shower, longed to wash the sleep out of her eyes as well as the memories of last night's dream.

'We're not going out now,' she said. 'I'm busy. I've got things to do, places to be.'

Yeah, like what?

The voice echoed inside her head, or maybe it came from somewhere else. She eyed the dog suspiciously. 'No,' she said, more firmly this time.

Jack's response was to trot back into the kitchen and lift his leg against the dresser.

'No!' In two strides she was across the room and had him by the collar before he'd managed to sprinkle her grandmother's prized possession. 'Don't even think about it.' The dog sent her a doleful look. 'Okay, okay, you win. You can piddle in the garden.'

She opened the back door for him, and obediently he headed for a flower bed at the end of the garden. Watching him in case he made a run for it, Lia sniffed the air, which was fresh after the rain, and decided to go for a jog.

When Jack had returned to the kitchen, she went upstairs to change into a tracksuit and pull her hair into a ponytail. On the bathroom shelf lay an old-fashioned metal comb with a few hairs in it, and if Lia stared hard enough, squinting her eyes nearly shut, she could almost see her grandmother

19

touching up her ice-blue perm. This was how Ivy Barrington had always brushed her hair as part of her morning toilette, and it was one of those little idiosyncrasies which made a person stay alive.

Another flash in the mirror, to do with water, a piercing shaft of insight, made Lia step back in alarm. Whatever it was, memory, vision, imagination, it lingered on the periphery of her mind like a bad smell. Then she pulled herself together. Her grandmother was dead, and Lia didn't believe in ghosts. Even if Ivy had come back to haunt the house, she meant no harm to her only grandchild. She finished tying back her hair and put her trainers on.

When she came back down, Jack was holding his lead in his mouth.

'All right, stand still,' she said and clipped the lead on to his collar. 'Maybe you're better brought up than I thought.'

And what am *I doing, talking to a dog? I don't even like them.*

Having locked the back door, she hid the keys underneath a flowerpot. The morning air was crisp, and her warm breath billowed out in puffs of steam. She pulled up the hood and set off for the lane leading to the main road, her rubbery soles squeaking against the crazy paving. Tugging at the lead impatiently, Jack dipped his nose to the ground here and there and lifted his head to catch an elusive scent. Lia unclipped the lead and watched him skitter ahead, delirious. She whistled for him, and he bounded back immediately.

'Good boy,' she said.

They ran along the quiet road for a while, their only company the kerbside trees, their trunks clad in ivy so that despite their winter nakedness they could maintain a degree of modesty. At a fork in the road she chose the left turning leading towards the beach. She'd gone the other way yesterday, to the village just to see if it looked the same as always. She hadn't met anyone, which suited her fine. She wasn't here to socialise and put down roots. Whatever roots she had in this godforsaken place, she was here to pull them up. Besides, Brett had money and came from a large family. He could buy her whatever roots she wanted or needed.

She glanced at Jack, who trotted along beside her with an impish grin on his two-tone face as if life was eternally fun-filled. She hadn't expected to inherit a dog and wondered what to do with him. She could find him a good home, but she hardly knew where to start. This was Ivy's village, and although she'd lived here for a while as a teenager and had visited once or twice in the last decade, she didn't know that many people herself. Mrs Larwood clearly had no intention of taking Jack. That left a rescue centre or, failing that, an injection. She frowned at the thought. It wasn't going to be easy.

The hedgerows of shaven beech trees started to thin and gave way to evergreens. When she came nearer to the beach, she noticed new pines had been planted since she was here last, and as she ran along the grassy kerb, avoiding the potholed track, she had to dodge a few tiny ones.

Jack sprinted up the bank and disappeared over the top. The bank was covered in prickly gorse and low, gnarly pine trees and served as a natural sea defence. Lia slowed down to walking pace. She had recently injured her knee during a game of squash and running uphill would put too much strain on the joint.

At the top she stopped to stretch her hamstrings. The North Sea was spread out in front of her like a smooth table hewn from slate, broken only by small ripples of foam in the distance. The sun had risen fully now, but it was unable to penetrate the heavy clouds, and the Earth was enveloped in a sheet of lead. Only Jack lit up like a white dot, a moving target in the surf.

The coast stretched away westwards on her left towards the Wash, and east to a spit named the Point. Beyond that was the town of Wells-next-the-Sea, but you couldn't see that from here until you reached the Point, which was where she'd planned to go.

She whistled for Jack. 'Come on. Let's see what you're made of.'

The dog let go of something he'd hauled up on the beach, seaweed or a dead animal, Lia didn't know, didn't care. She couldn't imagine what had possessed her grandmother to buy a dog after all these years without a pet. Loneliness, perhaps. Or had there been another reason?

But all Ivy had had to do was call. And Connie lived no further than the outskirts of Lowestoft. Lia shook her head and started to run. She would never know now, so why worry about it? There was enough to worry about already.

As she jogged, ice crystals in the sand crunched under her trainers. She knew she was being unfair. Ivy and Connie had a strained relationship; it would take a lot for Ivy to turn to her daughter. And Lia may as well have been on another planet.

When she'd met Brett, her move to the States became final. There everything was bigger and better. People talked more loudly, cars were bigger, guzzled more petrol, houses were more spacious and modern, distances more expansive, the sky higher, the weather conditions sometimes awesome. Even fat people were fatter. Worlds apart. It was easy to forget one's grandmother in windy old Norfolk.

Guilt gnawed at her as she ran faster. Running helped her to get away from all the things she didn't want to think about, didn't want to remember. Instead she forced herself to concentrate on the physical effects that the exercise had on her body; her breathing, the dull ache in her injured knee, her feet which made deep impressions in the sand. Mentally she tried to keep count of her strides. One thousand was about a mile. Jack kept up with her, obviously enjoying this new game, and she imagined it must be a welcome change from her grandmother's more sedate pace. They quickly covered the distance of more than a mile.

Panting, she flopped down on a timber groyne damp from the rain. Her clothes were wet too, both from the drizzle and from sweat. As she flapped her running top to cool down, another ghostly vision of her grandmother appeared in her mind's eye. The carefully powdered cheeks, the understated lipstick, and her sometimes prim pronouncements on the workings of the human body.

Women don't sweat, Ophelia. They glow.

The thought made her laugh quietly, but then a peculiar feeling of nostalgia set in, and she wiped her nose, dripping from sweat or rain or tears, on the back of her hand. Jack jumped up on to her lap, covering her in wet sand, and tried to lick her face. She pushed him down again and started back the way she had come.

'I don't need sympathy from a bloody dog!' she shouted. 'In fact, I don't need it at all. I'm in control. I'm cool.'

Ivy's death had come as a shock since despite her age, she'd always enjoyed good health. Naturally, it was always sad when people died, and there never was a 'right' time, and it *was* a shock because one didn't get up in the morning expecting something like this to happen.

But shock combined with jet-lag and the disorientation of her different surroundings was not enough to explain her underlying feeling that something was very wrong. It was as if her life had changed track without a clear indication exactly when this had taken place, and not being able to put her finger on it was extremely frustrating.

She ran faster, as if by running she could escape these confusing thoughts. She reached the trees by the path where she'd set out, sat down on the sand gasping for breath and in desperate need of water, but she hadn't brought any. Jack followed her, kicking up the sand with his hind legs, and sought out a small puddle of rainwater in the hollow of an old tree trunk. He lapped it up with loud slurps.

'Clever dog,' she said, as he sat down next to her looking as if he was game for more. Tentatively she caressed his ears. She hadn't really meant to touch him like this because it was easier to shove him away and relegate him to that growing pile of stuff she didn't want to deal with.

'You like that, don't you? You like having your ears scrumpled up like this, yeah?'

In response Jack put his head on her leg with a sigh and sent her a look of adoration. Something fell into place inside Lia. Whatever it was that felt so wrong, this, at least, was one thing she could make right.

Seagulls cawed and dipped in the sky, and a seal was bobbing up and down on the waves. A cool breeze rustled the needles on the row of fir trees behind her, and although Lia was beginning to feel the cold, she was too lazy to get up just yet. On this bleak stretch of coast she could be one with nature. Not at any old time, though. It had to be in that brief transition before the rest of the world woke up, before the headlights and the aeroplanes. It was like that now, and she'd forgotten how peaceful it could be. Jack seemed to sense it too.

The solitary seal was still cavorting in the water, this time closer to the shore. Lia hoped it wouldn't get too close, because she was sure Jack would see it as another plaything, and seals were known to be ferocious. Lia didn't fancy having to wrestle her dog out of its jaws. Now it was rising from the sea to its full length.

Rising . . .?

Standing up, she shielded her eyes with her hand. Seals didn't walk on two legs. Whatever was appearing from the sea was human.

The diver emerged, a black rubbery Triton, as dreamt up by Francis Bacon rather than Botticelli, complete with oxygen tank, neoprene suit, mask, and fins. He headed straight for where Lia was sitting, and a ridiculous impulse made her dip behind the fat trunk of a low pine tree in the hope that on this dull, grey morning her charcoal track-suit would be sufficient camouflage.

He didn't seem to have noticed her. Near where Jack had found rainwater to drink, he took off his mask and his hood, unstrapped the tank and leant it against the tree. He unzipped his suit by pulling at a long zipper which ran from his front on the right, across the back of his neck, and down to his chest on the left. Peeling the top half off, he let it dangle around his waist, then he bent down to pick up a towel which lay tucked behind the tree and began to dry his face and hair. Not once did he look in her direction.

She realised she was spying on him, which was completely out of character for her, but it did have certain advantages. She could watch him without worrying how her expression might be interpreted. Perhaps one should always look at other people like this, at first anyway, to see them as they really were and not how they wanted to present themselves.

'Hello, Ophelia,' he said suddenly, still without turning.

Lia wished for the ground to swallow her up. So he had seen her, after all, and he had noticed her hiding. How embarrassing. There was nothing for it but to come out from her hiding place, but she was hardly in a fit state to be seen. A V-shaped sweat stain had formed on her front, and there was a large sandy wet patch on her bum.

And how on earth did he know her name, let alone her real name? She'd forgotten how the sound of it could make her wince, and wondered briefly what had possessed her parents to call her that.

She stepped out from behind the tree, brushing the sand off her bum as best as she could. 'Excuse me, but do I know you?'

'Of course you do. Aidan Morrell. We were at sixth form college together.' He spoke with only a hint of Norfolk burr, several degrees removed

27

from Mrs Larwood's intonation, and held out a hand for her to shake. 'Down in Fakenham.'

She took his hand, expecting it to be cold and damp, but it was surprisingly warm. He must have good circulation, she thought, if he could maintain this kind of body heat after a dive in icy water. Then she wondered if the rest of him was just as warm and felt the blood rush to her cheeks. With a name like hers it was no surprise he remembered her, but she had no recollection of him at all.

'I'm afraid I don't remember. The time I spent there was passed in a bit of a daze.'

Laughing, he swung the towel over his shoulder. 'Just like the rest of us, then.'

As he stooped to pick up his gear, she couldn't help staring. His thick, curly brown hair, still wet, stood out in all directions instead of clinging unattractively to his skull and made him look like an animal shedding its winter coat. His arms and chest, with the remnants of a summer tan, were muscular, his hips slim, legs long, and he had a six-pack to die for. One word repeated itself over and over in Lia's mind as she tried to keep her cool.

Wow.

When he turned and their eyes met, Lia wished she had an excuse to look anywhere else. But there was only the sea and the sky and Jack at her feet, and even if she'd had the ability to make small talk about the weather or things like that, she wouldn't have been able to tear herself away. His eyes were a clear green, and behind them glinted the promise of something which made her swallow uncomfortably.

As she tried to figure out whether this promise was a warning to stay away from him, to leave well alone, she became aware that neither of them wanted to be the first to break the contact. A vague recognition stirred in her, but memory was such an unreliable companion that she couldn't be sure if she only remembered him because she wanted to.

She wanted to say something clever, maybe even glib, to break the spell and send her thoughts back where they belonged, but instead she blurted out, 'Don't you have a diving buddy? Isn't it rather dangerous to go out on your own?'

'It's not advisable,' he replied, 'not even for experienced divers like myself.'

'So, why are you doing it?'

He grinned. 'John, my buddy, is nursing a cold today; but don't worry, I was only in the shallows. You're quite right, though. Diving alone in the sea is pretty much frowned upon in the diving community. I expect I'll be drummed out if John finds out. Don't tell him, eh?'

'Sure.' Lia shrugged. It wasn't any of her business what Aidan did, and she didn't know this John character anyway.

Holding her gaze, he put down his diving equipment and moved towards her. Instinctively Lia took a step back, but he merely scooped Jack up in his arms. The unexpected attention made the dog lick his chin.

'I'm very sorry about your grandmother,' he said. 'She had some fine qualities.'

His measured compliment made Lia's throat constrict for the first time since receiving the news of Ivy's death. She looked to one side to blink away the tears she knew were expected of her, but which didn't quite come as easily as they should, and wondered if she appreciated his sympathy for the sake of it rather than because she needed it. At any rate she wiped her nose with her sleeve.

'Sorry.'

'It's all right, take your time.' Aidan patted Jack's head with his free hand. 'At least you've got this little fellow here.'

This made her laugh, because the whole Jack situation was just too ridiculous. 'Jack's a problem, actually. I never imagined inheriting a dog. Don't quite know what to do with him.'

'Couldn't you take him back to the States with you?'

Again he seemed to know more about her than she knew about him, and it was annoying. She wasn't going to take that one lying down. Who *was* he anyway? 'Hardly. I work long hours, and it wouldn't be fair.' She looked at Jack's upturned nose and the adoration in his intelligent eyes as he snuggled up to Aidan, and felt a stab of regret. However, it was short-lived. 'You don't know anyone who might want a dog, do you?'

'Not offhand, but I can ask around. He's rather appealing.'

This was exactly how Lia was beginning to feel, but letting herself get drawn in by energetic dogs or men with green eyes was a bad idea. She had to get back on track and find those last missing pieces of the puzzle. Regain her peace of mind. In the clear light of day she knew suddenly that those pieces waited for her somewhere along this deserted coastline.

Probably like stinging jellyfish.

'How about you?' she said. 'He seems to like you.'

Aidan opened his mouth to say something, but was drowned out by the ear-splitting noise from an aeroplane which shot across the sky from nowhere. They both jumped, and Lia looked up at the sky, but the cloud cover was too low for them to see what kind of plane it was.

Aidan didn't need to see it, he knew anyway. Living in Norfolk with air force bases dotted all over the countryside, he'd heard that particular engine noise a hundred times, and had even learned to distinguish between the various planes.

But unlike most people, for Aidan the sound brought back memories of war and loss, everything he just wanted to forget. The noise severed the easy camaraderie which had existed between himself and Lia up till then, and he put her dog down again. The silly creature grabbed hold of one of the sleeves on the drysuit he'd left dangling over a low branch, and tugged at it with a playful snarl.

'Tornado,' he explained when he'd freed the drysuit from the dog's sharp teeth.

'What?'

'It was a Tornado GR4. A fighter plane.'

Lia nodded, looking perplexed, and he smiled.

'They have them at RAF Marham.'

'You sound like a man who knows what he's talking about.'

'Oh, I do.'

'About Jack here,' she said, 'would you take him?'

Lia. Always to the point. No beating about the bush. He'd expected her to return for her grandmother's funeral, but when she didn't, he thought that he'd never see her again, like so many other people he'd gone to school with, although with more regret.

She hadn't changed much. She still wore her raven black hair long, with a severe fringe, and her pale complexion stood out in startling contrast. Dark rings, bordering on bruises, circled her blue eyes, but that was no surprise, really, with a death in the family. If she'd worn a studded jacket, smudgy black make-up and a safety pin in her nose, she could have been mistaken for a Goth, but she seemed far too straight-laced for that.

He'd dreamt of that face sometimes, over the years. Now she was here, after so long, and all she wanted was for him to take her stupid dog. He felt like saying no, just for the hell of it, but she looked so desperate, and the dog was rather cute, if a bit of a nuisance. Right now it was chewing on a piece of driftwood.

He decided to tell her the truth, or part of it anyway. 'It might complicate things.'

'What, have you got a hundred cats or something?'

He grinned. 'No, just the one. The cat isn't the problem, it's, er . . . how can I put it? I'm at a stage in my life where I'm tying up loose ends and eliminating problems, not adding to them.'

'You know, that's really mysterious and vague.'

He shrugged. 'Me in a nutshell.'

Crossing her arms, she cast him an irritated glance. 'Well, since you're so keen on eliminating problems, I need to find someone who knows how to operate a Rayburn. I came here two days ago, there's no heating, and the hot water supply is sporadic to say the least. The only thing I can get to work is the coal fire in the living room.'

'A Rayburn? I can help with that. When is a good time for you?'

'Now, actually.'

'*Now?*'

'I could do with a shower.'

She tugged at the front of her tracksuit, and only now did he notice the sweat stains. For some reason that made her seem human, even if she was more prickly than he remembered her. He assessed her for a second or two while trying to determine whether rejecting her dog meant that he owed her a favour in return, then made a quick decision, thinking he was probably going to regret it.

'Okay, then. I just need to get dried up and load this stuff in the car, but I can give you a lift if you'd like. Be quicker that way.'

He picked up his diving gear and walked ahead of her back to his car. He saw now that the way it was parked, half-hidden between the trees, seemed surreptitious somehow, and wondered if she'd thought the same when she'd gone down to the beach.

Maybe she hadn't noticed it at all.

He unlocked the door for Lia, who climbed in and slapped her thigh for the dog to follow, then he walked around to the back to change from his diving gear into a set of dry clothes. When their eyes met in the rear view mirror, he realised, with a jolt, that she was ogling him. Unashamedly.

Although the towel covered his scarred leg – he made sure of that – no one had looked at him like that in a long time. It made him feel absurdly pleased.

'Coffee?' Lia asked, holding up the kettle.

Aidan shook his head. He was kneeling on the kitchen floor, twiddling the knobs on the Rayburn, and wondering what the devil was wrong with the damn thing. 'How often do you use the oven?'

'I have no idea. The house has been empty for two weeks, but I suppose the neighbour must have kept it running, because it was warm when I arrived. Then it just packed up. I've been using the electric hob in the scullery, and the microwave.'

'I think that's the problem. The more you use a range cooker, the more reliable it is. This one's old, and they're the most temperamental.'

He rattled off a few simple instructions on how to keep the outdated equipment working at its most efficient, but she didn't seem to be listening. Instead she was staring at his hands, and he followed her eyes while he imagined what they looked like to her. His mother called them fisherman's hands, and they were certainly tanned and strong, but they were also nimble enough to hold a paintbrush.

What did Lia see? The hands of a painter or a fisherman? Or of a man trained to kill?

Probably best not to know, he thought when he noticed her shudder.

'Are you getting any of this?' he asked, masking his disappointment with irritation. 'Hel-lo?'

'Sorry.' She smiled. 'I was miles away.'

'Would it be easier if I wrote it down?'

'I think so.'

'In that case, maybe I'll have some of that coffee after all.'

As he tried to concentrate on the writing, he wondered about the sadness in her eyes. He suspected it had to do with more than the death of her grandmother, who'd had a good life. It made him want to get to know her better, although he doubted she'd be receptive to that idea.

35

At the same time she struck him as an interfering sort of person, a do-gooder even, and interference was the last thing he needed.

When he left, the sun was peeking out from behind the clouds, and he caught the look of recognition which crossed her pale face.

'I remember you now,' she called out as he was getting into the car. 'You used to sit at the back in your overcoat and draw pictures behind your school books.'

Grinning, he rolled down the window. 'I knew it would come to you in the end.' He saluted her as he'd learnt in the navy, with the side of his hand to his brow, palm downwards, got out his mobile and speed-dialled a number, then drove off with the phone glued to his ear. A sleepy voice answered.

'You'll never guess who's back,' he said.

Lia waved goodbye, but Aidan seemed to forget about her the moment he put the car into gear. She saw him put his mobile to his ear and say something with a smile.

Why's *he* getting a signal, and I'm not? she thought. Since she'd arrived back, her smartphone had been beyond useless, with no mobile signal and no internet connection because Ivy's house didn't have broadband. Brett had the number for the landline, but knowing him, he'd probably tried emailing her first, and it had never occurred to her to tell him this would be impossible. She'd have to get in touch with him herself.

Another thought crossed her mind, that driving while you were on the phone was both dangerous and illegal; but above all she had the overriding impression that this particular phone call had something to do with her.

She closed the door. Jack lay sleeping in front of the Rayburn, which was now warming up nicely, but he opened his eyes and cocked his ears when he sensed her looking at him. She ignored him and started tidying up, then opened the larder to put the cereal box back. Jack followed her, pushing his nose against her lower leg.

She tried to shoo him out, but he manoeuvred around her and stuck his head down in the narrow space between a small upright freezer and the wall. He whined when he got stuck, and Lia pulled him back.

'What did you have to go and do that for, you crazy mutt?'

Jack whined again, and Lia reached in to the gap and pulled out a paper bag as well as a mouse trap with the desiccated corpse of a mouse in it.

'Eurgh!'

Disgusted, she carried it to the bin and threw both mouse and trap away. Inside the bag were four neatly rinsed takeaway foil trays and a dated receipt which was stamped with The Goa, Indian Restaurant, followed by an address in Wells-next-the-Sea and a telephone number. It was such a thrifty post-war thing to do, to rinse out and save food trays, and so typical of her practical grandmother that it made

Lia smile for a moment. Unfortunately she was lumbered with the task of clearing out the house and had no need of the foil trays. She crammed them in the bin with the bag, but kept the receipt. A curry house on the doorstep might come in handy.

It wasn't until she carried the rubbish out to the wheelie bin that it struck Lia as odd. Ivy had been fond of spicy food, but she'd always been fiercely proud of her own home cooking, and Lia had never known her to order a takeaway. Perhaps she'd found cooking was getting a bit too much for her as she got older. Not for the first time, Lia felt a stab of guilt at the thought of her grandmother facing her old age alone.

CHAPTER 3

The last thing he wanted was someone else intruding on his life. But Lia was proving hard to forget.

When Aidan had tried, for the fifth time, to blend the exact grey of an underwater rockery and still could not get the colour just right, he threw down his palette knife in disgust.

'Sod it,' he mumbled and wiped the paint off his hands with a rag dipped in turpentine, then washed them in the small basin in his studio. There was only one thing for it.

He opened a large storage cupboard and reached for a folder on the top shelf. It was an old-fashioned artist's folder with a brown mock leather cover and fabric spine, thick with dust. Carefully he wiped it with his hand towel, then set it down on top of the plan chest he used for storing prints and watercolours.

He'd completely forgotten he had it until this morning; he'd just slung it in the cupboard when he took over the house, along with all his other art materials and bits and bobs.

The portraits were over fifteen years old, the paper

yellowed with age, and they were done mostly in pencil and ink pen, some hastily drawn as if the sitter was impatient or the artist in a hurry. Others were careful and more elaborate. Aidan had done them at sixth form college, and the subject was the same person each time.

Lia.

He'd had a massive crush on her when they were teenagers, but she was too aloof and he too shy to approach her, and that had been that. He'd settled for drawing her instead, from every possible angle: the back, the side, half hidden behind her hair, and, on a rare occasion, from the front.

He browsed through the folder, occasionally wincing at how much his skills had developed since art college. He felt mainly pride, despite the slightly amateurish style, because he'd managed to capture her various expressions. She'd looked sad even then. And furtive, as if she were carrying the crushing weight of a secret on her bony shoulders.

Of course, the latter had been his imagination running wild. When you can't get close to a person, you invent all kinds of things about them, he knew that.

He snapped the folder shut and returned it to the cupboard. It was a long time ago now, and besides, if he ever decided to show it to her, he'd have to explain why he'd drawn her so many times. How did you explain to someone that you used to have a crush on them, without sounding like an idiot?

She was bound to misunderstand and think that he was trying to pick up where he'd left off.

Things were different now. He'd been at a cross-roads so many times in his life, finding his way back was almost impossible. Being invalided out of the navy as no longer fit for active service had scarred him in more ways than one. The mental scars had healed, for the most part, but the idea of Lia looking at his injured leg, maybe even touching it, was one he refused to contemplate. He could imagine her revulsion all too easily.

Then there was that whole sorry business with his brother . . .

The meeting with Aidan stayed with Lia. Determined to get him out of her head, she'd called Brett to tell him about the dog and lack of mobile phone or internet service, but he was busy working on a case so they didn't talk long, and she was reluctant to disturb him again. She then spent three days moping around in the quiet house waiting for the solicitors to get back to her.

This is pathetic, she thought and made a snap decision. She'd reacquainted herself with the beach and Ivy's favourite walks, but there were only so many times she could trot the length of Holkham Bay to the inlet at Burnham Overy, or watch the changing tide. Hungry for company, she dropped in at Mrs Larwood's house.

Mrs Larwood showed her into a dingy room, which she called 'the parlour', and proceeded to ply Lia with weak tea and hard, shop-bought biscuits, while pumping her for information about her grandmother.

'I still don't understand,' said Mrs Larwood, 'her going like that. The picture of health, she was. Doctor Campbell said so himself last time I saw him.'

'Ivy's doctor?' Sipping her cooling tea, Lia was racking her brain for a suitable pretext to ask about Aidan. She'd confined her grandmother's death to a neat little compartment in her mind, and she didn't want to talk about it now.

'Been with him for over thirty years. Both of us have.' Mrs Larwood was saying. 'Now, my blood pressure was always a little on the high side, and Doctor Campbell usually takes me to task for that, he does. If anyone was in line for a heart attack, it would've been me, he said, not her.'

'It sometimes happens that way,' said Lia, thinking that the good doctor could learn a thing or two about patient confidentiality. Then again, perhaps there was no such thing with someone like Mrs Larwood around.

Mrs Larwood sighed, then sent her a look of such startling shrewdness, Lia was taken aback. 'Well, no point in me carrying on about that, now, is there? That's not why you're here. You want to know about young Aidan. Saw his car parked outside your house the other day, and thought you'd make a nice couple.'

Lia gaped. A busybody *and* a matchmaker?

'He was just helping me with the Rayburn . . .'

'Oh, yes? Hmm. You don't know him as I do. Injured in the Gulf, he was. So was . . . well, never mind. Here's the address. Used to be his parents' place, so I doubt as he'll be in the phone book, but he lives there on his own now.' A torn-off piece of paper with something scrawled on it was thrust into Lia's hand.

Before she had a chance to thank her for her hospitality, Lia found herself shunted outside again with Mrs Larwood's parting shot echoing in her head. 'Mind you treat him right.'

Infuriating woman.

Back at the house she hung around for another hour, undecided, while she fed Jack.

What was the worst that could happen? That Aidan was out? Or told her to go away? She could handle that.

In the larder she found a couple of bottles of wine, thick with dust, and a quick glance at the labels told her that they weren't your average plonk. She changed into her best T-shirt, a turquoise-blue stretch top with a deep V-neck, put on some make-up, and told Jack to behave.

Her grandmother's car, a very old hatchback, was parked in the garage, and after a couple of tries the engine spluttered protestingly to life. Lia spent a few minutes fiddling with the lighting controls and the unfamiliar heating system before setting off.

A hazy sun cast the last of its dim rays across the fields when she left the village, and she was glad she'd chosen the late afternoon to visit him. It wasn't too early in the day to open a bottle of wine, and if he turned out to be a teetotaller, it wasn't too late for a cup of tea, either. She only hoped he made a nicer brew than Mrs Larwood.

Aidan lived near Burnham Thorpe, six miles further inland. Getting no reception on her smartphone, she consulted a local Ordnance Survey map from the glove compartment and found the turning without any problems. The place was a typical Norfolk two-storey farmhouse, with a small courtyard and outbuildings on both sides. To the west the view further inland was partially obscured by four long, narrow greenhouses which lay end to end and next to the farmhouse opposite.

Lia hesitated. The farm was dark, except for a single light in the house, and had an air of disuse about it, though it wasn't exactly derelict.

Forlorn, perhaps, she thought as she made her way towards the green-painted front door. As if its inhabitants had packed their bags and left in the night without saying goodbye.

A single sheep bleated in the distance, and Lia felt her spine tingle. She cast a nervous glance over her shoulder, but there was nothing to see except the last light of day catching on the glass roofs of the greenhouses and setting them ablaze.

Another word sprang to mind. *Watchful*, that

44

was it. She felt as if the place was watching her, which was nonsense, of course.

She lifted her hand to knock on the door, but before she got the chance it was flung open, and Aidan stared out at her. His face was sullen, as if he wasn't in the mood for company, or had expected to see someone he didn't like. Lia stood her ground.

Since she'd met him on the beach, she'd revised her opinion about avoiding the locals. She'd never sorted out the estate of a deceased person before and had no idea how long it would take. If the last three days were anything to go by, she'd die of boredom. Or get lonely. And when you were lonely, you brooded, which was a Bad Thing. At least, that was how she justified seeking him out.

Curious now, she waited to see what his reaction would be.

Startled to find Lia on his doorstep when he'd just been thinking about her, Aidan stared at her while he tried to work out whether she was real or just a figment of his imagination.

'Will red do you?' she said, holding up a bottle of wine. 'Or I've got white in the car if you prefer.'

'What?'

'I wanted to say thank you, you know, for fixing my stove.'

Aidan realised he must be scowling when he saw the uncertainty creep into her eyes, and he forced himself to backtrack and start again. Hear knock, open door, smile – except she hadn't actually knocked, had she.

'I wasn't expecting anything back.' Touched by her gesture, he stepped aside to let her in. 'How did you know where I lived, anyway?'

Lia rubbed her hands against the cold and bent down to stroke a slinky tabby cat who brushed against her leg and marked her as his property. 'Bold as brass,' she said.

'Hmm. You or the cat?'

She laughed. 'Both of us, I suppose. I asked Mrs Larwood where to find you. It seemed like the safest bet.'

'Oh, yeah, the fount of all knowledge, she is. You'd better be careful what you tell that one, unless you want the world and his wife to know about it too.' He took the wine bottle from her. 'Red will be fine. You're welcome to share it with me. Through here.'

He led her into the sitting room to the left of the hallway. He was proud of this room. It was large, with sash windows overlooking the garden at the back of the house, and he'd furnished it with an eclectic mix of modern and traditional: dark brown leather sofa and matching chairs, a low Zen-style coffee table, bookcases made from Scandinavian ash, as well as a Persian rug and an old-fashioned wall clock with a rose pattern on the glass.

'What a nice room,' she said. 'Not quite what you'd expect from the outside. I was thinking more

46

cosy cottagey sort of feel. Flowered upholstery, frilly lampshades, that sort of thing.'

'We only met again a few days ago, and already you're prejudiced. My, my, I *am* in trouble.'

'Sorry.' She bit her lip. 'It's just that I haven't been back here in a long time.'

'No problem.' He indicated for her to sit. 'Make yourself at home, I'll just get us some glasses.'

He left her and went in search of glasses and a corkscrew. A lot of people thought as she did, that Norfolk was the back of beyond, and a place best forgotten once you'd left it. He'd felt the same once, when the rest of the world had beckoned, but he'd returned as if pulled by an invisible cord. He hadn't tried to rationalise it too much, just accepted it.

In the kitchen he opened the wine and dug inside a cupboard where he found two bog-standard wine glasses. Holding them up, it occurred to him that supermarket glasses didn't quite cut it, and he rummaged at the back of the cupboard for a pair of Bohemian crystal glasses he was sure his mother had left behind when she moved out.

The crystal glasses were dusty, but fortunately both in one piece, and he gave them a quick rinse under the hot tap and dried them on the cleanest tea towel he could find before returning to the living room.

Lia was perched carefully on the edge of an armchair. She didn't look as if she'd made herself at home exactly, but Aidan had to admire the economy in her quiet movements, like a blackbird on a high branch surveying everything around it without turning its head.

He wondered if she'd noticed his paintings. To most people they were just dark blobs, unrecognisable shapes. One woman he'd had a fling with about a year ago even commented that they made a nice contrast to the reds and ochres in the rug, and was that intentional, et cetera, et cetera.

'How long have you lived here?' she asked.

Aidan handed her a glass of wine. 'A couple of years. My parents used to own the farm – that is, my mother still owns half of it – but after my father died she moved away.'

'I'm sorry to hear that.'

'Oh, I'm not cut up about it. I never got on that well with my dad in the first place.' He took a large gulp of his wine. 'Miserable old sod. When we had that foot and mouth crisis, he took it personally, which didn't surprise anyone. Always moaning about his lot in life. And then a few years later he had to sell off all his dairy cows when milk prices made them uneconomic.' Aidan dropped down on the sofa and put his feet on the coffee table. 'I never imagined it'd be the end of him.'

'What happened?'

'He had a stroke. Wham, like that. Alive one day, dead the next.'

'It seems like everyone is dropping dead these days.'

Aidan took his feet off the table and leaned forward. 'Sorry, that was clumsy of me.'

Shaking her head, Lia twirled the stem of her glass. 'Don't worry about it. I couldn't help noticing the artwork. It's very, er, interesting.'

'That's one way of putting it.' He laughed. So she *had* noticed. It pleased him. 'My mother thinks they're ugly. She'd prefer it if I stuck to Monet-type landscapes, all cheery pinks and greens. The irony is, of course, that they are landscapes.'

'You did these?'

'Mm-hmm.'

'Is it okay if I take a closer look?'

He shrugged. 'Be my guest.'

Lia moved over to study the paintings and was silent for so long, he began to worry. She hates them, he thought. *Like everybody else.*

'I don't know much about art,' she said and turned to face him, 'so don't expect any comments on composition and all that, but I like the way you blend colour. I didn't know there were so many shades of grey, but I can see lilac and brown and blue as well.' On the largest of the paintings she traced the sickle-shaped contour of lighter grey with her finger. 'This is the Point, isn't it? Painted from that place by the footpath where we met the other day? It's almost like a black and white photo.'

'Well spotted.'

He rose to stand next to her and caught a trace of her perfume, something light and fruity, like melon. It suited her, and hinted at a softness beneath the briskness and the practical hair.

'Does anyone really *know* about art?' he said. 'Surely, it's about feelings rather than clever words. About what it does for us, how it moves us.' He took another sip of his wine. 'I believe everyone has a special take on the world, and you don't have to be an artist for that. Anyone who says so is full of shit. Pretentious. Like art critics who are so bloody up themselves you hope they brought a torch.'

Lia laughed. 'That's a very unfavourable view of art critics. I'm sure some of them can justify their big fat pay cheques.'

Not just softness, Aidan thought. There was humour there too. 'Yeah, some of them,' he said. 'So, do you like my work?'

She was quiet for a while, probably wondering how she could let him down nicely. He was used to it, he could take it. Even so, he'd hoped she'd be different.

'Your paintings remind me of something. Something inside me.'

'And that is?'

Her shrug was more of a shudder. 'I don't know, anger, perhaps. Sadness. Feeling insignificant in the big scheme of things, something along those lines. I couldn't say for sure.'

'So you *are* moved? Or maybe *you're* just pretentious.'

Lia smiled and punched him on the arm. 'Yes, I am moved, all right. Happy now?'

'Ecstatic.'

'So, tell me,' she said and turned her clear blue gaze on him, 'why do you see the world mainly in black and white?'

'I paint through goggles.'

'Diving goggles?' She raised her eyebrows.

Aidan nodded. 'Going back to Monet, of whom my mother is so fond, did you know that he had a cataract when he was in his eighties? Because of it, the tones in his work became muddier and darker, and when he'd had an operation on one of his eyes, he was literally so appalled by some of the work he'd done that he destroyed a lot of it.' He sighed. 'I'd have loved to see them. Imagine his famous water lilies without the pale blue.'

'It wouldn't be the same.'

'Exactly, and that's why I wear my goggles. They're my cataract, because what I see and the way I see it is not the same as the way another person will see it. The fact that it's goggles and not, say, rose-tinted glasses is just a device.'

Lia eyed him uncertainly. He'd never spoken to anyone before about his techniques because he was aware most people would think him a lunatic, and perhaps it needed to be elaborated.

'It's about what we see and don't see, what we choose to see or not. Our interpretations are often, if not always, selective. Does that sound crazy?'

Again that disconcerting bright-eyed look as if she could see right through him. To lighten the mood without being too obvious about it, he pointed to the other paintings arranged on the wall on either side of the one depicting the Point. They were smaller and painted in similar tones. 'So what do you think of these, then?'

'I don't recognise the place at all. It's not from around here. They're like eerie, alien landscapes.'

'Actually, it is. It's a seascape, from under water.'

'From under water?'

This time there was no doubt about it; she shuddered from head to toe, although she suppressed it quickly. Why? he wondered. They weren't that ugly.

'But how do you . . .?'

He laughed. 'I don't sit at the bottom of the sea with my easel and artist's palette. I take photographs when I go diving. With an underwater camera. Then I put my goggles on when I paint and see the photograph as I saw the real thing originally.'

'That's seriously far out; but having said that, I suppose it's the end result which matters. And that's very compelling.' Lia lifted her glass to her lips and drained the rest in one go. Aidan held out the bottle to pour her another, but she shook her head.

'I'm driving,' she explained.

'It's beautiful down there, you know,' he said and topped up his own glass instead. 'Peaceful and so full of life at the same time. A world free of interferences. The only sound you can hear is your own breathing.' He glanced at her and suddenly longed to push back a lock of her black hair which had escaped from her ponytail. Somehow it seemed synonymous with a part of her which was struggling to escape the tight control she had of herself. 'I could take you diving sometime, if you'd like.'

'I appreciate it, but I'm really not that good with the sea,' she said. 'The thought of having my head under water fills me with terror.'

'But you can swim?'

'I can swim.'

'Then you can learn to dive,' he said.

Lia decided to let the matter rest. It wouldn't take too long to clear out Ivy's house, and then she could put it on the market and stay at Connie's, if her mother would have her. She wouldn't be here long and could easily think up an excuse if Aidan should ask her again. Changing the subject, she pointed to a collection of photographs on the mantelpiece.

'Who are they?'

Aidan raised his eyebrows. 'What is this? *Twenty Questions?*'

'In my line of work you have to be nosy,' she said and wondered if he was going to ask her what she did for a living or whether he already knew. What else did he know?

Aidan pointed to a colour photo of a blonde woman crouching next to a beautiful little girl. 'Okay, this is Marcella and Niamh. My older sister and her daughter.'

'She's lovely.'

He nodded. 'She is. Sadly I don't see them much. They live in Liverpool. Marcella moved there soon as she was out of school. Doesn't get on with Mum, you see.' He pointed to another photo. 'This is a picture of my parents, before . . . well, some time ago, and these two' – he handed Lia an old sepia photo of a woman in a spotted dress, arm in arm with a British soldier – 'are my grandparents on their wedding day. I never knew them. I just keep it as a piece of social history.'

Lia thought of her grandmother's rinsed-out foil trays, another legacy of wartime Britain, and the closest she came to any social history in her own family. There were no photos on Ivy's mantelpiece, only a smattering of dusty china figurines. She returned the picture to the mantelpiece with a certain reverence.

'We don't have anything like that in my family.'

'You must have something somewhere.'

'Perhaps, but I've never bothered to look. We're not a family who dwell on the past. We were always forging ahead, and what went before, well, if it worked and had a function, it was allowed along on the journey; if it was broken or . . . or complex, it was best forgotten.'

She stopped. This was more than she'd meant to say. Aidan was watching her intently, and she felt a rush of adrenaline, a kick inside, when he smiled as if he knew her better than anyone else in the world. They'd shared a confidence, and for a moment she believed that virtual strangers could truly know each other, that they were capable of looking beyond words and seeing what no one else could. Then her thoughts turned to her fiancé, who was the safest thing in her life. *Brett* knew her. Of course he did.

Shrugging, she said, 'I don't know why I said that. I don't even know what it means.'

'I expect you said it because it's time to start looking.'

'Maybe it is.'

Looking at the dregs in her glass, it both amused and unnerved her that he had this ability to read her mind. She'd never felt quite so exposed before. Mentally backtracking, she refocused on the mantelpiece and picked up another photo, which was half-hidden behind some of the others. It was a colour picture of Aidan in uniform, which was no surprise as she remembered his goodbye salute the other day.

'I see you were in the army. When was that?'

Aidan slumped down on the leather sofa and took a large swig of wine. 'The navy, actually. That there is my older brother, not me. We're very alike. Outwardly, anyway.'

Sitting down on the footrest opposite him, Lia had an awful feeling that out of all her nosy questions, this was the worst one she could have asked. Aidan seemed to withdraw, his face closing down to an expressionless mask. At a loss for what to do, she tried to make conversation.

'I didn't know you had a brother, or a sister for that matter, but then again I never really knew much about you. So is he still in the army, then?'

'No,' he said, not meeting her eye, 'I'm afraid Gerald is . . . gone.'

Working in the trauma unit, Lia sometimes had to deal with bereaved relatives. She was trained to identify the needs both of those who showed their grief in a quiet, dignified manner and those who reacted with uncontrolled hysteria. With Aidan her training failed her. She'd never experienced being shut out like this. It was almost as if he hadn't wanted her to know. As if he was ashamed.

'God, I don't know what to say. I had no idea that . . .' she trailed off.

When Aidan failed to make polite noises and instead stared at his hands, she took the hint that not only did he not want to talk about it, he also wanted her to go. In hindsight it had been clear from the moment he opened the door that he hadn't wanted her company in the first place. Picking up her jacket, which she had slung over the back of the armchair, she rose, chewing her lip.

'Sorry, I shouldn't have come uninvited like this. You really look like you'd rather be alone.'

Aidan caught her sleeve. Startled, she looked down at his long, slender fingers flexing with strength and barely controlled emotion, then she met his eyes.

'It's okay, why don't you stay for dinner?' he

said. 'Neither of us has anywhere else to be, do we?'

Lia hesitated, then nodded. He was right, she wasn't exactly swamped with offers. It couldn't hurt to stay for a bit, surely.

CHAPTER 4

'Susannah lives around here now,' said Aidan. 'I expect your grandmother told you that.' He stirred the tomato sauce which bubbled slowly beside him, and savoured the tangy aromas of black olives and capers.

Lia was sitting at the old oak table in his kitchen looking far more at ease than she had in his living room. It couldn't possibly have anything to do with her surroundings, he decided. Disorganised at best, it was chock-a-block with books, newspapers, bits of diving gear, paperwork, iPod dock, brushes and paint, pet bowls, car head lamps, as well as a computer on a small table in one corner.

Enough to drive any house-proud person insane, but he liked the contrast: elegance and style in the living room, chaos where he spent most of his time.

'Susannah?' Lia glanced at him with a small frown.

'She was at sixth-form college with us. Lived on the far side of Fakenham, I think.'

'Yes, I remember,' she said. 'I just didn't know she'd moved here.'

'Your grandmother never said anything?'

Lia smiled. 'Ivy wasn't keen on Susannah. She was a bad influence, apparently.'

'I suppose she was a bit wild, driving that souped-up moped of hers.'

'And the rest of it. Bound to get respectable people's knickers in a twist.'

She laughed suddenly, and the whole room lit up. Aidan had a tremendous urge to give her a hug, but forced himself to hold back. Instead he strained the pasta and dressed it with the tomato sauce, then heaped it on to two plates. He put them on the table next to a hunk of Parmesan cheese on a plate and a grater.

'Weren't you two friends?' he asked.

'We were. We are,' she added, almost as an afterthought.

That was pretty much the same signal he'd received from Susannah when he'd mentioned that Lia was back. Something was going on here, but he was damned if he knew what it was. Maybe people just drifted apart.

Grating cheese over her food, Lia said, 'Mmm, this smells good. Does it have a name?'

'Pasta à la Morrell-i. I'll teach you how to make it sometime.'

Why did I say that? he thought when the tail lights from her car disappeared in the distance.

He didn't really want to get involved, with anyone, wasn't looking for a relationship of any

59

kind. He'd been down that route a few times, and it was more trouble than it was worth. She didn't want to get involved either, he was sure of it.

So what the hell are you doing, you numbnuts?

He'd practically invited her back with his MasterChef proposition. He could tell she was lonely, he would be too in her shoes, but he hadn't planned on making it his responsibility. Maybe it was those bright blue eyes and that nervous energy of hers which made him want to shake off the chains of his self-imposed isolation. Maybe he was just bored. He couldn't deny that he still found her attractive, perhaps even more so now they'd both grown up, and the thought of having sex with her was extremely appealing.

He shook his head. Bad idea.

Hopefully by rekindling her friendship with Susannah she'd find someone else to spend time with and let him get on with what he needed to do. There was so much she didn't know, and he wanted to keep it that way. It would definitely be better for her to stay ignorant of certain things.

He cleared up in the kitchen, then returned to his studio and the colour-blending problem he'd struggled with earlier in the week. With a sudden clear-sightedness he found that if he added a little ochre to the mix, he got the result he wanted.

The village shop Susannah owned with her husband was typical of numerous villages all over the country. Doubling as a sub post office and a local community hub, it sold a variety of goods as well as phone top-ups and similar services. Heavy condensation framed the posters in the window and the OPEN sign on the shop door. Outside, in a convenient lay-by, stood a post box, a red phone box, and a wooden bench with a planter beside it.

Lia could imagine the elderly villagers sitting on it, exchanging news and gossip. Her grandmother had probably sat on that bench, but not on a day like today.

It had started raining that morning, and though the worst of it had eased off, a steady drizzle persisted. Despite a fleece, jacket and waterproof boots, the cold sneaked under Lia's defences, gripping her as if it never wanted to let go.

The old-fashioned bell clanged as she pushed the shop door open. She thought of Aidan's certainty that she and Susannah were friends, but didn't share it. Right now it felt like walking into the lion's den.

She remembered the letter Susannah had sent her, after Ivy decided that it was best for her granddaughter's education if she boarded at Gresham's for the remainder of her A-levels. Shortly before, Susannah had become pregnant and dropped out before sitting her exams, and in the letter she'd accused Lia of abandoning her, saying that if Lia had stood by her, she'd have had the courage to continue.

In other words, it was Lia's fault Susannah didn't get her A-levels.

Of course, this didn't make sense to anyone, but for years the guilt had gnawed at her that she'd been too defensive to write back and insist they were still friends, that she'd ruined everything. She often wondered if Susannah had taken her exams later.

The shop was tidy with a small glass cubicle housing the post office, and brimming with produce. Canned soups and vegetables were stacked neatly to the edge of the shelves, and tube packets of biscuits lay on top of one another on the shelves without rolling off. Susannah evidently took pride in her presentation.

Nevertheless it was with some trepidation that Lia turned towards the woman behind the till.

'Ophelia. I heard you were back.'

The tone was friendly, the face gave nothing away other than the intention to please a customer, and Lia relaxed a little.

'I'm staying at Ivy's.'

'Of course, yes. It was very sad about Mrs Barrington.' Susannah clasped her hands together on the counter top, and it was then Lia noticed she was pregnant. She'd always been pretty, with sleek blond hair, but the pregnancy lent her a rosy-cheeked bloom, and although she'd filled out in other places, she still made Lia feel big and clumsy. All hands and legs.

'She was getting on,' Lia replied. 'It wasn't unexpected.'

'Still, she was a regular sight in the village. One of my best customers, too. She believed in supporting the local traders, unlike others around here.'

Lia smiled. 'She had her principles.'

'She came in here only the day before she died. With that dog of hers. What's it called again?'

'Jack.'

'That's right. Cute little thing,' she added, though she clearly didn't mean it. 'Anyway, she was looking rather peaky. Said she had some problems with her stomach. Heartburn or indigestion, I think. So I said to her, "Mrs Barrington, a woman your age should see a doctor, not buy over-the-counter remedies. You never know, it could be serious." But she wasn't having any of it.'

'I can imagine,' Lia remarked. The more she heard about Ivy's sudden illness, the more she felt she should have been there.

'Mind of her own, that one,' Susannah continued, then blushed as if she'd committed a terrible faux pas. Or maybe she just didn't want to lose a potential customer. 'I didn't mean to be rude or anything.'

'It was probably the curry she ate.'

Susannah frowned. 'Curry? She didn't buy it here.'

'No, she got it from some place down in Wells. The Goa. I was thinking of trying it out myself, though if it gave my grandmother indigestion, I don't suppose that's a great advertisement.' Lia laughed. 'Maybe I'll stick to spaghetti.'

She turned around in the shop to look for the

spaghetti. There were two unopened packets in the larder, but now she was here she had better buy something.

'Down there, on your right, next to the pasta sauce.' Susannah was all smiles again, and the defensiveness Lia had sensed in her was gone.

She found the spaghetti one shelf up from the bottom. It was stacked in exactly the same way as the biscuits, and when, without thinking, she took a packet from the bottom, the whole pile slid to the floor.

'For God's sake, be careful!' Susannah flared up. 'Spaghetti breaks easily.' She moved from behind the counter, a protective hand on her large belly, and knelt down with obvious difficulty to re-stack the packets. Her hand movements were as quick and practised as the rest of her seemed encumbered.

Next to her, tall and awkward, Lia teetered between admiration and being close to tears.

Susannah must have caught her look, or maybe customer care kicked in. She apologised. 'It's just that no one will buy them if they're broken.'

'I understand,' said Lia, wishing herself miles away.

'Listen, why don't you come in for a cuppa? Then we can talk about old times. I hear you have the most amazing job.'

Lia didn't want to talk about her job and certainly not about old times. For all her polish, Susannah still had an unpredictable streak. As a teenager she'd been rebellious, unconventional, fun, yet part of the attraction was that you never really knew where you were with her. Now, as she stood here with her shopkeeper's plastic smile, her unpredictability had turned to edginess, and Lia would be forever treading on eggshells.

But Aidan had said something about looking at the past to understand the present, and it had touched a chord with her. She straightened her spine surreptitiously. Susannah was part of that past. Perhaps it was time to face up to things, clear the air. Hiding away wouldn't help, that was for sure.

Swallowing a sigh, she said, 'Yeah, that'd be nice.'

Ten minutes later they were sipping hot, strong coffee in Susannah's kitchen with a packet of biscuits between them, full of broken bits. Another customer must have fallen foul of the stack 'em high trick, too.

'Sorry, it's not much,' said Susannah. 'It's hard to keep anything to myself in this house. If I buy a little treat and turn my back on it for just one minute, it's gone.'

'I wasn't expecting to be fed, so don't worry.'

The kitchen was light and airy, with doors leading to the hall, the staircase and the back of the shop. The units had been painted a calm sage green, the worktops were black slate, and the table and chairs, one with a plastic booster seat on top, were white like the walls. Next to the stainless steel cooker hood hung a large clock in a black frame, the kind one might see at a train station, and through the window to the garden at the back Lia could see the skeletal beginnings of a conservatory.

The stylish décor seemed out of character for the girl who had smoked behind the bike sheds and snogged any bloke she could get her hands on, but Lia supposed everyone grew up at some point.

Susannah kicked off her shoes. 'So tell me about your job.'

Lia's eyes dropped to Susannah's ankles, which were slightly swollen. 'Sorry, I couldn't help noticing your ankles. Are you all right with the pregnancy?'

'Fluid retention. Nothing for you to worry about.'

'Oedema is often the first sign of pre-eclampsia, but I expect you know that,' said Lia.

Susannah's eyes glinted dangerously, but her voice was level when she said, 'I do. This isn't my first pregnancy.' *As you well know.*

The words hung between them, and hot guilt welled up in Lia. 'I know. I just didn't know if you . . . if you kept the baby.'

'I did. She's fifteen. She's called Zoe, and she's a right madam.' Susannah smiled, and the mood passed. 'I also have a little boy, Ethan, who's four. He's with his grandparents today. But enough of me. I really want to hear about your job. I gather it's a bit like *ER*.'

'Alas, no George Clooney.'

'Oh, Glumsville.' Susannah made a face. 'How do you survive?'

'With difficulty.'

'And what's the name of your hospital again?'

'I'm at Penn U. Pennsylvania University Hospital.'

Susannah made an appreciative noise. 'Sounds glam. Your grandmother was always telling us about it. To anyone who bothered listening.'

Lia laughed. 'Ivy liked embellishing things. Sadly there's nothing glamorous about patching up people who've been shot or in an accident. All you can do is deal with it. You can't plan for it. And as for dishy doctors, well, when you've been working seventy-two-hour shifts and can barely keep your eyes open, the most attractive thing is your bed.'

Seeing Susannah's disappointment, she added, 'Having said that, I do enjoy seeing people get better. That's what it's all about for me.'

'But I hear you've found yourself a dishy barrister. I bet he isn't short of a bob or two.' Susannah looked suddenly sly, and Lia felt she was angling for something.

'They call them attorneys in the US,' she said to regain her ground. 'And, yes, he's doing all right.'

'Some people have all the luck.' Susannah sighed, but for once her comment seemed genuine and barb-free.

'You've not done so badly yourself.'

'I suppose not. Though I'll admit running a

village shop wasn't quite how I imagined my life would be. I wanted to do great things, something people would remember me by when I was gone. See the world, you know.'

'So why did you stay in Norfolk?'

'Nigel, my husband, is from Cley, and, well—'

She shrugged and looked at her hands. Lia noticed that her fingers were slightly swollen too, and that she didn't wear a wedding ring. Perhaps she'd taken it off when she became pregnant to prevent it from getting stuck. Lia was just about to ask her if she was having her blood pressure monitored regularly, when Susannah looked up again and caught her off guard with an expression of immeasurable sadness etched into her face.

'And what about you? Are you back for good, or are you just clearing out the house before taking off again?' It wasn't an accusation as such, and Lia understood that. It was just Susannah's usual blunt way of putting things.

'I don't know.' As soon as the words were out of her mouth, Lia knew it was the truth.

'We lead a very simple life here. This isn't glam.'

Before Lia could reply to that, they were interrupted by a loud knocking on the shop door. Susannah had flicked the sign to CLOSED earlier, but obviously the local clientele weren't that easily put off.

Brushing biscuit crumbs off her lap, Susannah rose. Lia took this as a sign that their conversation was over and followed her out. It was time to get back to Jack anyway.

A young woman rapped loudly on the glass, her outline blurred through the condensation on the window. When Susannah unlocked the door, she almost fell through the gap.

'What took you so long? I was getting soaked out there.'

Definitely not a customer, thought Lia. A customer would be politeness itself in a village this size. She looked at the girl, then back at Susannah, and the penny dropped. Susannah's daughter, the one she'd been pregnant with when Lia had left.

There was something else about her which seemed strangely familiar, but Lia couldn't put her finger on it.

With no concession to the weather, like a lot of teenagers Zoe wore shorts and black leggings, with skinny legs ending in a pair of caramel-coloured UGG boots. Her curly brown hair she'd arranged in a bun on top of her head, a Cath Kidston bag was casually slung over her shoulder, and in her hand she clutched a BlackBerry phone as if she planned to shoot someone with it.

So, your average teen, then, Lia thought; then reminded herself that appearances could be deceptive.

'Hi, are you the ER woman?' Zoe asked when she spotted Lia. It seemed abruptness ran in families.

'That'll be me.'

'Neat.' She brushed past them both and called over her shoulder to her mother. 'By the way, Mel's coming over later. She wants to copy my Lady Gaga downloads.'

'Fine,' said Susannah testily. 'When you and Mel have *hung out*, could you give me a hand in the shop as you promised, please?'

Zoe looked at her over her shoulder with the kind of cutting arrogance that was designed to slice a parent into little bits. 'I've got homework, haven't I?'

She disappeared at the back of the shop, and they could hear her heavy footsteps on the carpeted stairs.

'Teenagers,' said Susannah, but her shop smile had slipped.

Lia wanted to put her arm around her, but Susannah's posture didn't invite intimacy. Instead, Lia zipped up her jacket and stepped out of the shop just as two Humvees and an army truck drove through the village. Their heavy tyres hissed against the rain-washed street, and the tarpaulin covering the truck flapped angrily. The bow wave of the vehicles made the large shop window rattle.

'God, haven't they heard of the speed limit?' she said.

Standing in the doorway, Susannah followed Lia's gaze to where the red tail lights disappeared in the afternoon gloom. 'It's been happening a lot lately. Rumour has it they found some sort of explosive device at one of the military bases around here. It's been high alert ever since.'

It was hardly surprising to find the military on high alert in the current climate of international politics, thought Lia, but surely there wasn't much here worth blowing up.

'Do they have any idea who's behind it?'

Susannah shuddered visibly and hugged herself tighter. 'Oh, the local media have been accusing the usual suspects. The Real IRA, Muslim extremists, even Fathers 4 Justice. I don't think they have a clue.'

'Probably just some lunatic, then.'

Lia had expected her comment to elicit some kind of response from Susannah: further speculation, perhaps, or at least a non-committal grunt of agreement; but what she got, when she turned to her friend, was a look of pure hatred.

CHAPTER 5

Susannah hid her look so quickly Lia almost thought she'd imagined it. Still, it bothered her.

What did I do, she thought, for her to feel that way about me?

The answer was nothing.

The rain had turned icy by the time she returned. Before she'd even inserted the key in the lock, Jack was going bananas, skittering from scullery door to front door and barking so furiously that visitors could be forgiven for thinking he was a huge monster rather than a tiny terrier.

When she opened the door, another banged shut at the top of the house. The glacial charge which surged through her was brief. There was no one upstairs. Neither ghost nor burglar. Doors slamming inexplicably was what happened in old houses, and she was sure that if there had been a resident ghost, it would be a benevolent one. She felt no malice here, merely an air of sadness and regret.

Jack whimpered with puppyish delight, jumping up and down and snapping at her jacket sleeves.

Lia sighed and tried to bury the guilt that welled up inside her. She still hadn't resolved what to do with him. She'd meant to ask Susannah, but there hadn't been a right moment, and then there was that icy, hard-eyed stare which had unnerved her.

Shuddering, she pushed aside the feeling that somehow she ought to know why Susannah would look at her like that.

'Steady on,' she said, as she rescued her jacket from Jack. It was a soft black goatskin number, slightly punkish, with a zip at the front and a tie belt just above the waistline, and if she paired it with black trousers, the cut made her long legs seem endless. She had bought it at Macy's a year ago when she and Brett had taken a trip to visit some of his relatives in New York.

Jack didn't seem to appreciate the finer points of designer clothes, and instead went to sit on the doormat, with his nose to the small crack between the door and the door frame. He sniffed keenly and sent Lia a look which she'd learnt meant 'walkies'.

'Not now. I've only just got back.' Hanging up the jacket, she decided that she'd have to get herself something warmer and more substantial if she was to survive the Norfolk winter.

Jack whined, and she took pity on him. 'All right, you win. Again.'

Instead of her leather jacket, she put on her grandmother's old Barbour, still hanging from the scullery door. It was a waxed mud brown with a dark brown corduroy collar and tartan wool lining, and it smelt faintly of the lavender water Ivy used to wear.

Norfolk lavender for a Norfolk girl.

She heard her grandmother's words clearly, and wasn't sure whether she'd said them herself, or whether she just remembered them being said.

Completing the outfit with a waxed hat, also brown like the Norfolk dirt and with a fabric flower attached to the hatband, she tucked her long black hair inside the collar. Ready to brave the elements, she stuffed Jack's lead in her pocket.

It was getting darker now, as if nature had twiddled a dimmer switch during those few minutes Lia had spent indoors. Jack led the way, shining a dull yellow under the sodium light from the few scattered street lamps; tall, emaciated sentinels guarding the entrance to the village.

Soon civilisation was behind them, and they were heading to the beach along a different footpath from the one she'd taken the day that she'd met Aidan. The path was deserted. The wind which had whipped the rain against Susannah's shop windows and soaked Zoe to the skin had died down, and the only sound was rainwater dripping from the trees on to the rotting leaves on the ground. There were no signs of any animals, neither birds nor rabbits. Not even a nocturnal fox.

There was a sense of expectation in the air, almost as if nature was holding its breath. An oppressive quiet before the storm. An uneasy peace before Thor, the god of thunder, swung his mighty hammer.

Or something like that.

Lia smiled at the bizarre turn her thoughts had taken, but she couldn't shake off the feeling that an enormous weight rested on her shoulders. Jack seemed to sense her mood, staying close to her legs for a while. Then he stuck his nose to the ground, following a zig-zag trail across the path, and sped off.

She climbed the gorse-covered bank that acted as a natural sea wall, and her mood shifted. The sea lay spread in front of her, vast and lonely, glowing a silver grey. It promised freedom to those who dared sail across it and revelations to those who looked beneath the surface. You could travel anywhere on the sea, carve out your own path in life and not follow the one laid out for you. What seemed like a source of danger and dread to Lia was also the bearer of possibilities.

She stopped at the top and let the wispy night air kiss her face. Had she followed someone else's path or was it her own? It was probably more or less her own, with some outside expectations and well-meaning suggestions. At any rate, because of circumstances, she'd been placed in a situation where she had to make some tough choices, and this time she wanted to be sure she made the right decision for herself.

Low white-topped waves curled slowly up the

dark sand. The tide was rising, making the Point, which was only just visible in the distance, a more pronounced sickle shape. It wouldn't be long before the sea would be lapping the sand within feet from where she was standing.

Involuntarily she took a step back.

Eddie.

Lia thought she heard herself say the name of her little brother out loud, but maybe it was just an echo on the airwaves, like some stray radio signal caught in a time warp and transmitting from the past. That's where Eddie was; well and truly in the past. Was he the reason she was here, with this peculiar urge to stay, even though the thought filled her with dread at the same time?

Jack came back from his excursion and sat down by her feet. Caressing his ears, Lia spied a figure in the distance, walking across the sand towards the crawling surf.

Experiencing a strange sense of déjà vu – wasn't déjà vu always strange? A trick of the mind, a memory that didn't feel like a memory – she noted the black suit, the mask, and the yellow oxygen tank on his back. Aidan must have parked his car by the other path like last time they met, which would explain why she hadn't seen him on her way here.

Odd, though, that she hadn't heard the diesel engine in the still evening air.

Waving, she called out to him, wondering if he could hear her in all his gear. He turned around slowly as if seeing her here was the last thing he'd expected. That was odd too, since they'd stood and talked on this very beach five days before.

'Aidan!' She began to climb down the bank, her booted feet sinking into the sand. Now that he was kitted out it seemed a good time to tell him she would never have the nerve to dive, even if he insisted on teaching her. 'I need to talk to you.'

But Aidan had either read her mind that she wanted to back out, or he was in a hurry, because he didn't wait for her. He saluted her quickly, in that annoying way of his, the white skin on his palm standing in stark contrast to his black mask, and headed for the sea.

Pride stopped her from running after him, and when he waded out into the surf, she drove her hands in her pockets with a huff. 'Well, stuff you too.'

Behind her, on the bank, Jack emitted a low growl, and Lia felt a sudden tingling sensation on the back of her neck. She turned around. The dog stood in a cluster of gorse with his teeth bared, facing the sea.

She stepped up the bank to put his lead on, but Jack growled again, a guttural sound deep in his throat, and she thought better of it. The dog crept slowly forward, and then everything happened so fast Lia hardly had time to think. In a flap of wings a partridge flew out of the thicket. She gave a gasp of terror and felt the blood rush from her face. To stop herself from colliding with the bird, she dodged to one side, lost her footing, and tumbled back down the bank.

Jack chased the partridge for a few yards, then with a hangdog expression trotted back to where Lia lay sprawled in the sand.

Shock gave way to mortification. What if Aidan had seen her fall flat on her backside? She would never live it down. Laughter welled up in her as she spat sand out of her mouth. The whole thing was just so stupid, her running after Aidan, she who had never chased a bloke in her entire life and certainly not one who thought he was a penguin, and then rolling about in the sand because she got frightened by a bird.

'You're impossible,' she scolded Jack. 'Nothing but a goddamn pest.'

She spoke harshly, but it wasn't because of Jack's misdeeds. She couldn't shake off the feeling that there was a purpose to her being here, something to do with Eddie. With her dignity more or less intact she got up and picked up the hat, which had rolled away.

It made no sense, of course. Her baby brother had been dead for almost thirty years, and she'd been too young to truly feel the gap his death left behind. She hardly even remembered him, only in fragmented images. They were stronger here than anywhere else because she had too much time on her hands in which to brood.

She didn't believe in haunted houses, didn't accept that there was more between heaven and earth than what the eye could see. Here of her own free will, her only purpose was to sort out her grandmother's house and then get the hell out of town.

It had to be.

Returning to his car, Aidan stowed away his gear and reached for a towel. He'd seen Lia on the beach, but she'd been far away, although he was sure it was her. After their evening together, which he'd enjoyed – there was no getting around that – he'd thought several times how easy it would be to drive past her house on some pretext and invite himself in.

Seeing her in her grandmother's very distinctive coat, he'd thought, for one crazy moment, that Mrs Barrington had come back to pester him, in death as she had in life. By the time he'd recovered from the shock, the opportunity to approach Lia had passed.

They had nothing in common, anyway. A few shared memories of sixth form college – so what? She hadn't paid much attention to him then, and there was no reason why she should pay particular attention to him now.

He pulled on his jeans, then a roll-neck jumper. Through the knitwear he perceived movement nearby, and yanking his head through the neck opening, he swung around, pulse racing wildly.

Mrs Larwood stood on the sandy path about ten feet away from him, her wrinkled grey face a lighter disc in the twilight.

'Gave you a turn, did I?' she asked and came closer. She was dressed in sensible tweeds, a padded jacket, and sturdy brown shoes. A plastic rain bonnet covered her hair.

'I didn't hear you coming. What are you doing here, anyway?'

He finished dressing, pulled down the jumper and buckled his jeans. Mrs Larwood continued to eye him up, unabashed. The old crone had some nerve, which he could only admire even as he found it intrusive.

'You're built like my Howard was,' she said, ignoring his ill-tempered question, 'except for that . . . thing on your leg. Mind you, his scars were all on the inside. I know which one I'd prefer, any day.'

'Yeah, and which is that?'

'Oh, the outside kind. You know what you're dealing with, then. Everything is out in the open.' She put her fist over her heart. 'It's when it's in here, all kinds of trouble starts. No one can really see what goes on in another's heart.'

'True.' Aidan rested his foot against the tailgate and began lacing up his boots.

'Your brother, he was like that. On the inside, it was, all that pain and anger. He didn't cope well.'

Fumbling with the laces, Aidan said, 'No.'

'To imagine him going the way he did. A crying shame.'

With his back turned, Aidan clenched his fists and closed his eyes for a moment as she droned on.

'—always like that, even as a little boy. Remember when I used to clean for you lot, up at the farm? Always came running to me, he did, telling me he was going to do this, that and the other. Full of himself, thinking he could take on the world. But when it came down to it, he couldn't handle it, could he?'

'You favoured him, as I recall,' said Aidan.

'I did, that's right. Because I always thought you were the stronger one. You didn't need me telling you what was what; had it all figured out for yourself, you did. Turned out I was right.' She sniffed. 'Turned out you were the lucky one.'

Aidan rounded on her. 'Really? My brother thought his life wasn't worth living, and that makes me *lucky*?'

Mrs Larwood held his furious stare, not in the least bit intimidated by the differences in their size and physical strength, and Aidan faltered.

'You know what I'm talking about,' she said at last. 'Anyway, thought you might like to know that Ivy's granddaughter isn't selling.' With that, turning her face up against the incessant drizzle, she secured the strings of her rain bonnet under her chin and continued along the path as if their little interlude had never taken place.

Aidan watched her disappear over the top of the bank. That's all I bloody need, he fumed. *Her sticking her nose in where it doesn't belong.*

He stayed where he was as night fell, leaning on the tailgate and sipping hot black coffee from a flask cup. The rain which had been falling on and off all day tailed off, and the clouds dispersed as if by magic, revealing a clear night sky. Moonlit shadows appeared around him, and somewhere off to his right, further inland, they seemed denser and darker, like a black hole absorbing all the brightness of the world. When a fox cried out, the hairs on the back of his neck stood on end, and he gave an involuntary shiver, nearly dropping his plastic cup. He swore as hot coffee spilled over his hand.

Then he laughed. She certainly had a way of spooking people, that Mrs Larwood.

Lia's determination to look forward and not back lasted about two days.

When her mother's signature was required on some legal documents, she drove reluctantly to Lowestoft to see her. Connie's battered Ford Fiesta was parked in front of her house. Lia got out of her equally battered car. What was it about the women in this family that they chose to drive around in such clapped-out old bangers? Ivy could afford a new car but had chosen to be eccentric. Connie couldn't, but had chosen to renounce her inheritance.

The word 'pig-headed' entered Lia's mind, and she longed for the smooth driving experience of her Chrysler in Philadelphia.

Connie's house was a typical 1960s semi-detached, boxy-looking and built mainly of brick and weatherboarding at a time when urban developers had at least tried to shed the post-war tendency to slap up as many dismal houses as cheaply as possible.

Lia took a deep breath. Her mother would go down in history as the Woman Who Tried. She had tried to do a degree, to have a happy marriage, to bring up two children, and then to build a normal relationship with her daughter on the ruins of the other three.

There had been happy times too, and with that in mind Lia walked round to the back of the house and tried the door. It was unlocked, as it was whenever Connie was home, so she let herself in. The utility room held the usual clutter of coats, boots and umbrellas, as well as a small golf bag leaning against the wall. It was a half set, for someone who was playing golf on a lab assistant's budget. On a coat rack hung a pair of binoculars. When her mother wasn't golfing in her spare time, she was bird-watching, or 'twitching' for the initiated, another activity which didn't require the participation of her family.

The golf shoes on a newspaper next to the bag were coated in fresh mud. Lia hung up her coat next to Connie's golf jacket, which felt cold to the touch. Her mother played with a passion, whatever the weather.

Connie was in the kitchen peeling potatoes.

'Hi. Good day?'

A whole head taller than her mother, Lia bent to

kiss her cheek, as always marvelling that they looked so different. Connie had fair hair which had never really greyed, though it had turned coarser; her eyes were hazel, and she had that curious shiny complexion you got from spending hours outdoors. In her tartan golf trousers her figure seemed slightly dumpy, but she had an air of faded celebrity about her which made people turn their heads.

'Lovely, thank you, Lia. I did eighteen holes.'

'Did you get my message?'

Connie dropped a potato into a saucepan of water. 'About the documents you want me to sign? Yes, I got that.'

'And you're okay about it?'

'As long as I'm signing it all away.' Connie remained bent over her potatoes.

'Why don't you want anything?' Lia asked. It irritated her. Dealing with everything on her own was like a millstone around her neck. There must be something she could do to persuade her mother to take a lump sum at least. 'If you put your paw print on those documents, you will be signing it all away. To me. Is that what you want?'

Her mother fixed her with a stare. 'We've been over this before, and no, I haven't gone dotty in my old age. I won't need to be sectioned. It's for you to do with what you like. If you want to sell the whole boiling lot, that's fine by me.'

'And the dog?'

'No,' Connie almost snapped and turned back to her potatoes.

'He's cute.'

'I'm sure he is.'

Lia sighed. She took the envelope with the solicitor's logo out of her handbag and spread the papers out on the small kitchen table in the corner of the room.

Connie dried her hands on a tea towel, lit the gas ring under the saucepan, and sat down. Without bothering to read the documents through, she scribbled her signature on all the lines marked with an 'X', and returned them to the envelope. Smiling as if a great burden had been lifted from her shoulders, she turned to her daughter.

'There, all done. Now, would you like a sherry before supper?'

Over dinner Connie gave her an account of today's golf game: her best hole, the best shot she'd played, how far she was off her personal best round, the fox slinking along the periphery of the golf course. Seeing the animation on her mother's face, Lia tried to seem interested, but she couldn't help wondering how two people, mother and daughter, could live in such complete and mutual incomprehension of each other.

When there was a gap in Connie's endless stream of words, Lia broached a subject which had been on her mind.

'Mum, did you notice anything strange about Gran before she died?'

'Strange? In what way?' Connie's hand, with a

85

forkful of peas, stopped in mid-air. A few peas fell back on to the plate like beads from a broken necklace.

'Well, she bought a dog, for starters. I found takeaway cartons in the house, which isn't like her, either. Did she seem worried to you? Was she lonely, perhaps? Did she say anything or do anything at all which was out of character?'

Connie continued eating her peas without looking at Lia. One by one they dropped off her fork as she brought it to her mouth with a slightly trembling hand, and she replaced it carefully on the plate.

'I can't say that I noticed,' she said. 'Perhaps she was a bit lonely. That would explain her getting a dog, I suppose.' She folded up the cloth napkin which lay across her lap, and put it beside her plate, one edge flush with the edge of the table. 'As for being worried about something, well, Ivy was a tough one. Worry didn't come into it, you must know that. She did exactly what she pleased, whatever people said. Why ask for their opinion if she had no intention of listening to their advice in the first place? She was self-reliant, superior; and she always did The Right Thing. A hard act to follow.'

This was more than Connie had ever said about her mother, and it wasn't quite what Lia had expected to hear. Phrases like 'tough old bird' and 'moral rectitude', yes, but *superior*? Perhaps Ivy had always regarded her social standing to be

86

higher than certain other people's, but she'd been very much part of the community, so she couldn't have trodden on that many toes. Perhaps her superiority, as Connie put it, had more to do with striving for perfection in everything she did than with social status. It was true that Ivy had scorned failure.

Normally Lia would side with her grandmother, but Connie had been uncharacteristically frank, and instead she saw an opportunity to ask a question which had simmered inside her like a forgotten saucepan for well over a decade.

'Is that why I was sent to live with her?'

Connie's face closed down. 'I had no say in that.'

'But you're my mother. You must've had something do to with it.'

'I was unfit, wasn't I?' Connie gave a mirthless laugh. 'My husband had walked out. My son had died. I probably drank more than was good for me, too. How could *I* bring up a teenager and provide for her so she could meet those high expectations which had been crammed in with her baby milk? Your life was all mapped out for you. By her. I was taken out of the equation. End of story.'

'No, sorry, I don't accept that.' Anger welled up in Lia, or maybe it was that long-forgotten saucepan which had finally come to the boil. 'If Ivy wanted to provide for me, she could have done that while I was still living with you. We never had any money to speak of. She could've helped.'

'Oh, she did, in her own way,' said Connie with a dismissive gesture. 'You wanted to go to Fakenham Sixth Form College, and in all fairness it seemed like the ideal environment for you. You couldn't have commuted from here, and I didn't want to leave my job. It made sense for you to live with her. And you never wanted for anything, did you?' she added in a bitter undertone.

'No, she was very generous. That's not why I asked.'

Connie's eyes grew distant, as if she remembered an old pain.

'Then she sent you to Gresham. Something to do with a friend of yours falling pregnant, though what that had to do with you, I don't know. To begin with I didn't even know you'd gone. I thought you didn't want to talk to me.'

'I didn't. I was angry. I would've liked to have been consulted, and there were you and Ivy making plans over my head. I felt isolated.'

I still do, she thought. Withdrawing into herself and becoming inscrutable was a defence mechanism. She liked to think of it as the tortoise effect, and she used it frequently. It was only now, when she was completely on her own, it occurred to her that self-imposed isolation wasn't all it was cracked up to be.

'That was what she wanted,' said Connie. 'She wanted you away from me so she could work on you. So she could make you into this . . . this copy of herself.'

'You're being really unfair. I'm nothing like her.'
Or am I?

Connie's tight expression loosened a little. 'Well, thank God for small miracles.'

Lia reached out to take her hand when a sudden thought struck her, a thought so jolting that she pulled her hand back sharply as if she'd received an electric shock.

'Did you hate her?'

'Did I hate my mother? What sort of question is that? Do *you* hate *me*?'

'I just want to know.'

Sighing, Connie fiddled with the napkin she'd folded earlier, rolling it into a tube and letting it unroll. 'I hated her for what she said about Eddie.'

Lia had a flash of memory, like a series of negative stills. She saw herself, thumb in mouth, pushing her index finger inside the fat fist of a baby, heard his contented gurgles echoing down the years, felt his squinting eyes studying her face.

'What did she say?' she asked, although she could guess the answer.

'Horrible things.' Connie was wringing her napkin in her hands, making her knuckles go white. 'That he was only half human, a freak. That he should never have been born. He was only a Down's syndrome baby, for heaven's sake, not the Elephant Man! Although I'll admit she was good to me after he'd died. She stood by us, looked after you. Then she drove a wedge between us. Yes, I suppose you could say I hated her.'

CHAPTER 6

The temperature had plummeted when Lia left her mother's house, and her breath billowed around her in the dark like a genie emerging from a lamp. In the car she rubbed her hands together against the cold while she tried to remember which button did what. Although she was used to working with high-tech equipment, her grandmother's rudimentary car still defeated her, and it bothered her.

That wasn't the only thing.

Connie had said more about her relationship with Ivy in one evening than she had in twenty years, and Lia knew she ought to be pleased. Not only that, she'd got what she wanted from her – the documents had been signed, the ball would finally start rolling, and all the legal stuff could now be sorted out. Somehow, though, that was no longer enough.

What she hadn't got was peace of mind.

Their frank conversation had come as a surprise, because she'd expected to wade through the usual treacly evasiveness which had always characterised her relationship with her mother.

90

At the same time, the more she dug, the stronger became her urge to probe further, which made it more likely that she'd uncover something painful she could do without. Like finding out that her grandmother had been lonely. She didn't really want to know that, because of the guilt it caused, and she certainly didn't need to know what Ivy had said about Eddie. Her baby brother had been rejected by someone who should have loved him, and although Eddie himself would have been oblivious to that rejection, Lia wasn't.

No, she definitely didn't want to know, but she seemed unable to stop asking difficult questions.

Was it just human nature, she wondered as she turned on to the A149, this need to prod and poke until the bubble burst? With Connie admitting that she had hated Ivy, Lia couldn't help thinking that the bad feeling which had existed between the two most important people in her life had a lot to do with her.

At the same time, she couldn't shake off the suspicion that although her mother had been unusually open with her this evening, there was still a lot she wasn't telling her.

While mulling this over, Lia automatically dipped the headlights for an oncoming car. The driver didn't respond in kind, but raced past her in an angry blur, heedless of anyone other than himself. A series of starbursts scorched her optic nerve and half-blinded, she slowed down.

'Prick,' she muttered, but the experience had refocused her thoughts.

Like the Big Bang, everything had a starting point, as well as a point where it all settled into a certain order based on the laws of physics. That was where the answers lay. Scientists had telescopes which enabled them to see into the violent past of the universe, but people had their own internal telescopes too, or maybe antennae was a better word. All she had to do was point it in the right direction.

Looking in Ivy's house would be a start. She had to clear it out anyway, so if there were any answers to find, that would seem the most logical place to find them. Then, perhaps, she could get out of this curious state of limbo.

She thought of the quiet house almost with longing. She'd begun to enjoy the tranquillity, even though it was so different from what she was used to; but in contrast, the silence in the car was unnerving. She switched on the radio and twiddled the knob for a music station, but all she could find were talk shows.

'Oh, for heaven's sake,' she exclaimed, then pricked up her ears at the sudden mention of Aidan's name. What on earth was he doing on the radio?

Aidan adjusted the headphones while he braced himself for the female presenter's first question. Lottie Millar sat across from him in the sound booth, an earnest expression on her face, which was meant to invite confidences but instead made him feel like a fraud. She was grey-haired and had leathery skin from too many years in the sun, but her voice was like brandy, smooth and rich. Perfect for radio, he thought.

'Thank you for coming on the show, Aidan,' she said. 'Perhaps to start with you could tell us a little bit about your brother, and after that we'll move on to the reasons you're here today.'

Aidan cleared his throat. 'Er, well, Gerald was a bit of a hell-raiser. Left school at sixteen, lots of jobs, lots of girlfriends. A bit aimless, but always good-natured about it. A cheeky chappie, perhaps. And he always watched out for me and my sister, at school and at home. I suppose I looked up to him.'

'He sounds like a fabulous brother,' the presenter cut in. 'Me, I only had sisters.'

She was trying to put him at ease, and he appreciated it, but talking about his brother was always difficult. 'Yeah, he was.'

'What then? He joined the army, and . . .?'

'Yes. There's always been military men in the Morrell family. Later I was in the navy myself for a while. But Gerald was floundering, only joined up for lack of anything else to do. He was on his second enlistment when we went to war with Iraq in '03 so when he got orders to go, he was eager to do the job he'd been trained for. He must've been glad his contract was up after his tour in Iraq. He didn't re-enlist.'

'What was he like when he returned?'

'A bit subdued, but you'd expect that, wouldn't you? At twenty-odd years it's literally boys doing men's jobs out there. They're under attack every day, see their friends get killed. It would've been strange if he hadn't been affected.'

'Your family must've been relieved for him to be home safe.'

'Of course. We thought life was going to go back to normal. Within twelve hours of fighting in Basra he was basically sitting in my parent's living room like he'd never been away. It seemed so easy.'

'But life didn't go back to normal, did it?'

Aidan sighed. 'No.'

'What happened?' the presenter prodded.

'He had trouble adapting to civilian life. Couldn't find a job or a place to live. He tried for a council flat, but as a single man he was considered a low priority. Then he started drinking.'

'That's pretty normal in the army, isn't it? Work hard and play hard, and all that.'

'Sure, yeah. I mean, I should know. Except on his own it sort of took over. He got moody and angry, didn't like being around people. Would look for fights when he went out, got in trouble with the police. It was like he had something missing he was trying to replace.'

'This must've been difficult for your family.'

There was a moment of feedback from the microphone, but the presenter held up her hand to indicate that it was normal.

'They took the brunt of it,' Aidan said, 'My dad was getting on and needed him to help out on the farm and not "mope around" as he put it. So they'd row, which was pretty upsetting for my mother. I'd finished art college in Liverpool and was working there, living near my sister, Marcella. She didn't want to . . . get involved, so I decided to go back home, to mediate.'

'That was very noble of you, if you had other plans with your life.'

Aidan shrugged, then realised this would be lost on the listeners. 'I just wanted to help him get over whatever crisis he was facing. I was very naïve, really.'

'Naïve, because . . .?'

'Because I couldn't help him. Anyone who tried, he'd push them away. He'd changed, but we'd remained the same, and we expected *him* to be the same, because families do.'

'What exactly *had* changed for him?'

'Well, he'd gone from signing up to signing on. Had lost everything he had in the military, but didn't want to admit he was struggling, that he was now a nobody. And there were other problems too.'

'What sort of problems?'

Aidan cleared his throat. 'He couldn't settle or sleep. Would jump out of his skin if a car backfired or something like that. And he was having nightmares and flashbacks, triggered by sounds and smells, he told me later. Like a fuse box had blown in his brain.'

'Did he see a doctor?'

'He did, in the end, after having put it off for ages. And that was relatively quick – some wait years before they seek help. His doctor diagnosed post-traumatic stress disorder.'

'That must have been a relief for him.'

'Actually, it had the opposite effect,' said Aidan. 'All Gerald wanted when he got back was to make a contribution to society rather than become one of its casualties. He absolutely hated the idea that there was something wrong with his head.'

'Couldn't he just pull himself together?'

Aidan felt a flash of anger. She was incredibly cutting, but he'd heard her on the radio before, so more fool him for not preparing himself for that. Why she wasn't down in London, rubbing shoulders with Jeremy Paxman, instead of a local radio station at the back of beyond was anyone's guess.

Controlling his anger, he continued: 'It doesn't work quite like that. No one, not even doctors can understand what soldiers go through. Seeing mutilated bodies. Killing people. Do you know what a body bomb is?'

'I think I can guess, but why don't you explain it for the benefit of our listeners?'

'Okay.' Aidan took a deep breath. 'A body bomb is when terrorists implant a bomb inside a human being. Sometimes that person is alive, sometimes he's dead. And sometimes it's kids.'

'Nasty.'

'Yes, it is, and in the barracks they joke about all the horrible stuff because dehumanising themselves is the only way not to fall apart. It takes years to tease that kind of hidden problem to the surface. A diagnosis and a bottle of happy pills aren't enough.'

'Going back to your brother, what happened to him?'

'He withdrew into his own world. Became depressed and bitter, because he felt let down by the society he'd risked his life for.'

The presenter cut in. 'Can I just stop you there? The figures I have show that about four per cent of returning soldiers suffer from the condition, but I also know there's plenty of help available. So, why was it harder for him than for so many others?'

'There's a lot more awareness about PTSD now, but back then when Gerald had finished his tour, it was a relatively new thing. And as for "plenty" of help, it depends on how you look at it.'

'Care to elaborate?'

'It takes six months to convert a civilian into a soldier,' Aidan replied, 'but no time at all to turn a soldier into a civilian, or so it seems the Ministry of Defence believes. Some of them fall through the cracks, like Gerald, and when they do, there's no one to pick them up. Families aren't equipped to deal with these kinds of mental health problems.'

'What about the Armed Forces?' asked the presenter.

'It's not their job to prepare people for civilian life.

Their job is to defend the realm. Which they do extremely well, if I may add.'

'What measures would you like to see put in place?'

'I'd like to see a veterans' charter adopted in all parts of the country. Give returning soldiers a lifeline back into society. They're national assets, and deserve it. If we don't do something, it's like a time bomb in terms of mental health out there in the community.'

'You say "in all parts of the country". Does that mean this charter already exists in some areas?'

'In a few places, yes, but sadly it's the exception rather than the rule.'

'Surely there must be charities out there?'

'Oh, loads of them, and the public is very generous, but there's no real co-ordination between them. The message might be that these people don't need help, but they do.'

'What about The Royal British Legion, and Help for Heroes? Is that not their remit?'

'It is, and I'm glad you mentioned them because I was coming to that. The British Legion is perfectly placed to bridge the gap between life in the armed forces and life on civvy street. If the MoD could pass on the details of service leavers to them, they might be able to stop this happening, but the Ministry has refused, citing the Data Protection Act.'

'How does that make you feel?'

'How do you think it makes me feel?' Aidan couldn't help raising his voice. 'I'm extremely angry. Veterans like Gerald suffer on average ten to fifteen years before asking for psychiatric help. What else would the British Legion need that information for, if not to help? It's too late for my brother, but if the MoD weren't such dinosaurs, others could be helped before their problems got out of hand. Now we're nowhere.'

'It's too late for your brother, you say,' the presenter prodded gently. 'What, exactly, happened?'

The pain hit him in the stomach like it always did. 'He tried to take his own life. Cut his wrists. At the hospital my mother explained to the doctors that he was a danger to himself, that they had to keep him in somehow, or just do something.

'By then I was in the navy, working as a Clearance Diver, so she had to deal with this all on her own because my father had died a few months earlier and my sister still stayed away. They ignored her and discharged him. Then he just upped and left. Didn't take anything with him.' Aidan could feel his voice begin to shake. 'We, er . . .'

'Take your time,' said the presenter.

'We live on the coast. He'd left his clothes on the beach and gone into the sea at high tide. They never found his body, but speaking as a seasoned diver and one who knows the currents and the seabed around here very well, I can tell you that's no surprise.'

The presenter let the impact of his words sink in before her final question. 'So what exactly do you want to achieve with your campaign?'

'This has been pretty hard for our family and especially my mother. Like I said, it's too late for us, but people out there still need help. My aim is for the MoD to release those details to the British Legion, so they can provide that help. If not, the Ministry needs a wake-up call, and I'm going to make sure they get it.'

'Thank you, Aidan,' she said, rounding up the interview before taking questions from the listeners, 'for speaking on a subject which must be very painful to you. This is Lottie Millar for *Over To You*, your local mouthpiece. I see now we have our first caller on the line. Hello, please state—'

Pulling up outside the house, Lia switched off the radio, shaken by what she'd just heard. So that was how Aidan's brother had died. His dignified grief had moved her in a way she didn't fully understand. Clutching her stomach, which had tied itself in knots all of a sudden, she felt an overwhelming urge to go to him right now and just hold him.

Would he welcome it? Somehow she didn't think so.

She sighed and got out. Jack must have heard the car in the drive because he was barking loudly behind the front door. A good guard dog, Mrs Larwood had called him; not that Lia needed one.

But maybe her grandmother had.

CHAPTER 7

The light on the answer machine was blinking when Lia entered the living room. The telephone was on a low table next to a window. She pressed the Play button, absently snapping a leaf off a lemon geranium plant which stood on the windowsill. Crushing the leaf between her fingers, she breathed in the sharp citrus scent.

There was something spooky about listening to messages on an answer machine belonging to a dead person. What if the caller wasn't calling to speak to Lia but to her grandmother, like a voice suddenly filling the room with memories of the past? What did you say in situations like that? *You've got the wrong number, sorry.* Or *Ivy can't come to the phone right now.* She would have to tell the truth and then brace herself for the reaction of the person at the other end, which could be anything from embarrassment at having unwittingly intruded upon a grieving family, to shock and sudden anguish.

Fortunately none of the messages were for Ivy. One was from Brett, who was busy, busy, busy and would try to catch her again soon when things quietened down at the office. Lia half-snorted. When were things ever quiet? Brett was a whirlwind and usually left only a cloud of dust in his wake.

The second message was from Susannah, apologising for her abruptness the other day and offering to help Lia clear out the house, if she needed a hand. Lia smiled. She hadn't expected that, but she should have been prepared for surprises when it came to Susannah. She should have remembered that and not tried to over-interpret that strange look she'd received from her. After all, Susannah had never been able to hide exactly what she thought and felt. Lia wondered if Zoe was the same, but her impression when she had met her told her that Zoe probably was.

Why Susannah should hate her so much was something she didn't want to think about.

The last message was from Ivy's GP, Doctor Angus Campbell, asking her to call him. She double-checked the number he'd left against the one in her grandmother's address book. It was a different number, possibly his private line. She looked at her watch. Chances were that he'd gone to bed, but she tried the number anyway in case he was still up.

To her surprise he answered after only two rings.

'This is Lia Thompson,' she said.

'Ah, yes, Miss Thompson—'

'Doctor Thompson,' she interjected. She wasn't especially protective of the title, but she knew from her own experience with patients' relatives that he would probably talk to her differently if he knew he was speaking as one doctor to another.

'Ah. Yes. Of course.' There was a momentary pause. 'Thank you for returning my call. I, er . . . just wanted to tell you how sorry I am for your loss, and also to ask you a wee favour.'

'Oh?' Lia felt a niggle of unease snake down her spine.

'Well, your grandmother was as strong as an ox,' he said in a thin, reedy voice, rolling his 'r's like a true Scotsman. 'I still can't quite believe she went so quickly. Perhaps you can help clear up a few remaining issues for me.'

'What sort of issues?'

'I'd rather not say over the phone. Could you come by some time?'

Lia sniffed the scented leaf. 'I have a lot on at the moment. Is it very urgent?'

'I'm not entirely sure. It's . . . well, let's just say I'd prefer to see you in person.'

Lia could hear the undercurrent of tension in his voice, and she found herself agreeing to call in to see him on Monday. Hopefully that would satisfy him.

He gave her the address for the surgery, wording it very carefully as you might do for the benefit of a child or someone hard of hearing.

'I know where it is,' Lia assured him. 'I've been there before with my grandmother.'

Bidding him goodbye, she put the phone down,

quelling an exasperated sigh. Doctor Campbell was not much younger than Ivy, and should probably have retired by now. She suspected that he carried on out of loyalty to his patients. She had to admit she admired his dedication, and somewhere at the back of her mind an accusing inner voice piped up, telling her that old-fashioned commitment to the simple act of healing was conspicuously absent from her own working life.

Everything she did was a patch-up job.

And now, when she was slap-bang in the middle of yet another patch-up job, sorting out Ivy's estate so she could get out of here and on with her life, he wanted to share his lingering concerns about Ivy's death. It would no doubt delay her, and besides, she wasn't sure that she wanted to hear what he had to say. What did it matter now? It wouldn't bring Ivy back, and life went on. Life even had the audacity to go on when a young person died. There was no stopping it.

Yet when she lifted her hand from the phone, she saw that it was shaking, from tiredness or excitement or maybe from something else.

'A few remaining issues' – what could that mean?

The sheep bleated expectantly when Aidan rolled open the barn door, clattering the buckets of feed. The not-entirely-unpleasant smell of dirty wool, straw and fresh droppings greeted him, and he smiled to himself. If anyone had told him only a few years ago that tending these rather dumb animals could have produced this quiet content-ment in him, he would have laughed in their face.

Now, working almost on autopilot, pouring feed concentrate in the troughs, listening to the shuf-fling of gentle hooves, and feeling a skittish woolly head here and there, he found it particularly soothing after his bruising on the radio.

He didn't blame Lottie Millar for her cross-examination of him earlier. The interviewer was only doing her job, getting to the crux of the matter without worrying too much about how many toes she stepped on in the process. Some would buckle under it, some developed a rhino hide, and others, like himself, were somewhere in-between. And in all fairness, she hadn't asked the one question he'd truly feared: why had *he* joined the navy, after what had happened to his brother? In doing that, what had he been trying to prove?

'I'd have been hard pressed to answer that,' he said out loud. 'Still am.'

The sheep stopped and stared at the sound of his voice, then started eating again, unconcerned. One of the bigger sheep muscled in and shoved a younger one out of the way of the trough.

'You great big bully,' Aidan muttered, then grinned as the younger sheep came up from beneath the chin of the larger sheep and head-butted its way back in. 'Got a taste of your own medicine there, didn't you? Well, that's as it should be.' Both animals ignored him, munching intently, their dark eyes vacant.

He stroked one of them. 'You might ask what I was trying to prove. It'd be a fair question, even from a woolly-head like you.'

What *had* he been trying to prove? Nothing, because it hadn't even been a conscious thought at the time. Everything, because what had happened to Gerald wasn't going to happen to him. Although Gerald had been everyone's favourite, he, Aidan, was better, stronger, and nothing could shake his belief that he would be able to deal with whatever emotional and physical crap life flung at him, unlike his brother, who had crumbled.

'A fatal mistake,' he muttered, 'because, guess what, I crumbled too.' He had, if less spectacularly so, but had picked himself up again, had changed. He wasn't sure he liked the new Aidan any better than the old one, but at least the person he was now knew his own limitations. The residual anger he couldn't contain, though.

And now he'd found an outlet for it, beautiful in its simplicity, and so truly one of those slap-your-forehead moments he was almost appalled that it hadn't occurred to him before. He knew what his purpose was, and he was going to see it through, regardless of the consequences.

One person had thought his approach very wrong, but her opinion was no longer relevant. 'I'm not one for speaking ill of the dead, but my God, she was too nosy for her own good.'

As he prepared to shut up the barn for the night, he noticed a single sheep at the back of

106

the pen standing immobile and facing away from the hungry throng. Frowning, he put down his buckets and climbed over the railings and into the enclosure.

Instead of running away when he approached, the sheep continued to hang her head, appearing depressed and listless. From the number tag in her ear and the markings on her face he recognised her as a lamb he'd hand-reared in spring because the ewe had died. Tamer than most, she didn't flinch when he reached out and scratched her behind the ear, although her legs shook as if they would buckle under any minute.

'What's the matter, girl?' he whispered.

Without expecting an answer, he slid his hand down her side and rested it against her abdomen where he felt a ripple of minor convulsions. Realising she was suffering from lactic acidosis, he swore softly.

Not only was it very uncomfortable for the animal, it was also life-threatening, and the only way to treat it was to drench her with antacid and keep her separate from the other sheep. Trouble was the only space available was in the barn on the other side of the yard, and he wasn't sure the animal could walk that far.

There was nothing for it. Thanking his lucky stars that he'd had the foresight to change out of his interview clothes, he lifted her up and carried her out of the barn. Young as she was, she hadn't quite reached her mature weight, but it was still an arduous task carrying her across the cobbled yard while restraining her kicking, skinny legs.

When he'd ensured the sheep was comfortable in the makeshift pen, he fetched the drench gun and mixed up an antacid solution from bicarbonate of soda. Ignoring the animal's protests, he grasped her head firmly and administered the drench, ensuring that the liquid was put back far enough so she couldn't spit it out again.

'That'll teach you not to be such a greedy-guts,' he said when she tottered away from him, flapping her small ears in disgust. Despite his no-nonsense handling of the sheep he hoped she would make it.

Packing up the drenching equipment, he considered the further treatment. He would have to continue with the antacid for the moment, while he introduced feed to her diet again, increasing it slowly to give her system time to adjust. Which meant that the sheep would have to remain isolated in the barn away from the main pen so he could keep a proper eye on how much she ate.

Which meant coming in here.

He cast an eye over his shoulder at a bright blue tarpaulin at the back of the barn. He knew what was under there, recognised it as part of the process of what he had to do, but what it represented still filled him with dread.

He forced himself to look away and finished what he was doing, then closed up. The rusty latch on the barn door had become bent over the years and needed an extra lift in order to engage properly. He put his shoulder to it and gave it the required lift and shove, then yanked it to see that it was secure.

The wind had started blowing while he was inside, without warning as it often did in these parts, and fallen leaves skittered across the yard here and there, like a swarm of nocturnal locusts. The night was black as soot with not a single star in the sky. He pulled up the collar on his wax jacket when the first drops of rain began to fall.

The sheep gave a pitiful bleat when she realised she was to be all on her own.

'Get used to it,' he muttered. 'I have.'

Having fed Jack, Lia made herself a quick snack of scrambled eggs on toast and ate it balancing the plate on her lap while catching the tail end of a disaster movie. By her feet, Jack regarded her with big soulful eyes, no doubt hoping for a tidbit.

'I've already fed you.' She nudged him away with her foot, just as Godzilla went on a final rampage through New York City. 'What more do you want?'

Jack removed himself to the hearthrug and heaved a doggy sigh which made his jowls flap. She took pity on him and put some of the crust on the floor in front of him. He sniffed the bread, moved his head away, and looked up at her.

'What? Not good enough for you? Go on, I'm not trying to poison you.' She pointed to the food. 'Eat.'

Jack sent her one last look and hoovered up the toast, then licked his lips expectantly.

Lia had an idea. She put another crust on the floor, held up her finger, and said, 'Leave it!' in a voice you couldn't argue with. The dog stayed where he was, watching her every move intently. Then she pointed to the food and said, 'Yes.' Jack dived at it and consumed it in one gulp. She repeated the exercise with the last bit of crust, then sat back in her chair, slightly baffled.

Jack wasn't just any old dog. He was a *well-trained* dog, and Ivy couldn't have had him long enough to have trained him herself. So someone else must have done it. But who? And did it matter? She could see why an elderly lady might get a dog that was already trained. It made sense, saving time and hassle. The part which still didn't add up, however, was why Ivy had got a dog in the first place.

Jack hadn't come into Ivy's life simply to be a companion. His presence had served another purpose, and with the words of Doctor Campbell ringing in her ears, Lia realised how important it had become to her to get to the bottom of what that purpose was.

She thought of Aidan's radio interview and of how, by a certain stretch of the imagination, they found themselves in similar circumstances. Both of them had been left to make sense of the mess others left behind, and the sudden insight made her understand Aidan a little better.

At the same time it was probably best to stay clear of him if she could. The idea of flirting with him had been a pleasant, temporary diversion, but it didn't seem right to be playing games with him. And there were Brett's honeyed tones on the answering machine which had reminded her where her loyalties lay.

Or ought to lie.

Upstairs, out of habit she reached for her sleeping tablets, but stopped herself short of taking one. Barbiturates dulled the senses, shut your eyes. She needed to see things clearly if she was going to solve this little mystery of Jack and those 'remaining issues', whatever they were. What had possessed her to start taking the tablets in the first place?

Easy enough to answer. Stress at work, too much pressure, too many things unresolved. Drugging yourself was the easy way. As a doctor, she should have known better.

Resolutely, she put the bottle back on the bedside cabinet.

But natural sleep didn't come. The wind picked up in the night, and the pear tree on the lawn tapped and scraped its gnarled branches against the bedroom window. On the landing the door to the spare room kept blowing open and slamming again, each time eliciting a low woof from Jack, who slept on a blanket outside the bedroom.

As she tossed and turned, throwing off the covers and pulling them back up again, Aidan's final words on the radio kept coming back to her, louder and louder till the sound filled her head.

'. . . *A wake-up call . . . I'm going to make sure they get it.*'

CHAPTER 8

Lia was woken early by the phone ringing. With the duvet wrapped around her she pottered downstairs and reached the phone just as the answer machine clicked on. It was Brett.

'Did I wake you?' he asked in response to her incoherent mumbling into the receiver.

'No,' she managed to say.

'Liar.' She could almost hear the smile in his voice. 'I'm sorry about that. I still haven't gotten used to the idea of you being in England while I'm here in the big city. Things okay?'

'Mmm.'

Lia glanced at the mantle clock and saw it was not yet seven. Philadelphia was five hours behind, and that meant—

'Brett,' she said, a sudden note of concern in her voice. 'It's two a.m. over there . . . is anything wrong?'

'It's all right,' he said. 'I was up late working on some case papers. I was getting worried about you on your own. Any news on the house front?'

She climbed into an armchair with the phone tucked under her ear, and Jack trotted across the rug and settled himself at her feet, pulling the duvet down with his weight. She resisted the temptation to push him away, because after last night's revelation she was curious to see what he'd do next. She had a feeling she was going to enjoy this sport of watching Jack.

'Not much,' she replied, her eyes still on Jack. 'The paperwork should be done now, so the property will soon be signed over to me. Then I can put it on the market. Bit difficult at the moment.'

'Sure.' Brett sounded slightly distracted, as if his mind was really on other things. 'And the dog?'

Jack tilted his head backwards and looked up at Lia with his wet, pointy nose in the air as if he knew he was being discussed. 'No takers so far.'

'You want him, don't you?'

For an awful moment Lia had the feeling that Brett wasn't referring to the dog, but to Aidan, and that he'd somehow tapped into her subconscious and read her mind, which could only really be described as confused at the moment. There was a complex mixture of compassion, fascination, and misgivings swirling around inside her head when it came to Aidan.

And then there was lust, but that didn't mean she wanted him.

'No!' she protested.

'We can't have a dog in this apartment, you know that.'

'I know.'

'When he got here, he'd be alone all day. That's

unfair on the dog. Sure, we could get a dog sitter, but what's the point in having a dog if you have to rely on others to look after it?' He paused. 'When we have our house and some kids, a dog will be perfect. We've talked about that before.'

'We have.'

They'd discussed how it was all supposed to pan out, the house and the 4×4 and the further paraphernalia, including matching baseball caps for the entire family, but the fact that everything which hadn't happened yet had been planned down to the very last detail made her want to scream. Maybe she wanted that sort of life, maybe she didn't, but she wanted the chance to decide for herself.

She thought of Ivy, who had only had one daughter, to whom she wasn't particularly close. Even Lia, her favourite, since Eddie had never really counted, had been more of a fashion accessory, someone to show off, rather than to get to know. It was all she knew, this quiet household where you moved around on slippered feet, and she didn't want that; but even though she'd often envied Brett the luxury of his large and boisterous family, his alternative seemed too confining as well.

As if sensing this was a contentious subject, he returned to the matter of the house. 'Have you spoken to a realtor yet?'

'Estate agent. We call them estate agents.'

Brett laughed. 'Long may we continue to be divided by a common language. Whatever you call

115

it, have you taken any steps yet? And what's the housing market like in England right now?'

'I don't know, but it's probably a bit too close to Christmas to expect many viewings. Perhaps I'd better wait until January to put it on the market.'

She was telling Brett the truth, but it felt like procrastination. It was almost as if the house itself was willing her not to sell it until she'd unravelled its mysteries. Every creaking step, every banging door, every draught that found its way down the chimney and blew on the ashes in the grate spoke of memories and their subjective interpretations.

'I'm taking some time off at Christmas,' said Brett, 'and I'll be flying over to England to spend the holidays with you. And your mother, of course. What's her name again?'

'Constance,' said Lia and quelled her irritation at the way he would just spring things on her. 'But everyone calls her Connie.'

'Connie, yes. Well, I guess it's high time I met her.'

He then reeled off a handful of dates and times still available for transatlantic flights, and they narrowed them down to a couple which would be convenient to both of them. They ended the conversation on a note which left Lia with the feeling that there was more to be said, except that she couldn't think of what it might be.

She pulled the duvet tighter around her and stared out of the window. A white mist hung low

116

over the lawn like an insubstantial blanket, and the still air was saturated with moisture. A crow sat in the pear tree watching her through the window with beady, black eyes, then spread its wings and took off, croaking mournfully. Lia could feel the cold from the wooden floor creeping up her legs. Jack moved away and settled on the hearthrug, where he began to lick his front paws.

His ablutions made her think of showering. Draping the duvet over the armrest, she went back upstairs. Ten minutes under the hot tap followed by ten seconds of piercing cold water, and she felt halfway human again. She dried her hair and decided it was time for action.

On the kitchen dresser she found a Yellow Pages directory and carried it through to the living room. Why the phone book was in the kitchen she didn't stop to consider. In an English country household the dresser acted as general storage for a little bit of everything. Plates, keys, bills, photos, hand cream, postcards, pens, buttons. Bits and bobs. Odds and ends.

She opened the directory under 'E', found a list of estate agents, and selected the one with the largest advert, because she figured that the bigger the advertising budget, the bigger the company, and therefore there was a greater chance they were open on a Saturday.

Dialling the number, she watched as a couple of plump grey wood pigeons settled on the frozen lawn. The mist was slowly clearing, and a pale sun lit up the white collar on their necks.

A voice answered at the other end. 'Smith and Dallington, good morning.'

Lia opened her mouth to speak. Upstairs, the door slammed. Jack raised his head and growled, and the pigeons on the lawn flew away in a flurry of beating wings.

'Hello?' said the voice. 'Can I help you?'

Jack, snarling with his hackles raised, was staring right at her. She felt a shiver run down her back and disconnected the call. 'All right, keep your fur on,' she reassured him.

Again she'd allowed herself to be spooked by nothing, and she snapped the telephone directory shut in irritation. She didn't believe in ghosts or portents or omens, but the timing of Jack's growl seemed ominous, as if he knew she was trying to sell the house and didn't want her to.

Or perhaps it was simply the door blowing shut which bothered him.

When she put the Yellow Pages down, she noticed a curious dry brown stain on the spine. She scraped at the stain with her fingernail and sniffed her fingers. The substance smelt sweet and metallic, and she recognised it. It was a smell she often came across in her job. It hung around the staff in the emergency room, permeating their scrubs, their hair and their skin. They even smelt it in their dreams, or maybe she just imagined that part.

Blood.

It had to be Ivy's – hadn't Mrs Larwood said there was blood everywhere when Ivy had fallen and hit her head? Lia had thought the woman was exaggerating, but her grandmother must have hit her head very hard for blood to splatter on to a phone book which lay on the dresser.

Except it didn't look splattered. The blood looked like it had seeped in. Perhaps it hadn't been on the dresser.

Maybe Ivy had been about to make a call and then dropped the phone book when she had her heart attack. Nothing strange about that. Mrs Larwood had probably put the book back where it belonged when she found her, without noticing the blood on it.

Apart from the bloodstain, it looked in pristine condition, as if it had never been used, and the numbers of her grandmother's doctor, her dentist, and local services were keyed in to the speed dial function on her telephone. So who would Ivy be calling?

Lia shook her head.

I'm imagining things.

I'm paranoid.

What's the matter with me?

Ivy could have called just about anyone. A plumber, the council, a takeaway place.

A takeaway place.

Suddenly a half-formed theory made her run back into the kitchen for the receipt from the takeaway restaurant. She found it where she'd put it, in the top drawer of the dresser. She spread it out on the kitchen table, then grabbed a small bundle of utility bills which hung from a hook on the dresser, held together by a bulldog clip. On a very recent bill from British Telecom she ran her finger down the itemised list of called numbers. The number of the restaurant wasn't on the bill by the corresponding date. In fact, it wasn't there at all.

She checked it again in case she'd overlooked something and got the same result.

If Ivy had phoned for a takeaway from The Goa, she hadn't done it from her home number. Maybe it hadn't been Ivy who had ordered it at all.

Lia stared at a row of plates on the dresser in front of her, not really seeing them. Several seemingly unconnected strands were slowly becoming intertwined in her mind. A dog which shouldn't be there. A takeaway meal which didn't belong here either. Blood on the phone book. Doctor Campbell's strange concerns. And on the periphery of it all, a resentful, unhappy woman who hated her mother.

A feeling of dread curled around her spine. *It couldn't be*. No. She refused to believe it, to even think the thought to its natural conclusion.

'This isn't happening,' she muttered. It was in her mind. Her grandmother probably just knocked the phone book off the dresser when she fell and died of natural causes.

And that was that.

Jack had followed her into the kitchen, kindly dragging the discarded duvet with him, and was now lying by her feet, Sphinx-like, with his front paws just touching it.

She knelt down and scratched him behind the ear. 'What are you trying to say, boy? That I'm untidy?'

The dog snorted.

'I don't suppose you're trying to tell me something else, are you?'

Jack covered his nose with one of his paws.

'Of course not. What was I expecting, anyway? You're a dog.' And, though well-trained, maybe not too clever, either. One dog biscuit short of a packet, that sort of thing. However, she didn't say this out loud. Just in case.

She rose, returned the bills to the hook on the dresser, and picked up the duvet. Despite her shower earlier, her mind still felt fuzzy. Tougher means were needed. 'I'm going for a run,' she said to Jack. 'You coming?'

Hurriedly she put on a pair of nylon leggings, a fleece top, a scarf, and her running shoes, then stuffed her gloves in the pockets of the fleece. As she got ready to leave, the door to the spare room blew open yet again, creaking on its hinges, then slammed shut as if pulled by an invisible string.

She'd had enough of that door banging at all hours. It took only a few minutes of rummaging in the broom closet to come up with the solution: a length of plastic washing line. Fashioning a loop at one end, she slung it over the door handle, and tied the other end to the radiator on the landing, then stepped back feeling rather smug with her handiwork.

Whistling for Jack, she locked the front door and placed the key under a flower pot. Jack raced ahead of her, tongue lolling, but turned back and caught up with her when she turned off the main road in the direction of the deer park. Lia stopped and stretched. Jack inspected the low bushes, but the sudden squawk of a pheasant sent him darting back to her side.

'Wimp.'

She set off at a brisk walking pace. If only she could keep moving, she could keep a sense of who she was and leave behind all the unanswered questions and the issues she didn't want to face. Events from then and now. Those disturbing childhood images of water crashing over her. It was all too much.

Leaning forward, Aidan slotted a CD in the car stereo and cranked up the volume. Coldplay blared out of the loudspeakers.

He was on his way to deliver a commissioned painting which he hoped would lead to more work of the same kind. The sun was shining, the sick sheep was showing signs of recovering, there was a divers' meeting tonight. Life was good. All he needed now . . . no, that thought would take him nowhere except down a very rocky road.

When he recognised the lone jogger, he sounded the horn and pulled up beside her.

Big mistake. Lia gave a start and held up her arm as if to ward off a blow. Her dog barked in sympathy.

Oh, hell. Maybe this wasn't such a good idea after all.

'Fancy a lift?' he asked, now that he'd stopped, and wished he hadn't.

'No, thanks.'

'Why not?'

'I'm exercising,' she replied and started running again in a slow trot. Unable to resist a challenge, Aidan followed in a low gear.

'Who pissed on your parade?'

Lia arched an eyebrow, suggesting that he was to blame. 'Sorry, can't hear you.'

He turned the music down. 'Better now?'

'It's an improvement.'

'And I still can't give you a lift?'

'I told you, we're exercising.'

'Come on, don't play hard to get.'

She stopped abruptly and spun around. 'I'm not playing hard to get!'

Aidan laughed. 'I know you're not, but I couldn't help it. The look on your face is priceless.'

'Oh, you're infuriating.' Heaving a demonstrative sigh, she opened the passenger door and got in. Jack followed her and tried to climb up on her lap. 'Down,' she said. Obediently he curled up on the rubber mat by her feet.

This time it was his turn to raise an eyebrow. 'Have you been training him?'

'Not really, I've just been doing things with him that he's already learned.'

'I don't think your grandmother took him to puppy class.'

She patted Jack on the head. 'She didn't. I think someone who knew what he was doing worked with him before Ivy bought him. I also think she bought him for a specific purpose'

'I see.' Aidan glanced at Jack who yawned and put his head on Lia's shoe. 'Well, whatever that purpose was, it wasn't hunting.'

'Of course not. Where are we going?'

'To deliver a painting.'

'A commission?'

'Behind you. But keep your mutt away from it. It's worth four hundred pounds to me.'

She reached behind his seat for the painting, which he'd wrapped in an old sheet for protection, and pulled it on to her lap. Having untied the string, she gasped in appreciation. 'It's beautiful! Absolutely breathtaking.'

Aidan made a face. 'It pays the bills.'

'How do you do it? I mean, how can you create so many greys?' Lia held the painting close, then at arm's length. 'Amazing. When I hold it close, it's just rough brush strokes, but further away it's, I don't know, liquid with life, or something.'

'Thanks,' he said, touched.

'Who is she?'

'The model? She's the owner of the picture. It's meant as a surprise for her husband's birthday.'

'That's really romantic.' A blush spread over her cheeks, and she turned away.

Aidan glanced at the large ring on a finger on her left hand. 'Is your fiancé not romantic, then?'

Following his gaze, Lia held out her hand. 'Brett believes in grand gestures, but they usually involve a visit to an expensive jeweller's, where he buys something the shop assistant recommends.' She sent him an apologetic smile. 'Most men are not very good at shopping for what they think women might like.'

'What would you like?'

'I don't know. Books, maybe. Some nice hand cream. I get very dry skin in my job, you see.'

'Maybe he thinks you're impressed by price tags. A lot of women are.'

'I'd just like him to get me something a bit more "me", if that makes any sense,' she continued.

'Maybe you should tell him that.'

'Yeah, maybe I should.'

'As for the gesture behind that painting, I don't know how romantic it is,' said Aidan. 'It's a well-known fact in the community that this woman's husband has a roving eye and a pair of rather busy hands. I expect she's giving him a picture of herself to remind him which side his bread is buttered on and to keep an eye on him.'

'But you can't do that with a painting, unless you put a webcam behind it.'

125

'Ah, well, there are more things in heaven and earth than are dreamt of in our philosophy.'

She looked up. 'I beg your pardon?'

'Shakespeare. *Hamlet*, in fact.'

'Oh, him. Aren't you the clever one?'

'"Oh, him". Is that all you have to say about the greatest bard?'

She smiled suddenly, and Aidan felt as if someone had punched him in the gut. 'I'm sure you'd feel the same if you'd been named after the crazy girl-friend,' she pointed out.

'Fair enough. Anyway, take another look at the sitter's eyes.'

Amused, he watched her draw the picture close, then rock it slightly from side to side. The woman who had commissioned the painting had asked if he could make the portrait watch over her husband, and he was quite proud of the effect he'd created. With layers of paint it was as if there were several pupils inside each eye socket, and wherever you stood in relation to the portrait, the woman's eyes would follow you around the room.

Finally Lia drew away from the painting. She wrapped it in its protective sheeting and returned it to the space behind his seat. 'I see what you mean, it's quite disconcerting. But do you think the buyer will like it?'

'I hope so.' He grinned. 'Although I have a sneaking suspicion the errant husband won't. But, hey, she's paying.'

He slowed the car and took a left turn down a dirt track. 'Actually, I'm glad I ran into you. I've been meaning to call.'

'Oh?' She seemed wary.

'I bumped into Hazel Larwood a few days ago—'

'Hazel, is it? Tch.'

'—and I hear you're not selling.'

Lia's eyes widened. 'I never told her anything about not selling. I don't know where she got that from.'

'But is it true?'

She hesitated. 'I've thought about it, of course. I tried calling an estate agent this morning, then reconsidered. There's no way Mrs Larwood could've known that, though.'

'Sometimes she just knows things,' he said. *As I have discovered to my cost.*

'No, she doesn't. She's a mean old gossip who sticks her nose into other people's business, and then she puts her own slant on it.'

'That's a bit harsh.'

'You might say that, but I think she knows something about my grandmother's death, and she's holding out on me.'

Something curdled in his stomach. 'What's there to know?'

'Beats me, but now Ivy's doctor wants to have a word with me. It's all very disturbing.'

They drove on in silence, further down the dirt track and through a small wood. The red-brick farm buildings which greeted them when they emerged from the woods were very much like his own, except there were no greenhouses.

He undid his seatbelt and took the painting from the back seat. 'I won't be long.'

Aidan ambled across the muddy yard with the parcel under his arm, bypassing the front door and turning round the corner of the building. He knows where he's going, Lia thought. *He's been here before.* Of course he had – the woman had sat for her portrait, and they must have spent hours together while he painted, either here or at his place. Before she could put a lid on the thought, she felt a stab of jealousy. If this woman had a straying husband, perhaps she wasn't completely against the idea of straying herself, and Aidan was an attractive man.

He disappeared into the farmhouse, and Lia hid her face in her hands with a groan.

Hell, what am I doing? I have Brett. Why should it matter what Aidan does?

Whimpering, Jack jumped up on to her lap and attempted to lick her face, but caught the back of her hand instead.

'All right, Jack, I know you're trying to be nice, but I've already had a wash.' She gently pushed him down again as Aidan returned to the car. Smiling smugly, he started the engine, turned the car around in the cobbled courtyard, and pulled away. Because of the treacherous feelings she shouldn't be having, the smile irritated her. A little devil made her plunge in with her feet first without thinking.

'Another satisfied customer?'

He grinned, and his grin spoke louder than words. She quickly changed the subject, because she couldn't bear these thoughts any longer. 'You said you wanted to talk to me. Was it to do with your radio interview?'

Aidan's grip tightened on the steering wheel, and he hurtled the Honda through the small wood faster than was safe. 'So you heard that?'

'It explains a lot,' she said and let him make the next move. When it finally came, they were back at the main road again, and Aidan was turning left, away from the direction which Lia had come.

'That wasn't what I wanted to talk to you about,' he said, staring fixedly at the road. 'I hear Susannah has offered to help you clear the house. I just want you to know that she has a tendency to push herself too hard.'

Lia glanced out of the window to hide her disappointment. 'Is there anything people don't know around here?'

'Plenty. So you'll make sure she takes it easy? No heavy lifting and all that. I feel sort of . . . protective towards her, if you get my drift.'

'She has a husband, you know.'

'Yeah,' he said ambiguously.

'What I mean is, presumably he's looking after her and making sure she takes it easy.' She could feel the heat rising in her cheeks that Aidan might think she was suggesting something untoward. What consenting adults got up to in rural Norfolk had nothing to do with her. Soon she'd be back in Philly where there was safety in numbers and where you could hide among thousands.

'I know what you meant.'

He put his hand on her leg briefly. It was a friendly gesture, not intended to be sexual, but the sudden sensation of his warm touch through her thin leggings sent daggers of heat up to her crotch. She bit her lip to stop herself from gasping in surprise.

He didn't seem to have noticed. 'How about if I buy you lunch? I know this great place not far from here where they do an excellent ploughman's. Freshly baked bread and home-made pickles.' He glanced at Jack at her feet. 'And dogs are welcome too.'

Lia looked at her dirty trainers with dismay. 'I can't go like this.'

'This is Norfolk, not the metropolis. I doubt if anyone will notice.'

Except his eyes told her that *he* had noticed, and that he liked what he saw.

CHAPTER 9

Aidan took her to a traditional pub outside Burnham Overy and ordered a ploughman's lunch for them both. 'What would you like to drink?'

She hesitated. 'You might think it a little odd, but what I'd like more than anything else is a Guinness. It's not that it's hard to find in the States, but somehow it never quite tastes the same over there.'

'Not at all. Guinness it is.'

He ordered two half pints, and as they carried their glasses through the crowded saloon bar, they heard a familiar voice.

'Well, I never!' said Mrs Larwood. 'Fancy you two being here. And *together*.'

There was no mistaking what she was hinting at, and beside her Lia felt Aidan tensing. She didn't blame him, it was like being caught with your hand in the cookie jar. Then she drew herself up. There was no reason she should feel like that. Nothing wrong with two people having lunch, whatever Mrs Larwood's interpretation.

'What are *you* doing here?' she asked in return.

They were some distance from the village, and Mrs Larwood didn't have a car, as far as Lia was aware.

'It's our regular pensioners' outing,' Mrs Larwood replied and indicated a large group of people as old as herself and dressed in their Sunday best, taking up several tables. 'Been planning this one for weeks, haven't we?'

The people around her table nodded.

'Some of us don't get out much,' she continued, 'the old bones not being what they were, but Bernie there—' she pointed to one of the men at her table, a craggy-faced gentleman in a blazer and cravat '—has a grandson who runs a coach company. Always happy to take us, he is. Never too busy like most young people these days.'

Bernie nodded, and then continued nodding as if he couldn't stop his head from moving. Parkinson's, Lia suspected, but couldn't say for sure.

She smiled. 'What a splendid idea.'

It pleased her that Mrs Larwood's social life wasn't hampered by old age, but it made her wonder about her grandmother. Had Ivy joined such outings? Or had she sat at home, alone, waiting for her busy granddaughter to call?

The expression in Mrs Larwood's sharp button eyes provided her with the answer, and she felt the smile leave her face.

Aidan put a hand on her arm. 'Let's find a table. Around the back is very nice.' To Mrs Larwood's pensioners' group, he said, 'Lovely to meet you all.

132

Have a great time,' as he steered Lia away from them, through an archway, and into a small lounge where there was a low table and a couple of armchairs in front of an open fire. There the kind landlady had already placed a bowl of water on the floor and a couple of Bonios for Jack.

'Don't let her get to you,' Aidan said.

Lia dropped down into one of the armchairs and stretched her long legs out in front of her. 'I wasn't.'

'It didn't look that way to me.'

She shrugged. 'Okay, maybe she did, a bit. I couldn't help thinking of Ivy, alone in that house, just waiting for, well, I don't know, for everything to end, perhaps.'

Aidan tossed one of the Bonios to Jack, who caught it in mid-air. He'd paled a little, and she wondered why.

'It's probably best for your own peace of mind if you don't think like that,' he said.

'You're right.' Of course he was right, she reminded herself. He knew what he was talking about where the subject of loss was concerned. The guilt, the heart-searching, the apportioning of blame. What could I have done that I didn't do, what did I do that I shouldn't have, and all that.

Those feelings were not unfamiliar to her, either, and they had nothing to do with the death of her grandmother. But she wasn't going to tell him that.

Resolutely she put the encounter with Mrs

Larwood behind her and snuggled into the armchair while she took in her surroundings.

A copper jug with an arrangement of dried lavender, wheat, and gold-painted poppy seed capsules stood beside the fireplace opposite a log basket, and an oil painting in cheerful blues and greens – not one of Aidan's, definitely not – hung on the bare brick wall above the mantelpiece. A fireguard was attached to the wall on either side of the fireplace, to keep out children and dogs. Thus thwarted, once he'd finished his treats, Jack stuck his head in the log basket instead and fished out a piece of bark which he proceeded to shred into little bits.

This was Norfolk at its picture-book best, a fertile place of cosy warmth.

At the same time, ever since Lia had arrived she'd had a feeling that if she allowed the peaceful country atmosphere to beguile her, she'd miss something important. Sight alone was not enough to prove that the soil was hardened by frost. All her senses were required.

They kept their conversation light while they waited for their food. As they ate, mostly in silence, Lia's mind returned to the radio interview. Her gut instinct told her this was the key to understanding Aidan, but she couldn't work out how to bring it up again.

'When you and Susannah have bagged up everything, I'd be happy to take it to the dump for you,' he said over coffee. 'The seats in my car fold down flat, so I can fit quite a lot in. And you might want a hand to clear out the attic.'

'I appreciate it, thanks.'

'Then you and Susannah can pore over embarrassing school photos and dress up in old clothes in peace.'

Did she detect a note of over-eagerness in his voice? And why was she so suspicious of him? This was a village; people gossiped, but they also helped each other out. Besides, it would be nice to have someone around when she went into the attic.

'I suppose we might go on a trip down memory lane,' she said. 'You can hardly avoid it when you clear out someone's house, but dressing up? Probably not. Besides, I don't think there'll be much to sort out. My grandmother wasn't a great accumulator of junk.'

'Most people have stuff in the attic.'

And skeletons in the closet, she thought, but kept it to herself. Instead she replied, 'Most people aren't like my grandmother.'

'Isn't that the truth?' He went quiet and stared into the fire. Jack curled up and went to sleep, this time at Aidan's feet. Lia spotted an opportunity, but kept her tone casual.

'I saw you on the beach the other day. I called out to you, but you just walked off. I was rather cheesed off, actually.'

'The beach?' he blinked and stared at her.

'Wednesday, I think it was. You were kitted out

135

for diving, on your own. I probably asked you before, but isn't that rather dangerous?'

'Oh, yes, well . . . It's not recommended.' He seemed a bit flustered and hesitated before adding, 'Listen, I didn't mean to . . . walk off. Sometimes I get like that. Not wanting company. It's nothing personal. And for me there's no better place to think than in the sea. It's a completely alien world, it sort of takes you out of yourself.'

His face became animated as he spoke, and his green eyes shone as if just imagining himself in that strange watery world made him happy. Despite her own irrational fears she envied the easy way he could duck under the waves and leave everything behind.

One day, she thought. *One day I might do the same. Rediscover what I lost.*

By talking about diving, Aidan had hoped to divert Lia's attention away from the situation on the beach as well as from his radio interview, but although he could tell that her interest was piqued, he realised he hadn't quite succeeded.

'It must be difficult for you to stay on at the farm now with your brother gone,' she said. 'Have you ever thought of selling up?'

He assessed her for a moment. She sat with her long legs stretched out in front of her and didn't seem self-conscious like so many other women he'd met, who'd finger their hair and their jewellery suggestively, batting their eyelashes so hard he'd worry they had something in their eye. Over the last few years he'd built up an immunity to come-hither smiles.

But Lia, in her Lycra leggings and no make-up, her face rosy-cheeked and windblown from being outdoors, ignited a part of him which he'd worked hard to keep a lid on. Something deep and true.

Swallowing hard, he resisted the temptation to reach out and touch her. She was engaged, and although that kind of commitment meant nothing to a lot of people these days, it mattered to him. Besides, he wasn't sure she'd welcome it.

For the time being he'd be content with getting to know her better. Her expression, as she regarded him now, wasn't a direct challenge, but instead invested with the altruism of a person belonging to the medical profession. At the same time, he could tell that the person behind the doctor was definitely curious. It made him smile.

'It did occur to me,' he replied, 'but I like it around here. Anyway, a house is just a house, it doesn't hold the spirits of those who lived there before.'

Lia nodded uncertainly, as if she didn't quite agree with him. Perhaps she felt differently. Perhaps there was a presence in her grandmother's house which affected her. Although he didn't believe in such things, he hadn't considered that she might. It just seemed a little at odds with what he knew about her.

'Technically, I can't sell it,' he went on. 'One

half of the estate belongs to my mother. For various reasons she doesn't feel it would be right to sell at the moment. Possibly she's clinging on to her memories; I don't know, she hasn't said anything. I only agreed to take it on for a while because she's not as strong as she used to be, and you can't just stop running a farm from one day to the next. You have to wind down gradually, sell off animals, lease the land, et cetera.'

'That's very decent of you,' she said. Her smile seemed genuine and was very pretty.

'Not really.' He finished his coffee, grimacing because it had gone cold. 'Family is important. You're lumbered with the one you're given, and you might not like the people in it very much or what they do, but you have to do the right thing. Which is why I was a little pissed off when she married again.'

'Because of your dad.'

She *so* had the wrong end of the stick, and he laughed. 'No, she was well rid of him. It was unexpected, though. Gerald had only . . . well, been gone a year, and suddenly my mother's off with some bloke. An army man, of all things! I said some rather harsh things, I'm afraid. So did my sister.'

'You don't like the army?'

'Are you for real?' He replaced his coffee cup on the saucer with a sharp clink. 'I have a few issues with the MoD, and with the government, as you've probably worked out by now. For instance, can you explain to me what we're still doing in Afghanistan?'

'Trying not to leave things in too much of a mess, I suppose.'

'Bit late for that, don't you think?'

She shrugged. 'I have no real interest in politics, except the basics. I think that if I allowed myself to become too engaged in current affairs, not just Afghanistan, I'd be permanently angry.'

'Uh-huh. So you stick your head in the sand instead?'

Her colour rose. 'Perhaps, but we're not talking about me. I just don't see what Afghanistan has to do with your mother marrying again.'

'I was angry – am angry – with her because she isn't honouring Gerald's memory.'

'That's a bit harsh, isn't it? We don't choose who we fall in love with, and perhaps your mother didn't know he was in the army until it was too late?'

Lia was needling him, but he allowed it. She was right, you didn't chose who you fell in love with. Because she fascinated him, he wanted her, of all people, to understand where he was coming from. On more than one account.

'It's very simple, and I don't need a shrink to help me work it out. The army betrayed my brother, like it continues to betray servicemen and women even as we speak. And my mother is sleeping with the enemy.'

This was his usual defence when on the subject

of his mother but, pinned by Lia's blue eyes, he realised how banal it sounded. Her reaction was what he'd expected from someone with her intelligence.

'Oh, come on, it's a soldier's job to go to war, isn't it? And it's no secret that people die in wars. So where does betrayal come into it? Your brother knew what he was doing.'

Touché, he thought and rose. He'd wanted to satisfy her curiosity while still maintaining control of the conversation, but she'd managed to direct it where he didn't want to go. He had to admire her, even as he wanted to throttle her.

Why are we ripping into each other like this? Because there's no one else?

'Yes,' he said, drawing a deep breath, 'Gerald knew what to expect, in war. Or he thought he did. It was what happened to him in peacetime he couldn't handle. He did his sacred duty, and then came home to find himself on the scrapheap, with no support. Have you any idea how it feels to see someone you love slowly disintegrate, fall to pieces bit by bit, and know that there's nothing you can do? Absolutely fuck all.'

Lia looked at him for a moment, a little wide-eyed, then shook her head.

'I'd better settle the bill,' he said. 'See you outside.'

On his way to the bar he cursed himself. For a second back there he'd been so focused on his anger that he hadn't realised she probably found

140

it rather scary. Aidan, you klutz, he thought. It was time for a peace offering, and he knew the perfect thing. Something she didn't already have.

In the pub the pensioners were getting ready to leave. Mrs Larwood caught his arm as he walked past.

'Does she know?' she asked.

'I don't know what you're talking about.'

Narrowing her eyes, she dug her hand into his arm. 'It's not right, dear. A nice girl like that. Doesn't deserve you messing around. If you don't tell her, I will.'

'It's none of your business.'

'You're wrong there, it is my business. And Ivy Barrington felt the same, she did.'

Aidan shook himself free of her grip. The urge to throttle someone came back with a vengeance. Clenching his fists to stop himself from doing just that, he sent her a furious glare and walked off.

Some day the old crone would stick her pointy nose out a little too far, and he wouldn't want to be in her shoes when that happened.

Oh, shit, Lia thought. *Shit, shit, shit. I've done it now. He'll never speak to me again.*

She rose and put on her gloves and scarf. Jack woke from his sleep and yawned.

When she came outside, Aidan had reversed the car, leaving angry tyre marks in the gravel of the forecourt. The passenger door was open, and Lia and Jack climbed in. The silence in the car was

141

tangible, and Jack seemed to sense it too, staring from one to the other with his round, brown eyes.

Lia wished she'd jogged home, but wasn't sure Jack could have coped with such a long trek. Besides, it had started to drizzle. After a brief sunny spell in the morning the sky had been heavy with slate-coloured clouds, so the rain was no surprise, but bad timing nonetheless. What had got into her, to provoke Aidan like that? Usually she was a great believer in letting sleeping dogs lie.

'Look,' she said, 'I'm really sorry about what I said back there.'

Aidan made a dismissive gesture. 'It's not you, okay? I know you were only trying to make sense of it. Unlike some,' he added under his breath.

'I know I can't completely understand how you feel, because only you really know, and your feelings are unique to you. But I see people in your situation every day. They don't get up in the morning knowing that they're going to be struck by tragedy. They don't think, "today my life will change forever". It just happens. I can't repair them or take their grief away, but I am familiar with it. I just wanted to help.'

'My grief,' he mused with a curious smile on his lips. 'My grief is, well, complex. For starters I'm more angry than upset.'

'That's often how people show their pain.'

'I expect you're right.' He glanced at her. 'Doing anything tonight?'

His question took her by surprise. 'Honestly, only a minute ago you were ready to bite my head off, and now you're asking me if I've plans for the evening. It's a bit confusing.'

Not to mention that it caused a peculiar fluttering in her stomach. Perhaps it was his unpredictability which attracted her, even though she found it unsettling at the same time. Like a moth to a flame.

'Well, do you have plans or not?'

Her head told her to say she was busy, but the rest of her had other ideas. 'I might make a start on the tidying. Other than that, nothing. Why?'

They had reached the outskirts of the village, and Aidan slowed down to the required speed limit. 'I've got some of my diving pupils coming over for supper, plus my buddy who's also an instructor. Why don't you join us? Then you can hear their stories of how scared they were the first time they went diving and all that.' He smiled, but there was a tinge of sadness to it. 'I'm still convinced it's my destiny to teach you to dive.'

'You'll have your work cut out for you, then.'

'It'd be no fun otherwise.'

'But you've already bought me lunch. I can't let you treat me to dinner as well.'

Aidan swung the car into the drive in front of Ivy's house, then killed the engine. 'It's a bring-a-dish do. Anything hot and spicy will be just the thing. But remember, three of us are vegetarians.'

His tone was light, but she sensed the pleading behind it.

Why? she thought. *What do you want from me?*

Then she thought of the cold house and the aerial on Ivy's television which could only produce a grainy picture. Whatever her grandmother had done to pass the time in the evenings, it had probably involved a lot of thinking, and thinking was the last thing Lia wanted to do right now.

The alternative was the company of individuals crazy enough to let themselves be at the mercy of the sea. No competition really.

'I'd like that. Thanks.'

CHAPTER 10

Later Lia knocked on Aidan's door, bearing an ovenproof dish of pumpkin risotto. To her surprise it was flung open by a slender blonde.

'You must be Lia,' she said before Lia could open her mouth. 'I'm Rachel. Come in. Here, let me take that.' She took the dish from Lia and told her to leave her coat on a chair in the hall, already laden with overcoats, then called over her shoulder. 'We're in the kitchen.'

Lia shed her coat and put her gloves and scarf inside her hat and left it on the hall table. She followed the sound of voices from the end of the hall, while she wondered who Rachel was and what she was to Aidan. For some idiotic reason it hadn't occurred to her before that divers could be both male and female, because Aidan had been a navy diver, and she'd always thought the navy was exclusively a male domain. She was happy to have her prejudices refuted.

And she wasn't jealous, of course. She had no right to be.

A collection of oddballs were assembled in the

145

kitchen, which was warm and steamed up from cooking.

Rachel made the introductions. She started with her husband Anthony – not Tony – who was an accountant, and Lia experienced a curious sense of relief that she wasn't Aidan's girlfriend. Anthony-not-Tony was tall with a receding hairline and the modest beginnings of a paunch. He wore a striped Oxford shirt and ironed jeans.

'Chablis?' he said, with a wink, and handed her a glass.

'Please.'

She took the glass gratefully as Rachel introduced her to Finn, who wore a brown suit jacket, a knitted Doctor Who scarf and a mock professorial expression. It was on the tip of her tongue to ask him where he kept his sonic screwdriver, but he beat her to it with nosy questions of his own.

'So, you're Aidan's latest addition. What can I say, the boy has taste.'

She was about to demand of him what he meant by that when Bella, a plump ginger-haired secondary school teacher, was introduced. 'Do you work locally?' Lia asked politely.

'In Fakenham.'

'The sixth form college? I went there. A long time ago.'

Bella smiled. 'I know. So did Aidan. I gather that's how you met. Which reminds me,' she said to the room in general, 'where is he?'

'In the stables, doing something unspeakable to

146

sheep,' said Finn, earning him a roll of the eyes from Bella.

'Anyway,' she continued, 'I think it's fantastic that you've kept in touch all these years. So many people don't.'

We didn't.

'And *very* romantic,' Finn interjected.

'Finn, find someone else to pester,' said Rachel. 'Oh, and this is John.'

Finn was handing a bowl of nuts around. 'John's our local tree-hugger.'

'Actually, I'm a tree *surgeon*, which doesn't involve a lot of hugging.' John grinned and pumped Lia's hand in a bone-crushing grip. He sported a goatee beard and a lazy eye which seemed to turn in a different direction from whatever his other eye was looking at. Lia learned that he worked at Holkham Park, the grounds surrounding Holkham Hall, which was a privately owned estate a couple of miles from the village.

'Have you been there?' he asked.

'A long time ago,' said Lia, 'with my grand-mother, but we saw the house, not the park.'

'Try the park some day. There are some lovely walks. Here . . .' he handed her a business card, '. . . if you get the time, give us a call, and I can show you around.'

Lia pocketed the card, grateful that although he was an instructor like Aidan, so far he hadn't mentioned diving, as if he sensed this was still a touchy subject for her. 'I'll do that, thanks.'

147

'Hands off, John, this one's spoken for,' said Finn. 'Have you seen the size of that rock? What did Aidan do, rob a bank?'

Self-consciously Lia slid her right hand over her left to cover her engagement ring. 'No, this isn't—'

'He *knows*,' said Bella. 'He's just winding you up.'

Rachel put her hand on Lia's arm. 'Come and meet Peter. He's a GP in Wells, so you two should have a great deal to talk about.'

Peter was laying the table at the back of the large kitchen where Lia and Aidan had sat only a few days ago. It felt like ages. He welcomed her with an easy-going manner, asking her if she was enjoying her stay in the village, and offered his condolences on the death of her grandmother. Of medium height, brownish hair colour, and a reassuring baritone, he was exactly the sort of doctor a patient could confide in about an embarrassing illness. Lia began to relax a little. Finn was funny, without a doubt, but he put her on edge with his teasing, and Bella and Rachel must have been under strict instructions to entertain the newcomer, because their behaviour felt stilted. But Peter was okay.

And where was Aidan? He knew what time she was due to be here, that she didn't know any of the others, so why didn't he show up? It was almost as if he was testing her, but she had no idea why.

'Can I help?' she asked Peter, in order not to stand there like a lemon.

He nodded as if he'd read her mind. 'You could find us some clean knives. Try the dishwasher.'

It was clear they all knew each other extremely well, right down to where the clean knives might be hiding, and it made her feel even more like an outsider.

But she forced herself to make conversation, and after a while it turned out not to be as difficult as she'd feared. She found herself laughing at Finn's complete irreverence in all things, admired Bella's ankle-length stiletto boots which lent a few extra inches to her short, dumpy figure, was warmed by the obvious affection between Rachel and Anthony, and discussed the relative merits of Norway Spruce versus Scots Pine as Christmas trees with John.

There was still no sign of Aidan, but when they were all sitting down, a gust of cold air from the back door announced his return.

He came into the kitchen smelling deliciously of cold air and fresh hay. 'Sorry, sick sheep,' he said to Lia. 'I hope Rachel has looked after you.'

'Everyone has,' she replied. It occurred to her then that the test had been for her to deal with an unaccustomed social situation without any hand-holding, and that she'd done rather well. Habitually, at a gathering, Brett's hand would rest on her lower back while he steered her around the room in a manner which was both reassuring and infuriatingly proprietorial. She suddenly realised just how much she resented that.

Aidan, on the other hand, had dropped her in

at the deep end, and she was grateful for that, in a perverse sort of way.

He took the empty seat at the other end of the table and, with a comforting smile at Lia, turned to Bella beside him. Lia discovered common ground with Peter, and they were soon comparing notes between working as a general practitioner and in a hospital.

'I enjoy it,' he said, 'although I do sometimes miss the excitement of the wards. The advantage is that you get to know your patients on a personal level.'

Lia had a brainwave. 'Did you know Aidan's brother, Gerald?'

Peter glanced in Aidan's direction, but Aidan was in deep discussion with Finn and Bella and didn't look up. He turned back to Lia. 'I was his GP for a while,' he answered warily.

'Did he really take his own life?' When Peter didn't answer, she added, 'I'm just trying to understand Aidan better. I heard him on the radio, but he's obviously still very raw, and I don't quite know how to handle it.'

Peter smiled but the wary look remained. 'Should you be asking me this? You know I'm bound by doctor–patient confidentiality.'

'Fair enough, but I'm asking you both as a doctor and Aidan's friend.'

'I suppose that's okay.' Peter shrugged. 'When Gerald came to me, he was very depressed. He felt useless, emasculated, couldn't sleep, and when he did, he had terrible nightmares. So I prescribed antidepressants.'

'And that was all?'

'I can only cure what I'm presented with,' Peter replied, with a hint of defensiveness in his voice, 'and only some of the time. I don't have time to take the holistic approach.'

Lia feared he was about to deliver a lecture about how overworked doctors were – as if she didn't know already – so she merely nodded. 'But you were the one who diagnosed him with post-traumatic stress disorder, weren't you?'

Peter speared a forkful of food from his plate, then put it down again. 'I was, yes.'

'I thought there was help available for that.'

'There is now,' he said, 'but Gerald was one of the first lot to return from Iraq, and it wasn't really understood how prevalent it was back then, or how devastating its effects could be. I'd just set up in my practice, and it was only when I attended a medical conference that I began to focus on it. Sadly, by then it was too late for him.'

'Did he refuse help?'

'Not as such, but he couldn't accept that his problems were psychological. "I don't want a head doctor", he said, and I couldn't force him to see a therapist. What he really needed was a self-help group with other veterans, but as far as I knew, there weren't any. They came later. On my own time I offered consultations where we'd just talk, and he turned up a couple of times, then stopped.

151

As frustrating as it was, there was nothing more I could do for him as a GP.'

Lia looked up, worried that the others had over-heard their conversation, but it didn't appear so. Only Aidan met her eyes, briefly, and she got the impression that he knew what they were talking about although he couldn't have heard them from the other end of the table.

Even so, she lowered her voice. 'What about Aidan? Did he try to get involved?'

'I didn't know Aidan back then.' Peter sighed. 'If I had, perhaps things might have been different. Fortunately, he isn't angry with me.'

'He's certainly angry with the MoD. Says they let his brother down. Do you agree?'

Peter nodded. 'I do, actually. Although I don't think the way he's going about it will make a blind bit of difference.'

With that he turned to the food on his plate, and it was clear to Lia she wasn't going to get any more information out of him. Whether he had anything else to share or not, she felt as if she'd only been given half the picture.

Though Peter had gone conspicuously silent, the dinner party continued all around them as if every-thing was normal. Lia couldn't escape the feeling that it wasn't though, and it was making her feel uncomfortable.

On her other side, John was talking about the walks in Holkham Park. 'The one going around the lake is stunning,' he said. 'It starts in the village, and it's about four miles long. A great place to ponder the meaning of life and all that.'

'I tend to run more than I walk,' Lia said, trying not to stare at his peculiar eye.

'I don't see why you can't jog along the path as long as you don't disturb the wildlife. There's a nature trail too, but that's a bit more rugged and not really suitable for jogging.'

Suddenly the conversation fell quiet around the table, and everyone turned to look at Lia. Finn was the first to break the silence. Swinging one end of the knitted scarf over his shoulder – why was he wearing a scarf while eating? – he said, 'So, when are you going diving with us?'

Lia looked at Aidan, who sent her a teasing smile, and she added manipulation to his long list of crimes. How could she back down now, with all these nice people so eager for her join them?

'I've never tried it before. To be honest with you, I'm not one for the water.'

'You're afraid of it,' said Finn.

At that Rachel protested vehemently, and they all started to speak at once until their voices rose to deafening proportions. Lia could barely hear herself think as they babbled on over each other, all except Aidan, who was still wearing that irritating, self-satisfied little smile.

'But you know the basics, don't you?' said John over the din. 'You know about the equipment and the buddy check. And the signals.'

She shook her head.

Bella put her wine glass down on the table with a thump. 'Dammit, Aidan, what are you playing at? Murder us in our beds? Apart from you and John, only two of us have Open Water certification. What if something goes wrong?'

Some of the others murmured their agreement, although no one pointed out that in the frigid North Sea they'd be as far away from their beds as they could possibly get.

Aidan lost the annoying smile. Good on you, Bella, thought Lia.

'Take it easy, Bella. I'm not that unprofessional. Lia and I will start with the swimming pool. Then I'll take her out on my own a couple of times to get her up to scratch.'

'Would you like me to come to the pool with you?' John asked.

Across the length of the table Aidan met Lia's eyes, then shook his head, and Lia let out her breath, suddenly conscious that she'd been holding it. It was one thing for Aidan to know about her reluctance to go in the water, but a virtual stranger too . . .? She wasn't quite ready for that.

'No, we'll be fine. But thanks,' Aidan replied.

Finn made a suggestive noise. 'Private lessons. I see.'

'Shut up, Finn!' said Bella and Rachel in unison. Bella tossed a bread roll at him, and it hit him on the head with a thud then landed on the floor.

'Hey,' he protested, rubbing his temple. 'I was going to eat that.'

Private lessons, like hell, thought Lia. She hadn't even agreed to any of it. 'Excuse me, but could you please stop talking about me as if I'm not here. For your information I've no intention of going within fifty feet of the sea, with you lot or anyone else.'

A cacophony of apologies and explanations winged their way back in Lia's direction, and she felt mollified. Slightly.

Anthony, who hadn't said much up till now, reached for Rachel's hand. 'You ought to give it a go,' he said to Lia. 'It's the most amazing thing you'll ever do. Going down into this whole other world with people you like and respect, building up trust—' he squeezed his wife's hand '—well, it saved our marriage.'

'Which, of course, puts a totally different spin on the notion of water therapy,' said Finn.

'Oh, shut up.' Rachel passed the wine bottle across the table to Finn. 'Here, have a drink and don't interrupt while the grown-ups are talking.'

Finn lifted his glass in an ironic salute.

'Seriously,' continued Anthony unperturbed, 'it's very safe. In the beginning I felt like you do. I've never been much of a swimmer, but when Rachel got the bug, I decided to join in—'

'Keeping tabs on her, more like,' Finn interjected.

Rachel rolled her eyes. Anthony ignored him. 'It's not about being a champion swimmer, it's about breathing, about technique. Respect the

155

element you're in, and you become a part of it. It's a whole new kind of freedom. It's wonderful.'

Despite Anthony's slightly lecturing tone Lia listened with fascination to his first experience of diving, the feelings it had evoked, and what a revelation it had been for him. His honest account of both his fear and his elation had an effect on her she never imagined. The others were silent too, even Finn, as if they had all shared the same epiphany.

Images of water and hands pulling her down flashed before her inner eye, but this time she managed to quell them, thanks to Anthony's reassurances and references to teamwork. She wouldn't be alone in this, the way she always was in her dreams. They would be a group, there for each other.

It's only a stupid nightmare, she thought. Why be so scared of something which wasn't real? If other people could overcome their fears, she could too. Temptation tugged at her. It would be so easy to say yes and go diving with them, entrust them with her safety, let go of her restraint. But there were still a few unanswered questions.

'How do you communicate if one of you is in trouble?' she asked. 'Do you use radios?'

'Nope,' said Aidan. 'Radios ruin the experience. In a silent world you must use a silent language. We use hand signals.' He made a thumbs up gesture. 'This means "we're going up".'

He then ran through a series of the most common

signals among recreational divers. Lia copied them all, and Aidan got everyone else to go through them again. It turned into a silly party game of who was the quickest off the mark, which Lia lost, of course, because she was unfamiliar with the signals and slow to produce them.

Despite her misgivings she could feel herself getting excited by the idea of going on a dive, and it appealed to her sense of order that diving was technically so involved. Technology designed with the function of keeping the body safe and avoiding accidents was something she could relate to, and her respect for Aidan went up a notch.

She made a decision. Be brave and give it a go. After all, she'd be with Aidan and all the others. What could possibly go wrong?

John turned to Aidan as everyone was leaving. 'Er, listen,' he said, 'could I drop by another day and borrow one of your suits? I've put on quite a lot of weight recently, and well . . . . I'm a bit skint at the moment. Can't really afford to buy a new one just yet. You're a couple of sizes bigger than me, aren't you?'

'Sure. Any time. If I'm not here when you come, just help yourself. The back door is always open.'

John thanked him and left with Rachel and Anthony. Aidan waited until they were gone before sending a text. Then he jumped in the car and drove, with the headlights off, into the village, where he parked in a small side road a few doors down from Susannah's shop on the opposite side of the main road.

Huddling in his dark jacket, he watched the house. The bedroom right above the shop front was dark, but that didn't mean anything. Susannah would come. She always did.

Sure enough, about five minutes later he spied a flickering light in the shop itself – she always carried a torch – and a figure came out of the shop door.

Susannah paused and looked up at the bedroom window, then turned and crossed the road to where Aidan was standing, half-hidden behind the house on the corner of the side road. She was dressed in some sort of voluminous, woolly cardigan or fleece, but her legs were bare in her Wellington boots. Wordlessly she slid her arms around his neck and gave him a quick kiss, then drew away again.

He could barely make out her features in the dark, but the set of her shoulders told their own story. They were hunched, as if she'd been carrying a heavy load, which he supposed she was.

'How are things?' he asked.

'Okay.' She shrugged and drew her cardigan tighter around her.

'Nigel?'

'Sleeping the sleep of the innocent.'

'Good.' He put a hand on her shoulder, felt the tension beneath her layers of clothing, and longed to comfort her. 'Long may it last.'

She gave a mirthless little laugh.

'And Zoe?'

This time he thought he detected a smile. 'A royal pain. What do you expect? She's fifteen.'

'I know she's fifteen. I know everything there is to know about her. As I should.' He sighed. 'What I meant is, does *she* know anything? About what's going on?'

Susannah shivered.

'You're cold,' he said.

'I'm fine.'

'Here, take this.' He shrugged off his jacket and draped it over her shoulders.

'Oh, will you stop fussing! I don't want your damn jacket.' She made as if to take it off, but Aidan kept it firmly tucked around her, and she gave up fighting him.

'By rights I should be spending my life fussing over you,' he said.

'No, you shouldn't.' She smiled up at him. 'But thanks.'

'So Zoe is still in the dark?'

'I'm not sure. Ever since she saw Mrs Barrington, about a week before she died, I think, she's been absolutely impossible, just pushing, pushing, and pushing. I don't think I can hold out much longer. She must've said something to Zoe, but what exactly is anyone's guess. And if she hears more, what then? She'll want to . . .' Susannah tailed off.

'She's not going to,' said Aidan.

'What about Lia? They could've talked before Mrs Barrington died.'

Lia, thought Aidan with a pang. *Lia, Lia, Lia.* Life could have been so different if Susannah hadn't fallen pregnant, if Lia hadn't moved away. Both their lives. Everyone's lives. He might have had the courage to . . . no, it was no use thinking like that. He had to concentrate on the here and now.

'Lia doesn't know anything, and she won't either if I have anything to do with it.'

'What will you do?' Susannah frowned. 'Aidan?' she prodded when he didn't reply immediately.

'Find some way to keep her busy,' he said. Which would be no hardship, if it wasn't for the fact that Lia had her own secrets. He held open his arms, and Susannah stepped into his embrace. 'It'll be all right.'

'I know,' she said, muffled against his shoulder.

CHAPTER 11

Before Lia had time to put her resolution to the test, other more urgent matters intruded. On the third day after the dinner party, she had another call from Doctor Campbell. Guiltily she realised she'd forgotten her promise to go along to his surgery, and suggested that she drop in to see him straight away.

'Make it three o'clock, I have a busy schedule today,' he said in his quavering voice. Nevertheless, Lia could sense the steel behind it, so she agreed.

At three on the dot she pushed open the door to Doctor Campbell's surgery in the village. It was empty apart from the receptionist, who glared at Lia through a glass partition. 'You don't have an appointment.'

'I do. Sort of. Doctor Campbell asked me to drop by. It's about my grandmother, Mrs Barrington. She died a few weeks ago,' she added.

Thus thwarted, the receptionist pointed down the hallway. 'Down there, second door on the left.'

The door to Doctor Campbell's office was ajar. The doctor sat at his desk staring myopically at a computer screen. He'd pushed his glasses

161

up on to his forehead and was typing up his notes using only his index fingers. Beside the keyboard stood a mug with the Scottish flag on it.

'Take a seat,' he said without looking at Lia.

Lia sat without a word.

'This newfangled technology,' he muttered, perhaps more to himself than to his visitor. 'More trouble than it's worth.' He looked up. 'Do you ken, we've to keep all our patients' records on this wretched thing now. The time I waste when I could be helping sick people . . .'

Without modern technology, the entire medical profession would be back in the Middle Ages, Lia thought, but hoped her non-committal sound could be interpreted as agreement. She didn't want to antagonise this cranky old Scotsman, who was clearly losing his marbles.

He sent her a sharp look. 'And I'm not yet ready for my dotage, if that's what you're thinking.'

She blushed. How could he read her mind without even looking at her? Spooky. 'I wasn't suggesting anything of the sort.'

'Of course not.' He smiled, and his whole demeanour changed, becoming the epitome of the kindly village doctor. 'Your grandmother was a fine old lady.'

'Thank you.'

'A lady with secrets, I daresay, but a lady nonetheless.'

Lia raised her eyebrows.

'Oh, yes, indeed. Now, where was it? Ah, yes,

here we are.' He turned the computer screen towards Lia so she could read the entry. 'I miss the old paper records. Paper has such a comforting smell about it. Unlike this confounded thing.' He scowled. 'Anyway, where were we?'

'My grandmother's medical records.' And her secrets, Lia added to herself. *What secrets?*

Doctor Campbell pulled his glasses down on to his nose. 'Well, as you can read, your grandmother didn't come to see me much, and the few times she was here, I gave her a clean bill of health. For a woman her age, her blood pressure was remarkably sound; she had a healthy diet as far as I could tell, she took regular exercise—'

'And she died from a heart attack,' Lia interrupted. 'It happens. Sadly.'

'Aye, but to sum up, Mrs Barrington was a great deal fitter than many women twenty years younger,' he told her.

'It's true she looked after herself, but I don't understand where this is heading. You mentioned on the phone that you had some remaining issues. Are you saying that my grandmother *didn't* die from a heart attack?'

He shook his head. 'Oh, it was a heart attack all right. What I'm saying is that it came as a wee bit of a surprise to me that it should happen to a woman in such good health. Unless it was brought on by something else.'

'Like what?' Surreptitiously Lia glanced at her watch. Susannah was coming at four o'clock for tea, and afterwards they'd planned to start on the clearing out. She wondered how much longer this was going to take.

The gesture didn't pass him by. Leaning back in his chair, he steepled his fingers and fixed her with a penetrating stare. 'I don't know how much you've heard, but your grandmother was in quite a state when Hazel Larwood found her. I expect she may have spared you the worst of the details.'

'Well, she mentioned there was a fair amount of blood. She must've hit her head pretty hard when she fell.'

'She'd thrown up a wee bit. She was also in a mess in, er, her nether regions.'

Lia stared at him. Had the subject matter been anything other than a death, she might have laughed at his coy manner. It seemed ridiculous for a doctor to use a euphemism for a simple bodily function, especially to a fellow doctor. 'It's normal for people's bowels to open when they die.'

'Aye, but that's not what I meant. She'd suffered a rectal haemorrhage, indicating severe intestinal bleeding. That was why I referred it to the coroner in the first place.'

Lia swallowed. Mrs Larwood's words came back to her. *Blood everywhere.* Her neighbour hadn't been exaggerating after all.

'He authorised a post-mortem, which confirmed the heart attack as the cause of death. The cause of the bleeding was . . . inconclusive.' Doctor

Campbell leaned forward and pointed his finger at Lia's chest. 'Now, if it wasn't a sin according to the Good Book, I'd wager all my savings, down to the very last penny, that your grandmother died because she'd ingested poison.'

A peculiar cold feeling fanned out from Lia's stomach to the rest of her, and she shuddered. *Dear God!*

'Poison,' she heard herself saying. 'What kind of poison?'

Doctor Campbell regarded her over the rim of his reading glasses. 'Well, how many kinds do you know of? The kind that kills a person, I should think.'

Lia cleared her throat. 'I meant, was it accidental or deliberate? Did someone administer poison to my grandmother, or was it something that happened by mistake, like, say, from eating contaminated food?' Her mind went back to the carefully-rinsed foil trays. 'I found an empty takeaway bag in the kitchen, from a curry restaurant in Wells. Maybe she picked up a nasty bug from there.'

'Well,' he began, 'it's true that some foodborne infections can cause symptoms such as your grandmother's . . .'

Unaware that she'd been holding her breath, Lia let out a deep sigh. Her thoughts had been taking her in an uncomfortable direction, and she just didn't want to go there. 'Well, that's settled then,' she said, even though she had the feeling it was far from settled, and got up. 'I'll give the council a call and get the Health and Safety Inspector to take a closer look at that place.'

Doctor Campbell stopped her with a look from under his bushy eyebrows.

'But,' he said with such authority that she sat down again. 'you'd likely expect in that case that there'd be an outbreak of some sort in the locality, wouldn't you? And there was none. Besides,' he added, 'they tested for E. coli at the post mortem. And Campylobacter. And Salmonella. All negative. See for yourself.'

He handed Lia a folder which contained a copy of the post-mortem report. She scanned the pages, her trained eye rapidly taking in the information as he spoke. As well as massive bleeding in the lower intestine, there was evidence of liver and kidney damage, and the beginnings of systemic organ failure, doubtless brought on by dehydration.

'They tested for arsenic, just in case,' Doctor Campbell was saying, 'as well as bacterial agents. But since it's not unusual for gastroenteritis to cause fatal complications in older people, the coroner signed it off as cardiac arrest, exacerbated by enteric infection, cause unknown.

'And that would be that,' he said as Lia got to the end of the report. 'Except that I still find it hard to believe a woman as fit as she was would have died from a tummy bug. Elderly or no'. The pathologist's a friend of mine, and I'm minded to ask him to re-examine his findings, see if there's some toxin he might have missed. Post mortem results are only about fifty per cent reliable, as I recall. Your grandmother was cremated?'

'Yes. The hospital released the body the week after, and my mother wanted to get the whole thing over and done with as quickly as possible.'

'Was cremation her own wish?'

Lia's mouth dropped open. Was he being serious? Then she looked at the calculated expression in his eyes, and realised he wasn't joking. A feeling of dread settled in her stomach.

She couldn't remember if she and Ivy had ever discussed such matters. Her grandmother had seemed like the sort of person who would carry on forever. They talked about books and Lia's job, and Ivy had kept her up to date with the local gossip, which gave her a sense of still belonging even though she'd disassociated herself from it all. She'd never felt comfortable with the way wagging tongues could make or break a person in a small community.

At the same time her grandmother kept her cards close to her chest, almost as if a black spot existed somewhere in her psyche which she never shared with anyone. It was Connie who had said that Ivy wanted to be cremated.

'I imagine so,' she said. 'Isn't that the most environmentally friendly thing to do these days? I'm sure my grandmother would've wanted to do her bit for the planet.'

Doctor Campbell made a non-committal noise, which sounded like a contemptuous snort. 'It doesn't matter. He'll have his notes, and your mother gave permission for him to keep some tissue samples. They won't have been destroyed yet. You don't have any objections, I take it, if the pathologist takes another look?'

'Why should I?' Lia tried to outstare him but couldn't and looked away. 'Although I still think it must've been food poisoning which led to her heart attack.'

Even though I've never seen my grandmother eat a takeaway in my entire life, she thought.

She half-walked, half-jogged back, anxious to be there in time for Susannah and Zoe. Doctor Campbell had given her a lot to think about, even if she suspected he was overreacting. Who would want to kill her grandmother? So she was a gossip. So was half the village. If anyone should be in the line of fire for that reason, it was that old hag Mrs Larwood. Talk about telling tales. You couldn't sneeze within a two-mile radius without her knowing about it.

Yet, deep down, the suspicion gnawed at her that Ivy may have stumbled upon something that someone was prepared to bury at all costs, and no matter how hard she tried, the idea was fuelled by every single thriller she'd ever read. Serial killers, political intrigue, financial motives, all in one big muddle.

The thought that the answer could lie closer to home she pushed aside immediately.

The weather had cleared up, and the sky was a crisp blue with a few clouds further south pushed along by an onshore wind. She could hear the sea, and over the beach seagulls soared and then dipped with ferocious speed as if they had spotted something edible in the swell.

Lia stopped to listen, then wished she hadn't. Without warning, images of water closing over her head flashed before her like a film reel on fast-forward. Eddie's moon face, the rage in Connie's eyes at dinner the other night, the water again, pulling and dragging her, singing and laughing. She gasped and steadied herself against a tree by the roadside.

No.

It wasn't possible. Her mother couldn't have. She *wouldn't* have. It was unthinkable.

She forced herself to breathe deeply, then squeezed her eyes shut to banish the images. Plunging her hands inside the pockets of her grandmother's Barbour, she stomped back to the house.

Ivy's death was precipitated by straightforward enteritis, either from something she ate or from some bug she'd caught. Connie had nothing to do with it. No one had anything to do with it. The ancient doctor needed pensioning off.

End of story.

Aidan was putting his shopping bags in the car when he felt a tap on his shoulder. Preoccupied as he'd been with his own thoughts, it startled him, and he swung around.

'No need to look at me like that,' said Nigel. He was pushing a shopping trolley with Ethan in the kiddie seat. 'I'm not out to get you.'

It was said jokingly, but his dark brown eyes met Aidan's head-on.

'I didn't think you were. You just gave me a start.' Aidan smiled at the boy. 'Hi there, Ethan. Going shopping with Daddy today?'

'Say hi to Uncle Aidan,' said Nigel, with a nasty little emphasis on the word uncle. Aidan ignored him.

Ethan stuck out his bottom lip. 'Don't like shopping.'

'Don't blame you, my friend. It's dead scary. First there's all those horrid-looking vegetables you have to avoid, then there's the Eat-Me Eat-Me cookies. You don't want to get too close to those snapping little devils.'

Ethan giggled. 'You're silly.'

'Yes, Uncle Aidan is being very silly.' There was that snide undertone again. Spit it out, Aidan wanted to say, then realised Nigel couldn't because of the child.

'Remember I promised you could have a go at steering my Honda?' Aidan said to Ethan. 'Would you like to sit in the driver's seat for a minute while me and Daddy have a talk?'

'Yay!' Ethan did his best to disentangle himself from the shopping trolley, and Nigel lifted him down. Aidan opened the car and let the little boy clamber up on to the front seat, where he immediately started making engine noises and pressing all the buttons he could reach.

Aidan left him to it and finished loading the shopping in the boot. 'What's on your mind, Nigel?' he said.

'I know what you're trying to do.'

'Do you? I very much doubt it.'

Nigel's usually ruddy face went a shade deeper, and he clenched his fists at his sides. Aidan thought he resembled an angry carrot, but held his tongue because he didn't fancy a broken nose. As it was, he was sailing too close to the wind already.

'Susannah doesn't talk to me any more, and it's all to do with you. Can't you just leave us alone? Stop interfering with my wife and daughter.'

'Interfering with your wife . . .' Aidan scoffed. 'That's not how I see it. And Zoe's not your daughter.'

'I'm the only father she's ever known. I fed and clothed her and everything else, so you can get down from your high horse.'

Aidan slammed the boot shut. 'Surely I have some rights.'

'None whatsoever, and you won't bloody well forget that if you know what's good for you!'

'Are you threatening me?' Aidan raised himself up to his full height. Nigel was well built, but shorter, and he didn't have Aidan's muscle tone or agility, nor had he been trained to be a fighter.

Aidan felt confident he could stand his ground in a scuffle with Nigel, although he hoped it wouldn't come to that.

Nigel went puce, and for a moment it looked as if it would end in violence, but Nigel's good sense prevailed. 'I'm asking you to back down,' he said. 'Give my wife some peace.'

'That's not really up to me, is it?'

Aidan went to the front to help Ethan out of the car, effectively ending the conversation, but long after he'd driven off, he felt Nigel's gaze boring into his back.

He'd have to be very careful from now on.

There was just enough time to put out some scones she'd made earlier and bowls of clotted cream and strawberry jam on the table in the kitchen, where, thankfully, the Rayburn decided to behave, before Susannah and Zoe arrived on foot. Susannah was her old self, and Zoe had a great deal more to say for herself than your average monosyllabic teenager. She wasn't afraid to express her opinions, either, which managed to distract Lia from her earlier thoughts.

After tea they divided the house between them. Susannah would tackle Ivy's wardrobe, and Zoe volunteered to go through the books and various knick-knacks in Lia's old room. Lia pared the kitchen down to the few necessities she'd need while she was here and stacked the bags and boxes in the hall. Marked with their intended destination

– charity shop, dump, recycling – Aidan would cart them away as he'd promised.

She felt no sentimental attachment to Ivy's belongings – possessions didn't make the person – but going up in the attic on her own worried her. She stopped thinking like a rational human being and instead quailed inside at the thought of what might be lurking up there, just waiting to be uncovered. Eight-legged or otherwise.

After having lugged bags around for an hour, she made another pot of tea and carried three mugs upstairs as well as an unopened packet of biscuits. Drinking tea with friends was such a normal thing to do that Doctor Campbell's suspicions, or dark fantasies perhaps, felt almost surreal; as if she were going to wake up any minute now to discover that fantasy had become reality, but how she might discuss this with Susannah she had no idea. Or if she even wanted to.

In her old bedroom Zoe was emptying the shelves of ancient, yellowed paperbacks. Sitting cross-legged on the floor in her leggings and UGG boots, Zoe was plugged into her iPod, and in front of her were several piles of books. Jack lay with his head resting on her thigh and a look of the utmost adoration in his brown eyes.

Traitor, thought Lia. 'Tea?'

Zoe removed the headphones from one ear. 'Mm?'

'I made more tea.'

'Did you check if it was Fairtrade?'

'I haven't a clue. The tea bags were in a tin.'

Zoe accepted a mug and sniffed it suspiciously, but shook her head at the offer of a biscuit. 'They're full of hydrogenated vegetable oil.'

Lia scanned the ingredients. 'Not these ones.'

'They'll make you fat.'

'So will the scones but I'll run it off.'

'The sugar will turn to acid in your mouth and rot your teeth.'

Lia cocked her head to one side. 'So I'll remember to brush before I go to bed.'

'Oh, all right, then!' Zoe snatched a couple of biscuits with a put-upon look, but she didn't quite succeed. Perhaps in an attempt to divert attention away from the fact that she'd accepted something as lowly as a biscuit, she nodded towards a pile of books. 'I found these. Is it okay if I borrow them?'

'You can have them.'

Lia ran her finger down the spines. Sartre, Descartes, Plato, Aristotle, John Locke, Shakespeare, Simone de Beauvoir. Some of them were from her A-level Philosophy course, others seemed to have sprung from a prescribed list of worthy literature given to young people to ensure they grew up to become sensible, upstanding, right-thinking members of society. There wasn't a single, frivolous title among them. No sex-and-shopping novels, no light-hearted romances, no whodunnits. Strangely she didn't remember ever having read any of them, but she must have done because she flipped one open to see the inside cover carried her name in black biro.

'Thanks,' said Zoe, looking genuinely pleased. Lia had an awful feeling she must have missed some important point in her own teenage years if the acquisition of such serious books could bring on this kind of cheerfulness.

Whatever it takes, she thought. 'You're welcome. Are you doing Philosophy at school?'

Zoe shook her head. 'I'm just interested, that's all. I do mainly Art and Design. That's what I want to do when I finish. Design. I might try for Central Saint Martin's. You know, where Stella McCartney went?'

'That sounds exciting.'

'I hope so.' She patted Jack on the head, and he let out a sigh of pure pleasure. 'Mum's not so keen on the idea.'

'Oh?'

'She thinks the competition will be too stiff.' Zoe made a face.

'Well, you won't know until you've tried.' *And who am I to advise a teenager?* They were much more clued-up nowadays than she ever was at that age. It was ironic, sitting here in her old bedroom, having something like the sort of conversation she would have liked to have had with either her grandmother or her mother, but never did.

'I have some drawings if you're interested,' said Zoe.

'Sure. I'd love to see them. Drop by any time you feel like it.'

She left Zoe to the books and went to Ivy's bedroom. From the doorway she watched Susannah holding a black velvet evening gown up against herself then twirling in front of the mirror. It suited her, and she looked less like a beached whale and more elegantly rounded.

'It's yours if you want it,' she said and put the tea tray down on the dressing table.

Susannah tossed the dress aside and reached for her tea. 'I don't need handouts.'

'It's not a handout, it's a second-hand dress no one else wants.' Why was this family so prickly? 'Please take it. The way you're carrying everything on the front, black will look really good on you.'

Susannah shrugged and accepted a biscuit, obviously not so bothered about changing the world as her daughter. 'It does stick out a bit. They say that if you have it all on the front, it's a boy, and if the curvature is gentler and follows the mother's contour better, it's a girl. It's so like a woman to mould herself and not stick out and shout, "Here I am", don't you think?'

'Old wives' tales. Zoe doesn't strike me as the moulding kind.'

'Unlike me, you mean.' Echoes of the ferocious look she'd sent Lia on the day of her visit to the shop appeared on Susannah's face.

Lia shook her head. 'No, I didn't mean that. Listen, Susannah, I wish . . .'

What did she wish? That the old easy confidence still existed between them? It never had in the first place, and even then the lack of depth had felt like a loss. If their friendship had been deeper, would she have been able to say, hey, guess what, the doctor says someone poisoned my grandmother, and what if my mum did it? Or was it that she couldn't share this with Susannah, or anyone else, because she couldn't bear to think about why?

'Wish what? That you were here when Zoe was born?' Susannah took another dress out of the wardrobe and held it up against herself in an almost challenging way as if she dared Lia to protest. It was sleeveless and made of dark blue Indian cotton, which suited her hair colour. Lia had no recollection of ever seeing her grandmother wearing it, so perhaps it was new.

'I let you down,' she said.

Susannah tossed the blue dress on top of the black one, either because she'd decided to accept the black dress after all and now the blue one as well, or neither of them. 'Most people did. Don't beat yourself up about it.'

'Well, for what it's worth, I'm sorry.'

Susannah sent her a peculiar look. Then she laughed.

'Oh, for heaven's sake! It's such a long time ago. Water under the bridge and all that. Of course I was upset that my best friend wasn't there, but it's my fault too. It's not like you were in a different country or anything.' She took a further three dresses out of the wardrobe.

'You shut me out.'

'Yes, I suppose I did.' Susannah folded the three dresses and put them in a black bin liner.

As Lia waited for the old guilt to settle in its habitual place, she realised that Susannah was providing her with an escape clause, and some of the weight lifted from her shoulders.

Susannah drank the last of her tea and returned the mug to the tray. 'It's just as well you weren't there. It might've complicated things, with Zoe's father being what he is and—'

She stopped, and her eyes were on the open door behind Lia. Instinctively Lia turned.

Zoe stood in the doorway with a face like thunder. Something about her scowl reminded Lia of another person who had an ability to span the whole range of facial expressions in seconds. Someone who showed the same kind of impressive restraint, but still left you feeling that it wouldn't take much for the world to blow up.

Now she bothered to look, it was obvious. Zoe's bright green eyes and her elfin looks, her long, artist's fingers, the brown curly hair. So like Susannah, and at the same time not like Susannah at all.

A copy of Aidan's eyes stared back at her, and it all fell into place. Susannah sent her a pleading look.

'What about my father?' Zoe sneered. 'What is he? Or should I say, who?'

Susannah sat down heavily on the bed. 'Zoe, we've explained this to you before. He couldn't . . . commit himself.'

'You mean, he didn't want to know. How can you not want that? If it was my baby, I'd want to know. Even if I was forced to give it away, I'd want to know what happened to it.' Zoe crossed her arms defensively.

'That's just the way he . . . just the way it was. I don't want you to get hurt, that's all.'

'You don't get it, Mum, do you? I'm already hurting. In here.' She thumped her chest with her fist. 'And do you know why? Because you treat me like a child. You don't trust me and keep secrets from me about stuff I have a right to know. It pisses me off!'

She stomped back to the other room and slammed the door. Jack whimpered.

Lia's eyes met Susannah's. She knew some reaction was expected of her, but she couldn't face it. She didn't want to know all the sordid details of how Aidan had slept with Susannah, got her pregnant, and then dumped her. It didn't fit in with the picture she'd had of him back then, a loner, in his dark overcoat and fingerless gloves, always sketching, drawing, observing, and daring to stand out and be different.

It didn't fit in with the picture she had of him now either. She liked the guy, was attracted to

179

him and intrigued by him at the same time. God, she'd even flirted with him.

With burning cheeks she picked up the tray and left the bedroom without a word. Perhaps it was unkind, but she had to go somewhere else where she could deal with her jealousy before she gave herself away. Because it was jealousy, pure and simple, and it was something she wasn't supposed to feel. Not now. Not ever.

Susannah had had a baby with Aidan. The thought stung. It shouldn't, but it did.

On the landing she stopped, torn between wanting to stick her head in the sand and the curious sense that there was another purpose to her being here. Perhaps it was high time someone exposed the dirty little secrets which dominated life in this small, tight-knit community.

It was bad enough having to deal with Doctor Campbell and his suspicions about Ivy's death – not that there was anything to them, mind. Now there was unfinished business between Susannah and Aidan, and Lia had a feeling that she featured in it somewhere, although she couldn't think how. For that reason alone she wanted to blow it wide open. No more closed doors.

She opened the door to her old bedroom and was met by a scowl.

'I bet you know everything,' Zoe fumed. 'I bet on my twenty-first birthday I'll get, like, some stupid letter with the words "not to be opened before my death" written on it. And then I'm supposed to feel sorry for my poor mother because she had to carry the burden of some terrible, dark secret. It's such bullshit!'

Lia picked up Zoe's empty mug. 'You should be a novelist.'

'Bollocks to that.'

Lia laughed.

'You know something, don't you?'

'Sorry, not guilty. I was away at boarding school for the last year of my A-levels. I'm sure your mum told you that.' It was the truth, wasn't it? Susannah hadn't actually said that Aidan was Zoe's father, and Lia had only just noticed the likeness.

The door to the spare room banged on the landing, and they both jumped.

'It does that a lot. There's a draught coming in somewhere,' Lia explained. 'I've tied the door with string, but I went in there earlier and must've forgotten to put it back on. It keeps blowing open and then banging shut again.'

'Freaky.'

'It's annoying. I don't know why my grand-mother didn't get someone to sort it out.'

'What's in there?' asked Zoe, craning her neck towards the landing, but the door was further down the hallway and out of her line of sight.

'Nothing now. I've already emptied it.'

'But there must be something,' Zoe insisted.

'Just a single bed and an old wardrobe where Ivy used to keep her winter coats. Oh, and the loft hatch. I expect that's what's causing the draught.'

'To the attic? Have you been up there yet?'

Lia shivered as she turned to leave with the tray. 'No, I'm saving that for another time.'

'God! Aren't you dying to go up there? It must be full of all this really old stuff, maybe like what they have on the *Antiques Roadshow*. What if you found something that was worth a lot of money? That'd be, like, so cool.' The pitch of her voice rose at the end of the sentence the way it seemed to do when something fired her imagination. A teenage affectation, probably.

'Attics are . . .' Lia began but then lost track of what she meant to say while she fought a tight knot at the pit of her stomach. 'Things in an attic have the capacity to surprise . . . and hurt.'

'You're weird,' said Zoe, then her eyes widened. 'Do you think there might be something up there about my father?'

Inexplicably a lump formed in Lia's throat, and she felt a sudden, overwhelming urge to hug the girl, though she resisted it. Keeping secrets was hard enough, but perhaps it was even harder when things were being kept from you. 'Why would there be?'

Zoe's eyes flickered uncertainly. 'I'm not sure, but I think your grandmother knew who he was. I came to see her sometimes. We'd, like, have coffee and talk. About all sorts of things. I can't talk to my own gran, you know. I can't talk to Mum. Mrs Barrington never said, "do this" or "do that", she just listened. When I told her I wanted to know about my real father, she got this funny look in her eyes and said maybe one day she'd tell me what she knew, and that I shouldn't be disappointed. But it's not like I can be disappointed when I don't expect anything, is it? I just want to know.'

She stuck her chin out to appear tough, but it was pure bravado. I want to help this girl, Lia thought. She wanted to help Susannah, and Aidan, even the doctor with his wild goose chase. But most of all, she wanted to get out of here. An immense tiredness stole over her. Ivy was dead, and whatever she'd known about Zoe's biological father, the knowledge had died with her.

'I understand,' she said, 'and I expect your mum will tell you when she's ready.'

Without a word Zoe turned away and began, none too carefully, to fill a box with books. Jack whined and crept along the floor, then put his head on Zoe's shoe and castigated Lia with his raised eyebrows.

See what you've done. It's all your fault.

Lia made a face and left. On the landing she met Susannah, heavy belly protruding, carrying two full, black bin liners. Lia tried to relieve her of the bags, but Susannah brushed her off.

'Your grandmother,' she said, narrowing her eyes, almost as if in the absence of Ivy, Lia was a good substitute, 'your bloody grandmother just had to go and stick her nose into other people's business. She couldn't leave it alone.'

Just like you.

The unspoken words clung to Lia. Her hands felt clammy when she put the empty mugs in the scullery sink, and her pulse was racing.

I can't bear this, she thought. *I simply can't.* What was the matter with everyone?

CHAPTER 12

Lia offered Susannah and Zoe a lift home when they'd finished. Susannah appeared reluctant, perhaps because she feared that by accepting, she'd have to apologise for her earlier outburst, and wasn't sure she could to do it. Lia extended an olive branch.

'It's true Ivy was a gossip, but I don't think she meant any harm,' she said.

'Sure,' Susannah muttered. She had dark circles under her eyes and struggled to get her coat on. Lia took the coat and held it open for her. Susannah mumbled a thank you.

I've been selfish, thought Lia, roping in everyone to help with the house because I couldn't face it on my own. Susannah had enough to do, with her shop and her pregnancy. But if Lia was to repay her, it would have to be something which didn't offend her fierce pride.

A tricky one.

'You know, apart from those dresses you found,' she said, 'if there's anything else you've seen and that you'd like, please say so. Otherwise it'll just be thrown out.'

185

Susannah buttoned her coat and picked up her scarf. 'Zoe?' she called over her shoulder.

'In a minute,' came the muffled reply from upstairs. 'I'm in the loo.'

Sighing, she turned back to Lia. 'Are there any photos?'

'Photos?'

'Mrs Barrington took quite a few photos of the village and the beach. And my shop. I think she snapped everyone at some point. Out at all hours with that digital camera of hers, she was. You gave it to her, didn't you?'

Lia sent her a puzzled look. 'You want the camera?'

'Just to borrow it, so I can download them on to my computer. They won't be of any interest to you, but . . .' She shrugged.

How do you know what will be of interest to me? Lia hadn't seen any photos. Come to think of it, she hadn't seen the camera either.

'I haven't found it, but if I do, I'll pass it your way.'

'Thanks.' Susannah shouted for Zoe again. 'There is something else, though, if you don't mind.'

'Sure.'

'Your grandmother made the most delicious Bakewell tart. I think it was her own recipe, and she kept it in one of her cookery books.' Susannah nodded to the books on the dresser, which Lia hadn't sorted through yet. 'Okay if I take a look? I know it's a bit personal.'

'Not at all. Help yourself.' Pleased that Susannah had accepted her peace offering, Lia went back upstairs to fetch the last of the bin bags. Then it struck her that this was exactly the right thing to do. What better way to remember a person by than something in their own handwriting, even if it was only a recipe?

Zoe was lying on the floor playing with Jack. Being in the loo was a fib, then. She wondered if Zoe was in the habit of fibbing a lot.

'Cute dog,' said Zoe.

'He's a horror.'

'Can I have him, then?'

'No,' said Lia as if on autopilot and then wondered why she'd said that. It wasn't that long ago she couldn't wait to get rid of him.

Zoe shrugged. 'Worth a try.'

When Lia returned to the kitchen, the cookery books were still on the dresser, and Susannah was going through the drawers.

'What are you doing?'

Susannah flashed her a startled look, then shut the drawer. 'The recipe doesn't seem to be in any of her books.'

'Well, you won't find it in there. I've gone through that. Ivy was a tidy person. She'd have put the recipe in the relevant book. Here.' Lia handed Susannah a tattered copy of an old M&S cook book. 'It might be in there.'

Susannah took the book and rifled through the pages at random. Then she did the same with a book on cake-making, breaking the spine. It seemed a brutal way to treat the belongings of a dead person, but Lia reminded herself it was the person that mattered and not their earthly possessions.

'Aha!' Triumphantly, Susannah held up a piece of paper which looked like it had been torn from a jotting pad. 'I knew it would be in her hand-writing. She told me it was her own recipe. I'll just copy it down.' She caught Lia's eye and smiled.

Lia felt her scalp prickle with unease and a feeling that she was being manipulated. What had Susannah hoped to find in the dresser?

Poisoning is said to be a woman's method of murder. The insidious thought hissed through her mind, startling her.

'No, it's all right,' she said, pushing the ridiculous notion aside. 'You can have the one in her handwriting.'

But the unease persisted, and she couldn't shake the feeling that Susannah had been looking for something else. Was it the camera? And if so, what on earth was on it that meant so much?

Outside it had started raining, a subdued drizzle. Lia let the engine run to warm the car up before setting off.

Zoe slouched on the back seat with teenage panache and plugged herself into her iPod. Jack scrambled in after her and dropped his head in

188

her lap with a big sigh. Lia frowned. She hadn't invited him to come.

Once on the road, Susannah cast an eye over her shoulder to check that Zoe was safely ensconced in her own world, before turning to Lia.

'I hear you've been seeing quite a bit of Aidan.'

'News travels fast.' Lia sneaked a peek at her. Susannah had sounded jealous, but it was too dark in the car to see anything other than blandness on her face. You don't fool me, Lia thought, but acknowledged that in similar circumstances she might have felt the same.

'This is a small community. Once one person knows, the rest of the village knows by sundown. It takes a little getting used to.'

'That Mrs Larwood isn't helping.'

'Don't get me started!' Susannah lowered her voice, so Lia had trouble hearing her over the noise from the engine and the ceaseless *chi-chi-boom* from the back seat. 'You know about his brother, don't you?'

'Yes, he died. The awful thing is, I never knew he had a brother.'

'Well . . .' Susannah started to say something then changed her mind. Her shoulders tensed, and she stared straight ahead. The tension which had hung between them most of the afternoon was back with a vengeance.

What did I do now? Lia thought. She was at a loss as to what triggered Susannah's ever-changing moods, and silence seemed the easier option, so

189

she concentrated on her driving instead. The road was slippery with rain, and she slowed to a crawl when they rounded a sharp bend.

'Aidan went a bit funny over it,' said Susannah finally. 'Became sort of obsessive.'

'I heard him on the radio the other night.'

'Oh? I missed that, but it's not the first time. He's also written letters to the newspapers, demonstrated outside the army barracks, and in Whitehall too. I think he's set up some sort of network of people who've lost relatives the same way. Or maybe he just joined an association. I don't know, but a lot is run over the internet.' Turning away, Susannah looked out into the darkness. 'He even invited everyone here in the village to sign a petition, but I don't know how much he got out of it. Things seemed to quieten down after that, except, of course, that radio interview which I didn't hear.'

Lia dipped the headlights for an oncoming car. 'Why the warning? It's not like I'm interested in him in that way.'

Pull the other one.

Susannah could almost have spoken out loud if the expression on her face was anything to go by. 'Just think about it,' she insisted. 'You have your rich fiancé and a totally different life. Aidan can't compete with that. I'm only saying this because I'm . . . well, very fond of him.'

Or maybe you just want to have your cake and eat it, thought Lia uncharitably. Then she realised

190

she was guilty of the same thing, that Aidan was a pleasant diversion for as long as she was stuck here, and then she was off back to her safer life in the murder capital of the world. Or was that Washington DC? Whether she liked it or not, Susannah had a point.

She was overcome by the urge to shake up the suffocating community. She wanted to shout, 'Wake up, there's a world out there: it isn't perfect, but neither is this place, behind its picture-postcard prettiness.' Susannah was so smug, with her now-so-respectable matron attitude and holier-than-thou warnings. So what if Lia wanted to have a fling with Aidan? It was none of her business. Susannah had had her chance. Aidan was a free man.

But I'm not a free woman. Her conscience made her grit her teeth and curse the solitude which made her think about everything so much.

Driving into the village, she changed the subject. 'I was called in to see Ivy's doctor this morning. You know, Doctor Campbell?'

'Yes, I know him. We're with the other one.' When Susannah turned to Lia, the orange street light reflected in her eyes. 'What did he want?'

'He had a few interesting theories about Ivy's death.' Lia paused.

'Well?' said Susannah, an impatient edge to her voice.

Honestly, Lia thought, this village. *They're all as bad as each other.*

191

She kept Susannah waiting for another few seconds on purpose. 'He seems to think she didn't die of natural causes. In fact, he suspects someone poisoned her. I didn't—'

Susannah gasped. Glancing across, Lia saw that her eyes were wide, and she'd gone pale.

'You don't seriously believe him?' Lia asked, more puzzled than anything.

Placing a protective hand over her belly, Susannah waited a moment before answering. It was enough for Lia to get a peculiar feeling in her chest. 'Of course not. It's just . . . Why would he say that? He should know better than setting the tongues wagging. He lives here, for Pete's sake! People will think he's gone dotty or made a mistake. Either way he'll lose patients.'

'Maybe he didn't think it would get out.' Lia pulled up on the forecourt in front of the shop and turned off the engine.

'Oh, believe me, it will. One way or another.'

'He seemed very adamant,' Lia said. 'Listen, did Ivy mention anything the day she came into your shop?'

'No, she didn't.' Susannah snapped the seat belt off and reached for the door handle with difficulty.

'Here, let me,' said Lia and reached across in order to open the door.

'I don't need any help.' Susannah pushed her hand out of the way and half-rolled, half-climbed out of the car. 'Mrs Barrington never said anything to me, and Doctor Campbell is wrong.'

Light streamed out of the shop window, and a man and a boy appeared in the doorway, silhouetted against the light. Susannah brushed past them without a word, and so did Zoe with her box of books. Abandoned by his playmate, Jack hopped down, whining, but the little boy sat down and patted his head, and Zoe was immediately forgotten. Lia got out of the car to retrieve him.

'Finished clearing out, then?' the man asked, sticking out his hand. 'We haven't met before. I'm Nigel. Susannah's husband,' he added unnecessarily. A large, burly man with a reddish complexion which matched a shock of fox red hair, he spoke briskly, with a Norfolk burr, and his hand was warm and calloused as if he spent most of his time working outdoors.

'Ophelia.'

'Yes, I know. That's quite a name to be lugging around.'

'You have no idea.'

'Would you like a cup of tea?' he asked. 'I'm afraid I can't offer you anything else. I'm sort of hopeless in the kitchen. I can boil an egg, but . . .' He shrugged.

He was tactfully trying to cover up the rudeness of his wife who was obviously not prepared to offer Lia any thanks for giving them a lift. Lia liked his rugged, straightforward manner, so different to Brett who covered his hands in baby lotion and could rustle up a soufflé in a matter of minutes.

193

She declined politely, extricated Jack from the little boy, and left.

The call came while Aidan was in the barn. Seeing Susannah's name on the display, he answered immediately.

'I've just been to see Lia.' She was breathing rapidly, as if she had been running. 'Apparently Doctor Campbell told her that her grandmother was poisoned.'

'Poisoned?' Aidan frowned. 'She died of a heart attack, didn't she? Has he lost the plot or what?'

'I don't think so. He's not one for making mistakes, even if he's getting on. Remember when Zoe was nine and had that red patch on her arm, and our usual doctor said it was just a mosquito bite and nothing to worry about? Well, on my way out, Doctor Campbell asked if he could take a look and then said it was a tick bite, and that there was a danger she could get Lyme disease. I thought of changing doctors back then and—'

'Yes, I remember,' said Aidan, cutting her short. 'But why would he say a thing like that to Lia?'

'I can't be sure, but Mrs Barrington did mention—'

'Mention what?'

'I'm getting to that, if you'd stop interrupting me!'

'All right, I'm sorry. Tell me everything, from the beginning.'

Susannah took a deep breath. 'Well, it was like

this. Mrs Barrington came into the shop, asking for antacids, the day before she died. She said she had a stomach upset or something like that. I sold her some Rennies and told her she should see the doctor. Then Lia turns up about two weeks later and says her grandmother had eaten a curry and maybe that's why she was having stomach trouble. Then I said—'

A curry. Aidan felt as if a sliver of ice slid down his back. Mrs Barrington had fallen ill after she'd eaten a curry. 'Okay, slow down,' he said. 'Take it easy, don't hyperventilate. The story will still be the same for being told without you hurrying.'

Susannah gave herself a minute to calm down. 'Then I said to Lia,' she continued more slowly, 'that Mrs Barrington didn't buy it from me, and that I had nothing to do with it. And she said, of course not, and that her grandmother got it from that new curry house in Wells. It was only when I heard Doctor Campbell thinks she was poisoned that I put two and two together.'

And ended up with what? thought Aidan. Where was Susannah going with this train of thought?

'You use that place, don't you?' she asked.

'All the bloody time.'

'Maybe you shouldn't.'

Aidan laughed, but even to his own ears it sounded hollow. 'I'm sure I'll be fine. I've not heard of anyone getting food poisoning from there.'

'What if it wasn't food poisoning?'

'Then it has nothing to do with the restaurant.'

He cleared his throat. 'Mrs Barrington died of a heart attack. The coroner saw no reason to doubt it. Why's Doctor Campbell stirring it up again now, in any case? It doesn't make sense.'

'But, Aidan—'

'Yes?'

'I think Mrs Barrington suspected that . . . well, you know.' Susannah stopped, as if she couldn't quite bring herself to say the next words. Aidan didn't particularly want to hear them spoken out loud either.

'Maybe,' he said.

'And we both know how some people are likely to react.'

Aidan stiffened. It was a possibility. Then he pushed the thought aside. It was simply too far-fetched. 'Listen,' he said, as calmly as he could, 'there's nothing to worry about. Mrs Barrington was too nosy for her own good. She went rooting around in matters that were none of her business. With someone like her, always taking the moral high ground, it'd be no use explaining, because she wouldn't understand. And then, she died. It's a terrible thing to say, but it couldn't have come at a better time. I won't pretend I'm sorry.'

'Not even in front of Lia?' The question was voiced pleasantly enough, but he caught the caustic undertone.

Would he pretend in front of Lia? He figured he probably would. Anything to avoid shattering that brittleness he sensed in her and which she tried

196

so hard to hide beneath an air of no-nonsense efficiency. He wondered if her fiancé noticed these things about her, or whether it was simply coming back to this place which had brought it all to the surface and maybe ripped open old wounds.

Recalling her guardedness on the evening of the dinner party, he doubted that he'd ever get to the bottom of what those wounds were, unless she began to open up. And there was no real reason why she should.

'I would, in front of her,' he said. 'Though having said that, I don't think she's all that sorry herself. . . Look, Susannah,' he went on, with more assurance than he felt. Why was life always so difficult? 'try not to worry. You need to look after yourself and stay calm. I'll think of something, I'll sort it out.'

Damn Doctor Campbell, he thought as they hung up.

Instead of heading straight home, Lia drove to Wells and bought fish and chips and a portion of samphire from a chip shop on the harbour. A local delicacy known as marsh weed in these parts, it was marketed to yuppies as 'sea asparagus' although it wasn't related to asparagus at all. She returned to the car and ate her food in the dull light from the street lamps. Jack had a little portion of his own which he munched through in no time, smacking his lips loudly.

She knew just what Brett would say about the British national dish: high blood pressure, pimples, type 2 diabetes, gout, death. Relieved that he wasn't there, she wondered what he was doing right now and realised, with a shock, that she didn't care.

The feeling was immediately followed by terrible guilt. Wasn't absence supposed to make the heart grow fonder?

With greasy fingers she whipped out her smart-phone, delighted to get some service at last. Quickly she tapped in Brett's email. The tempta-tion was to spill her guts about what had been going on, but something held her back. Certain things were best discussed face-to-face, and she wasn't quite ready to confide in him yet. Instead, feeling like a liar on both counts, she told him that she was fine, and that she couldn't wait to see him at Christmas.

Their hectic life together in the city should have been more complicated than the one she was living here, except it was the other way round. In this place, on this deserted stretch of coastline, life seemed infinitely more complex, an ever-shifting maze of secrets and lies and pussy-footing around trying not to step on anyone's toes. By rights she should loathe it – and a part of her did – but she couldn't help deriving a certain wicked pleasure from it too. Here was a mystery to solve, if Doctor Campbell's suspicions and Susannah's reaction were anything to go by; but underneath the many layers was an element of herself waiting to be discovered. That part of it wasn't quite so appealing.

When she had finished her fish and chips, she

licked the salt and grease off her fingers and put the oily paper in a bin on the harbour front. Immediately a seagull swooped down and settled on the railing beside it. Soon it was followed by several others, and they cocked their heads and ogled her with eyes that didn't miss a trick.

'Trust me, it's empty.' She returned to the car, and the birds took off, mournfully.

The car stank of grease and fish, and she rolled the window down. It was the sort of smell which was perfect while you were eating, but not so pleasant when it lingered.

She thought of Susannah's little boy. He was a lovely-looking child, with his father's colouring and his mother's blue eyes. Did women subconsciously choose men who would produce beautiful offspring? Was that what had attracted her to Brett? Because any child of his was likely to be absolutely gorgeous.

'We'll have a house in the suburbs, with a picket fence, and a dozen kids,' he would say. 'Do the whole Disney thing.'

Was that what she wanted? She no longer knew.

Images of picket fences and ginger-haired boys cuddling puppies stuck in her mind, and she switched on the radio to quell them. Searching for a station, she finally left the dial on Radio 1, which apart from Radio 3 and Classic FM seemed the only music station Ivy's ancient car radio was able to pick up. It was cold in the car with the window open, and she bent forward to roll it up again.

The handle stuck, and she pushed it hard just as she rounded a bend in the road.

She didn't see the figure in the middle of the road, until it was caught in the full beam of the headlights. Shocked, she hit the brakes too late, and the car careered for another twenty feet before screeching to a halt. The seatbelt slammed tight across her chest, knocking the wind out of her, and she felt a sharp pull in her neck as her head was yanked forward. Unable to stop it, she knocked her face against the top of the steering wheel. In the foot well of the car Jack did a somersault with a startled yelp.

For a moment, blinded by pain, she sensed nothing but the music. Then as she became more aware of her surroundings, she realised Jack, unscathed, had climbed up on the passenger seat and was snarling and barking furiously. The dog stood with his front paws on the dashboard and his nose pressed against the windscreen, misting up the glass with his warm breath. Hackles up, fangs bared, his two-tone face was puckered up with feral hatred.

Despite the searing pain in her neck she raised her head. There, two feet in front of the car a man was standing, slightly hunched over, as if he was hiding from something, although he was in plain sight. He was wearing what looked like an old pair of camouflage trousers and a heavyweight weatherproof parka which was torn and had clearly seen better days. The hood was pulled up so that his face, which was blackened and streaked with dirt, was in shadow, and all she could see was his glinting, wild-looking eyes.

Glaring at her through the windscreen, he thumped both hands down on the bonnet of her car, making her jump, and then he was gone, pushing his way through the undergrowth at the side of the road.

CHAPTER 13

Lia surveyed the damage in the bathroom mirror. She hadn't broken her nose. It was sore and swollen, but she was more concerned about her neck, which felt stiff. Her throat hurt, too, from the pull on her muscles.

Not good, she decided. Probably a minor case of whiplash. She rummaged through several worn packets and sticky bottles – another room to clear out – before she found some Nurofen tablets and a tub of Tiger Balm, something Ivy had always sworn by. She could almost hear her grandmother now.

No point in calling the doctor out for a few aches and pains. Doctors are busy.

Too right, she thought, and swallowed a couple of painkillers. Then she ran herself a bath, wincing as she pulled her sweater over her head. She dropped her clothes on the floor, and Jack, who'd stayed glued to her since they returned, lay down on top of her clothes and sighed.

After her bath she smeared a generous amount of the camphor-scented ointment on to the back of her neck. The pungent aroma filled the room, bringing on a sudden warm tiredness, and when the effect of the Nurofen finally kicked in, she pottered into the bedroom with a cup of camomile tea. Just inside the door, she stopped. Something wasn't right.

The walls had been stripped of pictures, and the wardrobe was empty and hanging open. That wasn't it though. That had been her and Susannah, clearing Ivy's things. It was something else.

Instinct made her hone in on the anomaly. She kept her own clothes in the dressing table. It was an ancient piece of furniture with drawers that stuck if you pushed them in too far, so she never closed them completely. Now, however, they were all neatly shut.

Susannah was her first thought. The way she stacked shelves in her shop, it must have offended her sense of order to leave them open. Still, she decided to check them all the same.

She hadn't brought much, unaware that she was going to be marooned here for so long, and a cursory glance told her all her things were still here. A second, more thorough look showed they were all jumbled up, as if someone had been searching for something.

But what? She had no secrets.

Maybe it was Zoe. Was she just curious about the woman with the cool job, or had she been looking for something to flog? If so, she hadn't looked particularly well, because Lia's jewellery roll was still there, underneath a pile of socks.

Irritated, she half-shut the drawers again. For the second time today she felt she was being used, spied on, weighed and found wanting. What did they expect from her?

She eased herself into bed, but sleep eluded her. Tossing and turning, she threw the bedclothes off to cool down, then pulled them back up again, shivering.

The scene on the road kept playing in the back of her mind. The darkness, the two elongated cones of the headlamps meeting in the distance, that terrifying moment when she'd nearly killed someone because she hadn't been paying attention.

Jack raked his claws against the closed bedroom door, whining. She pulled her pillow over her head to shut out the sound, but when it became apparent that he wasn't going to give up, she let him in. He jumped on to the bed, circled around a couple of times, and settled down.

'It's just for tonight,' Lia grumbled. 'Don't get any ideas.'

Ignoring her, he kept his eyes trained on the door, his ears cocked. Lia had an urge to turn around and look at what might be behind her on the landing, but common sense prevailed. There was nothing out there, because if there had been, Jack would have barked. Still, she left the door ajar, so at least she would hear it if anyone or anything walked across the creaking floorboard.

With the added warmth from Jack, exhaustion

finally won over, and she was granted a fitful sleep. She was woken by the sound of a slamming door. Sitting bolt upright with her pulse racing, she tried to penetrate the darkness, but it took a moment for her eyes to adjust.

Jack was no longer in the bedroom, but she could hear him moving about on the landing. She grabbed her dressing gown and peered out into the dark before switching the light on.

The dog was standing by the door to the spare room with his nose to the gap, sniffing and pawing at the frame. The washing line she'd used to stop the door from blowing open had snapped off and was trailing on the floor. Inspecting it, she found it ragged with deep teeth marks in the plastic. She turned to Jack. 'Did you do this?'

Jack snorted.

'Right, that just about does it. It's the RSPCA for you.'

He snorted again and clawed at the door frame. The door swung open, and a blast of freezing air from the unheated room billowed out on to the landing. Lia pulled the dressing gown tighter around her. Why was this house always so cold? She reached out to shut the door, but Jack was too fast. He evaded her, skittered into the almost empty room, jumped on to the bed, and started barking.

'What?'

He jumped down from the bed, then up again, and did a three hundred and sixty degree turn.

'What is it?' she asked again. 'What do you want?'

He barked again, tilting his head so his nose pointed to the ceiling.

She followed the direction of his gaze. The loft hatch. 'There's nothing up there. Just old rubbish. I'm not going up now. Not on my own.'

Jack whined.

'Yes, I know, but you don't count.' She turned to go, but Jack jumped down from the bed and grabbed her dressing gown with his teeth.

'Stop it, you stupid dog!' She disentangled herself roughly from his hold, then regretted her outburst and sat down on her haunches with his face between her hands. 'You're either the silliest creature on Earth' – he put his head to one side as if he was listening – 'or you're trying to tell me something. Trouble is, I don't think dogs are sentient beings.' He whined. 'Not much, anyway. The only thing in that attic is dust and rodents.' She got up and massaged her neck. Excitedly Jack bounced up and down snapping at her sleeves.

Unsure what to make of him, Lia regarded the dog for a moment. Sometimes, just sometimes, he seemed almost human. In the car their feelings had been completely in tune. Now he wanted to go into the attic, in the middle of the night. Was this through intelligent reasoning or just the whim of an empty-headed mutt?

Lifting her sleeves out of his reach, she decided to give him the benefit of the doubt. 'Let me find a torch first.'

He barked angrily when she left him. After a few minutes of rummaging – which was ridiculous because after her house-clearing she ought to know where everything was – she found a large black rubber torch on the top shelf of the larder.

Back in the spare room she felt on top of the dusty wardrobe for the long stick with a hook on the end, which she'd seen when clearing this room earlier, and yanked at the loft hatch with it. The fold-down stairs came down with a tremendous clattering, and she secured it on the floor. Before she could stop him, Jack ran up the metal steps with amazing speed.

'Will you come back this instant! Jack!'

He ignored her, and she could hear him skidding around in the attic, then a thump followed by a crash. It was the last thing she needed, the bloody dog wreaking havoc before she'd had a chance to go through whatever was up there.

She sighed. Attics were strange places in the daytime, full of cobwebs and dust and things which had been put away to be remembered later, and had then been forgotten. She needed someone with her, and Aidan seemed the most obvious choice. She wanted his moral support and his company, and probably he was the only one who understood her need for catharsis as well as her reluctance to begin the process.

Stuff and nonsense, she thought. Aidan knew nothing of the sort. She put her foot on the flimsy bottom step; Jack needed to come down, and that was that.

The attic was even stranger at night. Accessed by the hatch at one end of the house it ran across the entire first floor from east to west, flanked at each end by a wide chimney breast. The uninsulated ceiling sloped dramatically on both sides, and it was only possible for Lia to walk upright in the centre, right under the roof line. To either side under the eaves a few boxes and rickety pieces of old furniture were arranged in a way that left a wide path in the middle. Realising that there was a bare bulb hanging near the top of the stairs, Lia left the torch by the opening, and turned on the light. The room was immediately bathed in a white light, almost blinding in its intensity.

The crash she'd heard was a pile of boxes which had toppled over, and she righted them, calling for Jack. He came trotting back looking pleased with himself and she caught him by the collar.

'What did you think you were doing, scarpering like that?'

No answer, but of course she hadn't really expected one. Instead he did a couple of twirls and settled down on the cold floor.

Well, I'm here now, she thought, so I might as well make a start.

But where? It looked like an almost impossible task.

Wrapping her dressing gown around her legs, she sat down and began by pulling a box towards her and opening it. After a few minutes this didn't seem like such an impossible task after all. Always an orderly woman, Ivy had labelled each box with a black marker pen, and a quick search through each of them confirmed that they contained what it said on the front.

There were boxes of unwanted crockery, still intact, but unfashionable, a collection of old photo frames, saucepans, lampshades, assorted ornaments. One box contained model railway magazines, though what had happened to her grandfather's little railway Lia didn't know.

Another box yielded the unexpected treasure of old *Vogue* magazines, all of them with pictures of Ivy on some of the fashion pages.

'Oh, my God!' she squeaked out loud. She'd forgotten her grandmother had been a model, and she put the magazines aside in a pile of other things she wanted to keep.

A large trunk held all Connie's schoolbooks and report cards, revealing that her mother had been an exemplary student and very bright. She'd obviously had great potential. Why, then, had she ended up as a lowly assistant in a school chemistry lab? Now Connie had golf on the brain and had given up pursuing anything worthwhile. Life was strange.

Removing a layer of old newspaper from the trunk, Lia almost squealed with delight. Underneath the yellowed paper was a framed photo of her granddad as a serviceman in Burma, leaning against the bonnet of a Jeep, healthy and svelte-looking, with a smiling fellow officer. Next to the picture frame was the hat he wore in the picture. Reverently, Lia lifted it out of the trunk and turned it over to look at the underside of the brim. There, exactly as her grandfather showed it to her as a child, was the striking signature of Vera Lynn.

We called her the Forces' Sweetheart.

She remembered little of her grandfather except his voice. Soft and slightly playful. Here was the piece of family history she'd complained to Aidan that she didn't have, and she could feel tears pressing in her eyes.

Jack whined, and she wiped them away. Her grandmother was only recently gone, and Lia was moping over someone she hardly remembered.

Another voice spoke to her from the past, but who and where was lost in the mist of time.

He never got over that poor little boy.

She pushed the unhappy thought aside and lifted another layer of newspaper out of the trunk. There on the bottom, cushioned by an old blanket, lay her grandfather's kukri knife, a wartime souvenir given to him by a Gurkha soldier. Excited, she examined the decorated handle in the unnaturally bright light, then pulled the fifteen-inch knife from its wooden sheath. The curved blade sang.

'How about that, Jack? That's a fearsome weapon, isn't it?'

But Jack was nowhere in sight, and even so, it was unlikely he'd have appreciated her find. She could hear him padding about at the end of the long attic room.

Lia rose, stretched, and massaged her aching neck. In her eagerness to get through some of the junk in the loft, she'd forgotten about the pain. Now that the cold was creeping up on her, and she'd found some mementos she wanted to keep, she longed for bed.

She turned towards the stairs, then noticed a box she'd overlooked. She hoisted it up to take downstairs, then reached for the light switch. As she did so, something in the corner behind the staircase caught her eye. Her hand froze in mid-air, and she nearly dropped the box.

In the corner was something which by rights shouldn't be there, couldn't be there if the laws of physics were to prevail. Maybe there were ghosts after all?

She was fairly certain, though, that they didn't leave foot prints in the dust.

These were made by a pair of large shoes, a size ten perhaps, starting in the corner behind the hatch and running, as far as she could see, along the width of the house right under the eaves before doubling back on themselves and ending back where they started.

As she stared at them, three things went through her mind: the intruder, whoever he was, would have had to crouch; the foot prints were not completely fresh, because a thin layer of dust had settled in the shape, which explained why Lia hadn't spotted them to begin with; and whoever had made them had gone.

Thankfully.

She still rushed down the rickety steps with the box under her arm, shooing Jack unceremoniously in front of her, then slammed the hatch closed and wedged it shut with the pole. Dashing from room to room on the first floor, she switched on all the lights, then leaned against the door to the spare room, breathing hard. Confused, Jack whimpered.

The rational side of her mind told her the owner of the size ten shoes was no longer in the attic, the irrational side was convinced there was a monster lurking in every dark corner of the house waiting to gobble her up. The knowledge that she'd left the sword up there, for someone to pick up, didn't help.

Even though the kukri was used as a woodcutting tool, it was said the knife was specifically weighted for the purpose of slitting the throat. She'd read that even a dull blade could cut quite viciously, because of the forward curve of the knife.

Which was not a comforting thought.

Either she had to go back upstairs to fetch it and then hide it somewhere safe, or she needed to make sure that no one else went up there. But how? A piece of chewed up washing line wasn't going to keep anyone out of the room, let alone the loft.

She put the box down, took a steadying breath,

and went back up into the attic. Even if the knife was useless for stabbing, it was quite fearsome to look at, and it would make her feel a lot safer to have a weapon in her hand.

Just in case.

It lay where she'd left it, next to the hat and the copies of *Vogue*. She grabbed her hoard, climbed down the steps as fast as she dared and secured the hatch again. Laughing with relief, she felt a certain triumph that she'd overcome the fears caused by her over-active imagination. There was, of course, a perfectly logical explanation for the footprints in the corner.

She just had to find it.

After the phone call from Susannah two things occurred to Aidan in rapid succession.

His first thought was that Mrs Barrington, who'd had a knack for unearthing people's secrets – he knew that from personal experience – might have confided in Doctor Campbell. *How much had she told him?*

The second was that he didn't want Lia to be on alert like this. It didn't fit in with his plans.

As soon as he had finished up in the barn, he jumped in the car without bothering to change. Parking it down the lane from Lia's house, he locked the car behind him and went on foot the rest of the way. Why, he wasn't really sure.

Impulse had taken him here, but now his good sense told him you couldn't go visiting someone

213

unannounced at this time of night. He needed an excuse, and he didn't have one. Lia was probably in bed by now, anyway.

Or maybe not, he thought, as the house came into view from behind the conifers which surrounded the property.

Light blazed from every single window, and although the curtains were drawn, it cast long shadows over the frozen lawn.

Aidan stopped and debated with himself what do to do.

Knock?

No. If she was awake – and there was a good chance she was since all the lights were on – she'd jump out of her skin.

Call her from his mobile and tell her he was outside?

Could do, but then she'd wonder why he hadn't driven all the way up to the house instead of sneaking up the lane like a prowler.

'Damn,' he muttered. Nothing appeared to be straightforward with Lia, and this was just as much to do with his own complex emotions as with her.

There was a place and a time for everything, his mother had said once. He couldn't remember the exact occasion, or maybe there had been several occasions, and she'd been fond of that particular saying. It certainly stuck in his mind. The cliché had since morphed into reality when he missed an opportunity with Lia at high school because life went pear-shaped.

214

And now when fate had allowed him another chance, things were going pear-shaped again.

'What the fuck am I going to do?' he said through gritted teeth.

Making a snap decision, he decided to call her. If she asked why he'd left the car down the lane, he'd simply respond that he didn't want the noise to wake her, and that he'd only planned to knock if he thought she was awake. Then take it from there.

He pulled the phone out of his jacket pocket, but it slid from his grasp and disappeared in the darkness. Cursing softly, he dropped to his haunches and felt it on the lawn. He found it in a small depression, a hole of some sort, and once his fingers had closed around the phone, out of curiosity he slid it open to shine a light on the hole.

It was a large footprint. Old too, because the ground had since frozen, leaving the mark behind for posterity, or at least until spring. Without thinking, he placed his own foot in it, noticed the perfect fit. He'd visited Mrs Barrington many times before, had even stood on her lawn, but had he ever stood here, sheltered by the conifers?

He supposed he must have. If he hadn't, the print had been left by someone else.

Sliding the phone shut, he drew back. Maybe Lia had good reason to be on her guard. *He* was the one bringing danger and insecurities with him, which was the last thing she needed right now.

Returning to his car and leaving her was a wrench, but he couldn't think what else to do.

When he got home, he opened the drinks cabinet and hit the bottle. Hard.

In the kitchen Lia reached for the camomile to steady her nerves, then abandoned it for a cup of strong black coffee with a slosh of whisky. She wondered if she should call the police. Someone had turned out her chest of drawers, and someone had been in her grandmother's attic.

It wasn't a difficult decision to make. What would she tell them? The footprints probably belonged to a workman. Vaguely she remembered Ivy mentioning that the attic needed to be insulated more efficiently. The police would laugh at her if this turned out to be the case. As for her chest of drawers having been searched, she suspected Zoe and didn't want to get her into trouble. Nothing was missing anyway.

She warmed her hands against the mug, then opened the box.

The first object inside sent her heart racing. It was a photo of herself with Eddie on her lap. She couldn't have been more than four, and Eddie two. She sat with her arms around her brother who squinted happily at the camera.

Carefully she put it aside, then, puzzled, pulled out a stack of family photos all in a jumble, pictures of Connie and of her grandfather. Ivy had practically no photos around the house except for Lia's graduation picture; yet a whole box full of them was stored in the attic. It seemed like an odd place to put the pictures of your loved ones.

As if they had a mind of their own, Lia's fingers sought out pictures of her baby brother, and she spread them out on the table. There were over twenty of Eddie, sleeping, holding a beach ball, drinking from his bottle. There was something about the way he'd been captured in everyday poses which told Lia that Connie must have taken them. Only a mother photographs her child doing unremarkable things; only a mother fully appreciates the daily developments.

In Eddie's case these had been very slow. He'd taken forever to learn to sit up, to hold on to a toy, and even longer to learn to let go of the toy again. In his short life he'd never completely learned to walk, talk or even say 'Mummy', but he was always happy and smiling, always ready to cuddle. What he'd been unable to say with words, he said in spades when he put his small fat hand in Lia's.

She remembered his soft baby smell, the way he gurgled with laughter because he saw the whole world as created solely for his amusement. She remembered the bitter wrench, the gaping hole in her chest as if someone had punched through her, when he was no longer there.

For years Lia had dreamed of his death, not knowing if it was the very nature of dreams that made them so vivid, or if they were really a memory.

But seeing his face again, she knew. Poor little Eddie who drowned in the bath during a moment without adult supervision.

Slowly she returned the photos to the box, except the one of herself and Eddie. By closing the lid she could make believe she'd never seen the contents. On impulse she twisted it round to see if it had been marked as neatly as the other boxes.

On the back it read, in hastily scrawled black lettering, 'junk'.

Lia blinked at the word. The tears pressed again, but this time they weren't caused by the joy of finding a treasured item long forgotten. They stung in her eyes like acid, and a sour taste welled up in her throat. To know that what had meant so much to her, and to Connie, had meant so little to Ivy.

Junk? Eddie?

She hid her face in her hands and broke down.

CHAPTER 14

idan sat on a bench in the large farmhouse scullery, nursing a killer hangover. From the top of the washing machine the cat watched him intently as he tended to a pile of diving suits on the floor in front of him.

He'd collected a number of them over the years, one- and two-piece wetsuits for summer use and all-in-one drysuits for the winter, and although several of the older wetsuits were repaired with tape where he'd managed to rip them, he preferred them to the newer and smarter ones, which were less flexible. Now he had seven in total.

He paid particular attention to the drysuits, checking the adjustable exhaust valves, which could get clogged up with fluff from the undersuit and thereby compromise the function of the valve, but everything was as it should be.

A million thoughts were running around inside his brain, refusing to leave him alone. Worry about Lia, coupled with anxiety over what she might uncover. Concern for Susannah who seemed on the verge of a collapse, although she'd never admit to such a weakness, least of all to him. Not to mention that he'd been warned to stay clear.

And then there was the ever-present anger, which had been with him for so long he couldn't recall his life before it, an all-pervasive poison coursing through his veins and infecting every heartbeat. It made him so tired.

With a groan he picked up another wetsuit, ran his hand through the sleeves and legs, splaying his fingers to check for tears. The suit was fine, and he reached for the next.

He suddenly noticed he seemed to be missing one, a drysuit, and he checked carefully to make sure. True enough, there were only two. What had happened to the third?

John, he thought. Hadn't John said something about borrowing one? He must've been here while Aidan was out and just helped himself as they'd agreed. Not only that, but he'd helped himself to Aidan's favourite, a well-worn Poseidon unisuit which was the easiest to get into on his own. The one he'd worn when he met Lia on the beach.

Damn.

It wasn't the end of the world. Aidan had another, similar, cold-water suit, but the neoprene wasn't as flexible as he'd have liked. John obviously knew a good thing when he saw it.

The cat jumped off the washing machine and on to his lap, pointing out with a plaintive miaow that he hadn't been fed yet.

Aidan put him on the floor. 'Okay, in a minute.'

He returned the outfits to their special hangers and hung them up on the pegs in the scullery while he reminded himself to be around next time someone needed to borrow something from him. Having fed the cat, he grabbed his car keys and stuffed a bag of croissants from the bread bin into his rucksack.

He'd promised to help Lia with her house-clearing, and he was running late.

She wasn't there when he knocked.

Strange, he thought. They'd agreed this morning, and she didn't strike him as the forgetful sort. He glanced at the kitchen windows, saw that the curtains were still drawn, then knocked again, this time more forcefully. A furious barking could be heard from within. At least the dog was there. Lia had probably fallen back asleep after his phone call had woken her.

As he got out his mobile in the hope that she kept her phone next to the bed, the scullery door was suddenly flung open, and Lia appeared on the doorstep in her dressing gown, a fearsome-looking knife in her hand.

'Whoa!' he said, backing off. 'I'm only fifteen minutes late. Give a guy a chance.'

'What?'

'Tell me you're not PMS-ing.' *Or unbalanced*, he thought and cursed Doctor Campbell for unsettling her with his stories.

'Premenstrual?' she echoed.

221

He pointed to the knife in her hand. Her eyes were puffy as if she'd cried, and her face appeared drawn and pale.

'Oh, that. I see what you mean. Sorry.' She gave an embarrassed laugh and returned the knife to the sheath. 'That's just my grandfather's kukri knife. I found it in the attic. Anyway, it's not a particularly good weapon for stabbing.'

'Lucky me. So you went up in the attic, huh? I was under the impression you didn't want to do that until I could come with you.'

'I thought I heard something.' She stood aside to let him in.

He raised his eyebrows. 'A woman alone in a house hears a bump in the night and decides the smartest thing to do would be to go up into the attic and investigate? How very Gothic. Did your candle blow out? Did you scream and faint?'

'Oh, shut up,' she muttered and sent him a dirty look which made his lips twitch with amusement. Turning away, she switched the kettle on, then put her hand on one of the Rayburn lids. Aidan noticed the range cooker had gone out again. No wonder this house was always so cold.

'There was nothing there.'

Perhaps just the ghosts in your mind, he thought. *We both have them.*

'Oh, yeah?' He dropped his rucksack on a kitchen chair and lifted Jack up. The little dog writhed frantically in an attempt to lick his face. 'Did you help Lia? Good boy. You're a great guard dog, aren't you?'

Spooning coffee into a pot, Lia snorted contemptuously. 'Guard dog? He's a Jack Russell. He couldn't guard a doll's house.'

'Maybe not, but I imagine that's why your grandmother bought him.' He stopped when he realised he was just as bad as Doctor Campbell now. 'What happened to your nose?' he said to change the subject.

She shrugged. 'Some idiot ran out into the road in front of me last night. I had to slam the brakes on quite hard, and knocked myself on the steering wheel.'

'You okay?'

'I'm fine. Just feeling a little delicate.'

I'd say, Aidan thought, and prickly too. He'd have put a comforting hand on her shoulder if he hadn't feared he'd get skewered. He put Jack down again and picked up a curious hat which lay on the kitchen table next to a cardboard box. 'Was this in the attic too?'

She nodded and handed him a steaming mug. 'It was my grandfather's, from the war. Go on, turn it over.'

Frowning, Aidan flipped the hat upside down and twirled it in the light. Then he felt his eyes widen. 'Vera Lynn signed his hat? I *am* impressed. You said your family had no memorabilia to speak of. Well, you've found this. How does that make you feel?' He followed her gaze to the box on the table and wondered what it contained. From her expression, he'd guess it was something painful.

'Sort of happy,' she replied.

'Only sort of?'

'It's . . . not that easy.'

'It never is,' he said and popped the hat on his head. 'How do I look?'

'Ridiculous,' she said, but her smile told a different story.

He laughed and put it back on the table, then opened his rucksack and tossed her a paper bag. 'Here, I almost forgot. I brought croissants. They're not completely fresh, but a few minutes in a low oven should do nicely.'

She caught the bag. 'It'll have to be the microwave. The Rayburn has packed up again.'

'Yeah, I noticed. Would you like me to take another look at it?'

Without waiting for an answer, he bent down in front of the Rayburn and fiddled with various settings. She was standing close to him, closer than ever before, and as she leaned over the cooker to pull down a baking tray from a shelf above, her dressing gown fell open.

Aidan tried not to stare but he couldn't stop his eyes from following the contours of her bare legs. A well-toned thigh was just inches away from his face, and he had an overwhelming urge to slide a hand up the back of her leg and press his lips to her skin. He was willing to bet it would be soft and warm.

Looking up, he saw that she'd caught him ogling

her. She didn't look cross, just . . . well, *challenging,* as if she dared him to follow his impulse.

For the first time he sensed a real fire in her, a genuine hunger lurking just beneath the surface, and wondered what she'd be like in bed. All he had to do was get up, carry her upstairs, then screw her senseless. The provocative look in her eyes made it clear to him she wouldn't object, that she'd be a willing participant.

Except he didn't want to get laid for the sake of it. He wanted the whole hog: the love and the commitment, and everything that went with it. She'd already made that commitment, to someone else, and Aidan knew he could never be content with less from Lia. It was all or nothing.

As if suddenly self-conscious, she drew the dressing gown tight and covered herself up. Aidan looked away. The spell was broken.

'You have nice legs,' he said, which sounded a bit lame.

'Thanks.'

He adjusted another button, and the Rayburn rumbled back to life. It was ironic, he thought, that this was the second time he'd brought warmth to her house. He wondered how Mrs Barrington had coped with the cold, but suspected she'd probably known how to handle the temperamental cooker.

'I know what your problem is,' he said.

She was placing the croissants on the baking tray, but swung around, almost startled, when he spoke. 'You do?'

225

'You've covered the air intake on the fire door.'

'Sorry?'

'Look.' He held up a bath towel, which hung over the rail to dry. It was still damp. 'If you cover the intake, this will cause the cooker to stifle and put itself out.'

'Oh.'

'This is where the air comes in.' He pointed to a small grille. 'No air, no fire. I'm sure they taught you that at school.'

'I'm afraid not. Or if they did, I wasn't paying attention. I had better things to do back then.'

Yeah, Aidan thought sadly, *and they didn't involve me then any more than they do now*. Without further comment, he stood up and turned towards the sacks by the front door. 'So is this all for the dump then?'

Yep, the spell was well and truly broken.

What had possessed her? Lia thought, as she watched Aidan load the car.

She'd virtually invited him to have sex with her, with that provocation. When he'd knelt in front of the cooker, she'd wanted to reach out and run her fingers through his unruly hair. Then he would have got up, they would have kissed, gone upstairs. She could almost see it happening.

Whatever Aidan did, he seemed to do with a passion. She could imagine him embracing love-making with the same intensity, and the thought made her shiver with a mixture of pleasure and panic. Her love for Brett caused no such anxieties in her, but with Aidan it would be different. He'd take over and demand all of her, and she'd be consumed by those green eyes of this.

Then what?

She'd be hurt, that's what.

To cool off, she hopped in the shower. When she came back downstairs, she found Mrs Larwood in the kitchen, a self-satisfied expression on her face.

God, could the woman walk through walls? Then she realised Aidan had left the front door ajar while he was carrying the boxes outside.

'Sorting the place out, I see. Must be a mite difficult for you.'

Muttering platitudes, Lia offered her coffee. There were no croissants left, and Lia carried the empty baking tray into the scullery before her neighbour began pecking at the crumbs.

'I heard your car last night,' the older woman said.

Lia returned to the kitchen. 'I wasn't aware Ivy's car sounded different to any other car.'

'Gone for a walk, I had,' Mrs Larwood continued as if she hadn't noticed the sarcasm, 'when I heard wheels screeching. Went to investigate, naturally—'

'Naturally,' said Lia and put a mug down on the table in front of her neighbour.

'—and that's when I saw you speeding up. As if you were fleeing from the devil, you were. Something frighten you?'

Lia sensed that she was being put to a test somehow. 'There was a man in the road. I nearly ran him over. I'd never seen him before. He looked like he might have been living rough. It gave me a bit of a jolt, that's all.'

'Mmm, the wild man. Yes, I've seen him around. Mind you, he's no ordinary tramp.'

She waited for Mrs Larwood to elaborate, but instead she slurped her coffee loudly and nodded in the direction of the hat and the kukri on the table. 'Your grandfather was quite a dashing man.'

'You knew him?'

'Lived here for years, he did. Long before Ivy. She wasn't from around here.'

That sounded like an accusation. Unsure what to make of it, Lia decided not to comment.

'Know quite a bit about your family, I do.'

I bet, thought Lia. *And you're dying to tell me all the details.* Pursing her lips to hold back a smile, she looked out of the window at Aidan, who'd finished loading the car and was heading back towards the house. Relief flooded through her.

'Been in the attic, have you?'

'Yes,' Lia replied tersely. *What was taking him so long?*

'Horrid places, attics. Never know what you might find. I hope there weren't any nasty surprises waiting for you up there. People aren't always what you expect them to be.'

Mrs Larwood's small button-eyes bored into hers as if she could see right through her. Lia

228

considered confiding in her, then thought better of it. Sometimes family stuff belonged in the family, no matter how tempting it was to unload on to an outsider.

Aidan came in through the scullery door, and a blast of icy air followed him into the kitchen. From his usual place on the jute rug Jack lifted his head, whining a welcome and tapping his tail against the floor like a metronome.

'Wipe your feet on the mat, please,' said Lia and then blushed at how cosy and wifely this sounded.

Mrs Larwood's face crinkled in a knowing grin. She rose, arthritically, then buttoned her coat and tied her headscarf under her chin. 'Best be off then. Mr C will be waiting.'

'Mr C?' said Lia to Aidan, once she was out of earshot.

'Cunningham. He lives in the village. She cleans for him on Mondays.'

'She *cleans* for him? But she's ancient. I mean, she can hardly sit down without her bones creaking, let alone swan about with a mop and bucket.'

Aidan warmed his hands on the Rayburn. 'You mustn't let yourself be fooled by that one. She'd pretend to be at death's door if it would land her the latest gossip. She knows everything that goes on around here.' His jaw tightened, and he looked away.

Recalling Mrs Larwood's knowing look, Lia said, 'She certainly seems to know things that haven't happened yet.' *Or never will.*

'That too. As I've explained to you, she has a reputation for being a bit of a witch.'

Lia laughed. 'You're kidding me. That is so small town.'

'You may laugh, but it's no fun for those who get caught up in it.' Aidan pulled his car keys out of his pocket. 'I've loaded as much as will fit in my car, but I'll be back for more later.'

'Thanks, you're being a real friend,' she said.

He held her gaze longer than was strictly necessary, then he grinned. 'Pure self-interest.'

When he'd left, Lia decided to give Doctor Campbell a call to see if he had got any further with the pathologist. She would have preferred the matter to be closed, but had a feeling this was far from the case. The surgery receptionist took the call and informed her that Doctor Campbell had gone to stay with relatives and wouldn't be back until after Christmas.

'Is it something urgent? If it is, I can book you in with Doctor Lorimer—'

'No, I don't need an appointment,' said Lia. 'Is there another number where I can reach him?'

'I'm afraid not.'

'How about his mobile? Only this is rather important. He's aware of the situation.'

'I'm not at liberty to give out private telephone numbers. Out of the question.' The receptionist was firm.

Lia tried again. 'Do you think you could be so

kind as to call him yourself and ask him to get back to me?'

'You people,' the battleaxe snapped. 'The doctor has a fifty-hour working week. If it's important, then I'm sure he's taken the paperwork with him and will ring you over the holidays. If he doesn't, it'll be because he needs a break.'

Lia felt the frustration building inside her, but she kept her head. It wouldn't be the first time she'd dealt with an unhelpful person in a general practice – in fact she had a sneaking suspicion that the support staff were chosen purely on the basis of their forceful personalities and no-nonsense attitude, and that their primary function was to simply scare sick people into feeling better all of a sudden. She tried a different tack.

'I've recently lost my grandmother,' she said, 'and Doctor Campbell had some concerns about the cause of death. He was going to speak to the pathologist, and . . . well, to be honest, it's very unsettling to have this hanging over us.'

'You're Ivy Barrington's granddaughter.' This was a statement and not a question, but Lia was beginning to get used to the notion that in this community everybody knew everything about everybody else.

'She was well liked around here. Why didn't you say so?' said the receptionist, appeased. 'Hold on, I'm fairly certain that Doctor Campbell left me a note in case you rang while he was away . . . yes, here it is.' There was a brief silence, evidently while she scanned the contents of the note. 'He says that with the pathologist's caseload and the time of year, he thinks it unlikely he'll hear from him until the first week of January, but that he'll let you know as soon as he does. Does that answer your question?'

'Yes, thank you, that's fine,' said Lia, and hung up, feeling that it was anything but. She didn't want to believe there was anything untoward about Ivy's death. If the pathologist had missed something, it would be evidence of a viral or a bacterial infection, not anything more sinister. But since Doctor Campbell had raised those nagging doubts, she wanted to be certain, one way or the other. She didn't like the direction her thoughts took, as long as she wasn't sure. And now she would have to live with her doubts until the new year at least.

CHAPTER 15

Aidan returned after lunch, and they spent the next couple of hours clearing the attic. Lia almost laughed when she went back up there. It was amazing how different everything looked in the clear light of day. The attic room seemed warmer, and a watery sun spilled in through two small windows at either end of the house, reflecting the dancing dust they kicked up as they worked.

She let Aidan take whatever he wanted, which included a Bakelite radio, an old floor lamp and a Chinese ornamental birdcage made from white-painted metal.

'What do you want that for? The only birds you'll catch around here are seagulls.'

'Oh, I don't know,' he said, looking her up and down.

'Very funny.' She shook her head, willing herself not to blush.

'I don't intend to cage anyone,' he said, and this time she did blush.

When they'd finished in the attic, Lia offered him a brandy and took it through to the living room.

The house was warmer now after Aidan had tended to her Rayburn, but there was still a slight nip in the air, and Lia pulled her feet up under her on the sofa and curled into a ball. Aidan didn't appear to be bothered and sat cross-legged on the hearthrug, looking every bit the eccentric he seemed to be these days.

Absently, he scratched at Jack's ears when the little terrier came into the room and settled down next to him. They looked very comfortable together, and Lia, frowning, found herself feeling jealous of the dog – she wanted Aidan to touch her instead, like he'd nearly done earlier, but, of course, that would be wrong.

'Something's on your mind,' he said. 'Anything you'd like to share?'

Lia sent him a startled look, expecting a mischievous or even flippant grin but got an open, sincere expression. He wasn't trying to be funny, he wasn't trying to extract information from her for the sake of it, he really meant it. His green eyes shone with genuine interest, and something else, concern perhaps. The colour reminded her, as once before, of precious stones. With such expensive eyes, she thought, I can hardly fob him off with a cheap answer. She took a deep breath.

'Have you ever discovered that a person you respected and relied on turned out to be different from what you'd thought? That they might do or have done something you never in your wildest dreams imagined they would?'

He was all ears. 'Are you telling me your grandmother was a bad person?'

'No, not quite like that. It's just, I don't know, I've discovered a different side to her, a whole other facet I hadn't bargained for. A mean and unfeeling side. An undercurrent of selfishness.'

'Aren't we all a bit like that?' he said and moved closer to where she was sitting.

'I like to think I'm not.'

He laughed quietly. 'Oh, come now. I've told you all my secrets.'

Have you? she thought.

'Have you never lied?' he asked. 'Never had a bad thought? Never wished that someone you don't like would just get run over by a bus?'

'Of course I have. But I keep them to myself. I see no point in hurting others for the sake of having my say. Besides, thoughts like that are more likely to poison your own mind than the person they're directed at, wouldn't you say?'

'Well, how about that? It looks like I'm in the presence of a saint.' Aidan swirled the brandy and sent her a teasing grin over the rim of the glass.

Irritated, she regarded his profile. Curse him. Why did he have this ability to twist everything she said?

Suddenly she felt overwhelmed with tiredness, and her neck had started aching again. She slid her hand over the back of it and, rubbing it gently, she blessed her lucky escape. Jamming the brakes that hard could have caused a lot more damage.

The car could have overturned, and she could have ended up with more than a sore neck and a bloodied nose. Thinking of her nose, she was grateful the swelling had gone down. She wasn't interested in Aidan – or was she? – but she didn't want him to find her unattractive.

'Are you feeling all right?' he said. 'Is something the matter with your neck?'

'It's nothing. Just a minor case of whiplash.'

'Shouldn't you see a doctor?'

'I am a doctor.' Lia wished he wouldn't fuss. No one ever fussed over her.

'Who was the fool who stepped out in front of you?' he asked. 'Someone local?'

'No one I knew,' she said. 'I couldn't really see him. His face was all streaked with dirt. Mrs Larwood called him "the wild man"'.

Aidan frowned, managing to look both worried and disapproving at the same time. 'I still think you should see someone.'

'Maybe I will.'

He put his glass on the floor and sat on the sofa beside her. 'Here, let me,' he said and placed a cool hand on her neck. She flinched at his touch.

'I don't think massaging it is a good idea.'

'I wasn't going to. Just relax, will you.'

Reluctantly Lia turned her back towards him, bent her head forward and allowed Aidan to part her hair to expose her neck. She felt the light pressure of his thumbs, almost smoothing her skin as if he was following the contours of each neck bone.

The rest of his fingers moved forward, tracing the outline of her jaw, and slid gently down the front of her throat. A sudden crazy thought entered her mind. She hardly knew him, but what she'd seen of him so far raised questions about his emotional stability. What if he decided to apply just a little more pressure to her throat? Would she be paranoid if she pushed him away? Then again, it was better to be paranoid than dead.

As she felt herself tense, he lessened the pressure and massaged the lower part of her face with only the tips of his fingers. Gently he eased her head backwards, letting it rest against his chest, and continued to stroke her face, her chin, her cheeks and her brow. It was like being touched by butterflies. Lia closed her eyes and gave in to the simple enjoyment of his touch.

'Do you believe in love at first sight?' he asked.

Lia jumped at the question and attempted to sit up, but he pulled her back with a firm hand. She was reminded of all her thoughts of seducing him, for herself mostly, but perhaps also to wind Susannah up, and here he was, possibly doing just that to her. Part of her wanted to get up and re-establish the distance between them, another wanted her to remain where she was, for as long as he intended her to. She had never let go of herself like this before, and it was as if she'd missed out on something unique and precious.

'Not really,' she said in answer to his question.

Aidan made a little indistinguishable grunt, and

she thought he must be smiling, though she couldn't tell for sure.

'In my view,' he said, 'it's those who've never experienced it who tend to disbelieve. It's a bit like believing in God, I guess. You won't truly get it until it hits you.'

His argument seemed reasonable enough, so much so it was almost too much for her, and she wanted to get away from him but found that she couldn't move. He dropped a kiss on her cheek. It was the lightest touch, and almost brotherly, but it sent a bolt of electricity through her. She rose from the sofa quickly and shook her shoulders pretending to loosen the stiffness.

'I think you'd better stop now.' She began to clear away their empty glasses. 'I'm feeling a lot better, thanks.'

Aidan merely smiled, an enigmatic sort of smile, which should have infuriated her but instead made her want to sit back down and pick up where they left off.

This will never do, she thought as she clattered with the glasses on the drinks tray. It wouldn't be fair on Brett.

Sensing her withdrawal, Aidan turned his attention to a photo, which was propped up against a single remaining ornament on the otherwise empty mantelpiece. He'd never seen it before, not while Lia's grandmother was still alive, so he assumed Lia must have found it herself and put it there.

Only a week ago she'd been picking up photos from his mantelpiece, he thought wryly. It was odd how their roles seemed to have been reversed in the short time since they'd met again. Was this what happened when people started giving a little of themselves? Were he and Lia on an emotional see-saw, taking turns in being high and free-falling or low and in control?

When he looked at Lia again, he saw that his action had given her the chance to regain her poise, but there was no way he was letting her off the hook that easily. He wanted to get to know her.

'I recognise you, but who's the baby?' he asked.

'My brother. He died, a long time ago. When I was a child.'

Gently he returned the photo to the mantelpiece. 'I'm sorry to hear that. How, if you don't mind me asking?'

'He drowned in the bath, if you must know.'

Lia seemed determined to maintain the distance between them and went back into the scullery with the tray, but he followed her closely, Jack hot on his heels.

'What was his name?'

She put the glasses in the sink. 'Eddie.'

'Lia and Eddie?' he mused. 'An odd combination of names for siblings.'

'Surely it's no worse than Gerald, Marcella, and Aidan,' she said.

He grinned. 'I suppose not.'

'It's short for Edmund. And my mother is Constance, but we call her Connie. We're all named after tragic Shakespearean heroes and heroines, who come to a sticky end.' She gave a little shrug. 'My grandmother's idea.'

'An odd thing to do to your family.'

Lia grimaced. 'You're telling me.'

Aidan leaned languidly against the fridge and watched her while she rinsed the glasses and put them on the draining board. 'Is it because of your brother that you don't like the water much?'

'I don't know. Maybe.'

As she turned away and reached for a tea towel, he noticed the set of her shoulders, rigid, unapproachable. They'd had a nice time, there was no reason for her to act like this all of a sudden. Unless it had something to do with that photo.

Stepping closer, he rested a hand on her back. 'It must be hard for you, being here with all those memories.'

She turned, suddenly, and threw her arms around his neck. Because of the unexpected force of her embrace he had to steady himself against the fridge before he could return it. Then he pulled her close and cradled her against his chest, enjoying her scent, a mixture of brandy and that fruity perfume she always wore.

'Why don't you tell me what's really bothering you?' he whispered into her fragrant hair, his lips almost touching her ear.

He felt her pull back and loosened his grip but

only so he could still hold her by the arms. He wasn't letting her go. Not yet.

'I'm sorry,' she said. 'I don't know what came over me.'

'Don't be sorry, just tell me.'

'It's . . . it's about my brother.'

'He drowned in the bath, yes, you told me.'

'I think . . .' She paused. 'I think it might have been my fault.'

Aidan smoothed back a tendril of her black hair. 'Why would you think that?'

'Because I was there.' Her voice rose. 'I remember it. It was finding the photo that did it. I suddenly remember *being* there. I think I was supposed to look after him. I'm to blame!'

She wrested away from him and would have run from the scullery if he hadn't caught her arm. 'Lia, listen to me. It wasn't your fault. It was an accident. Just a dreadful accident.'

'How do you know? You weren't there!'

'And you were, what, five?'

'Four.'

Her jaw was clamped tight as she struggled hard to keep her tears at bay. Aidan released her to preserve her pride, and it had the desired effect because she got herself under control. He'd learnt this about her, that if you cornered her and got a strong reaction, it would only cause her embarrassment, and she would withdraw further into her shell. He wanted to avoid that.

'I was four,' she repeated.

'Then how can it be because of something you did or didn't do? Let those who were the grown-ups at the time carry the guilt, not you. You were far too young to be given that responsibility, anyway. Wouldn't you agree?'

She sent him a sceptical look. 'Yeah, I suppose so.' Then she smiled, a little sadly, he thought, and the moment passed when he could have kissed her for real. 'You know what?' she said. 'In a funny sort of way, you're actually quite good for my peace of mind.'

'That's not what a guy wants to hear.'

Fully recovered, she rolled her eyes at him and tossed him the tea towel. 'Here. You can do the drying.'

He took the towel, pretending to be put out by her ordering him about, but pleased that she'd recovered enough to do so. He wanted her to open up more and hoped he was beginning to unravel the mystery that was Lia.

His words stayed with her long after he'd left with the usual naval salute, a gesture which had both annoyed and puzzled her in the past, but now left her with a feeling that something was missing. The opportunity had been there to kiss her, so why hadn't he?

Am I that repulsive? she thought.

Then her cheeks flamed as she realised why, and she glanced at her engagement ring, which felt uncharacteristically tight all of a sudden. Stuffing her hands in her jeans pockets, she wandered back into the living room to watch the slowly setting sun. The sky went languidly through the spectrum of colours, from yellow to indigo, and a large scarlet cloud in the shape of a Chinese dragon ambled across it.

Aidan was right, her mind was playing tricks on her. It had been doing that a lot since she arrived here.

She turned away from the window as the telephone rang.

'Mrs Barrington?'

'No, I'm her granddaughter,' Lia answered. 'What can I do for you?'

'This is Steve from Lambda Security Services. Just phoning to let you know that we're ready to install the security system now, and I was wondering if we could agree on a date which would be convenient to Mrs Barrington.'

'My grandmother ordered a security system from you?'

'That's right. On the fifteenth of November to be exact. We now have an engineer ready to go on site.'

Lia felt a righteous anger bubbling to the surface. You heard such stories of ruthless salesmen who preyed on the elderly. She could just see this Steve character, turning up on her grandmother's doorstep and not leaving until he'd got her to sign away her life savings. 'My grandmother died four weeks ago,' she said sharply, 'and we won't be needing your services. And now we are on the subject, I have to say that I don't take kindly to the way you people operate, exploiting the fears of elderly people like that.'

Steve was quiet for a moment. 'I'm very sorry to hear your grandmother has passed away. Please accept my deepest sympathies and my sincere apologies for intruding on your grief. If I'd known, I'd have . . .' he petered off.

'Well, you'll have to find someone else to rip off.' Lia was in full stride, her anger building further. Where did it come from, all this pent-up fury?

'As I said, I'm deeply sorry for your loss,' he repeated, and this time there was a hint of annoyance in his voice, 'but I assure you we're a reputable company. Your grandmother contacted us, back in early November, asking us to install a comprehensive security system in her house as soon as we had a space in the diary. Unfortunately we've been snowed under with requests. It seems everyone wants an alarm system before they go away for Christmas.' He paused. 'Seeing as you won't be needing our services, I'll return the deposit to your . . . the estate immediately. Where would you like it sent to?'

Lia sighed, feeling vaguely guilty for jumping to conclusions like that, and rubbed her forehead with her fingers. 'You can send it to me. I'm the executor of the estate.'

She rattled off the necessary personal details for him to send a cheque to her. When she'd hung up, she stared out into the garden, surprised and slightly spooked that the darkness had crept up on her when her back was turned. Then she was spurred into action by the thought that she couldn't see anything in the dark, whereas anyone out there could see her as clear as day. With a quick, almost frantic movement she pulled the curtains.

It was all coming together, although she'd done her best to ignore the signs. A level-headed old lady who suddenly acquires a guard dog, of sorts, and orders a security system, was either coming to terms with her own vulnerability, or she'd discovered something which gave her genuine cause to be afraid. Maybe Doctor Campbell was right, and Ivy had had real reasons to fear for her life.

But what could those reasons have been?

CHAPTER 16

'**A**re you sure you're up for this?' Aidan asked Lia.

They were driving along the A149, heading towards the public swimming pool in North Walsham. It had taken some persuading, but she'd finally agreed to give diving a try. Night had already fallen and the darkened landscape flitted by, broken only by the lights from a few scattered houses and the naked trees by the roadside.

'I know I said I was going to teach you or die trying, but it was just a joke. If you really don't want to, we can turn around, and I won't think any less of you for that.'

She wrapped her grandmother's old Barbour jacket closer around her, looking uncomfortable, he thought. 'No, it's all right. It's time I got over myself. Nothing can happen to me in a swimming pool, right?'

Aidan grinned. 'I'll look after you.'

'Though I don't see why we have to do it this late. Couldn't they fit us in at a different time?'

Aidan shook his head. 'It would mean

re-arranging their programme. I could've put you in with my regular session, but then you'd be with a group. I thought you'd prefer it to be just us the first time.' He sent her a sideways look. 'Eight o'clock isn't that late.'

'No, I guess not,' she said. 'It just doesn't seem right that my first re-acquaintance with the water should happen in the dark.'

'It won't be. We'll turn on the lights.'

'Of course,' she replied and shuddered visibly.

Aidan was tempted to turn around and try for another day, but just then the swimming pool came into view, a modern building of yellow bricks and tinted glass.

It's now or never, he thought, and parked in a bay designated for the disabled. Lia tutted.

'There's no one here,' he said, 'and we've got a lot of equipment to carry. Don't you ever get tired of being such a goody two-shoes?' He opened the back of the car and handed her a large diver's bag.

'I'm *not* a goody two-shoes,' she protested and stumbled a little as the bag almost pulled her backwards.

'Careful.' He steadied her with his hand, then when he was sure she wasn't going to collapse under the weight of the heavy gear, he hoisted a similar bag over his own shoulder. Perhaps it wasn't the gentlemanly thing to do, but divers, male as well as female, needed to be able to carry their own stuff. The sooner she got used to that, the better.

He led the way to a door at the back of the building, which was built on an incline. Behind what was a single-storey section at the front, it rose to at least two storeys and consisted of large glass panels held together by criss-cross metal framework. Aided by the full moon, one could just about make out the pool behind the glass, and it appeared as flat and still as a mirror.

Lia sent him a questioning glance as realisation dawned on her. 'We shouldn't really be here, should we?'

'Nope.'

'You're not planning to break in, I take it.'

Aidan laughed quietly. 'I've got a man on the inside.'

'I see,' she said, but clearly didn't. He sensed a rising panic in her as her breath came in short, silent gulps.

'Relax. The security guard is a mate of mine. I taught him to dive, you see. It's just easier this way than having to go through all the official channels, booking a time slot, and, er, well, paying for it. It's not cheap to rent a whole swimming pool.'

'No, I'm sure it isn't.' Lia hoisted Aidan's rucksack further up on her shoulder. 'What's in this bag, by the way? Bricks?'

Just then there was movement behind the darkened glass, and the fire exit door was pushed open from the inside. Aidan's friend stuck his head out. He was wearing dark blue trousers and a shirt in a lighter blue colour with a logo on the breast pocket.

'Lambda Security,' Lia muttered. 'Small world.'

'I beg your pardon?' said Aidan

'Nothing.'

The guard ushered them inside. 'I've left the pool lights on because they won't show from the outside. Just remember, they switch off automatically at nine.' He glanced at his watch. 'It'll have to be a short lesson.'

'We've got plenty of time for what I have in mind. Thanks, Jim. I appreciate it.'

'And I don't need to tell you to lock up,' said Jim. 'I could get in real trouble if anyone finds out.'

'Sure. I know.' Aidan clapped him on the shoulder and secured the fire door firmly after he'd left. Then he unpacked his rucksack.

Lia dumped her burden next to his and began to do the same, but he stopped her. 'I'd rather do it myself. I know this equipment, and I'd like to pack it and unpack it in a certain order, if that makes any sense to you.' He handed her a large, flat packet wrapped in brown paper and tied with string which lay at the top of the bag. 'I've got a present for you.'

'A present?' She arched her eyebrows.

'Go on, open it.'

Suspiciously she untied the string and pulled the coarse paper aside, then lifted out the two-piece wetsuit. It was a smart-looking outfit of black neoprene with reinforced sections in bright blue at the knees and over the shoulders, and the inside was a cheerful magenta. A girlie get-up.

For a moment she seemed speechless, then she said, 'Where did you get this?'

'I bought it.'

'But I can't accept it. It must be hugely expensive!'

He shrugged. 'You said you wished someone would buy you something personal. Well, it doesn't get any more personal than this. I could've bought you lingerie, of course, but I didn't think it'd be appropriate.'

'Damn right it wouldn't.'

He grinned. 'At least try it on, eh? Over there. I won't look.' He pointed to a row of plastic chairs bolted to the floor about ten yards away from them.

'You wouldn't get anything out of it if you did. I'm wearing a swimming costume under my clothes.'

'Oh, bum.'

She laughed, a carefree teasing sound. Saucy even. It warmed him to see her like this for a change, because he knew she was nervous, and he hoped she'd accept his present. It pleased him that he'd been able to choose something personal for her, despite the price tag.

He continued unpacking the gear, then found himself a private spot at the other end of the row of chairs and changed into his own wetsuit, careful to keep his scarred leg facing away from her in case she looked. When he'd finished, Lia was still wrestling with hers.

'Are you decent?' he asked

'Always,' she replied sourly.

'Why the long face? You'll be quite safe, I promise.'

'It's not that,' she said, coming towards him with a look of dismay. 'I think my zip is stuck.'

'Here, let me.'

Before she could protest, he unzipped her jacket again which she'd only managed to close halfway. As he reached his hand inside to examine the back of the zip, he brushed against her breast accidentally and felt her nipple go as hard as a pebble. She gasped, a sort of strangled squeak, and he moved his hand but caught her eyes. Her lips had parted and were begging to be kissed.

Framed against the moonlight she looked like a sorceress, enthralling him with her long, dark hair and translucent skin. At first, she didn't move, as if any action on her part would shatter the moment and force them back to reality, but then she reached out and placed his hands on her hips underneath her open jacket. Following her lead, he tightened his grip, his long fingers almost encircling her slim waist, then pulled her closer till their pelvises met.

She gasped again when she felt the proof of how much he wanted her. He made no attempt at hiding it, but instead pressed himself against her, showing that he was willing if she was.

Then he came to his senses. She was engaged, and there were things about him and his past she might not like, or even understand. He shouldn't be doing this.

Bad idea.

He let her go, and without a word she turned away and zipped up her jacket. This time the zip worked without any problems. Their unspoken desires hung in the air between them. To return to their easier footing, Aidan said, 'You look good in a wetsuit.'

Which was about as lame as that comment he'd made about her legs a few days previously.

She smiled, and after that she was strictly business, as if the interlude hadn't happened at all. They sat at the edge of the pool where the underwater lamps gave sufficient light for him to go through the equipment step by step.

'This is your buoyancy control device, or BCD for short, and it consists of the diving cylinder and regulator,' he explained and put an inflatable jacket over her wetsuit. 'The BCD is a like a bladder where you can add air or remove it so you either have buoyancy on the surface or neutral buoyancy under water. The cylinder—' he tapped the canister and indicated three hoses attached to the valve at the top of it '—is the air supply. It's obviously not pure oxygen, but a mixture of oxygen and nitrogen, same as what we normally breathe.'

He adjusted the vest over her shoulders and closed it with a clip at the front, carefully avoiding any further contact with her body. 'There are two stages: the first stage, which we call the reduction stage, and where you use this regulator.' He placed a small black mouthpiece over her mouth. 'The air in a bottle like this is under pressure, and the first stage from the tank reduces it to current atmospheric pressure. This is to compensate for depth. The second stage is the demand valve, or mouthpiece if you like—' he held up a larger, blue mouthpiece, '—which you breathe from when you're under water. You know what the bends are, don't you?'

'Sort of,' she said. 'I know it's decompression sickness and how to deal with it if someone is suffering from it, but that's it.'

'Right, well, when you dive, because of the pressure from the water around you, you need to breathe gas at a higher pressure than on the surface, and that difference needs to be compensated for gradually when you re-surface. In other words, if you come up too quickly, your body can't adapt and you risk getting the bends.'

Lia sent him a wild-eyed look, and the vein on her neck throbbed visibly. He liked the idea that this was caused by his nearness, but more likely it was because of the forthcoming dive. He wished he could kiss it better.

'Are you listening?' he asked when she didn't respond.

She nodded.

'Okay. Now, you don't have to worry about the pressure for the moment. It'll be minimal because we aren't going deeper than a few meters.' He smiled at her doubtful expression. 'Have you never fetched a diving stick in a swimming pool?'

'My grandmother insisted that I had swimming lessons when I was eight. I never went in the water before that.'

'And did you enjoy it?'

'I hated it. I only did it to please her.'

Aidan squeezed her shoulder lightly. 'Today we're in a swimming pool, but when we dive in the sea . . . it's the most beautiful place on earth. I promise you, you won't look back.'

'But one step at a time, eh?' she said, and her voice quivered slightly.

'One step at a time.'

He explained the rest of the equipment and went over the explanation once more to make sure she'd understood everything, then placed a console in her hand. It had three dials and was attached to the regulator set. 'This isn't just a fashion accessory,' he said. 'Here you have your compass, and your depth gauge, and, very importantly, your SPG.'

'Es-pee-gee?'

'Submersible pressure gauge. It shows the actual pressure in your bottle and how much air you have left. You always need to make sure you have enough for a potential emergency.'

She gave a jerky nod and held up an extra hose from the regulator set with a bright yellow square on the mouthpiece end. 'And what about this?'

'That's your octopus, or secondary demand

valve. You clip it to the diver's harness where it's easy to see and where both you and another diver can reach it if for some reason you need to share air. That's why the hose is longer; it lets you swim in single file while you're sharing air.'

Lia nodded again, a determined look in her eyes, but she couldn't disguise a slight trembling of her lips.

It won't be relevant today,' he said gently. 'Ready?'

'Don't I need a certificate or something?' she asked.

He recognised her question as a last-ditch attempt at getting out of the dive without losing face, and rolled his eyes theatrically. 'Listen, I'm a PADI-certified Master Scuba Diver. You're in good hands.'

Looking at her more closely, he took in her pinched mouth, the dilated pupils, and read genuine fear. Lia was absolutely terrified, and he felt for her, but he also knew that if he let her off the hook now, he'd never get her this far again. He decided to give her the option, but in a challenging way.

'But if you really don't want to do this, we can stop right here. It's not advisable for an instructor to dive with someone who's going to panic, because you run the risk of hyperventilating. Being a doctor, you know what that means.'

'Not enough carbon dioxide in the blood,' she snapped. 'Yes, I know. I'm not panicking.'

'All right, if you're sure.'

'I am,' she said, and sounded far from sure.

'You probably think all this stuff is incredibly tedious, but you can't dive until you know the equipment inside out. Who's going to help you if you forget the basics once you're underwater?' At her startled expression, he smiled. 'I'll be there, of course, but you do need to know your own gear.'

'As does any professional.'

'Quite.' Aidan checked the fit of her vest, yanking the straps to ensure they were sufficiently tight. 'Damn,' he muttered.

'What?' Panic rose in her voice.

'Your weight belt. You're not wearing it.'

'Do I need it? I mean, it's only a swimming pool.'

'You need it to compensate for the positive buoyancy of your suit, yes.' He rummaged in both diving bags, frowning. 'I'm sure I packed it. It must be in the car. I'll just pop out and get it. Just stay where you are, or dangle your feet in the water if you like. Don't go in until I'm here.'

'How will you get back in?'

'With this,' he replied and held up a child's polystyrene float. 'I'll wedge the door open. Stay cool.'

Lia watched him anxiously from the poolside as he pushed open the fire exit. Briefly he was bathed in moonlight, a slick, dark silhouette against the pale light, as he placed the polystyrene float between the door and the door jamb, then he was gone.

He'd be back in a minute, she reassured herself, and as she sat with her feet dangling in the water as he'd suggested, images of numerous swimming pools, and just as many exasperated swimming teachers, floated back up to her. With them came her memories of the utter revulsion she'd felt for the water in front of her and of her grandmother whom she couldn't disappoint, waving encouragingly from the spectator stands. A skinny child, she'd shivered in her costume as she dipped a tentative toe and experienced the chill of the deadly element.

But things were different now. Cocooned in neoprene and emboldened by the alien gear on her back designed to keep her safe, she slid down into the unheated pool. He'd said to wait, but if she stayed right here, by the edge, she was sure it wasn't dangerous. She'd expected to feel cold, but as the water penetrated the wetsuit, it was heated up by her own body and acted as an insulating layer.

It was the most peculiar sensation, like being wet and not being wet at the same time.

I could get used to this, she thought. The water didn't seem quite as threatening and unforgiving as it had done in the past, and she forced herself to let go of the tiled edge, pushing herself further away and slowly into the centre of the pool. The underwater lights bounced off the shiny black hoses of the regulator, and her paddling feet seemed almost bloodless in the greenish water. Laughing quietly, she lay back and, held up by the suit and the jacket, floated like she had never dared do before.

'Yes!' she laughed again. 'This is so good. It's wonderful!'

Her words echoed in the empty hall, bouncing back from all the hard surfaces, and brought her up short. It wouldn't do if they were caught here. They would get fined for trespassing, and the guard would most likely lose his job. Lia didn't want to be the cause of that.

She continued to float but this time enjoying the sensation in silence, and she'd almost lulled herself into a trance, when the pool lights went out. The shock of it sent her flailing and splashing, and for a moment the water closed over her head despite the buoyancy of the jacket. She surfaced again, hacking and coughing, and began to swim toward the edge when something stopped her.

Out of the corner of her eye she caught a fleeting movement among the tiered spectator seats at the far end of the pool. There was something there, she was sure of it. Something . . . not right. She strained her eyes but the moon which had lit the pool from the outside, muted by the tinted glass panes, had gone behind a cloud, and the darkness inside was almost impenetrable.

'Aidan?' she called out tentatively.

No response.

'If it's you, stop playing games.'

The silence in the pool hall was watchful, almost condemning, broken only by Lia's attempts at staying afloat without panicking. She remained in the centre of the pool, because if there was someone, or something, in here, she realised, in her near-panic state, then she would be most vulnerable if she tried to climb out. But she couldn't stay here forever either.

'Aidan?' she cried out again, this time uncertain. He wouldn't do this to her, would he? It didn't make any sense, but if he was playing games with her, the question was, why? Why would he when he knew how anxious she was?

A crash and a clang of metal came from the direction of the door. 'What the hell do you think you're doing?'

Relieved, Lia swam towards the edge of the pool where his voice was coming from. 'The lights went out,' she panted from exertion. 'I was floating and suddenly, bam, no light.'

Strong arms pulled her out, and she sat down beside him unable to make out more than the faintest contours of his face.

'I told you to bloody wait for me, didn't I?'

'It's okay. The water's only chest high at this end anyway.'

She tried to reassure him, but the shock of being plunged into darkness and the peculiar feeling that someone else had been in the building with her was making her pulse race, and her breath came in short, shallow bursts.

'It's *not* okay,' he snapped. 'We haven't even started yet, and you've just gone and put yourself in danger. As your instructor your safety is *my* responsibility, so from now on you listen to what I say. Got it?'

He sounded incredibly angry, more angry than she'd ever heard him be, and for some reason it got her back up. She was tempted to bite back, to say that she was perfectly capable of taking care of herself and had done so for years, thank you very much, but an undertone in his voice warned her not to. Instead she sighed and put his ticking-off down to experience. She knew she had a lot to learn.

'Got it. Sorry.'

'Ah, never mind.' She felt rather than saw him shrug. 'Odd about the lights, though. 'They weren't supposed to go off until nine.'

The moon peered out from behind the cloud and bathed the pool in a ghostly, white light. Lia glanced at the wall clock just above the fire exit. 'It *is* nine.'

Aidan pressed a tiny button on his wrist watch. 'Hm, it looks like my watch is slow. How annoying.' He rose and took off his watch, then tossed it into his diver's bag. 'Let me just find the fuse box, and we can carry on.'

'Aidan?'

He turned. 'Yep?'

'When you were out, I thought I heard something. Shouldn't we investigate?'

He held out his hand, and she allowed him to pull her up. 'There's nothing in here, Lia. Just us two and the pool.'

'But—'

'It's in your mind. You were alone in here, the lights went out. It's enough to spook anyone, but that doesn't mean there's anything to be spooked about. You've got to let it go. Tell it to go away. Banish it. Lock it up and throw away the key. It's the only way forward. Trust me, I know what I'm talking about.'

They left the public pool shortly after ten o'clock, once Aidan had checked and double-checked that the fire door was closed properly behind them. Before leaving he asked her to pack the bags for him while he held up every piece of diving equipment in turn, saying out loud what it was, so they wouldn't leave anything behind by mistake.

He was silent in the car, but Lia was grateful for that. Her head was spinning with all the instructions Aidan had given her, relating to diving and to the equipment, as well as the exhilaration from the dive itself and the threat that they might be arrested any minute.

She sighed heavily, causing a patch of condensation on the passenger window. She had no idea she could feel so liberated. So at ease with her body. It was as if a burden had fled her insides and left her weightless, and with the feeling that she could do anything if she wanted it enough.

Smiling to herself, she glanced at Aidan and

couldn't help thinking of his earlier reaction to her. He obviously found her sexy, but wanting her was a different thing altogether. Then she thought of the sound she imagined she'd heard when she was alone in the pool and of Jim, the security guard, who worked for Lambda Security like that Steve character. She wondered whether these were coincidences, or whether they were significant in some way. They were pieces in a puzzle she couldn't quite fit together because she didn't know if they were all part of the same game or several mysteries with pieces missing.

Aidan stopped the car rather abruptly, and, sitting up, Lia saw a roadblock with three military trucks parked on the soft kerb. Two soldiers, in full combat gear, with machine guns nesting in the crook of their arms, were waving them slowly through the barrier. They signalled to them that they were clear to carry on. Lia watched them out of the rear window as Aidan sped up on the other side of the barrier.

'What was that all about?' she asked.

'I expect it's an exercise or something.' He shrugged, but kept his eyes on the road. His fingers were gripping the steering wheel tightly all of a sudden, so tightly she could see his white knuckles in the dark.

'At this hour?'

He glanced at her. 'Oh, come on. You've lived here before. When you stayed with your grand-mother. You know what it can be like. They're just doing what soldiers do in times of peace. Don't give them a bad name,' he added cryptically.

'I don't remember it being quite like this.'

'Selective memory.'

Isn't that the truth, she thought.

CHAPTER 17

idan's reaction stayed with her until the
following day. The obvious explanation
would be the tragic circumstances
surrounding his brother's death and Aidan's subse-
quent anti-military campaign. That made the
anger understandable. He hadn't seemed angry in
the car, only . . . well, nervous, now she thought
about it. Yes, nervous. Why, she couldn't fathom.
Unless he was doing more than just protesting?

Lia sighed as she waited for Brett's plane, which
had been delayed. The display in Heathrow's
Arrivals lounge showed that yet another plane had
landed, but not Brett's. Cursing inwardly, she
bought herself a coffee and settled down to an
even longer wait.

If only I'd known, she thought, I could've slept
a bit longer. Then she felt instantly guilty. Brett
would be jet-lagged, and she worried about missing
a couple of hours sleep.

Sipping her latte, she thought about Brett coming
all this way to spend Christmas with her, when
he could have had the most wonderful, lively get-
together with his own family. At special occasions

his parents' home was always filled with brothers and sister, uncles and aunts, nieces and nephews. They'd all be milling around, serving food, opening bottles, squabbling amicably over who was to bring what and who was to sit where.

Although longing to be part of it, Lia had found it difficult to carve out a niche for herself and had accepted the role of observer by default. Though she wasn't really needed in this micro society, she realised that for Brett to forego the family Christmas this year meant he was upping the pressure. She couldn't put him off forever.

Two hours and three lattes later she fell into his arms, jittery from too much caffeine. He hugged her tight, and she thought that perhaps there was no need to put him off after all. Maybe she should just go with the flow as she'd always done, forget her ghosts, pretend that the past had no influence on the person she was today.

'It's good to see you,' he said. 'I've missed you. We all have.'

He looked smart in a reefer jacket and Timberland shoes. Perfect for the Norfolk weather. 'We?'

'Mom, Dad. They keep saying I shouldn't ever have let you out of my sight.' He paused. 'They're pressing for a date.'

'Oh.'

'But I told them to lay off. I said that some people take a little longer making their minds up. I'll do all the pressing that needs doing.'

She turned away and began pushing the airport trolley towards the lift to the car park.

'I'll take that,' he said. 'You just lead the way.'

'I see you're dressed for the part,' she said as she paid for parking at the ticket machine.

'Oh, my clothes. Do you like them?'

She nodded.

'I googled Norfolk and read up on it. It's all windy salt marshes, so I thought I'd get the right gear.'

And he had, Lia had to admit, but couldn't figure out why this efficiency should irritate her so much. It made sense to keep warm.

'Sadly there aren't any salt marshes where we are, but it can be pretty nippy. Cold,' she corrected. 'Nippy' was a very British term. 'We have some nice beaches, though, and there are some lovely walks. Jack just loves—'

'Jack? Is that dog still with you? I thought you were finding him a home.'

'I am, I just haven't had much luck yet. My neighbour's looking after him, but only for today.' She opened the boot, and Brett loaded his bags, while she returned the trolley to a trolley station.

'What have you done to your hair?' he asked in the car.

'Nothing.'

'It's a bit wild.'

She laughed self-consciously. 'I haven't brushed it today.'

'Is that what they do in Norfolk, don't brush their hair?'

'Some do, some don't.' Frowning, she joined the motorway traffic. Surely, he'd seen her with morning hair before? Or maybe not, she couldn't remember. What was it Brett's sister Vicky had said once? That her husband didn't know what she looked like without make-up after five years of marriage, because she always went to bed with the lights off and got up before him.

For a second Lia felt she couldn't breathe and opened the window.

Brett rubbed his hands against the cold. 'So tell me about the famous house. I can't wait to see it. What's it called? Holk-ham Hall.'

'Holkham,' Lia said, pronouncing it 'holkum'. 'We don't say the "ham" bit. There are quite a few places named something-ham in Norfolk. I think it means "small village". There's Dereham, spelt D-E-R-E-H-A-M, but we say Deram.'

He whistled. 'I'd never have gotten that.'

She smiled at his confusion. 'My personal favourite is W-Y-M-O-N-D-H-A-M. It's simply shortened to Windam.'

'So, er, *Holkum* Hall, is that where you grandmother lived? You never told me she was – what's the phrase? – landed gentry.'

Lia laughed. 'Sorry, I think that might be an Anglo–American misunderstanding. My grandmother owned some land, like most people in Norfolk, because there's quite a lot of it to go around, but she wasn't landed. Also, you might call her genteel, but she wasn't gentry.'

'An Anglo–American misunderstanding, huh? Why, you stiff-assed Brit.' He threw her a smile to accompany the phrase she'd heard so often, a standing joke between them which seemed to encompass how different they were, but in a good way.

Lia laughed again. It was good to have him here to lighten the mood. 'Holkham Hall is a manor house quite near to where we are. We can visit it if you like. But my grandmother's house is just a glorified two-up two-down.'

'Two-up two-down?'

'Four rooms, plus a box room. Though they're a good size.'

'Ah, well, I can't wait to see it. It sounds really quaint.'

He was going to be disappointed, she thought. 'There isn't much to see. I've cleared out almost everything. There's only a few bits of furniture left, and the place echoes.'

'There is a bed, I hope.' He sent her a sideways glance.

'There is a bed,' she answered, wondering what the hell Jack was going to do when he was ousted from the bedroom. Howl, probably.

When they reached the last roundabout before the village, Lia found the usual exit blocked. A Humvee and an armoured security vehicle were parked across it, and two Redcaps from the military police were redirecting the traffic. Lia sighed and took the next exit, which meant quite a detour.

'What's going on?' asked Brett.

'Probably to do with the bomber.'

Brett turned in his seat. 'The *bomber*?'

'Oh, don't worry, it's pretty low-key. Just some unknown individual who's been placing IEDs at the various army facilities in the area. They never go off, but the army takes it seriously enough. As they should.'

'Do they know why?'

Lia shook her head. 'How can they? They don't even know who.' And neither do I, she thought. Never mind that Aidan had been speaking out very strongly against the Ministry of Defence and fitted the profile worryingly well. She changed the subject. 'So tell me, what's been happening at work?'

When they reached the house, Lia showed him around, though there wasn't much to see. Brett had his hand around her waist all that time, and when she showed him the bedroom where they would be sleeping together, he pulled her down on the bed.

'Brett!' she said with pretend indignation, though her whole body tensed. 'I've got to—'

'Come on, Lia,' he whispered into her ear, his breath hot against her neck. 'It's been a long plane journey. At least you could reward a man for his determination.'

The temptation to make up an excuse was strong, but Lia realised she didn't have any basis for not having sex with him. Brett was her fiancé; that's what people did. So she let him make love to her, while all the time she felt nothing. Nothing at all. And the look in his eyes told her, with gut-wrenching insight, that he sensed her remoteness.

'How awfully nice to meet you.' Lia's mother held out her hand to Brett but kept the rest of her body at a distance. It was hard to gauge what Connie felt, but Lia wasn't surprised at her mother's cautious welcome.

Brett appeared not to have noticed. He beamed a smile at his mother-in-law-to-be and handed her a parcel wrapped in garish crimson cellophane with an enormous bow that looked completely over the top. 'We brought the Christmas pudding. I've no idea what it is, but Lia assures me it's a national speciality.'

'You could say that,' said Connie and seemed to thaw a little.

Lia led the way into the kitchen at the back, lured by the homely smell of roast.

'What a cute little house,' said Brett. Lia's hackles rose.

Connie sent him an apologetic smile. 'Sorry, it's not very grand,' she said and hung their coats on the coat stand. 'I'm sure you're used to a lot more.'

Brett was, and it showed on his face, but perhaps it was only because Lia knew him well that she noticed. She sincerely hoped her mother hadn't. 'Anything we can do to help, Mum? I can tell you've already put the turkey in, but would you like some help with the veg?'

'Just make sure Brett is comfortable in the lounge, then you can help me in the kitchen. The tomato salad needs preparing. There's a bottle of sherry on a tray with those nice little glasses you gave me once.'

Lia recognised a pretext when she saw one. Brett didn't seem to mind being ushered unceremoniously out of the kitchen. It happened a lot in his own family where his mother, his aunts and cousins ruled, but there he'd have other people to talk to. She promised herself she would be as quick as she could so he didn't feel too lonely.

'Looks like I'm being dismissed,' he said and reached for the sherry. 'Harvey's Bristol Cream. Never heard of it. Is it any good?'

'It's sweet. Mum likes her alcohol sweet.'

'Well, I like mine plentiful.' He filled three glasses almost to the top and handed one to Lia.

She looked out into the small back garden. A string of coloured fairy lights wrapped around a lonely fir tree shone like beacons against the settling dusk.

Brett joined her. 'Those lights are pretty neat.'

'They are, aren't they? It's funny,' she said, 'but Gran always used to say that coloured fairy lights were vulgar, and that anyone with any sense of style would choose white ones.'

Brett sipped his sherry, then pulled a face and held the glass away from him to look at the liquid. 'That's not very nice.'

Lia stared at him, wondering how it was that he'd managed to say what she'd always wanted to say, but never dared. 'No, I don't suppose it was. My grandmother said a lot of not very nice things.' She would have said 'nasty', or 'horrible', except she'd never used such words in connection with Ivy. 'I never thought about it before, and I know one shouldn't speak ill of the dead, but—'

'Mm? No, I meant the sherry. It's too sweet.' Brett put his hand on the back of her neck and gave it a friendly squeeze. 'Lia, it's Christmas. Lighten up. As for those lamps . . .' He shrugged. 'Whatever their colour, you need something bright around here. I've never been in such a gloomy country before.'

Leaving him to find more faults with her nation, she went into the kitchen to help her mother.

'Well, he seems very nice.' Connie sipped the sherry Lia had brought her.

Lia was slicing tomatoes and arranging them in a flat dish. She poured a generous amount of virgin olive oil over them, then she picked a few leaves off a basil plant from the windowsill, breathing in the aroma before sprinkling them over the tomatoes and oil.

'He is,' she replied finally. 'Almost too nice.'

'How can a man be too nice? Don't look a gift horse in the mouth, Lia.'

'I'm not.' Irritation prickled between her shoulder

blades, unreasonably, because she'd have said exactly the same thing to a friend in similar circumstances. And she did see Connie more as a friend than a mother. They'd never been close, but close enough for them to have this sort of conversation. Perhaps it was up to her to take the first step towards bridging the gap between them. 'I like him a lot. And I respect him.'

'But you don't love him.'

Lia considered her answer carefully. 'I don't know any more. I'm just so confused. This whole thing with Ivy and the house . . . well, I've been finding stuff—'

'What sort of stuff?' Connie's voice was sharp.

'Things that have made me realise she wasn't quite what I thought she was. And that's made me think maybe no one is. Least of all myself.'

'Then it's time you found out. And you can start by being honest to that nice young man in there.'

Between Christmas and New Year, Brett wanted to play the tourist, now he was finally here. The distraction stopped Lia from mulling over her true feelings.

They watched live glass-making in Langham, and Norwich Cathedral rendered Brett speechless. For once he wasn't referring to things as 'quaint' or 'cute'. He stood in stunned silence for ten minutes while Lia was making faces at the gargoyles in the ceiling through the cathedral's viewing mirror.

'That's one hell of a church,' he said as they left.

'Imagine uneducated peasants building such a monument to God. Makes you think, doesn't it?'

She nodded. 'Bit of a contrast to their humble medieval huts. In the face of such splendour they'd have to believe in God.'

'Without the help of cranes and computers, too,' said Brett.

Lia opened her mouth to broaden the discussion, then stopped. What could she say? Again they'd talked at cross purposes. Of course Brett was right in his observation. He was intelligent and well educated, but it irked her how he never seemed to tap into her thoughts. How could she not have noticed this before?

New Year's Eve was a cosy twosome in front of the fire in Ivy's living room, and Lia dithered. It struck her that she'd deliberately chosen a man who was different to her so she could make believe she was a different person herself. Whether this was good or bad, she couldn't decide. If she'd changed, with Brett being the catalyst, it didn't mean her own personality had been subordinated, did it?

But a rebellious streak reared its ugly head and told her this was the coward's way out. Instead of facing up to her own demons, she was hiding behind Brett's persona and trying to ignore her own tangled emotions. Of course a person could live like this, temporarily, but it wouldn't give her any lasting happiness. To achieve that, she had to find out for herself.

New Year's Day they went to a church service in Wells. St Nicholas's was crowded, but they managed to squeeze in on the back pew next to an elderly couple. Lia wasn't religious, not like Brett and his family, but as the service progressed she felt herself soaring on a wave of warmth and goodwill. She soaked up the atmosphere and delighted in the sermon which was well-written and delivered with conviction.

A lot of familiar faces were there. Lia nodded to Mrs Larwood and the doctor's receptionist, for whom she was beginning to feel a grudging respect. Susannah too, with her husband and children. Nigel waved a cheery hello, and Zoe beamed at her, but Susannah didn't turn around once during the ceremony, and instead kept her face studiously averted.

Slightly peeved, Lia ignored her rudeness. She had other things on her mind than worrying about Susannah's complexes. I'll patch it up with her next week, she thought, although why it was up to her, she had no idea. Susannah hadn't exactly been proactive with regards to their friendship either.

A part of her was relieved that Aidan wasn't there. Every night since the dive at the swimming pool she'd relived the feel of his hands on her hips, the sparks sizzling between them. Having Brett and Aidan coming face to face would stir up a hornet's nest of questions and emotions she couldn't face right now.

At the same time she yearned for a glimpse of him, but she suppressed the feeling ruthlessly.

Outside, they shook hands with the vicar, and Brett went back into 'quaint' mode. The stone church was 'picturesque', the vicar was 'quintessentially English', the sermon 'outlandish', and the whole town smelled of fish. Lia laughed it off even as she ground her teeth.

Despite the smell she persuaded Brett to take a stroll along the harbour. Fishing boats were moored next to the pier and had an air of disuse about them, and the ever-present seagulls croaked and flapped their wings in the hope of receiving a tidbit. The harbour was deserted except for a solitary figure at the end of the quayside.

The person she'd both hoped and feared she would see.

Aidan saw them coming from way off. He'd placed his easel facing the boats bobbing quietly in the harbour and was working on a painting commissioned by a boat owner. As with the portrait it was a departure from his usual seascapes, but it paid well.

Lia and her companion were walking towards him, with purpose, it seemed, both smiling broadly. The man wore tan desert boots, thick denims and a navy blue jacket, and had completed his outfit with a striped Breton scarf and leather gloves. Ambling along as if he'd just stepped out of a catalogue and was testing his new clothes, he could have been just another weekender. The type who played at boating on one of the many leisure crafts in the harbour without having a clue what he was doing. Aidan hated him on sight.

So, this was what he looked like, that fancy lawyer. Brett or whatever his name was.

What was she doing, parading her boyfriend in front of him? He hadn't forgotten her reaction to him at the swimming pool, and knew he could have had her there and then if he'd chosen to act on it. Noble ideals had held him back, but now he realised he'd been a fool. She very likely didn't share those ideals if she could rub the existence of her fiancé in his face like this.

Was she completely clueless about the effect she had on him, both emotionally and physically? Or had she played fast and loose with his feelings? It didn't tally with the Lia who had thrown herself into his arms, distressed by her findings in the loft, or the girl whose eyes went wide with fear of the water. Then again, what did he know?

Looking at her more closely, he noticed her discomfort. It wasn't every day a person had to square up to an almost-lover and a current one simultaneously. He found himself admiring her dignified posture and the way she gesticulated and chatted to her fiancé as if nothing had happened. He couldn't hear what she was saying, but suspected it was mainly small talk.

He made his face as expressionless as he could, to show he didn't mind at all. Lia halted for a moment, then walked on with her head held high and the smile still in place. It had slipped a little, he saw, become brittle.

God, I'm such a cad, he thought. He didn't smile back, though; instead he sent them a scowl and turned his attention to his work.

His attempt at intimidation had no effect on the lawyer. Catalogue Man came right up to stand behind him, peering over his shoulder like so many did when an artist worked *en plein air*. Usually Aidan found this flattering and amusing. It was as if the observers were waiting for him to make an inspired stroke, now that they'd honoured him with their acknowledgement. Sometimes he obliged, earning himself praise.

This time his hand shook and the brush wobbled under the scrutiny. Cursing inwardly, he scraped the paint off the small area with his palette knife and tried again.

'Aidan,' said Lia, 'this is my fiancé, Brett Melrose. Brett, meet Aidan Morrell. We were at school together. He's an artist,' she added unnecessarily.

'And a very good one, too,' said Brett.

Aidan stopped what he was doing and arched an eyebrow at Brett. 'You know about art?'

'I know what I like, and I like what you're doing. Take those orange trawl floats on that boat there.' He pointed to a fishing boat in the harbour with a row of net floats on the side. 'Now, back to the painting – up close you don't see the floats, they're just rough brush work, but when you step back, you get the whole picture. You see them clearly for what they are. You're good.'

'Well, thank you.'

'Don't mention it.'

'I hear you're a lawyer.' Aidan couldn't resist. 'Are you a good one?'

'The best.' Brett smiled pleasantly, but there was no mistaking the determination behind his eyes.

Aidan could picture him easily, formidable in a courtroom, winning more than he lost. In a game of one-upmanship over Lia, Brett would emerge as the undisputed victor. He was suave, successful, rich. Probably on first name terms with the President. Unscarred. Anything Aidan could offer her – and that wasn't much by any stretch of the imagination – Brett could give her ten times over.

So what?

Setting his testosterone pride aside, he had to admit Brett was okay. He'd wanted him to be another brash and uncultured American so that he could mock him and feel superior. Instead the other man had shown him, not that he was an art connoisseur exactly, but that he appreciated Aidan's skills at face value.

A quiet respect rose in him. Lia could be happy with Brett. The prospect pained him, but his presence in her life lately had clouded her judgement, and he had to step aside so she could decide for herself what was right for her.

Acting the unpredictable eccentric, he saluted

ironically and noticed Lia bristling at this. Brett, however, wasn't deterred.

'I see you're a navy man,' he said.

'Ex-navy. What gave me away?'

Brett smiled, displaying the kind of teeth an orthodontist could only dream of. 'The way you saluted just then. In the old days the Limeys used to have dirty palms from handling ropes, so when they saluted their superior officers, they held their palms downward to hide the dirt.'

'How do you know all this stuff?' Lia said. 'This isn't even your country.'

'I wasn't always a lawyer. I've been around. And I read.'

Add well-read globetrotter to his list of assets. Smart alec, Aidan thought, and returned to his canvas. 'Nice meeting you.'

'Yeah, nice meeting you too. I wish you every success with your painting venture.' Brett's delivery was as smooth as a marbled egg.

They left, and Aidan watched out of the corner of his eye as the American gave Lia a little squeeze and a kiss on the temple. Something he said made her laugh, a carefree sound which cut through Aidan and made him wish he hadn't witnessed their easy intimacy.

Well, what did he care? His life was complicated enough as it was without adding his feelings for Lia to the mix.

CHAPTER 18

On the morning of Brett's return to the States Lia persuaded him to come for a walk on the beach. She let Jack loose, and he scarpered ahead of them, oblivious to the wild beauty around them. The sea, a flat granite slab, extended into the distance and blended with the sky, only separated by a narrow white line on the horizon. Squinting, Lia could just about make it out.

'What are you doing?' asked Brett, linking his arm with hers.

'Trying to see where the sea ends and the sky begins, but you have to squint. Go on, try it.'

'What am I looking for?' he asked, squinting obediently.

'A white line on the horizon.'

'I can't see anything. Can we move now, before I freeze to death?' He shuddered in his many layers, though it wasn't that cold. 'Why do you like this place so much? It's just a beach, and I find the surroundings, I dunno . . . oppressive, I guess.'

Lia shot him a look. 'Just a beach? It's an official Area of Outstanding Natural Beauty, I'll have you know. Anyway, don't you get a great sense of space, the way it stretches on forever? Think of all the worlds out there, and all the possibilities.'

He shook his head and retreated further into his coat. 'I don't get it. To be frank, I feel as if the sky is going to fall on me. It gives me the creeps.'

Lia shaded her eyes with her hand and looked out over the sea. 'I'm sorry you feel that way.' More sorry than you can imagine, she thought. Since his arrival she'd tried to bridge the gap between them but had been unable to. It was as if she'd been asleep for years and only just woken up to discover where she truly belonged.

And it wasn't in Brett's world. Nor was he at home in hers.

Later, at Heathrow, she hugged him tight. When she pulled away, she read the puzzled sadness in his eyes, as if he knew they'd come as far as they could and was unable to explain why.

'You're the best thing that's ever happened to me,' she said.

'But not the right thing.'

She let go of him. '*I'm* not right.'

'You have a lot of ghosts to deal with. I knew that when we first met. I tried to ignore it, hoping it would go away.'

'But it didn't.'

She slid the diamond ring off her finger and handed it to him. He twirled it in his hand for a moment, then dropped it in his pocket.

'Coming over for Christmas,' he said, 'I realise you've left something of yourself behind here. I hope you find it.' Smiling, he brushed her cheek lightly with his finger. 'And if you do find it, and want to come back, I'll be there. Just don't leave it for too long. I'm a practical sort of guy. In the meantime I'll arrange for your things to be sent back.'

'I'll pay for it, of course.'

He shook his head. 'Let that be one last thing I can do for you.'

'If you insist,' she said. 'Thank you. For everything.'

'No problem.'

She watched him stride towards the Departures lounge without turning around once, and her eyes fell on his new Timberland boots. There wasn't a scratch on them, even though he'd worn them for over a week; an unlooked-for sign that they belonged to two very different worlds. For a while she'd allowed herself to be beguiled by it all: now she had to deal with what was waiting for her here, whatever that may be.

By the time she and Jack had returned to Norfolk the wind had got up, and instead of going home, they headed for the beach. The little dog had waited patiently in the car at Heathrow; now he was rewarded with the freedom of running wild. The wind lifted and tossed Lia's hair as she strolled across the damp sand to the filmy, grey sea. The tide was low, and a ray of sunshine was fighting with the drifting pewter clouds for possession of the sky. For a moment she just breathed in the flatness and the emptiness of it all.

Having squared things with Brett, a burden had lifted from her shoulders. One down, one million to go, she thought wryly. In Philadelphia she had, without realising it, felt hemmed in by the bright lights and the sirens in the night, the TVs blaring from neighbouring apartments with canned laughter till five in the morning. The city was in your face, and it had stopped her thinking. For that she needed space.

Here, every house, every tree, every dip in the landscape spoke of history; and the sea, like people, kept secrets. They bubbled beneath the surface, and occasionally one was given up, reluctantly, to a lucky finder. The answers lay here, where nature ruled. She was certain of it.

Walking away from the beach, she sobered. Not everything had been resolved yet. There was still the matter of Ivy and her strange behaviour before her death. Not to mention the other odd happenings and her own reaction to them.

Shivering violently, and not just from the cold, she made her way back, her good mood gone.

At the height of a cold snap in January, Aidan finally managed to persuade Lia to come diving in the sea with him. They'd been back to the swimming pool a few times, courtesy of Jim, but in the daytime, to Lia's obvious relief, and in a sectioned-off area of the deeper pool, away from screaming kids. She'd kept him at arm's length and concentrated on the business of learning to dive, and he wondered if she was angry with him for the way he'd acted when he met her fiancé, but decided some things were best left unsaid.

He did speculate about her lengthy absence from work, and broached the subject finally, over coffee. They were sitting in her kitchen, which was warm for a change.

'I've resigned,' she replied. 'I've inherited enough from my grandmother to live on until I've made up my mind what I want to do. And then there's the house, which I'm hoping to sell.'

'I thought you enjoyed your job.'

Lia shrugged in a way which could be interpreted as both a yes and a no.

'Why did you pack it in?'

'It was time for me to come home.' Another cryptic response.

The boyfriend, Aidan thought. Something was up with the American. It was none of his business, of course, but a little devil made him prod further. 'So, when's the Yank coming back? Valentine's Day?'

He prepared himself for a terse reply, but she merely looked at him, for a moment expressionless, as if she had no idea to whom he was referring. Then she smiled, a tentative curve of her lips. The smile caught him unawares, and his heart skipped

285

a beat or two. This was the real Lia, the object of his teenage infatuation, and he was still in danger of losing his head. *Damn.*

'He isn't,' she said. 'We broke up. Now, can we get on with this diving lark, before I get cold feet?'

He opened his mouth to say something, then realised there would be plenty of time for that another day. She'd smiled when she told him, which was nothing if not encouraging, but her insistence that they focus on the diving – something he knew she feared – was clearly a signal to back off. Besides, he needed to retain his own focus.

'Sure.' Pushing the thought aside, he went through some of the basic safety measures again in connection with a dive and the use of the diving equipment, just in case she'd forgotten. Picking up the console from the kitchen table, he said, 'Remember this? Your compass, your depth gauge and your SPG. Very important.'

'I remember.'

'And you're sure you know the drill? All the steps we went through in the pool?'

'Yep, I won't forget. Promise.'

'Good.'

They changed into drysuits. Although he'd given Lia a wetsuit as a present, it wasn't suitable for winter diving, and he'd hired a woman's drysuit from an equipment hire service. A quiet breeze ruffled her black hair as he loaded her change of clothes into the Honda. The morning was crisp and clear, but the sun was still low in the sky, and there was a definite nip in the air.

Telling the dog to stay put, Lia shivered, from anticipation and maybe cold. 'Will I be warm enough in this? The water must be absolutely freezing.'

'You'll be fine for the length of time I'm planning for us to be under. Unlike a wetsuit, where your body heats up the water, a drysuit seals you off from the water and keeps you warm. Even in these sea temperatures.' He glanced at her as he turned the ignition. 'Are you cold now?'

Lia shook her head. 'Not really.'

'Any other questions?'

'Oh, only like half a million,' she muttered.

He laughed and checked a large, square watch on his left wrist.

'That's a strange-looking watch,' said Lia.

'It's a dive computer, and it costs an arm and a leg, just so you know. I used to plan my dives, but now it's all on here. It tells me the depth, dive time, and whether I need to stop for decompression when I'm going up. That sort of thing.' He handed her a piece of paper from the dashboard. 'And because I'm old-fashioned, I always check the tide.'

'Tide a.m.,' she read. 'High tide eleven thirty-five, height very low. I'm sorry but that's mostly gobbledegook to me.'

'We need to dive within the quiet period between the turn of the tide. Diving at eight a.m. should be just right for us. That'll be before the tide comes in. The other figure means that the height of high tide today is very low, and that in turn means that the water doesn't come particularly high up on the beach. The direction of the wind is ideal as well, onshore. It doesn't get much better than that.'

He turned the car into the narrow dirt track, which led to the section of the beach where he'd first seen her again, and switched off the engine. Running a hand through his hair, he turned to look at her. 'There's still time if you want to get out of it.'

'I know.'

'I won't be cross if you back out now. I'd rather postpone the dive than push you when you're not ready.'

She nodded, and he sensed her struggle from her slightly jerky movements. Or perhaps it was impatience.

'What will you do if I decide not to go?' she asked.

'Go home, I suppose. Or dive on my own. Although I probably shouldn't.'

'On your own?' That seemed to decide her, but whether it was the thought of him alone in that vast expanse of icy, grey sea, or the worry she'd be bored waiting for him, he couldn't tell. He hoped it was concern for his safety. 'I'm fine,' she said.

They left their bags by the hollow tree stump high up on the beach and headed for the water's edge in their lead weight belts and BCDs, carrying their fins and masks. The beach was potholed with puddles from last night's high tide, and a thin crust of ice had formed on top.

'First the buddy check,' he said when they reached the water, and he showed Lia how they would take turns checking each other's BCDs. 'We need to inflate them before we go in, to compensate for the weight of the equipment.

'Okay.'

'Can you reach your primary mouthpiece if it dangles down your back instead of your front?' he asked.

Lia slung the blue mouthpiece over her shoulder, then reached for it and moved it to the front again. 'I can reach it. Can you reach yours?'

'Yes.'

'Is that it?'

'Patience. The last thing I need to know is if you remember the most important diving signals.'

Lia groaned. 'As if I could forget that evening of utter humiliation.'

She copied all the signals correctly, to his relief. 'Once you get used to the idea of non-verbal underwater communication, they're quite self-explanatory, aren't they,' he said. 'Okay? Excited?'

'Er, sort of. I understand it's not something you do lightly. Actually, I find it technically involved. A bit like some of the medical equipment I use in my work, really. *Used* in my work, I should say,' she added with a shrug.

289

'Regrets?'

'None.'

As soon as the words were out of her mouth, Lia realised the truth of them. She had no regrets. It was like running a marathon, coming around a bend and realising that the end was in sight if she could just overcome that one last hurdle. Whatever secrets the past still had to reveal, for the first time in years, a viable future was within reach.

And the first step into that future meant getting her head under water.

Aidan took her hand. 'Ready for some resort diving, then? That's what we call it because some people learn basic scuba when they're on holiday in the tropics.'

'This is hardly the tropics.'

'Same difference.'

When the water had reached their waists, they put on their diving fins and dived under the wave to avoid being knocked over. Beyond the swell Lia turned her head and gasped when she noticed how far they were from the shore. The beach was just a thin dun-coloured line, and the low trees on the dunes a cluster of dark dots. Her heart beat faster, and suddenly this didn't seem like such a good idea any more.

'Aidan . . .' she began, her breath coming in short gulps.

He was a few yards away from her. 'Yes?'

'H-how deep is the water here?'

'About eight feet. Why?'

'It's too deep.' The bottom was only a couple of feet below her, but she pictured herself hanging suspended over an endless depth, the gaping mouth of Hell. 'We'll drown,' she rasped and tasted panic at the back of her throat.

Aidan was by her side in two strokes and put his hands on her shoulders. 'That's why you're wearing an air cylinder. To stop you from drowning. If we go further back in, we'll dive right in the swell, and that gives us less control.'

'I don't have much control now,' she said, her teeth clattering.

'Yes, you do. Look at me. Look into my eyes.' His face behind the mask crinkled in a warm smile. 'You are in control. You're beautiful and successful, and you are in control. Say it.'

'I'm in control,' she whispered.

'Good. Now listen. You fear the sea. Of course you do, it's natural. You'd be a fool if you didn't. It's so deep and dark, and there's so much of it. The planet is practically covered in it. It's full of secrets and dangerous animals, and, let's face it, fish fuck in it.'

She laughed, despite herself. 'That's supposed to make me feel better?'

He put his gloved hand to the part of her cheek which wasn't covered by her mask and her hood. The neoprene felt soft and scratchy at the same time, like a hard sponge. 'We all have to conquer our fears sometime. It's the only way to move forward.'

'Yeah, who says?' She'd been thinking exactly that just a few minutes ago. Had he read her mind?

'I do. So, are you ready? We won't be going deeper than twelve metres, not until you have the proper qualification, but if you want to postpone it, we can. Just say so now.'

She shook her head, put her mouthpiece over her mouth, and made the OK sign with her thumb and index finger. Aidan did the same, and they submerged slowly, holding hands.

Below the water was a different world, grey-green and dappled with shafts of light from the winter sun above them. Lia could hear the sound of her own breathing rasping loudly in her ears and the muted gurgling noise of her body moving in the water, more gracefully than she'd ever thought possible. She was no longer a diver, she was a bird or an astronaut floating in space, weightless and free of her troubles. There was no Hell waiting, just beauty and independence.

Aidan let go of her hand and indicated for her to follow him. He made a short triangular diving circuit, and she copied the way he swam using only his feet and diving fins. He kept his arms by his side, and the up-down movements of his legs enabled him to swim entirely on his front. It looked easy enough, but Lia found that she had a tendency to be more or less vertical in the water herself. She kicked out hard with her legs and forced her body forward.

The surrounding water grew darker to a teal green,

as they descended further into the murky depths. Still struggling to remain in the horizontal position, she propelled herself forward, using the sea bed as her guide. A few yards ahead of her Aidan was suspended in the water waiting for her to catch up, bubbles circling around him and rising smoke-like as she came up beside him. He signed 'OK', and she signed back and followed him, tracing her hand along the sand and rocks on the sea bed.

A hermit crab felt for food with its long striped antennae. Lia picked it up, and it retreated into its shell immediately. She examined the shell. A colony of little polyps was growing on the surface of it, forming a rough, brown layer, and a bald patch indicated the spot where the crab had been dragging its borrowed house along.

Inside her a bubble of happiness rose at the perfection of it all and the possibility of such oneness with nature. She hadn't expected this richness of life. Carefully she put the little crab back on the sand and could have sworn it sent her a look of silent disdain. Next, with Aidan bobbing alongside her, she examined a starfish curled on a small rock. In the diffuse light, the starfish was buff-grey with five prickly arms, and she remembered finding the same kind on the beach when she was a child. Dead ones, of course, but this one was very much alive, and she returned the rock to the bottom.

Something big suddenly flew up from the sand and almost collided with her mask. Her breath exploded in bubbles, and the mouthpiece fell out of her mouth. She flailed around trying to find it again but it was dangling out of reach.

The octopus. I need the yellow octopus.

Her brain issued the command to unclip the other mouthpiece from the front of her jacket, but her arms were not responding and instead signalled 'can't breathe' to no one, because Aidan wasn't there.

Up, up, up. The instinct was to surface, to return to her natural element.

Someone grabbed her from behind.

Turning her around, Aidan jammed the mouthpiece back in her mouth. She forced herself to take deep regular breaths, but her lungs were greedy and swallowed the concentrated air in loud gasps. Large green bubbles encircled them, and she kicked furiously with her feet to return to the surface. Terror struck her as Aidan held her back with a firm grip on her waist, and she hit out at him in slow motion, impotently.

He's going to kill me.

Signalling 'up' with his other hand, he held her tight, and they began to resurface, rising no faster than the bubbles escaping them.

Noise crashed over them as they surfaced. Waves breaking, gulls screeching, Lia spluttering and crying. Aidan inflated her jacket, and she floated flat on her back, unable to move from shock while he loosened her lead belt and cupped her chin to hold her head back.

'It's okay, it's okay,' he whispered close to her ear. 'You're all right, you're doing fine. Absolutely fine.'

Her breath was coming out in loud sobbing gulps, and it took several minutes and a great deal of effort for her to try to breathe normally. Slowly, however, her heartbeat calmed and she could think rationally again.

'I'd never let anything happen to you, you know that, sweetheart.' He kept his arm around her as they stayed afloat in their jackets. 'You had a fright. It's normal, nothing to worry about. A lot of navy men panic the first time. Big guys, twice your size.'

'Where were you?' she managed to say.

'I was right beside you.'

'I didn't see you.'

'You were panicking, that's why. Somehow your brain just didn't register I was there.'

She sent him a doubtful look. 'And what was that *thing*?'

'A turbot. A bloody great big one actually, at least three feet long. It had camouflaged itself to look like the sand.'

'A turbot?' she repeated, unable to equate the large shape launching itself at her with a dinner table delicacy.

As if reading her mind, he said, 'If I'd had a harpoon, I'd have caught it and cooked it for you.'

'But you're a veggie,' she protested numbly.

'Can't pull the wool over your eyes, can I? Well, I'm glad to see you're back to your normal self. Now you can take us back in safely.'

295

'Me?'

'Yes, you.'

They changed in the car, and Lia tried hard not to look at him. Not only did the sight of him in top-to-bottom neoprene – and what she'd seen of him out of it – do funny things to her innards, she also had a feeling she'd failed him somehow.

Maybe not completely, she thought as he dropped her off at the house, kissing her quickly on the cheek.

He'd called her sweetheart. No one had ever called her that before, certainly not a grown man of the right age, the right height, and possibly the wrong temperament. But what to make of it? It had come naturally to him, she could tell. She was the one reading too much into it.

One thing she did know. She had to get her head round this diving lark, and not just to please him.

Aidan stopped in the village to pick up a few groceries, feeling pleased with the morning so far, despite the slight hiccough with the turbot.

Susannah was out the back, but came into the shop when she heard the bell. Noticing his still wet hair, she said, 'Been diving?'

'Couldn't have asked for a better day.'

'With Lia?'

Placing his purchases on the counter, Aidan looked up. 'I have, as a matter of fact.' What's it to you, he nearly added, but her pinched expression stopped him. 'Something wrong?'

'It's Zoe.'

'What? Where is she?'

'I don't know!' She was wringing something in her hands, a piece of tissue, he saw, and her red-rimmed eyes glared back at him as if it was his fault her teenage daughter had gone walkabout. 'We had a row, and she just took off. Nigel's gone to see if he can find her. Thought he'd search by your farm. Zoe seems to like it there.' She sniffed.

Good old Nigel. Dependable, trusting Nigel who had no idea what he was dealing with. A feeling of unease settled in Aidan's stomach. 'I'll go and help him,' he said.

'Yeah, you do that.' Susannah twisted the tissue in her hands, now shredded beyond recognition. Without looking at him, she rang up his groceries, the silence between them palpable.

'I've kept my side of the bargain,' he said.

'I know, but how long for?' she flashed back at him.

'For as long as it takes. You've never disagreed with me before.'

'I don't . . . I don't disagree.' She put her hand over her mouth as if that would stop her lips from trembling. 'I just wish we could have an end to all this.'

'What sort of end do you have in mind?' he countered, unable to disguise the bitterness in his voice.

Before she could answer that, a car pulled up outside the shop, and two men got out. Clad in suits and overcoats, they scanned the road in both directions with what seemed like practised ease, then headed into the shop.

'Excuse me,' said the older of the two men, addressing Susannah. 'I wonder if you could give us directions to the Barrington place. We have the address, but I'm afraid my colleague here has got us lost.'

The other man held up his hands, not as an apology, but as if he habitually had to defuse a tricky situation. Aidan didn't need his military training to recognise the good cop, bad cop routine. That and the reference to 'the Barrington place' smelled of an official visit.

Susannah explained the best way to Lia's house, using a makeshift map drawn on a till receipt, and the men left, Good Cop giving Aidan the once-over as he closed the door behind him.

Aidan looked back at Susannah just as she spoke the word which was on both their lips. 'Police?'

After Aidan had left, Lia took Jack for a walk. When she returned, Connie had left a message on the answering machine.

'Just thought I'd warn you,' she said, 'but two detectives were here asking me about Ivy's death. I've answered all the questions I can, but they took a great deal of interest in her will and the fact you inherit everything. Of course, I explained to them that you were about three thousand miles away when she died, but it seems they want to hear it from you.' She paused. 'What's going on, Lia? It's not as if we murdered the old bat.'

Lia frowned. She hadn't wanted Doctor Campbell's concerns to be correct, but the pathologist had obviously found something suspicious, otherwise the police wouldn't be making inquiries.

But what? Had someone poisoned Ivy? That begged the questions, what with, who and when?

As her mother had pointed out, Lia had been halfway across the globe at the time. But what about Connie herself? Lia realised with a slight frisson of heightened awareness that she had no idea of her mother's movements. Connie rarely visited Ivy, but had she gone to see her that day?

Bringing a takeaway curry, perhaps?

CHAPTER 19

The police wasted no time. As Lia was making herself a cup of tea, a car drove up, and two men got out. Taking a deep breath, she prepared herself for the visit, and opened the door. Although she'd talked to the police many times in her job, it always brought out a feeling of having done something wrong, even though she hadn't. Seeing the way the two men moved as one, with purposeful steps, their expressions serious, this reeked of bad news.

'Doctor Ophelia Thompson?' said the shorter of the two.

'Yes, that's me.'

He introduced himself as DCI Sommersby of the Norfolk Constabulary and gestured towards his colleague. 'And this is DS Cromer. We have a few questions relating to the death of your grandmother, Ivy Barrington. May we come in?'

'Of course.' Swallowing hard, Lia stepped aside. 'I was just making tea. Would you like some?'

They declined, and she showed them into the living room. Jack followed close behind, clearly curious, but not enough to leave the relative safety behind Lia's legs.

DS Cromer clapped his thigh, and Jack trotted across the floor to him, his initial reluctance forgotten. 'That's a lovely dog you've got there.'

'You can have him.'

The sergeant grinned back at her. 'I'm sure you don't mean that.'

Lia frowned. What did he know about what she meant or not? He didn't know her at all. She caught his eyes – hazel and peculiar-looking in a rather attractive face, blinking rapidly like a lizard's – and had an uncomfortable feeling he could read her mind. She considered feigning ignorance of what was going on, but thought it unlikely she'd fool anyone, least of all Lizard Eyes here.

'Perhaps you could tell me exactly what this is about,' she said.

DCI Sommersby cleared his throat. 'There have been disturbing new developments regarding your grandmother's death. It seems there's some doubt she died entirely from natural causes.'

'Oh?'

'The cause of death was given as a heart attack, am I correct?'

'That's right.'

'And it was your family doctor who referred her death to the coroner?'

The information was probably in the papers on his desk, so why was he pussy-footing around whatever it was he wanted to say? Lia quelled her impatience and answered evenly.

'Yes. My grandmother had been with Doctor Campbell for as long as I can remember. He thought something wasn't right about her death, but I must admit I didn't take him seriously. He's getting on a bit.'

'Do you or anyone else remember her complaining about stomach cramps at all?'

Lia recalled that Susannah had sold antacid tablets to Ivy the day before she died. 'She told our local shopkeeper she had indigestion.'

'When exactly?'

'Well, you'd have to ask her, but as far as I know it was the day before she died.'

'The shopkeeper told you that herself?' interjected Lizard Eyes, still stroking Jack.

'Er, yes.'

'Did anyone else see your grandmother in the days leading up to her death?' asked Sommersby.

Lia looked from one to the other in confusion. 'I really don't know, I wasn't here.'

'And you can prove that?' This was from Lizard Eyes.

'I can show you my airline ticket if you like,' she replied, slightly taken aback by the directness of the question.

'That would be a good start, but I'm afraid we'll need witness statements as well.'

'Really?'

'Yes. Now can you think of any enemies your

grandmother might have had? Anyone she'd fallen out with?'

The box with 'junk' written on the side and Connie's hatred flashed into Lia's mind, but she quelled it. 'No, she was well liked and respected around here. That's why I initially dismissed Doctor Campbell's suspicions. But when he wanted the pathologist to take another look, I had no problems with that. Although . . .'

'Although?' Sommersby raised an eyebrow.

'Well, I've lived in the States for the past six years, and it's possible that there was someone I didn't know about. And I've noticed a few signs that she might have been afraid of something. Just little things, mind you, nothing unusual to an outsider. Recently she arranged for a security system to be installed, and she also bought that dog there. The security system I can understand, but not the dog. She didn't like animals very much.'

The detectives exchanged a look. 'You're a doctor yourself, aren't you?'

'Yes, and my job is to keep people alive, not the opposite. The Hippocratic Oath, which I'm sure you've heard of,' she added sarcastically.

Sommersby's face remained impassive. 'Did you read the post-mortem report?'

'The coroner sent a copy to Doctor Campbell. He was kind enough to show it to me.'

'If you were to think of a poison which your grandmother might have ingested, accidentally or on purpose, what immediately springs to mind?'

Lia frowned. 'She wouldn't have done that to herself. She wasn't that kind of person. Anyway, why are you asking *me* this? Shouldn't you be speaking to the pathologist?'

'Indulge me. Professional interest.'

'Okay,' she said and thought for a moment. 'There's various wild mushrooms around here. She was very careful, but it's possible she could've picked the wrong one by mistake.'

'And if it was given to her without her knowledge?'

'Well, poisonous fungi again, disguised in something. And strychnine too, which is found in pesticides. Only a mad person would kill himself using that. It's a horrid death. Victims tend to bend double because of severe muscle contractions. And it would've shown up on toxicology. As would the mushrooms.' She shrugged. 'There's cyanide, but that doesn't cause the same sort of symptoms my grandmother suffered. I can't think of anything else, except arsenic, and I know that they tested for that.'

Lia's feelings of guilt returned. I should have been here, she thought. 'Doctor Campbell mentioned it was a messy death, but I didn't see that as unusual. Not at the time, anyway.'

Sommersby weighed his words carefully. 'I don't want to be alarmist, and I suppose it's always possible the pathologist has made a mistake, but he's gone over his findings again, and it seems there's a toxin he overlooked the first time, because cases in which it's involved are very rare. He's carrying out further tests, but he says that the internal damage your grandmother suffered could be – and he stresses the "could be" – consistent with ricin poisoning.'

'Ricin!' she exclaimed. That was one she hadn't considered. She knew that there'd been security scares about terrorists using ricin powder, but that was inhaled, and caused respiratory failure. Ricin orally ingested wasn't something she'd encountered herself, either from her studies or – so far – from her patients. Her surprise was genuine enough to register with the detectives.

'As I understand it,' said Sommersby, 'the poisons you mentioned are something like four times as likely to be detected in the body as ricin, and fungi more than twice as likely. He's still exploring other possibilities, and is obviously keen not to make any claims about something which could easily look like something else. Nevertheless, if someone did poison your grandmother, it's our job to find out who.'

Lia swallowed hard. *Deliberately poisoned? Dear God* . . .

'Ricin poisoning? How is that possible?'

She'd called Doctor Campbell, who was back at the surgery, the minute Sommersby and his sidekick had left. He'd had the news from the pathologist, and had been about to call her, not knowing that the police had beaten him to it. She tried to get the number for the pathologist out of him. He refused to give it to her. 'He won't talk to you anyway,' he said. 'Not now when he's under scrutiny.'

Lia wasn't having that. She needed some answers, and she needed them now. No more secrets and half-truths. 'Well, can you tell me then? How could my grandmother have ingested ricin?'

'I don't know, to be frank. But it would probably have been in some food she ate. It's unlikely to have been in powdered form, because even though it's possible to dissolve that in water, you need to know some chemistry to produce it. It's far more likely to have been in the form of castor beans,' he said, 'since they're where ricin comes from. You need to crush them up, though, to release it. Some people who swallow them accidentally are lucky, because the whole beans pass straight through without doing any harm.'

That was a start, thought Lia, but it still didn't answer the question of how ricin had ended up in her grandmother's food. 'I need to ask you something else. Let's just say for argument's sake this wasn't a mistake, but deliberate. How would you go about administering it?' When she was met with silence at the other end, she added, 'I'm asking *you* because there's no internet access here, and I didn't exactly study it as part of my degree. I'm not planning to bump anyone off.'

Doctor Campbell cleared his throat. 'Hmm, well, I've just looked it up myself, as you can tell. I suppose there's something to be said for this modern technology after all. I do know you can't just give someone ricin to eat and expect them not to notice. It causes a burning sensation in the mouth, so you'd have to disguise it by hot, strong-tasting food, like coffee or something spicy.'

Lia felt the little hairs on the back of her neck stand on end. Ivy had eaten a takeaway curry two days before she died. 'A curry?'

'Aye, a vindaloo would do the trick.'

'How much would you need? Off the top of your head?'

'You'd just mash up a handful of beans. Eight for an adult, three for a child, or thereabouts, and Bob's your uncle. Castor oil's a purgative, as of course you know. I once read that Mussolini's fascists used to force dissidents to drink huge quantities of castor oil. Basically they'd have it coming out both ends until they died from dehydration,' he continued, matter-of-factly.

Both she and Doctor Campbell dealt with death in the course of their work, and with the desensitisation it brought with it. Nevertheless Lia experienced a sudden light-headedness which threatened to overwhelm her. This was her own grandmother, after all.

'And where would you get the beans?' she asked, swallowing back the bile.

'They're not really beans. They're the seeds of the castor oil plant. It's grown here as a garden ornamental. An annual, I understand – it doesn't survive our winter. You can get the seeds from some nurseries, or on the internet. Councils up and down the country used to plant them in parks and such, but it's not so popular now. Given all that fuss about ricin, you can imagine why.'

She thanked him for his time and hung up.

For a while afterwards she stared out of the window. What had started out as a brilliantly clear day had turned misty, and the watery sun hung low in the sky. The wind had dropped, and the trees in the garden, their black branches held high in a last act of defiance, seemed to have accepted finally that this was the season of death.

Jack lay at her feet with the dog lead in his mouth. He whimpered as if he knew what was on her mind. A couple of weeks ago she'd have dismissed the idea. Not so now.

She knelt down and stroked his bony head. 'You know something, don't you, Jack?'

He whimpered again and rapped his tail against the wooden floor.

'If only you could talk,' she said. Then again she didn't need Jack to tell her that something was very wrong. The question was whether it was connected, and if so, how?

'We'd better go for another walk. I need to clear my head.' Jack didn't look like he minded in the slightest; as far as he was concerned she could walk all day and he'd happily come along.

When the little dog headed in the direction of the beach, she whistled for him to come back and snapped the lead on his collar. 'Not that way.' *I've had enough of the water for one day.*

Instead she decided to take the walk through the woodlands around Holkham Hall which John had recommended. From the village, they headed through the pedestrian access and into the Park, and the track took them past the sluice, and along the main route to the Hall itself. Two impressive bronze lions guarded the entrance, and Jack snarled, but Lia kept a firm hold on his lead.

She kicked up the leaf litter as she walked, deep in thought.

Ricin. A terrorist's weapon.

Bomb threats had been aimed at the military bases which were peppered all over Norfolk, British as well as American. Lia had had a hard enough time getting her head around that, but the idea that her grandmother had somehow got herself embroiled in it was just too bizarre to contemplate.

Ricin was one of the most deadly substances known to man, yet its powdered form, the most lethal, was harder to produce than many internet sites made out. Still, a competent chemist could do it in a school laboratory.

Images of Eddie's death suddenly surfaced in her mind, and with them came a blurred memory of her mother shouting out her grief and rage at Ivy, at everyone. And the last puzzle piece started to slot into place.

Aidan had accused her of having a selective

309

memory, but he probably didn't realise how right he was. She'd been blind in so many ways. Blind to the likeness between Aidan and Zoe, blind to how she felt about Brett, and to what was happening in her surroundings.

Fuzzy at the centre, the memory kept pushing itself forward, and she kept fighting it, but it wouldn't go away. In the end she gave up pushing back and opened herself to a terrible, dreadful, painful secret she'd carried alone for years.

Her sleeves had been wet.

Eddie's death hadn't been an accident.

Aidan spotted Nigel's car as he drove into the yard, but there was no sign of either Nigel or Zoe. They could be in the open barn, or even the house. The thought made him sigh because he didn't relish the prospect of walking in on an argument on his private turf.

The sliding door to the nearest of the greenhouses was open, and he could see movement inside. When he got closer, it was as he'd expected. They were having a blazing row.

'You're not my father! You have no right to tell me what to do!' Zoe was shouting at the top of her voice as angry tears slid down her cheeks. 'Absolutely no bloody right!'

Nigel tried to reason with her. 'I may not be your biological father, but it takes more than sperm to make a dad.' He turned as he sensed Aidan in the doorway. 'A hell of a lot more,' he added.

'Euw, that's just too gross,' Zoe sneered.

'Come on, let's go home, have a cup of tea, and talk about it. You can always talk to me, Zoe, you know that.'

'Don't you come anywhere near me!' she yelled as Nigel held out his hand.

'Cool it, Zoe,' said Aidan from the doorway. 'My plants are going to wilt if you shriek like that.' Zoe was standing next to a hip-high cannabis plant, and Nigel was too intent on his stepdaughter to notice. Probably just as well. Aidan didn't think they'd see eye to eye on that either, even if it was purely for his own consumption.

'I don't *shriek*,' Zoe protested, but her lips curved in a semblance of a smile when she realised where she was.

Aidan gave her a wink.

Nigel, seething with resentment, looked from one to the other, then fixed his eyes on Aidan. 'Surplus to requirements, am I?' Clenching his fists, he turned away and would have stormed past if Aidan hadn't caught his arm.

'Nigel—'

'I've just about had it up to here. See what you can do if you're so bloody perfect. Please,' he added.

He left the greenhouse and returned to his car. Aidan glanced at Zoe in the cannabis forest. Her shoulders were slumped, and she looked very much like the little girl she'd been such a short time ago. Their special bond still existed, but

311

though he was flattered by Nigel's confidence that he'd be able to sort things out, he couldn't help thinking Nigel had backed down too easily.

'Ouch,' he said and made as though Nigel had hit him.

'Yeah.'

'Looks like we both have some grovelling to do.'

She shrugged and went back to being surly.

'Well, I'll grovel, and you can make the tea.'

'It's not really his fault,' she said grudgingly. 'I just got so hacked off with Mum. Then Nigel got involved and was backing her up, and it's the two of them against me. It's like that all the time.'

'Parents have to present a united front.' Aidan smiled. 'Or so I've heard.'

'Why isn't anyone ever on my side? It pisses me off!'

'No one's against you, Zoe.'

'Don't you even want to know what it was all about?' she asked, coming towards him.

'Other than you being a terrible teenager, you mean? I can't imagine.'

She pulled a face at that, but he saw the beginnings of a smile before she turned serious again. 'I found a photo. I know who my father is.'

'Do you?'

Zoe took his arm and dropped her head to his shoulder with a sigh. 'You should've told me.'

'It wasn't my secret to tell.'

'Oh, yeah?' she challenged, but he decided it was safer to stay quiet.

She only came up to the top of his arm, and he rested his head on hers for a moment, breathing in the warm scent of her hair and something youthful and fruity; lip gloss, perhaps. 'Let's save this conversation for another time. Right now we need to see about that tea, okay?'

In the end, Nigel and Zoe stayed for lunch, both thawing considerably when Aidan rustled up an omelette and a rocket salad. They didn't say much, but at least they seemed to have agreed on a temporary truce.

Afterwards, he cleaned up his diving gear and retreated to his studio. He'd placed a canvas over a stretcher, and was stapling it to the wooden frame with a staple gun, when the phone rang. He looked up in irritation. He only had the corners left to do, and they had to be hospital corners, which required concentration. If not, they'd end up saggy, and he'd have to start all over again.

To his relief the ringing stopped, and he folded the first corner, then held the stapler over it. When the ringing started up again, he jerked in surprise, the stapler slipped, and the staple scraped his hand.

'Bugger,' he muttered and reached for the phone with his good hand, while sucking on the injury. 'Mmm . . . hello.'

'Is that Aidan Morrell?'

'M-yep.'

'It's Doctor Campbell here, from the surgery in the village. What's the matter with your voice?'

Aidan rested the handset under his ear and reached for a rag to stem the bleeding. 'I just cut myself. Stapled myself, to be more precise.'

'Well, you might want to put a wee bit of TCP on that. And come down to the surgery for a tetanus injection.'

'I had a jab last summer.' Aidan wrapped the paint-smeared rag around his hand. Traces of turpentine made the wound sting, but he bit back the pain. He'd lived through worse. 'When I stepped on a nail stuck in a bit of driftwood.'

'Aye, so you did.' Doctor Campbell sounded distracted. 'Anyway, I was calling to ask you if you would do something for me, if you wouldn't mind.'

'Go on.'

'I understand that you're friendly with Doctor Thompson, Ivy Barrington's granddaughter . . .'

'I don't see that that's any business of yours—' Aidan began.

'Calm down, laddie. I'm not concerned about your private life. What does concern me is Doctor Thompson. I'm asking you to look out for her, keep an eye on her. Make sure she's all right.'

'Why wouldn't she be?'

'Well, I had a notion her grandmother's death wasn't due to natural causes—'

'Yes, I heard. It sounded crazy to me. Who'd want to kill a harmless old lady?'

'Not so harmless as that,' said Doctor Campbell,

'and you know it. If you ask me, Mrs Barrington knew something someone didn't want her to know. And it seems I was right, because the pathologist's found new evidence that she might have been poisoned – with ricin.'

Aidan's blood ran cold. He'd hoped that Doctor Campbell's meddling would come to nothing, and now it seemed his suspicions were all too real.

'Ricin?' He kept his voice level. 'That's what terrorists use. I don't mean to be rude, but don't you think this is a bit improbable?'

'What about those bomb threats, laddie? That's an act of terrorism, or I'm a Dutchman.'

'I'm aware of that,' Aidan snapped, more sharply than he'd intended. 'And they've got nothing to do with it.'

'Oh, aye, and you seem to know an awful lot about it.'

'Of course not; I just meant it doesn't seem likely that those are connected to Mrs Barrington. They're two separate issues.' *At least, I bloody well hope they are*, he thought.

'You're probably right, lad.' Doctor Campbell cleared his throat. 'There's something else you should know. Mrs Barrington's granddaughter had a visit from the police. After that she asked me a whole lot of questions about ricin: how you'd get hold of it, how you'd use it, and so on.'

'And? You'd already told her you thought her grandmother was poisoned. Now she knows how, so what?'

'Aye, but the difference is she believes me now. She didn't before. Thought I had a screw loose.'

Her and me both, thought Aidan, ruefully.

'If she's anything like her grandmother,' Doctor Campbell continued, 'she's going to do her damndest to find out for herself whoever did this. And that person seems to me to be too ruthless for words.' He paused for emphasis. 'If you ask me, she could be in danger.'

CHAPTER 20

The pretext had been for Lia to fetch Eddie's towel from the rail on the Rayburn. She returned to frantic splashing noises, small legs thrashing wildly, muffled cries, then a sudden stillness. Ivy was bent over the bath, firm and unmoving, with her hand on Eddie's chest, and Eddie's eyes were staring at nothing. Then Ivy was framed against the bathroom door, her wet hand stroking Lia's hair.

'It's for the best. One day you'll understand.'

But she didn't understand, not then, not now. An innocent child, a life snuffed out. A gaping hole inside herself which could never be patched up, a longing for a replacement she could never find, a beloved brother lost.

She'd tried lifting him up, she remembered now, but he was too heavy for her slight frame, a dead weight, and his body slipped under the water again. Her grandmother watched from the door as her four-year-old self frantically tried to bring her dead brother back to life, her only thought that if she could just get him to sit up he'd be all right.

I left you. I'm a bad girl.

Now, clutching her chest and her stomach, she hardly noticed as her legs buckled and she slid to the ground. Her breathing consisted of rasping sobs which racked her body, and her insides were as hard as lead. Now that they'd finally emerged, the images washed over her again and again like a film on a continuous loop. Guilt and pain held her in a relentless grip.

She didn't know for how long she lay among the dead leaves, but slowly she returned to reality. A warm, pink tongue was licking the tears and dirt off her face, gently as if she was a newborn puppy.

'It's all right, Jack.' She put a tired hand on his two-tone head and gave him a quick hug. Sitting up, she felt the pain course through her body, but this time it was physical, as if she'd aged a hundred years in minutes. 'I'm okay,' she repeated, to convince herself as well as the dog.

Jack whimpered, circling her anxiously as she rose and brushed herself down. She'd carried the guilt for years, suppressing it in order to live with herself. But the crime wasn't hers. Her grandmother had committed it; out of some misguided sense of eugenics, perhaps.

A grim determination set in. If Connie was behind Ivy's death, Lia would do everything she could to protect her, even if it cost her her career and her freedom. She wouldn't stand idly by and see her mother go to prison for committing a murder no one in their right mind could blame her for. Justice was paramount in this matter and needed to be upheld.

But to protect Connie, she needed to know what had happened. And if Connie was innocent, she had to find out who else might have done it and why.

She used her break-up with Brett as an excuse to see her mother. Once there, however, she found it difficult to broach the subject. She was still too agitated to think clearly.

Connie placed a mug of tea in front of Lia. 'He was a nice young man, but I'm not surprised.'

'It wasn't lack of niceness which made me end it.' Lia sipped her tea and managed not to grimace. Her mother made the strongest tea in the world, enough to strip the enamel off teeth. At the same time it reminded her of home, of family. What was left of it.

'I'm sure it wasn't.'

'Brett was too nice, if that makes any sense.'

'It does, in a way. You don't consider yourself worthy of someone that nice, is that it?'

Lia shrugged.

Connie took Lia's hand and gave it a squeeze. 'You are worthy. But if he isn't the right man, that's all there is to it. Better to realise that now than after you've had a few kids. Pity, though. I was looking forward to a real American wedding,' Connie went on with a wistful expression on her face. 'White shaker-style church with the prairie grass waving softly outside and you walking up the aisle like Grace Kelly in *High Noon*.'

Lia smiled at the image, knowing she'd never look like Grace Kelly. 'That was a civil wedding, and they were Quakers.'

'Whatever. Better still, a wedding in Vegas with you in a white Stetson and a fringed leather outfit.'

'Yeah, like that was going to happen,' Lia spluttered into her tea and wiped up the spillage with her sleeve. 'It would've been a lavish affair with zillions of people I don't know and don't want to know. Lots of designer outfits and air-kissing. People who feature on the Philadelphia society pages. Brett's mother would've had something to say about that, I can assure you.'

'Ah, well, mothers.' Connie's mouth was set in a tight line. 'Anyway, he wasn't right for you, and that's what matters.'

Yes, mothers, thought Lia. Now might be a good time to raise the subject, but gently, because she had a hunch Connie would clam up. After all, it wasn't every day you had to ask your mother if she had murdered your grandmother.

'What sort of mother was Ivy?' she asked.

Connie looked taken aback. 'Why do you ask? You knew her as well as I did.'

'Yes, as a grandmother. I asked what she was like as a mum.'

Connie stared at a point over Lia's shoulder. 'What was she like as a mum? A bit bossy, I suppose. Always watching me in one way or another, always there even when she wasn't. I suspect I was a disappointment to her in some ways. It was liberating to leave home. Not that I went wild or anything.'

Lia regarded her mother in a new light. It had become second nature to think of Connie as incapable, but after her find in the attic and the resurrected memory of that fateful day, everything had been turned on its head. As she tried to make sense of it, one thing became clear to her: not only had Ivy taken her brother away from her, she'd also undermined Lia's relationship with her own mother, through years of pithy remarks which – it shamed her to think of it – had found fertile ground.

'After your father and I got married,' Connie continued, 'I became pregnant very quickly. Ivy seemed happy with you, and your grandfather was delighted. Called you his little black diamond because of your hair, but you probably don't remember that.'

Lia shook her head. The only memories she had of her early years were the ones that were clawing at her insides now.

'Then we had Eddie, and though he was born with Down's, we were happy enough, despite Ivy's comments. A child is a gift, no matter how different. When he died, we . . . we fell apart.'

'He didn't just die, he drowned,' said Lia.

Connie went on as if she hadn't heard her. 'Then your grandfather went, probably because of grief, and your dad couldn't bear being near us, took off for Australia. I don't suppose you ever hear from him?'

'Now and again,' said Lia. 'I get a card on my birthday. When he remembers. But I don't want to talk about him. I want to talk about Eddie. And Ivy.'

'What's there to say? She didn't want a grandson who was retarded, and then he died. Why are you asking me this now? Why bring it up again?' Connie's small, nimble hands rested on the table, and only the way she picked at her cuticles betrayed her anxiety.

'Because Eddie didn't just die, did he? It wasn't an accident. And you knew. You knew that—'

Connie rose abruptly, scraping the chair against the floor, and fled the kitchen. Lia followed her. 'You knew Ivy drowned him, didn't you? I know because I was there. I saw it all.'

When Lia caught up with her in the living room, Connie escaped into the conservatory with her hands over her ears as if by not listening she could ignore what had happened.

'I know how easy it is to forget the truth,' Lia said. 'The trouble is, it festers.' Connie clamped her hands over her ears even harder, so Lia raised her voice. 'I always thought it was an accident, because that's what I was told. Staying at Ivy's house, it's almost as if the house itself has been making me face up to the reality that my grandmother – your mother – murdered my brother. And you don't want to talk about it. You don't even want to listen. How do you think that makes me feel?'

As she followed Connie into the conservatory, the sleeve of her woollen jumper caught on the door handle, and a long thread was pulled out of the knitwear.

'Blast!'

Connie stopped. 'Oh, that lovely sweater. Here let me have a look at it.' She folded the sleeve up over Lia's elbow, turned it inside out. 'Ah, yes, all I need to do is guide the thread through to the other side and attach it so you don't catch your fingers when you pull it on.'

'It's not important.' Lia released her arm. 'You knew, didn't you? All these years, and you never told me.'

'I have a darning needle somewhere. I know because even though I don't do much darning, one should always have at least one in the house, and I said to myself if I throw it away I'll need it one day.'

Connie pushed past her back into the living room, then out in the hall and up the stairs with Lia trailing behind her to the spare bedroom, which was cold with disuse and filled with odds and ends.

'Mum . . .'

'Let me just have a look. I think it might be in here.' Opening a cupboard, Connie pulled out her sewing box and rummaged in a small drawer. 'No, well, I'm sure I'll find it, just give me a minute.'

'Mum, please . . .'

'Oh, here it is. I knew I'd kept one, because you never know. If you'll just hand me that sweater I'll sort it out for—'

Lia snatched the darning needle out of her mother's hand and tossed it across the room. 'Who cares about a damn sweater? Just shut up and listen to me! Look at me. Eddie was my brother. I loved him, and I saw him die, Mum. I saw him *die*. I saw Ivy holding him under the water until he stopped moving.'

Connie's face went grey. Wordlessly she dropped down on the edge of the bed. Lia sat down beside her and put her arm around her shoulder. The bed was covered in a threadbare, pink candlewick bedspread, and Lia recognised it as the one she used to have on her own bed when she lived at home. Unexpectedly tears welled up in her eyes. It was a hopelessly old-fashioned bedspread, yet Connie had kept it all these years.

'You knew, didn't you?'

Connie nodded. 'I guessed it.'

'Why didn't you report it?'

'She was my mother.' Connie sounded tired, as if the years of repressing the horror of her suspicions had finally caught up with her. 'Besides, who'd believe me? Outwardly she was a supportive and loving grandparent, a pillar of society, whereas I . . . well, I was working part-time, struggling with motherhood, and my marriage was going down the pan, long before Eddie died. How could I report a crime I hadn't even witnessed and expect to be taken seriously? It wouldn't bring him back.'

'But it would've been justice.'

'Justice?' Connie gave a mirthless laugh. 'If there was justice in the world, he wouldn't have died. He wouldn't have been born with Down's. I'd have had a happy marriage with a handful of healthy children, a good job, and plenty of money. I wouldn't be spending my life teaching high-school kids how to distil water or boring everyone to death with my talk about golf. And my mother certainly wouldn't have taken both my children away from me. But she did, one way or the other.'

'Ivy didn't take me away.'

'Oh, yes, she did. In a moment of weakness I let her take you. Schooling was the pretext, but there was something deeper at stake. She didn't want you to be too close to anyone. Then she moved you again to get you away from that friend of yours.' Smiling sadly, she touched Lia's cheek. 'But you came back.'

They sat close together, on the bed in the cold, austere room, more attuned to each other than they'd ever been before. A last question still hung between them, but Lia didn't want to ruin the moment just yet.

'The police have evidence that Ivy may have been poisoned,' she said finally. 'Did you have anything to do with that?'

Connie's response was a wide-eyed look of horror.

'Well, did you?'

'Wh . . . where would I get poison from?' she replied, her voice trembling. Then she got herself under control and said more firmly, 'No, I didn't kill my own mother. But I want to congratulate the person who did.'

Did Lia believe her? She wanted to, so much, but she hardly knew what the truth was any more.

After Doctor Campbell had rung off, Aidan stood for a moment just holding the receiver, stunned, then he slung the dirty rag across the room with an oath.

He spent the next ten minutes pacing up and down in the studio in an attempt to collect his thoughts, much to the dismay of the cat, which retreated under the table, glaring and hissing occasionally when he got too close. In the end, to calm himself, he rinsed his hand under the tap and found a plaster in the first aid box he kept in the studio.

The house of cards he'd built so carefully around him was set to tumble. He'd tried to do the right thing, God knows, he'd tried. And it had worked, for a while, until Lia's grandmother started prying and threatening everything with exposure.

That danger had been averted, but now Lia was taking an interest too and the police were involved. He had to stop her before she got herself or someone else hurt in the process. Buy some time.

Picking up the phone again, he dialled her

number at the house, but it rang endlessly before the answering machine kicked in. He didn't leave a message. Instead he tried her mobile, which went to voicemail immediately. She'd either switched it off or was getting no signal wherever she was.

He thought of driving by her house, but figured that if she'd been there, she'd have picked up the phone. She had no reason not to.

The cat stalked out from its hiding place, eyeing him uncertainly as if it feared he would turn into a wild man again.

'Of course!' He slapped a hand to his forehead, and the cat made itself scarce again. The dog, she'd be taking her dog for a walk, on the beach most likely. Yes, the beach, that's where she'd be.

Aidan grabbed a coat and his car keys from the hall, and slammed the front door behind him. The car beeped as he pressed the key fob, and he launched himself into the driver's seat. With the key already in the ignition, he forced himself to stop for a moment and apply some logic. If he came haring after her like a bat out of hell, she was bound to get suspicious.

He closed his eyes and took a few steadying breaths, then, as the first snow flakes began to fall, he drove off, determined to find her.

CHAPTER 21

Outside the sky had darkened, and the wind had picked up, icy and coming from the north.

'Are you sure you don't want to stay the night?' Connie asked. 'It looks like snow, and I worry about you being on the road.'

'Thanks, Mum, but I have to get home to feed Jack.'

'Can't you get someone to do it for you?'

Huddling in her coat and the expensive, matching scarf and hat Brett had given her for Christmas, Lia thought of Mrs Larwood. 'It wouldn't be fair to drag anyone out in this weather. I'll be fine. Jack's good company, and I've finally got the hang of the Rayburn. At least I think so.'

Connie pulled her cardigan tighter around her. 'Well, if you're sure.' She cast an anxious glance down the avenue of naked trees. Their dry branches were shiny with ice and rattled as though an invisible army were shaking them hard. 'It doesn't look good.'

It was too cold to remain immobile, so Lia waved and got into the car. Another time they would talk about Eddie some more, but right now she needed space to think.

On the edge of town she stopped. The heating controls were playing up, and the rear window was still covered in a fine layer of ice. As she scraped at it, snowflakes pricked her face and her hands were frozen. Hopefully she'd be back before it started snowing for real.

She'd lost the gloves which matched the hat and scarf. She had a sneaking suspicion Jack had appropriated them. He'd behaved strangely over Christmas, taking soft and cuddly objects into his mouth, then gently lifting them into his dog basket and licking them, like a bitch with her pups. Lia shook her head. She'd given up trying to figure Jack out and the reason why he was there. He'd grown on her, as Mrs Larwood had predicted, and she couldn't possibly get rid of him now – whether she chose to stay in Norfolk or go somewhere else in England, he'd have to come with her.

The snow was falling in heavy drifts now, and she switched on the windscreen wipers. They swung backwards and forwards a couple of times, then stopped uselessly in the middle of the windscreen. Snow immediately collected in two semi-upright columns of shimmering white, obscuring her vision.

'Oh, bother.' She got out of the car to free the flimsy rubber strips, but when she got back in, it was almost as bad as before.

She shrugged. There was nothing for it, she'd

have to carry on like this. Fortunately she knew the way, if not her position on the road, and hoped she wouldn't meet any oncoming cars. As she rounded a bend, the car skidded sideways, and she slammed the brakes on. Immediately, she knew it was the wrong thing to do, but it was too late. The car spun round and landed nose down in the ditch on the opposite side of the road.

'Goddammit!' she grunted when the steering wheel hit her full in the stomach.

It wasn't a bad accident, only a minor mishap, but it was still a disaster. Switching off the engine, she eased herself out of the car, careful not to slip on the ice, which had formed on a puddle in the muddy ditch. It wasn't a particularly deep ditch either. But how was she going to get the car out?

Chewing her thumbnail, she assessed the situation. She could probably reverse out. Returning to the car, she put the gear into reverse, but when she floored the accelerator the front wheels spun without getting anywhere.

'Elbow grease it is, then,' she said and got out of the car.

With her back against the bonnet she pushed the car as hard as she could, using her feet as leverage, but though the ground was frozen it wasn't hard enough to withstand the pressure, and Lia's boots sank.

Knowing even before she began that it was useless, she nevertheless tried to lift the car out of the ditch, but it didn't budge an inch. Thwarted, she kicked the wheel.

'Bugger, bugger, bugger!'

The last of her frustrated kicks sent a shooting pain up her leg, and she yelped in agony, tears pricking behind her eyelids. She tried to support her weight on the leg, but she'd aggravated her old squash injury, and she found it difficult.

What a stupid thing to do. She never lost her cool like this.

All the recent revelations and upheavals had shaken her more than she wanted to admit, and it was making her act out of character. As she blew on her frozen hands, she tried to talk some sense into herself.

It was an old car. It could have copped out at any time. Anyone could skid on an icy road without being more of an idiot than the rest of the world.

Returning to the car, she got out her phone, but there was no signal here, and she flung it back in her handbag and locked the car. She'd have to walk to the nearest village, or maybe farmhouse, and call from there.

Cocooned in her own breath, she hobbled along the road. Brett would have had a go at her for this, but that was Brett for you. The thought brought with it a certain wistfulness. She hadn't loved him, not really, but his kindness and efficiency had made her feel safe. Not having him in her life made her realise how alone she was.

Especially now, when a bit of masculine reassurance would have come in useful.

Maybe the wistfulness wasn't entirely about him. It had been a strange day. She'd opened a can of worms, and there was no stopping it now. Everything was happening too fast for her to adjust. She needed time to come to terms with the horror of what she now knew to be the truth.

After she'd walked for about a mile there was still no sign of a village, or even a farm. Puzzled, she tried to remember the location of different landmarks on this stretch of road. Surely the village of Stiffkey wasn't so far from here, back the way she'd come? Or had she gone the wrong way? Perhaps the spinning of the car had disorientated her. Even so, she must be somewhere between Stiffkey and Wells, on a road of nothing much except deserted plantations and disused gravel pits, with at least two miles in either direction.

Lia shuddered. Her feet were stiff in her thin boots and her hands were numb from the cold. Maybe leaving the car hadn't been such a great idea. She stopped to wipe away tears caused by the biting wind or from something overflowing inside her, she didn't know which. Crystallising on her cheeks, they made her skin feel raw.

As she was debating with herself whether she ought to return to the car, where at least there would be some shelter against the cruel wind, a vehicle appeared in the distance. Lia leapt out in the middle of the road, waving her arms for the driver to stop.

After he'd searched for Lia in the places where she was most likely to be, Aidan drove around for another hour. About a mile beyond Wells he noticed a car had gone off the road and into a ditch. He stopped to check that the driver was all right, then noticed to his horror that the car was Lia's. Heart pounding and half-expecting her to be injured, he looked through the window, only to find the car empty.

'Where *are* you?' he muttered.

She must have gone for help, but he'd only just come from there and had met no one. It couldn't have been long since she'd left the car, because although it was snowing heavily now, the snow hadn't yet completely covered the tyre tracks.

Had she gone the wrong way? If she had, there would be nothing for three miles.

Casting around, he saw her footprints, rapidly filling with fresh snow, but heading off, as he had feared, away from Stiffkey.

He jumped back in the car and followed her tracks. To his relief, after a couple of miles he spotted a familiar figure standing in the middle of the road waving her arms and pulled over. He opened the passenger door with the engine running, and Lia scrambled in.

'What are you doing out here?' He grabbed a blanket from the back seat and tugged it around her. 'You must be freezing.'

She merely nodded.

'I noticed your car back there. Are you all right? You're not injured, are you?'

'My foot hurts,' she said, through clattering teeth.

'Your foot?'

'I kicked the car,' she explained.

'You *kicked* the car?' Aidan felt his mouth twitch. 'That is the dumbest thing I've heard in a long time.'

Lia glared. 'Yeah, well, I don't exactly need you to rub my nose in it.'

'Sorry. No, I mean it, sorry,' he repeated when laughter threatened to bubble over. Lia had difficulties keeping a straight face too, he noticed.

'Instead of having fun at my expense, perhaps you could take me back there and help me push it out of the ditch.'

'Now? You must be joking. We've got to get you warmed up. I'm serious. You can call the AA in the morning. The car will be perfectly safe. No one's going to run off with that old banger.'

'I wish they would. I hate it.'

'Then why don't you buy a new one?' he asked and put the purring Honda into gear. 'I expect you've got enough money.'

'It's not really my money, is it?' she muttered.

'If you say so,' he replied and left it at that. She would tell him what was eating her if she wanted to.

★   ★   ★

'You can't stay here,' said Aidan when they returned to her house. 'It's colder than outside. What happened to the cooker? I thought you'd got the hang of it.' He put a hand on top of the Rayburn. It was like ice.

Lia tucked a shivering Jack inside her coat. 'I'm not sure,' she said. 'I filled it up with coal this morning, but I've been at my mother's all day. It must've run out.'

'You should've called. I could've topped it up for you.'

If she had called, he could have saved himself a couple of hours of driving around aimlessly. On the other hand, he wouldn't be standing close to her right now, breathing in her scent. Having left the farm with the intention of talking to her, diverting her if possible, he now found himself in the role of the rescuer. It wasn't often Lia needed rescuing, and he realised he rather liked this side to her.

'I didn't think about it,' she said. 'Why is this always happening? It's annoying.'

Jack was wriggling in her arms and Aidan lifted him out of Lia's coat. 'It's old. That has a lot to do with it. Even if you fill it up now, it'll take ages before the house warms up.'

'I wish I lived somewhere warmer.'

'Look, my house is as warm as toast. Why don't you pack a few things? You're more than welcome to stop over.'

She sent him a haughty look. 'Concerned for my welfare?'

'Always.' He smiled. 'I have a spare bed *and* a sofa bed. Bring the dog too. And don't worry, you're safe with me.'

'Am I? What a shame.'

Hobbling, she disappeared up the stairs to fetch a bag. Her innuendo hung in the air like the crack from a whip. Was he prepared to go that far to keep her preoccupied? He felt a grin tugging at the corners of his mouth. *Hell, yeah.*

They ensconced themselves in his studio. Lia dropped down on to a paint-smeared sofa, and Aidan tossed her a blanket made from numerous little crocheted squares in a multitude of colours.

Snuggling under it, she said, 'Nice blanket.'

'Thanks, my mother made it. A long time ago.'

'For you?'

'For the house. She left it here when she moved out.'

Lia fingered the blanket almost reverently. 'I'm surprised she had the heart to leave it. It's very fine.'

'I'm not,' he said. 'I suspect a poor man's blanket didn't fit in with her new lifestyle with the retired colonel.'

She looked up from the blanket. In the studio light her eyes were exceptionally blue. 'That's harsh. Maybe it was a gift.'

'Yeah, maybe.'

He went into the kitchen to make her something hot, and when he returned, Lia's dog had discovered the cat which lay in its usual place on top of the radiator shelf. Jack snapped in the air for the dangling tail. The cat curled his tail just out of Jack's reach, the tip signalling feline wariness, and sent him an arrogant look through narrowed eyes. Failing to get a rise out of the cat, Jack settled down to gnaw at Lia's boots.

Lia pushed the dog away with her good foot, and Aidan tossed Jack a bouncy ball in a sock, which the dog caught in the air and hauled under the small table in the corner. 'Here, drink this,' he said to Lia, and handed her a tumbler.

Having sniffed it, Lia took a sip and the colour slowly returned to her face. The smell of peat and malt filled her nostrils. 'Mmm, I love toddies.'

'Don't drink it too quickly, it's quite strong.'

'I'm not a child,' she said.

'If you were a child, I'd have made you a hot Ribena.'

'Are you trying to get me drunk, then? So you can have your wicked way with me?' Her smile seemed a little forced.

His eyes didn't leave her face. 'No, but I do find that a bit of alcohol loosens the tongue.'

'And why would you want to loosen my tongue?'

'You were in quite a state when I found you. Want to tell me why?'

'No.'

He took her hand. 'Please, I'd like to know.'

She turned away but kept her hand in his. He followed her eyes to Jack, who was busy tearing the cat's plaything to shreds. The cat had stopped pretending to be asleep and was sitting bolt upright on the marble shelf, statuesque and dignified, though watching the dog intently. Aidan wondered if animals could be jealous when someone else played with their toys, just like children. The cat's muscles tensed under his stripy fur and he looked set to jump.

The antics of the animals seemed to decide her. 'You're right. I was in a state. I was feeling lonely and abandoned, if you must know. I told you about breaking up with Brett. I think being alone in the snow sort of brought it home to me, that I was truly on my own now.'

'There are worse things than being on your own.'

'Like what?'

'Being with someone you don't love. Makes you guilt-ridden something rotten.' Aidan ran his hand along the backrest of the sofa, brushing off imaginary dust. Their knees were close to each other. All he had to do was reach out and touch her. He wondered how she'd react. 'I take it you didn't love him,' he said.

Lia made a circle along the rim of her glass. 'No, but I didn't realise until now. Stupid, isn't it?'

'It happens. I've been in relationships like that.'

'Were you ever in a serious relationship?'

He shrugged. 'They were serious enough at the time, but whenever things weren't working, I always found comfort in my one true love.'

Lia frowned, and he wanted to run a finger down

338

the frown line and tell her she'd get wrinkles if she didn't stop.

'Your one true love? Your art, you mean?'

'I want to show you something.' He fetched the folder from its hiding place at the top of the cupboard, dusted it down, and laid it flat on the table.

Wrapped in the blanket and with a bemused expression, Lia joined him at the table. He lit a lamp attached to the shelf above, and the cone of light reflected off the folder's surface, shiny with age.

'Go on,' he said. 'Open it.'

'Are you sure? It looks like a treasured possession.'

'I'm sure. I've been meaning to show you this for a while.'

Lia's hand shook a little as she untied the ribbons, from excitement perhaps; it was hard to tell with her. Lifting the heavy cover, she looked through his artwork, piece by piece. When she realised who the model was, she sent him a startled look.

'It's me,' she said.

'I did them at sixth form college.'

She smiled. 'You're lucky Pinch didn't catch you.' Pinch had been their English teacher and had earned his nickname because his nose looked as if someone had pinched it and pulled it long and thin.

'You were a great subject. You still are. You said

you remembered me drawing behind my books? Well, this is what I produced.'

'Just me? You only spied on me?'

He arched his eyebrows at her accusation. 'I drew a lot of people, actually. Things even, but it had to be a proper setting. I'm not much of a still life person.'

'So where are they?'

'I didn't keep them. They weren't very good.'

'But you kept these. Why?'

'Even you can't be that thick.' He reached out and smoothed a strand of her hair behind her ear. She flinched a little at the touch but didn't move away. Aidan reminded himself that she'd practically just broken up with her boyfriend, and perhaps it was a little too soon to make overtures in that direction.

Still, it cost him to let his hand fall and concentrate on the drawings instead. He handed her one particular drawing on paper from an ordinary tear-off block.

'You wore your hair in exactly the same way you do now,' he said, 'with a straight edge and a fringe.'

She smiled. 'It never really occurred to me to change it, which is odd, because I've changed everything else about my life.'

'Maybe your hair stayed that way because a part of you remains unchanged. Have you thought of that?'

'Sorry, that's a bit deep for me.' She laughed and turned the pages in the folder one more time, as if she was searching for something. Then the light left her face, and she shook her head. 'I seem so sad. Did I ever smile?'

Aidan examined his own drawings critically. He was so used to them, but now that he'd showed them to her, he tried to look at them as she might see them. On every single drawing her face, even in profile, carried the same expression. There were no facial lines, because she didn't have them then – she didn't have that many now either – and he'd used only light and shade to recreate her look of utter dejection.

'You were sad and beautiful,' he said. 'Perfect for studying and for trying to guess your thoughts.'

'And did you? Guess my thoughts?'

'No, you're a complete mystery to me.'

'Surely not,' she said. 'If I was to hazard a guess, I'd say you know me better than most people.'

'Perhaps I do. It'd certainly explain why I felt you were trying to fob me off earlier. Because you weren't really bemoaning the loss of your relationship status, were you?'

Shaking her head, she closed the folder and returned to the sofa, drawing the blanket around her. Aidan handed her the remains of her toddy, which was lukewarm but still effective.

When she told him the true story of her brother's death, about the visit from the detectives, her find in her grandmother's attic, and her face-off with her mother this afternoon, a lot fell into place. The vulnerability she'd tried so hard to hide suddenly stood out and made him realise he'd have to tread carefully in order not to expose her even more. That damned pride of hers wouldn't allow it.

At the same time he had a strong urge to draw her close, to soothe away her troubles, but this wasn't the right moment. He'd have to wait until she took the first step.

'No wonder you have hang-ups about the water.' He ran his hands through his hair to drive away the images. 'Christ!'

'It's in the past, but I'm glad it's out in the open now. I can move on.'

'But it's not completely over, is it?'

'What do you mean?'

'Someone poisoned your grandmother. Don't you want to know who? Could it be your mother?' He regretted playing the devil's advocate when all colour left her face.

'My mother has nothing to do with it.'

'Are you sure? In most murder cases, the murderer is known to the victim. She had a good reason for wanting to be rid of your grandmother. So do you.'

'Don't be ridiculous,' she protested. 'I think they've made a mistake.'

Aidan raised an eyebrow. 'A mistake? With that kind of poison? I don't—'

He was interrupted by a yowl from the cat, who had leapt off the radiator shelf and pounced on Lia's dog. Jack defended himself to the best of his abilities, but had met his match, and he scrambled on to the sofa and under Lia's blanket, leaving the cat in possession of the sock ball and bristling like a hedgehog.

The moment had passed, and Lia had clammed up. Perhaps she regretted confiding in him. Perhaps she'd sensed he was trying to steer the conversation in a particular direction. Although Lia didn't believe her mother had murdered her grandmother, it would be rather convenient if she had.

With the toddy working its magic, she sank back against the cushions and closed her eyes. Aidan pulled the blanket up around her and the dog.

'You better stay here while I make up your bed,' he said.

Though the snow had abated, Lia made herself and Jack cosy in one of the spare bedrooms, where she fell at first into a dreamless sleep, but woke in the night to find herself living once more through Eddie's last moments. The terror and confusion he must have felt when he died was enough to make her almost physically sick. She'd told Aidan she was ready to move on, but it was going to be some time before she could get those images out of her head. Years, perhaps, or maybe never.

Barefoot on the wooden floor, she opened the door to the landing. Everything was quiet, and she crept downstairs to the kitchen for something to drink. At the bottom of the stairs she noticed a faint light coming from under the closed living-room door. Tentatively she put her hand on the door handle and pressed it down without a sound.

Aidan sat on the sofa with a half-empty bottle of Scotch in front of him. As she retreated he must have heard her for he turned his head. His face looked haggard, with dark circles under his eyes and a smudge of stubble on his chin. Well, she supposed, a man would look like that after downing half a bottle of whisky, or however much he may have drunk.

'You couldn't sleep either,' he said, and it wasn't a question.

'I woke up again. I keep seeing Eddie in my mind.'

He nodded. 'We both have a lot of ghosts to battle.'

'That's what Brett said.' Lia sat down on the sofa next to him. 'When he left.'

'Not so dim after all, your lawyer friend.' He lifted his glass, but before putting it to his lips, he offered it to her.

'I never said he was dim.'

It wasn't whisky she longed for but something quite different. She touched his hair. It was soft and thick, like she'd always imagined it would be, and she twisted a brown curl around her finger.

'Maybe we can face them together, our ghosts,' she said before she had time to rationalise it. Ironically she'd gone halfway around the globe in search of a closeness which had always eluded her, and all along it might have been here, right under her very nose.

'Maybe we can,' he whispered and brought his face close to hers. Their lips met, cautiously at first, then with a hunger which surprised them both.

Lia let him pull her night T-shirt over her head, while she tugged at the waistband of his tracksuit. Her giggles over their almost youthful fumblings stopped in her throat when he cupped her firm breasts in his hands. This was no laughing matter, but a meeting driven by desire, by a raw need to obliterate their demons. Aidan wasn't tender or romantic, but almost ferocious in his passion. She let him enter her in the way he needed to, as *she* needed him to, and clung to him as he possessed her.

Later, warm and sated, she lay pressed against his chest. He kissed her sleepily and murmured close to her ear, 'There's something I haven't told you.'

'Tell me later,' she said, nearly dropping off. 'For now, just hold me.'

CHAPTER 22

They woke to an unnaturally bright light penetrating the pale Roman blinds in the living room. Aidan turned on his side and studied Lia. She was still in that half-conscious state between waking and sleeping, and she stretched and groaned from having slept on a sofa hardly big enough for them both. Then she came to, fully and with a start, as if she hadn't expected to find herself in his arms.

Smiling, he touched the tip of her nose. 'Morning, beautiful. Welcome to Narnia.'

'Eh?' She sat up, then snatched the blanket to her chest when she became aware of her nakedness.

'It snowed a lot last night. The whole world is covered.'

'What time is it?'

Aidan glanced at his watch. 'Just gone eight. Why? Are you in a hurry?'

'I have to be at Susannah's at ten for her to show me around the office. I've agreed to look after the shop when she's having her baby. Me and her mother.'

346

Playfully he tugged at the blanket covering her breasts. 'Then we've got time for a quickie.'

'No!'

In the cushioned snow world her protest sounded almost too loud, and he was startled by the force of it. Looking away, he tried not to give in to disappointment. 'Another time, then.'

As she fumbled for her bra which was draped over the backrest, he found his trousers and managed to pull them on without revealing his scar. 'I'll make us some coffee while you call the AA, then I'll give you a lift to your car if you need me to.'

'That'll be great, thanks.'

'What are friends for?'

Friends.

The word echoed in Lia's head as she sat in Susannah's small, windowless office, stacked high to the ceiling with lever arch folders and cardboard boxes for filing. She tried to concentrate on how to deal with the shop's paperwork, but her concentration kept slipping. Aching inside, both physically and mentally, and suffused by a deep longing, she didn't know whether to be relieved or miffed that Aidan hadn't stopped her leaving. He could at least have tried.

'Why the hangdog expression?' Susannah asked.

'What do you mean?'

'Something's bothering you. I can tell.'

Lia attempted to focus on the purchase ledger file in front of her.

If you only knew, she thought. *My mother might be a murderer.* How was that for a conversation stopper?

Briefly she thought of confiding her fears, then she caught Susannah's smirk. A sudden anger rose in her. This was no joke, not a subject for gossip. Connie may have done something terrible, but to Lia it would almost be excusable. What did that make her? An accomplice? And what would happen when the police really started digging?

A wild thought occurred to her. They could make a run for it, she and Connie. Clear out the bank account and go to India or Africa. Except it would never work. They'd be tracked down, or a holiday-maker might spot them on a beach somewhere. Running never solved anything. She'd been running all her life and ended up right back where she started from.

Keeping her voice steady, she said, 'It's just that I'm so undecided about a lot of things.'

'As long as you're not undecided about Aidan.'

'What's that supposed to mean?'

'You like him, I know that, but you don't know him the way I do. Aidan's a gem. He's had a rotten time and doesn't deserve you toying with his feelings.'

'I'm not,' Lia protested. It seemed an odd thing to say about a person who abandoned you when you were pregnant at seventeen.

'Aidan belongs here. He finds his inspiration in

348

this godforsaken place. Oh, and don't bother saying that it isn't, because it is. Out here is the last row of potatoes. Where the crows have to bring their lunch boxes. You don't come unless you live here or have roots here, because there's nowhere else to go apart from the sea.'

Lia smiled weakly at the image of crows with lunch boxes clutched in their scaly claws.

'If you take him away from here, you'll break him.'

Lia felt her face redden. Susannah went too far sometimes. 'Who says I will? Maybe I'm just as much a part of this landscape as—'

Just then Susannah's four-year-old son came charging in, declaring that he wanted a drink and a DVD. Easing herself out of the chair with difficulty, Susannah grimaced and put her hand to her stomach, then she took the boy into the kitchen immediately behind the office. Lia listened to the homely sounds of family life, the fridge opening, the child's protests, high-pitched and excitable, when he didn't get what he wanted, Susannah's firm but dulcet reassurances.

Lia would have been about Ethan's age when Eddie died. Had her home ever rung with such everyday squabbles? She couldn't remember.

A few minutes later Susannah came back. Relieved that she hadn't confided her suspicions about her mother, Lia considered that perhaps the security system Ivy had wanted installed was a clue in itself and pointed to someone outside the family. Perhaps her grandmother had said something to Susannah.

'You saw my grandmother the day before she died,' she began cautiously. 'Did she say anything about a security system she was planning to have installed?'

'No. Should she have?' Susannah's attention was on her files.

'I thought she might have.'

'All that happened was I asked her what might have caused her indigestion. If she'd been for dinner somewhere and eaten something unusual.' Intent on filing a few stray pieces of paper, Susannah kept her face averted. 'You know, just making polite conversation.'

More like acting as the village telegraph, Lia thought. Then it struck her, from Susannah's pose, that Susannah knew more than she was letting on, and had drawn her own conclusions. The shock of it was enough to render her speechless, and when she'd gathered her wits again, her head was brimming with scenarios.

Perhaps she'd been barking up the wrong tree. What if Susannah knew exactly who it was, and was protecting him or her? That brought on another question. If Lia voiced her suspicions, what would Susannah do? She'd have to think very carefully before letting on.

As she racked her brains for a safer subject, Ethan reappeared in the doorway, wanting to play outside.

'Sweetheart, it's raining.'

'But I want to play in the sandbox! You have to take the lid off.'

Susannah was about to get up, when Lia stopped her.

'Let me do this. You should rest, you know.'

A spark of irritation flashed across Susannah's face. 'Rest! When do I ever get the time?'

'Ethan, show me where your clothes are,' said Lia, ignoring her outburst.

'But I can't find my wellies!'

'Then show me where they normally are, and we'll look for them together.'

Ethan stuck his chubby hand inside hers with the kind of trust that children seemed to bestow randomly. She persuaded him to wear his raincoat with the hood up and opened the back door. An icy wind curled around her as she traipsed across the muddy lawn in her jumper, but Ethan didn't seem to be bothered by the cold.

The lid on the sandbox had blown off, and the sandbox itself was half full of water. She began to scoop out the water with a small bucket, and Ethan enthusiastically joined her, using a shovel. His small hands scooped, lifted, and poured, and she had a sudden memory of another set of very small hands engaged in water play. Pain lanced through her, and she swallowed. Eddie had loved playing in the water.

'This is fun,' isn't it?' she said, forcing her tone to sound jolly.

'Are you going to make a sand castle with me? The man does.'

'What man?'

'Mummy's friend,' Ethan replied as if this was the most natural thing in the world. 'Sometimes when Mummy's not looking, he plays with me.'

'What does he look like, this man?'

'He has long hair. It looks all crinkly.'

Lia sucked in her breath. From the description it sounded like Aidan, but why would he play with Ethan behind Susannah's back?

Leaving Ethan to his game, she went back inside. 'It's pouring down,' she announced. 'I don't think he'll be out there for long.'

'Let's hope he gives us a few minutes. I'd like to go over the ordering procedure with you,' said Susannah, but soon afterwards she slammed the order book shut and said with a catch in her voice, 'I can't even find my son's boots for him. What sort of mother am I?'

'I'm sure you're doing your best.'

'My best just isn't good enough.'

Lia thought of Connie. 'Perhaps all mothers feel that way now and again, that they could do better.'

'Yes, well, what do you know of motherhood?' snapped Susannah and jammed the file back on the shelves. 'You have all the answers, don't you? You with your perfect life and more money than you can spend. But you were the one who ran away, while I stayed and faced the bloody music. Don't you talk to me about motherhood.'

Aware of how the anger was rising inside her, Lia grabbed her handbag and jacket. Then, when she was sure she could speak without shouting like a fishwife, she turned and faced Susannah.

'Since my return you've been rubbing my nose in the fact that I left you down in Fakenham when you got pregnant, as if I had something to do with that, which is ridiculous. It was your own stupidity for having unprotected sex, and I resent the way you're trying to make me feel guilty.' She shrugged. 'Hell, maybe I did feel like a bad friend for a while, but that's not why I'm helping you now. I'm doing it because I can see that you need it. And, you know what, there's no shame in needing other people. I realised that when my life took a bad turn, and I discovered some painful things I might never come to terms with completely.'

'Listen, Lia, I'm sorry—' Susannah began.

Flinging her jacket on, Lia interrupted her. 'I'm not going to patronise you by saying you wouldn't understand, because I'm sure you would. You're not stupid. But as long as you labour under the misapprehension that I *owe* you in some way, or I sense you deriving *Schadenfreude* from my misery, I'm not going to share them with you.' She swallowed hard to contain the angry tears that threatened. 'My life is not perfect. Far from it. One thing I've never done, though, is to blame other people for my own bad choices. Think about that, before you hurl accusations next time, okay?'

She left without giving Susannah a chance to reply.

Stalking home in the snow gave her a chance to cool off. It had felt good giving Susannah a piece of her mind, and if she'd jeopardised their future friendship, so what? She was past caring about that.

All the same, she didn't really think that Susannah knew something. If she had, she would surely have gone to the police. She was a village shopkeeper, leading an ordinary life and dealing with the commonplace issues marriage and parenthood brought with them. Bored, petty, and hormonal maybe, but not embroiled in murder.

Lia would have to look elsewhere for her answers.

After Lia had left in the AA van, Aidan went straight into the studio while the memory of their intimacy was still fresh in his mind. He brought out a new canvas which he'd prepared and primed with white paint only a few days before.

Wearing only a pair of tracksuit bottoms, his hair still wet and uncombed after a hasty shower, he began to work, sketching her image with a thin brush. He wanted to capture her expression from that morning before she was fully awake, and when everything between them still seemed okay.

He wondered at her reaction. Had she been embarrassed by his suggestion that they make love in daylight? It was a possibility, of course; he'd met girls like that before, not shy exactly, but self-conscious about their bodies. Or maybe she'd just wanted a one-night stand to take her mind off things, and he'd fitted the bill. She'd certainly succeeded in distracting him.

Oh, boy.

Recalling her longs legs wrapped around him and himself deep inside her, heat rose in his groin, and the brush slipped, leaving a smear where the curve of her chin should be. Cursing, he wiped the offending brush stroke away with a rag dipped in turps and traced it again.

Somehow the idea of Lia in mindless pursuit of hedonistic pleasure didn't quite tally with the picture he had of her. She was far too sincere. Not only that, she was fiercely independent, a trait he both admired in her and found exasperating at the same time. She wouldn't need to use other people to feel better about herself, she'd find ways of achieving this through her own efforts, by looking inside herself, not outside. That much he knew about her.

But that didn't explain her reaction.

In his mind he went over last night in detail. Finding her in the snow, bringing her here. Showing her his drawings, then more or less accusing her of being obtuse when she didn't react the way he'd expected. What *had* he expected? Eternal gratitude that he'd taken notice of her at college? Girly giddiness at being an artist's model, albeit an unsuspecting one? A romantic and starry-eyed look?

'Come *on*,' he muttered. He might as well hope to win the Turner Prize.

Instead she'd been baffled, even a little put out, claiming he'd spied on her. Which he had. Sort of.

Later, after that horrendous revelation about her brother, she'd fallen asleep on the sofa, while he got the spare bedroom ready. They'd both gone to bed, separately, and that had been that, he thought.

Except she'd sought him out in the middle of the night and found him at his most vulnerable, had exposed her own soft underbelly while she clung to him. He'd poured himself into her, in more than one sense – to her breathless reassurances that she was on the pill – and had given back as much as he took. What their lovemaking may have lacked in finesse, it made up for in intensity.

It was only now it occurred to him that she may not have enjoyed it as much as he did, and that wounded his masculine pride, in the same way her rejection of him this morning left him confused. He thought of calling her, but dismissed the idea. Whether or not they were heading for something serious, he didn't want to appear too needy.

Having sketched her features, he stepped back, wiping the brush. Filling in with colours was the next stage, but the greys he normally blended seemed inadequate for Lia. In the end he left the painting as it was, an outline in rust-red oil.

He'd captured her in a rare moment with her guard down and feared that adding colours would obscure it.

He would call her. Eventually. Right now he had a task to complete.

When Lia got home, the house was freezing as she'd expected. She let Jack out for a runaround and got the Rayburn going again, congratulating herself for doing it without Aidan's help. Then she lit a fire in the front room as well because it would take the Rayburn ages to heat up the house properly.

The wood spat and hissed as the pine resin burned, and a couple of times the wind found its way down the chimney so a cloud of smoke billowed into the room, making her cough and her eyes sting. Nevertheless, lighting the fire had been the right decision. She was sick and tired of feeling cold and lonely. The cold she could do something about, but the loneliness was a different matter.

Aidan might be her lover, but there was a part of him she couldn't quite reach. Susannah had taken a perverse delight in reminding her of a debt she could never repay – although Lia had put her right on that score. Ivy was dead, but they'd never been close in the first place, and closeness to her mother meant facing up to painful memories she'd rather not think about.

Even Jack seemed to have abandoned his usual place by her feet and was now lying on the hearthrug eyeing her warily, his ears cocked.

'Judas,' she muttered.

The dog changed his mind when she went to make something to eat. He drooled and whined pitifully as she heated a tin of baked beans for herself, and eventually she took pity on him and opened a tin of dog food.

'You certainly know a good thing when you see one, don't you?'

He'd finished every last morsel in his bowl, and Lia had eaten as much as she could bring herself to swallow, even though the food had tasted of sawdust.

Jack licked his chops and jumped up on her lap. He tilted his head back against her chest with a look of adoration in his brown eyes. Staring back at his peculiar black markings and into the depth of his eyes, Lia wished he could talk. If any dog was capable of knowing what went on in the human world, that dog would be Jack.

She caressed his ears. 'Who's a clever dog?'

His response was a snort, and he stuck his nose nearer to her half-empty plate, sniffed it, then looked back up at her.

'Go on, then.'

He polished off her bread crusts in a matter of seconds, and as he continued to lick his mouth and nose clean of every last scrap of food, making contented little noises, she stroked his silky head absently. She understood now why people said that dogs could help you to heal. He may not be able to talk, but his presence was comforting.

Without warning, Jack suddenly went rigid on her lap, his muscles tensing down along his small body. With a low growl he jumped down and stalked into the scullery. Lia followed him. He had his nose to the back door, and from his chest came a low rumble. Ignoring her, he snarled furiously all of a sudden, his jowls curling up over his sharp, pointy teeth. Lia went cold, and a shiver ran from her scalp down her spine.

Someone or something was out there.

She stepped back from the door. What should she do? In the building where she and Brett had lived together, security had been tight, with plenty of locks, a doorman in the lobby guarding the lift to the upper floors, as well as swipe cards and security cameras. For them to be attacked by a stranger in their own home was virtually impossible.

Here the only thing separating her and whatever was out there was thin wooden door with a simple Yale lock and a bolt at the base. Her eyes slid to the bolt; it had been pushed back. She couldn't remember doing that, but she must have. Maybe when she took the rubbish out.

Jack's growling intensified, and he scratched at the door. Lia made a quick decision. In the cupboard under the sink she found an aerosol can with air freshener. Lily of the Valley. That'll do the trick, she thought grimly. If anyone attacked her, she would spray them in the face and perhaps buy herself enough time to shut and bolt the door and then phone for help.

With the spray can in one hand she turned the lock very quietly. Then, holding the aerosol can in front of her, she yanked it open.

There was no one out there. It was pitch black, and all she could hear was the dull tapping of melting snow dripping somewhere.

Jack remained on the doormat, still snarling though not quite so viciously. Then he whimpered and turned tail.

Lia yelled out into the night. 'I'm not afraid of you! I'm no little old lady, and you don't scare me!'

Her voice fell flat in the dark, cushioned by the snow, and the blackness seemed denser, watchful somehow. She shut and locked the door behind her, then tugged hard at the bolt for good measure to ensure that it was securely fastened. Jack lay on the jute rug with a melancholy look on his face, either deploring the lack of heat, or apologising for getting her worked up over nothing more than a prowling cat, perhaps.

'Dogs,' she grumbled, contradicting her earlier thoughts. 'Who needs them?'

Lia could no longer deny that Ivy had had good reason to fear for her life, but as she checked the window locks and the front door, she couldn't help thinking that it couldn't have been Connie she'd been afraid of. Why suddenly now, after all these years, when nothing had changed between them?

No, it had to be someone else. But who?

The question plagued her as she got ready for bed. The words she'd flung at Susannah, truthful though they were, joined with the cacophony of other jumbled thoughts inside her mind, and soon she was tossing and turning.

Camomile tea held no appeal. The aroma always promised a taste experience it couldn't quite deliver – like jam without fruit in it – and instead she headed for the bathroom and her tablets. To hell with dependency. She needed to sleep right now.

She'd put the tablets in the bathroom cabinet when she'd stopped taking them, to remove them from easy temptation. At least, she was sure she had, but they weren't there. She rummaged in her washbag, tipping it into the basin in irritation, but they weren't there, either. Frowning, she tried to remember when she'd last seen the bottle. She hadn't taken one since . . . when had it been, before Christmas? Perhaps she hadn't relegated them to the bathroom after all.

She piled its contents back into the washbag and returned to the bedroom. The bedside cabinet drawers were empty. She pushed her hand right to the back, but there was nothing. Someone must have taken them. Zoe? Why would she, there was nothing exciting about Temazepam. Susannah? Not while she was pregnant. Who, then?

This was crazy, they must be somewhere. Maybe she'd left them on the dressing table. No joy. The tablets weren't there. And something else wasn't as it should be. A candlestick lay on its side as if it had been knocked over, and the mirror had been flipped 180 degrees – *How had she not noticed that when she'd gone to bed?*

Stepping backwards with a horrible, horrible feeling in her gut, she stumbled over her suitcase and put her hand on the wardrobe to steady herself. Her fingers caught on the silky fabric of the only dress she'd brought with her, and which she'd packed on a whim though it was hardly suitable for the Norfolk weather. It hung from a wire hanger on the outside of the wardrobe door. Had she put it there? She couldn't remember.

Sweat sprang out on her forehead, and her heart hammered wildly. Leaving the bedroom, she suddenly saw everything with a sense of déjà vu. Jack's blanket was on the landing floor against the opposite wall to where it normally was. Jack was lying on it, still bristling. He followed her as she felt her way along the wall touching familiar objects with her hands because she wasn't entirely sure she could trust her eyes.

The washing line securing the door to the spare room had been snapped, the sofa cushions were upside down, the phone was off the hook, the photo on the mantelpiece of herself and Eddie was lying face down.

Somewhere at the back of her mind Lia knew that she was being stupid. If someone had been in the house, the only sensible thing to do was to call for help, not wander around in a daze exposing herself to danger. Yet who would she call? The police? She could almost hear how the conversation would be played out.

'Is anything missing, Madam?'

'No.'

'Has anything been disturbed?'

Herself, pausing. 'Well, no. Yes. Er, I'm not sure.'

'What makes you suspect that someone has been in your house?'

Herself, voice rising. 'Because the sofa cushions are upside down, and my sleeping tablets are missing.' Yeah, right.

Should she call Susannah? No.

Aidan, then? She reached for the phone and dialled his number. She let it ring ten times and hung up, before it switched to voicemail, with a strange sense of relief. She was quite possibly going mad, and Aidan had had enough madness to deal with to last him a lifetime.

Someone had poisoned her grandmother, but that didn't mean that this person wanted to kill her. Why would they? As Susannah had pointed out so accommodatingly, she wasn't part of the community. She hardly knew the people who lived here, had no inkling of whatever secrets they may be harbouring. She knew nothing.

But perhaps whoever was out there – if it wasn't just a prowling cat – thought she did. Perhaps the intruder intended to come back.

What then?

CHAPTER 23

Two days later, Aidan was just about to give in and reach for the phone, when a car drove into the yard.

Unfortunately it wasn't Lia as he'd hoped, but his mother. He'd spent the day before clearing snow from the courtyard to the main road, but Eileen Morrell had lived on this farm long enough to come prepared. Her slim legs in sturdy boots swung out of the Jeep with practised ease.

To Aidan's relief she'd come alone. At the same time he couldn't resist a jab at her when he opened the door and saw her looking almost happy. He greeted her with a dutiful kiss on the cheek.

'Where's Derek thingie today, then?' he asked, regretting it the instant her face closed up and became a smooth, expressionless mask.

'I dropped him in town. He was meeting with some old chums.'

'Army mates, I suppose.'

'I didn't ask.'

'Well, what can I do for you today, Mother? Would you like some tea?'

Her lips tightened at his use of the title. Don't

call me Mother, she'd said to the three of them once, a long time ago when things were still all right and no one had died. *It makes me feel I have to stand to attention.* So Aidan let her stand to attention.

'No, thank you,' she replied, not rising to the bait. 'I really only came to check how my seedlings are doing. And you, of course.'

'Of course. Well, I'm about to have some, so if you'll excuse me?' He hadn't planned on drinking tea just now, but it gave him something to do while he collected his thoughts. There were things he ought to tell her, but he wasn't sure how. Nor was he convinced she really wanted to know, but with everything seemingly coming to a head, did he have a choice?

She followed him into the kitchen. Instinct made him clear things away to avoid parental disapproval over the mess, and he removed a pile of papers from the nearest kitchen chair so she could sit down. Having put the kettle on, he began stacking the dishwasher.

Eileen sat down, with her legs crossed and hands neatly in her lap. His mother was a striking woman, he'd always thought, with clear eyes and salt-and-pepper hair in an elegant style. In her pencil skirt and cashmere twinset she was a walking advertisement for genteel retirement in the Home Counties.

Her boots, on the other hand, which she'd kept on to avoid walking on the cold floor in her stockinged feet, were designed for rough wear, for shovelling muck or taking large, boisterous dogs for walks across frozen, arable fields.

'I see you still have my old crystal glasses,' she said.

'What, these ones?' Aidan held up a wine glass which he'd left to drip-dry on the draining board to spare them from harsh treatment in the dishwasher.

She nodded and smiled for the first time since she'd arrived. 'They came from my mother's home, you know.'

'If they're so precious, why did you leave them behind?'

'I thought you might like something nice around the house.'

Her smile faded, and she twirled the string of pearls she always wore around her neck. When she became conscious of his stare, she dropped her hands in her lap again.

Hadn't Lia said something similar? About his mother leaving the patchwork blanket behind as a gift? The crystal glasses too by the sound of it. He did a mental inventory of other items she hadn't taken with her when she'd handed over the farm. The clock in the living room he'd loved as a child, the marquetry wardrobe in his bedroom, probably very old and worth a fortune. Even the photo of his grandparents on the mantelpiece, his mother's parents. She'd been very fond of them, he recalled.

'I do,' he said, 'like something nice, I mean. Thank you. Sure I can't get you some tea?'

In the end they skipped the tea, and they wandered around in the greenhouses, while she talked about plants, feeds, compost, and watering schedules. Eileen prodded her finger into the earth of a seedling pot made from folded newspaper, then pushed the earth around the base of the seedling down a bit. There were rows and rows of her pots and Aidan wondered when she found the time to plant them all.

'They seem to be doing fine. They'll need planting out in the main beds in a week or two.' She brushed the wet earth from her fingers. 'I'll come and do it when the time is right. Any other problems?'

'I've had a couple of sick sheep, but nothing else. Acidosis, both of them. One's cleared up now. Greedy little bu . . . beggars,' he corrected when he caught her disapproving frown.

'I'm very pleased with the way you've been looking after things,' she said. 'Your dad would've been proud, you know.'

'Would he?' At the mention of his father Aidan's irritability returned.

'Of course. Mind you, we always meant for Gerald to . . .'

He finished the sentence for her. 'Take over the farm, yes, I know. You've told me a million times.'

'Have I?' Her fingers sought her necklace again, and she looked at him without really seeing him. 'I'm sorry if it upsets you.'

'It doesn't. Not any more.'

367

He'd learned long ago that soothing away her grief was beyond his capabilities, but it hadn't stopped him trying. Ironically it seemed her new husband, a man completely unconnected with their family, had managed to do what Aidan never could. Or perhaps by adopting her new lifestyle with the colonel, she was able to contain it better, to edit out that part of her life as if it didn't exist.

What rankled most was knowing that he couldn't even begin to fill the gap left behind by his brother. His sister had felt the same and had stayed away from all of them to keep it from eating away at her.

Now there was finally a chance he could prove himself worthy. He never expected anyone to approve of what he was planning – even he could see that his methods were questionable – but no one could be in any doubt he was doing it for the right reasons.

Lia had been a spanner in the works in a way he hadn't anticipated, but as long as he could keep the issues separate, she would stay safe.

He didn't say any of this to his mother. Instead they continued on their monthly tour of the greenhouses. Glad of her company, he talked about his painting, ideas he was toying with, commissions he'd had, despite the knowledge that she neither grasped his passion nor understood his art. It didn't matter. Lia's insight was making him see her in a different light.

Later, she declined his offer of lunch and

re-buttoned her coat after the heat in the greenhouses.

'I have a message for you,' she said. 'From Derek.'

Aidan's good humour left him so abruptly it was as if he'd caught a sudden chill. 'Derek? What can he possibly have to say to me?'

'It's about your campaign. It hasn't gone unnoticed. Your "uncompromising views", as he calls them, of the army and of the MoD, will land you in trouble, he says. Serious trouble.'

'How does he know?'

'He may not be in active service, but he hasn't completely retired from the army scene. One never does, I think. He still hears things, from the inside. Your protests are no longer low profile. Someone's going to make a connection between what you've been saying and those bomb threats—'

'How can they, if there isn't one?'

'Isn't there?' She regarded him steadily, and he was the first to look away. 'I often wonder if Derek might've seen what was up with Gerald if he'd known him, but we hadn't met when . . . when Gerald . . .'

'I doubt it. The rest of us didn't see it coming, so why should he, a complete stranger?'

She shrugged and smiled. 'No use thinking like that now, about the what-ifs. It'll do no good.'

Now is the time, Aidan thought. *Now is the time to tell her.* Then the image of his mother's new husband, the colonel – Colonel Mustard, as he thought of him privately – with his sun-bleached moustache and framed letter from the Queen, made him change his mind.

'What does darling Derek want me to do?'

She sent him a reproachful look. 'I do wish you'd be a little less critical when it comes to Derek. He only has your best interest at heart.'

'Oh, sure.'

Ignoring the sarcasm, she went on, 'He says not to draw any further attention to yourself. You might get a visit, but apparently it's just routine. Shouldn't be anything to worry about.'

'Thanks, I'll remember to hide my arsenal of illicit weapons.'

'It's no joking matter.'

She held up her cheek for a goodbye kiss. Aidan obliged her. Then she held his face between her hands, and he could hear the rasping of his day-old stubble against her skin.

'I've lost one son,' she said. 'It's the worst loss imaginable, like having my insides scooped out with a spoon. Don't make me lose another.'

He put his hands over hers. 'Mum . . .' he began, when a familiar car drove into the courtyard and parked behind his mother's Jeep.

The spanner in the works.

Lia had had enough of feeling lonely and frightened, but when she'd decided to seek out Aidan, she hadn't bargained on meeting his mother too.

The former Mrs Morrell wasn't what Lia had expected of a twice-bereaved farmer's wife. Not only would she have looked right at home in the fashionable streets of London, but where Lia had expected brittleness and vulnerability beneath a jovial, mustn't-grumble exterior, Aidan's mother seemed more airy-fairy and sort of quiet and sad.

Feeling suddenly like a scruffy schoolgirl in the presence of an imposing headmistress, she let the struggling Jack down, brushed the dog hairs off her sweater, and shook hands politely.

Jack, catching the scent of the animals, took off and disappeared into one of the barns.

'I'm sorry,' Lia said when Aidan swore under his breath. 'I'll go get him.'

He shook his head. 'Don't worry, I think I know where he is. Back in a minute.'

Lia watched him head off with his roll-neck jumper pulled right up to his chin, and wondered, stupidly, if her running after him would be considered rude. She stayed put beside Aidan's mother, thinking it a little too convenient that he should go searching for her dog, not vice versa. He probably wanted them to get to know each other, so she did her best with the small talk. She'd learned by now this was the only way to get to know anyone around here.

'I knew your grandmother,' said Eileen.

Lia felt a slight pang. 'Seems like a lot of people did. I never realised she was so popular.'

371

'Oh, she was. She did a lot for the community. Patronised the local shop, campaigned for hedge-rows to be protected. Kept an eye on the sea defences, what state they were in, and had the council down there to plant new trees after that terrible storm we had. Everybody liked her.' Eileen paused slightly before continuing. 'Even my husband Derek liked her, though he reckons she was a woman with a secret. He's funny like that, seeing things.'

Eileen spoke with the same burr as Mrs Larwood, but without the double confirmation at the end of her sentences. She still sounded Norfolk born and bred, which made Lia feel more at ease.

'I suppose we all have secrets, when it comes to it,' she replied, not in defence of Ivy, but from a desire to keep her family's dirty linen private.

'How well do you know my son?' Eileen asked.

Lia hadn't expected such a direct question, and the colour rose in her cheeks before she had time to get herself under control.

'I see.' Twirling her necklace, Aidan's mother smiled, but the smile didn't quite reach her eyes. 'Well, perhaps you can do me a favour, then.'

'Of course. What would you like me to do?'

'I'd like you to keep an eye on him for me. Make sure he doesn't do anything . . . he might regret.'

'Like what?' Although she felt both mystified and flattered, at the same time Lia experienced a sudden rush of anger at being put in this situation. Aidan's mother was practically asking her to spy on him. She couldn't imagine why.

Eileen hesitated. 'I don't know how much you know, but he's been saying things about certain organisations . . .'

'Yes, I heard him on the radio.'

'Well, perhaps you can talk some sense into him. Tell him it's okay to be angry, but there are better ways to channel his anger.'

Lia shrugged. 'I can try, but there seems to be something driving him, something he has to do before he can let it go. Perhaps it would be best to let it run its course.'

'Perhaps.' Eileen didn't sound convinced.

'It's not as if he's doing anything wrong.'

'No, of course not.'

Aidan was walking back towards them with Jack in his arms. He handed the dog to Lia, and she felt his small body shake with fear. A growl rose from deep down in his throat and turned into a vicious snarl.

'Jack! What's got into you you?' She glanced at Aidan. 'What happened?'

'Don't look at me. I have no idea.'

Cradling the dog, Lia fondled his ears. 'There's nothing in there, you silly billy. Only rats, and they're smaller than you.' She clipped on his lead, which she'd put in her pocket earlier, and only then did she think it safe to let him down.

Immediately he stood on his hind legs, straining in the direction of the barn.

'Honestly, dogs,' said Aidan.

'Well, I'd best be off.' Eileen held out her hand to Lia. 'It was nice meeting you.'

'What did you and my mother talk about while I was in the barn?'

Aidan was chopping greens for a salad. Lia was warming her hands on the Aga but her attention was on Jack, who sat by the back door with his nose to the crack. He'd been in the same position for the last ten minutes, not moving except for ripples of tension along his body and an occasional rumble in his chest. What *was* the matter with him?

Aidan repeated his question.

'Mmm? Oh, she wants me to keep an eye on you.'

'I thought as much. And what did you say?'

Lia rubbed her hands, which were still cold. 'What could I say? She seems to think we're sufficiently close for me to do that.'

Aidan put the knife down and joined her by the Aga. 'Are we?'

'I don't know. Perhaps.'

Where do we go from here? Lia thought. It seemed a huge leap from having had sex and then no contact for days, to suddenly become intimate again. Who took the first step towards something more?

Maybe I do.

She reached up and wound a finger around one of his brown curls. She'd fantasised about those curls, how she would thread her fingers through his hair, then pull his head down and his mouth on to hers.

Aidan beat her to it. He caught her hand and brought it around his waist instead, then drew her close. He tasted of coffee and red pepper and something intrinsically him. Lia couldn't get enough. She wanted his mouth fused with hers, his hands on every part of her, his skin against hers. Impatiently she pulled at his clothes, his belt, his hair, and fought against his hands when he stopped her.

'This time, bed.' His breath was hot on her cheek, and she squeaked in surprise when he lifted her up as if she weighed nothing.

In the bedroom she let him peel off her jeans while she yanked her bra over her head and tossed it aside. Writhing with need, she was aware, from the gleam in his eyes, that he was teasing her, pulling down her knickers agonisingly slowly. She reached for him to help him out of his clothes, but he rolled out of her grasp and stood up beside the bed, undressing with his back to her.

Admiringly, she ran her eyes down his back, took in the broad shoulders, the curvature of his spine, the dip before . . . well, wetsuits didn't lie, but, oh, nothing could have prepared her for the glorious shape of his backside. She reached up to touch him, but he pulled away.

Lia frowned. With a body like that Aidan had no reason to be coy. So why didn't he face her? They'd had sex before, and she certainly hadn't been disappointed by his size. It was almost as if there was a part of him she wasn't allowed to see.

'Aidan, turn around,' she said. 'Please.'

'I can't.'

'Why not?' She put her hand at the base of his spine. 'Tell me what's bothering you.'

Slowly he turned, and Lia was literally face to face with an enormous scar covering his entire thigh. Her years of medical practice kept her from flinching, but the thought of the agony Aidan would have suffered when he acquired it was enough to make her swallow hard.

'So, you have a scar. Why wasn't I allow to see it? Were you afraid I would reject you because you weren't physically perfect? Who is?'

'I'm not exactly proud of it.'

She smiled. 'Believe me, I've seen worse.'

'They don't come any worse.'

'Oh, yes, they do,' she whispered and pressed her mouth to the scar despite his protests. She slid her hand up the back of his thigh and held him as she explored the ridges and the puckered skin with her lips. Closing her eyes, she created a map of him in her head, of every dip and line, the texture and smell of his skin.

Her senses sang with the feel of him, and when she opened her eyes again, she saw the tenderness in his.

'I dreamt of you, for years,' he said, with a catch in his throat. 'And here you are, in my bed, all black-haired and milky white. So perfect, while I . . .'

'You *are* perfect. Come.' She held out her hand to draw him down on the bed, was scorched by his heat as his body covered hers.

'It was always you, Lia.' He spoke softly as he slid inside her. 'Always.'

When Lia woke, it had turned dark outside. The branches of a tree in the back garden tapped against the window like Hitchcock's birds pecking their way through the glass. She stretched, feeling mellow, then turned over to seek comfort in Aidan's arms.

The other side of the bed was empty.

Her first thought was, why had he left her? The second, that there had to be a perfectly good explanation. She sat up, pulling the covers around her, and switched on the bedside light, squeezing her eyes shut until they'd adjusted to the sudden brightness.

Jack stood by the half-open door, whining.

'What's up?' You need to go outside, is that it?'

Lia got out of bed and wrapped herself in Aidan's dressing gown. It smelt strongly of aftershave and more faintly of him, a pleasant, warm scent. Downstairs Jack headed not for the front door as she'd expected, but for the door to Aidan's studio, and softly scraping at it, he whined again.

She glared at Jack for hauling her out of bed so he could go cat-chasing. The next minute, remembering how Jack seemed to sense things she couldn't, she went cold all over.

Aidan's mother had warned her he might do something stupid. Lia had seen no signs that he was a danger to himself, but how well did she know him? She rushed to the door, nearly tripping over the dressing gown belt, which had come undone, and flung it open.

At a first glance, the studio looked as if it had been burgled. Rags and brushes were strewn all over the floor, some still wet with paint. A jar of turps had been knocked over, the liquid seeping into the rag rug on the floor. Painted canvasses were everywhere, on every available surface, on the table, the lower shelves, or stacked against the backrest of the sofa. Even the cat's favourite place on the radiator shelf had been appropriated, and Lia noticed cat hairs sticking to the wet paint.

Aidan had clearly been here and left again not long ago. If the still wet paintings weren't enough evidence of that, a bottle of whisky and a half-empty glass confirmed it.

Lia went closer to inspect the paintings. He must have worked like a madman in order to produce five pictures in the time she'd slept. How long *had* she slept? A glance at the wall clock told her five hours. It was still only early evening.

As usual, Aidan's tonal painting style came into its own. Aside from his usual colours – grey, stone, granite, mocha, pewter and slate – he'd highlighted his motifs with spruce and moss, blue charcoal, dirty white, periwinkle, icy violet and rust. His brush strokes were less precise, more passionate perhaps, angrier, and the paintings were the most beautiful he'd ever done. They were also the most grotesque.

One set of pictures told the story in three parts of a naked man, from body perfect to a state of clinical dismemberment, like when a butcher separated a slaughtered animal into various sections of meat. His severed bones shone a dull white against the backdrop of a windswept shoreline, and his rust-coloured blood corroded the sand in stripes, like gangrene infecting a limb.

'Yikes,' she muttered.

The next wasn't as unpleasant as the first. A man hung from a rope by his neck, but instead of being dead he seemed alive in an uncanny way. The rope, thin and silvery, appeared to be swinging, not much, but enough to make a person blink, and on closer inspection a mischievous grin was transformed into a leer. Depending on how close the viewer stood, the painting seemed to move.

She didn't know what to make of them. Although fascinating in their own individual way, these paintings were also gruesome, horrible, fantastic. Oozing raw power, they were a far cry from the commissioned portrait he'd shown her once, and if the style hadn't been uniquely his, she'd have thought these were done by another artist.

The last painting was a pretty seascape, with underwater rocks and seaweed, and it was easy to overlook its significance among the stronger images, but when Lia studied it more closely, she thought she could see the hint of a face among the seaweed, cleverly painted so it blended in with the background. Although initially less disturbing, this one was worse than the others.

She drew back, shuddering. Aidan had painted an image of her very own nightmares as if he'd reached inside her mind and just plucked them out.

Only a genius could do that.

A gust of wind rattled the window frames. Jack growled, and, hugging herself, Lia left the studio. She checked the kitchen and the living room, with Jack trailing behind her. Then she checked the other rooms on the first floor, including the spare bedroom in case he'd decided to sleep in there instead of sharing his bed with her, but Aidan wasn't there. Nor was he in the bathroom.

At the end of the landing was another door, which turned out to be a set of stairs and not a cupboard as she'd first thought. The stairs led to a loft room, and she mounted the steps without worrying whether she was allowed up there or not. Jack followed her, tongue lolling, as if all this trotting up and down stairs was a new game she'd invented.

She wasn't prepared for the sight which greeted her. The walls were covered in army memorabilia – caps, photos, bayonets, medals and other paraphernalia. The bed was draped in a large Union Jack, and three smaller ones as well as an Iraqi flag had been tacked to one of the sloping walls with drawing pins. At the far end of the room, in the gable, hung a tattered cotton cloth which served as a makeshift curtain for a small, low window.

At first she thought it odd that he'd kept all this army stuff in his house when he clearly hated everything the military stood for. Then the answer struck her.

Aidan had built a shrine to his dead brother.

Did this mean he was as unhinged as his mother had hinted at? She knew him better than Lia, and now after having seen this, as well as those disturbing paintings, Lia had to agree that perhaps Eileen had a good reason to worry about him.

But what could Lia do? She could hardly tell him not to honour his dead brother. This was exactly what he accused his mother of not doing, after all. She thought of her own brother. Eddie lived in her heart, not honoured in any perverse manner, such as this strange and unsettling display.

Perhaps she'd bitten off more than she could chew with Aidan.

Jack was at the far end of the room with his paws on the narrow window ledge and his nose stuck to the glass. He snorted contemptuously when she called him and didn't move.

'What's up with you now?' Lia didn't have the patience for this, and she wanted to leave before Aidan found them up here.

Scooping Jack up in her arms, she cast a brief glance out of the window at the slowly falling snow. It mesmerised her. Perhaps it was its ability to cover everything up, all the dirt and ugliness in the world, leaving behind nothing but a cold, beautiful blanket. Or maybe the promise of a new start,

The outside light was on, turning a section of the white blanket into glistening diamonds. Lia frowned as the light revealed footprints between the barn to the right of the farmhouse and the house itself. Then she saw Aidan coming out of the barn and breathed a sigh of relief. So he hadn't abandoned her after all.

Spotting Aidan, Jack growled low in his throat and struggled to get down, but she kept a firm hold on him. 'It's Aidan, you silly dog,' she said. 'You like him.'

They met him in the hall. Recalling the paintings, Lia said nothing about her visit to the loft room. She hadn't touched anything, so there was no way he'd find out she'd been there. And Jack couldn't talk.

'You went outside,' she said instead.

'I have a couple of sick sheep that needed tending to. That's a farmer's lot for you.'

Sensing that he'd rather not elaborate, she accepted the explanation. Let him have his secrets, she thought.

It wasn't until much later, on the brink of sleep, when they lay entwined in his bed, that she had a peculiar feeling that there had been two sets of footprints in the snow.

CHAPTER 24

This time Lia wasn't in a hurry when they woke up. After Aidan had fed the animals, cat and dog included, they spent a languid morning in bed.

As she lay against his chest, he toyed with her hair. 'Sorry if I was acting strange yesterday. I always feel odd after I've seen my mother. And as you've noticed, I'm touchy about my scar.'

'That's an understatement and a half. You can be a bit of a Jekyll and Hyde character, can't you?' Lia grew serious. 'Want to tell me how it happened?'

Aidan drew in a deep breath. Did he? He wasn't sure. It brought back so much he wanted to forget.

As if she'd read his mind, she said, 'I find it helps to talk about things like that. I've seen it before with some of my patients. Doesn't seem so bad if you share it with someone.'

'I'm not sure where to begin.'

'The beginning?'

'Well, aren't you hilarious?'

Lia grinned. It seemed a good time to distract her with a kiss, but it didn't work. She looked at him expectantly, so he went on.

'I was on board a minehunter in the Gulf, deployed as a navy MCD – a Mine Clearance Diver. Do you know what that is?'

'Not offhand.'

In layman's terms, it's a bomb disposal diver. We dealt with any unexploded ordnance below the high water mark, and it requires a steady hand, let me tell you. The Iraq War itself was over by then, but we were part of an ongoing joint mine clearance exercise with the US Navy, making sure the Gulf was safe for shipping.

'Was it a terrorist bomb that gave you the scar?' Lia asked. 'You were lucky you didn't lose the leg completely.'

Aidan shook his head. 'Ironically, no. It was a stupid accident. When we weren't diving, the MCD team was just like any other member of the crew, with the same duties and so on. I'd been asked to run a message to a petty officer. Someone said he was in the galley, discussing supplies with the chef. He wasn't, as it happens, but I didn't know that then.

'It was stormy that day, with very high seas, and the ship was lying up against the wind. Whenever she lurched, you just had to grab on to something otherwise you'd find yourself flat on your face. Chef hadn't seen Chapman – that was the petty officer – and he was in a pretty foul mood anyway, shouting at his assistants. Don't really blame him, it must've been difficult running a kitchen under the circumstances.'

He stroked Lia's cheek. 'Memory is a fickle friend. Sometimes it's the most unimportant things that stick in your mind while the big stuff is a blur.'

She nestled further into the crook of his arm, but said nothing. This was his time for confessions, and he knew she understood what he meant about memories.

'I remember one of the assistants peeling this mountain of vegetables, and being surprised that he was able to do it in those conditions. Another was moving to close the safety lid on the deep fat fryer. They must have just taken something out of it. The ship wallows and the fryer spatters hot oil on to this guy's hand and arm. He yells blue murder and lets go of the lid, and as I'm nearest to him, I instinctively go to help him. I wasn't thinking about the fryer at all.'

Aidan closed his eyes and gritted his teeth as the memory flooded his brain, but he was determined to tell Lia the whole story.

'Just then, the ship pitches one way and rolls back the other, and it sets up a massive wave of boiling hot oil in the unfastened fryer. It shoots out and pours over my leg, and I . . . I don't remember much after that. I must've passed out.' Aidan shrugged. 'When I come to, I'm in a bed, battling through a haze of pain. I was told later that the navy surgeon had to remove a section of my trousers which had been burnt into my skin. Then I spent three weeks in hospital waiting for the skin grafts to heal, and a further three weeks when one of the grafts failed and became infected. Worst experience of my life at the time.'

Lia put a hand on his chest, and he squeezed it. It felt good to get it all out at last.

'Then what?' she asked.

'They discharged me. The scarring they couldn't do anything about, obviously. I mean, I had severe second-degree burns, as if I'd been splashed with napalm, they said. Even with plastic surgery, the scars would limit the elasticity of my skin, and that'd inhibit the normal movement of my leg. In other words, I'd walk with a limp.'

'You don't. Although perhaps you tend to favour one side of your body, now I think of it.'

'Only very slightly. It's improved over the years. It could've been better, maybe, but I never really had the nerve to face the knife again.'

'Does it still hurt?' Lia ran her soft fingers down over the scar, a healing touch.

'Sometimes. I get stabs of pain during certain weather conditions, kind of like as if someone's sandwiching my thigh bone between two nail beds and pushing down on it.'

'Ouch.'

He smiled, then grimaced. 'The worst thing was when a colleague of mine got blown up a week after my discharge. We both signed up for this, knew the risks, but he's the one who cops it. He was a friend.' He clenched his fist as the pain of that memory welled up inside him again.

'I should've been there,' he said hoarsely. 'I let them down.'

'No, you didn't,' Lia protested. 'Don't think like that, please. It's not like you asked to be in an accident. Come on, Aidan, you're an intelligent man. Shit happens, and it's just fate. There's nothing to say that you could've stopped him from being killed if you'd been there. It's not your fault.'

Aidan looked into her eyes and saw that Lia would always fight his corner, to her very last breath if necessary, if she perceived him to be in the right. He had to believe her words to be the truth and move on.

He could also tell from her fierceness that he'd be in serious trouble if she ever found him to be in the wrong . . .

Facing him, she rested her head on her elbow. 'I saw your paintings last night. They're . . . um, different.'

'Did they scare you?'

'A little bit.'

He cupped her chin and kissed her lightly. 'You don't have to be frightened of me.'

'I'm not frightened of you,' she said, 'only of what's in your head, because I don't completely understand it. I guess I do now though. Sort of.'

'There's nothing to understand. It was just some ideas I've been playing around with for a while but not committed to canvas before. I've been painting pretty pictures long enough. Yesterday I was spurred on to express another part of me.'

387

Lia shifted sideways and curled one of her long, long legs around him. 'What brought on the change?'

'You,' he replied simply as a lazy heat rose in him. 'You inspire me.'

'Not the landscape?'

'That too, but not as much. You always did, even when it was only the thought of you.' He put his hand on her hip and drew her closer, enjoying the way her blue eyes darkened with lust. 'Let's dive today. The weather is perfect.'

'It's Sunday,' she complained. 'What happened to the day of rest?'

Rolling on top of her, he spoke softly in her ear. 'We've rested long enough. It's time for some action.'

The sun was bright and defiant, and last night's snowfall glittered an icy blue. Despite the perfect conditions, when they parked at their usual spot and went through the buddy check, Lia experienced a mixture of reluctance and anticipation. She'd come a long way from the child who didn't want to go in the water, but didn't think it was entirely because of Aidan. It was as if she'd waited for this moment all her life, as if she was meant to be in the water. He'd just been the catalyst.

Still, she made sure she paid careful attention during the checking procedure, and was able to reach her secondary mouthpiece in case of emergencies.

As they headed into the surf, he indicated the Point in the distance, clearly visible today and dotted with elongated brown specks. 'The seals are out in force.'

Lia squinted against the sun's glare. 'Seals? Here? I thought they congregated at Blakeney Point.'

'They usually do, but that's not the only place. Did you ever go on a seal tour as a child?'

'No, we could never afford things like that.'

He regarded her sympathetically. 'You didn't have an easy childhood, did you?'

'Some parts were okay,' she replied with a shrug, shielding her eyes with her hand against the glare. 'Isn't it dangerous to dive near seals?'

'As long as you keep your distance, they won't harm you. They're mostly curious. I think they like to show off their swimming skills.'

Lia looked at him as if he'd gone mad.

'No, really,' he said and fastened his diving mask. 'They'll swim towards you like a bottle-nosed torpedo, then just as you think they're going to collide with you, they'll swerve up and around, showing you their belly, and swim back the way they came on their backs. I swear they're having a laugh when they do it.'

'I'm not entirely comfortable with that idea.'

Aidan grinned. 'It's the Great White you have to watch out for.'

'What?' She spun round. 'Sharks? As in *Jaws*?'

He nodded.

'Oh, Jesus! Now he tells me!'

389

She stopped in the swell, and he took her gloved hand. 'I won't lie to you. There have been sightings of the Great White around the coast of Britain, but it's very rare. They're warm-bodied creatures and don't like this cold water much because they haven't got the same layer of insulating fat as the seals. Don't worry, I'll never let you come to any harm. Besides, humans are far more dangerous than anything else.'

'Isn't that the truth?' she muttered and followed him into the water.

The dive went without any mishaps this time and no big fish scares, although she kept close beside Aidan while he collected various underwater plants and creatures to bring ashore.

He showed them to her when they came out of the water, fronds of green as well as slimy brown algae, leaves and branches of seaweed, some shells. One find in particular seemed to please him, and he held it out as they were walking back up the beach.

'What is *that*?' she asked and examined the ivory-white lump in his hand.

'It's a soft coral. An animal, actually, related to the sea anemone. It's quite common in Britain. You sometimes find them in rock pools as well. Here, d'you want to hold it?'

He put the white mass in her gloved hand. It was slightly curved, almost in the shape of a cup, with thinner protrusions growing from around the rim, and not as soft and squidgy as she'd expected from the way it looked.

'It looks like a small hand,' she said, handling the strange creature gingerly. 'Does it have a name?'

'The shape is a giveaway. It's called Dead Men's Fingers. Quite a memorable name for such a harmless little thing.'

The moment the words were out of his mouth, he recognised his mistake. Lia thrust the coral back at him with a barely suppressed shiver of revulsion.

'It's horrid,' she said. 'Please get rid of it.'

'Okay, if that's what you want.'

Being so used to the sea and the amazing treasures it contained, it hadn't occurred to him that she'd react like that. Lia had watched her brother drown, and he, Aidan, had just handed her something shaped like the hand of a drowning victim. He should have known that an experience like hers wasn't something a person ever recovered from fully. Retracing his steps, he put it back in the water.

How could he have been such a tosser?

Fortunately, she forgave him, and linked her arm with his as they walked down the footpath to the car. Mrs Larwood was waiting for them, dressed for the bracing air in a tweed skirt, Wellington boots, Barbour jacket, and a tartan headscarf.

'Been diving, have you?' she asked, stating the obvious with her particular brand of irony as biting as the air. 'Bit chilly for that, isn't it?'

Aidan merely nodded and opened the boot, which

he'd left unlocked. They put their diving gloves back in the bags, and Lia unzipped the jacket of her drysuit. Easing her hands out of the armholes of the jacket, she dried her upper body, pulled on her jumper, and reached for the thermos they had brought.

'Would you like some coffee?' she asked Mrs Larwood. Just as well, Aidan thought, because the old crone didn't seem like she was going to leave them alone.

'Thank you, my dear, don't mind if I do.' She took off her brown leather gloves and accepted a plastic mug of steaming black coffee.

Unperturbed by Mrs Larwood's presence, Aidan stripped to the waist and accepted a mug from Lia too. Sipping it, he caught the look of interest on Hazel Larwood's face as she stared unashamedly at his naked torso. She was eyeing him up, and he noticed from Lia's expression that she'd seen it too. She had trouble containing a smile.

'It's a fine young man you have there,' Mrs Larwood said to Lia. 'Almost as fine as my husband.'

Aidan nearly spluttered into his coffee. The old gossip mill was as ripe as ever, but this was fast even for Mrs Larwood. He looked away under the pretext of rearranging his gear in the boot, and could only imagine Lia's chagrin. If he met her eyes, there was a real danger he'd find himself rolling on the ground with laughter.

'Of course, my Howard was in the navy too,'

Mrs Larwood went on. 'The merchant navy, during the war. Worked on the convoys sailing from America to England. Carried all sorts of goods necessary for the war effort, they did. Torpedoed three times, was my Howard, twice in the Atlantic and once in the North Sea, and had to go in the boats. Cold like death itself, he told me.' Nodding for emphasis, she slurped her coffee. 'They called them wolf packs, the German submarines. Very appropriate name if you ask me. Sneaky.

'He wasn't the same when he returned. Suffered dreadfully from his nerves, poor thing. Technically he was a war invalid. Couldn't work, woke sometimes in the night screaming from his bad dreams. It was all I could do to calm him down.' She finished her coffee, handed the plastic mug back to Lia, and tightened the knot on her headscarf.

'Mmm, yes, horrible', said Aidan, who didn't want to hear any more.

Lia sent him an irritated look. 'It must have been difficult,' she said sympathetically.

Mrs Larwood nodded knowingly in Aidan's direction. 'Oh, it was. Seeing someone you love suffer like that, it does something to you. Makes you angry. Makes you want to take it out on the whole world. Mind you, nothing much has changed, has it. It's still happening today. Not that the army and navy do things the same way, but to all intents and purposes they're alike, aren't they? Two sides of the same coin.'

This rather one-sided conversation had taken a

turn in an uncomfortable direction, and Aidan scowled, his good mood gone. Lia appeared to have stopped listening and was gathering up the mugs. He hoped that Mrs Larwood would take the hint and leave them alone.

She did. Thanking them for the coffee and exchanging a few polite words, she continued up the bank towards the beach. At the top she stopped and looked back at them, but instead of waving, she gave a mocking salute. Aidan noticed Lia frown.

'What was that all about?' she asked when they'd changed and were driving back.

'Mm?'

'Well, her and her Howard. My grandmother and Mrs Larwood knew each other for a long time, but I've never heard that story before.'

'I have. She loves drawing parallels between her husband and the situation with my brother.'

'And are you as mad at the world as she suggests?'

'You know I am.'

It had started snowing gently, but it was small, insubstantial snowflakes which melted the moment they hit the windscreen. Aidan kept his eyes on the road, mulling over the exact same question Lia had posed. After a while, he said, 'Actually, I don't know, to be honest. People her age live by their own rules. She must be getting on. Maybe she's going senile. I think that makes you look back rather than forward.'

When they returned to the farmhouse, Aidan excused himself and headed for the studio, closing the door. Lia took this as a sign that he didn't want to be disturbed or wanted to be alone. Or both.

Cursing the old witch for ruining the rest of their day together with her remarks, Lia wrote him a note promising to pop in the next day, gathered her few belongings together, and rescued Jack from the cat. Again.

Driving home, she had a peculiar feeling Mrs Larwood had been trying to tell her something, but she hadn't a clue what it could be.

Since Brett had explained the history behind Aidan's navy salute, palm facing downwards and inwards to hide the dirt, she'd paid more attention to it and would recognise it again. The trouble was, Mrs Larwood's salute had seemed to be subtly different, although Lia couldn't put her finger on what that difference was, much less what it was supposed to mean.

What am I missing? she wondered.

She wasn't surprised to find DCI Sommersby and DS Cromer waiting for her. They were, after all, investigating a murder.

She parked her car, let an excited Jack out, and greeted them as politely as she could.

'We've verified your witness statements, Doctor Thompson,' said Sommersby, who now on his second visit reminded her of the Pilsbury Dough

Man, 'but I'm afraid we need another moment of your time. You remember the sergeant?'

'Of course.' Lizard Eyes, she almost called him out loud. A narrow escape, but his unwavering, watchful gaze could make anyone feel they'd broken the law, even if they hadn't. 'Come in.'

She ushered Jack indoors, and he headed straight for the kitchen and started whining. 'You don't mind if I feed my dog while we talk?'

'Be my guest.'

The officers followed her into the kitchen. Again she offered them tea which they declined, like last time. They clearly meant business, and a sliver of unease ran down her spine. Her throat had gone dry, and she made tea for herself. Holding a mug gave her hands something to do and stopped her fidgeting.

Sommersby watched as Jack gobbled his food as if his life depended on it while Cromer produced a notebook. 'He's a hungry little fellow, isn't he?'

'He's been held hostage half the day,' she said without thinking, then mentally kicked herself for having used the word 'hostage', which was bound to set alarm bells ringing inside the head of a police officer. She added quickly. 'By a vicious cat.'

'Poor thing.' The DCI tutted sympathetically to Jack, who cocked his ears. Then he looked back at Lia. 'Your cat?'

'No, my, er, boyfriend's.' She tried the word out for size and found that it was the closest one for describing their relationship. He wasn't her fiancé

396

or husband, but at the same time he was more than a friend. Lover might do, but that implied an illicit affair.

Lizard Eyes looked up from his black notebook. 'And what's the name of your boyfriend?'

Lia blushed. This was a big thing. She was about to step from the world of things unsaid, to where labels were used. 'Aidan Morrell. He lives a few miles from here.'

The sergeant and the DCI exchanged a brief look. 'Doctor Thompson,' said the sergeant, changing the subject, 'your grandmother was cremated, I believe.'

'Yes.'

'Was there any particular reason for this?'

Knowing what he was really asking, Lia looked him squarely in the eye. 'Doctor Campbell and I have already had this discussion. It's what she would have wanted.'

'Very well,' he said. 'And do you by any chance know how to make ricin?'

Lia suppressed another shiver. 'Why ask me? I've told you I wasn't even here when my grandmother died.'

'Just answer the question, please.'

'Yes, I know how to prepare it for ingestion. At least, in the form of castor beans. I asked Doctor Campbell, and apparently it isn't hard to do.'

'When did you speak to Doctor Campbell?' asked the sergeant.

'After I'd spoken to you. After New Year.'

'Can he verify that?'

'I'm sure he can. In fact, I thought he'd have been on the phone to you lot right after speaking to me, but maybe he didn't think it was important. I could've got that information from any number of websites, of course, but there's no internet access in this house.' She looked from the sergeant to the DCI. Jack had put his head in Sommersby's lap, and the inspector was patting him.

Bloody dog, she thought vehemently. 'I was curious,' she said. 'I wanted to know how easy it was.'

The DCI smiled his Pilsbury smile. 'Your mother works in a school laboratory, doesn't she?'

Nodding, Lia looked at her hands and curled them around her mug to stop them from shaking.

'Isn't it reasonable to assume that your mother knows how to extract this substance too?'

'I suppose so.'

The DCI stopped patting Jack and leaned forward with his arms resting on the kitchen table in front of him. His voice was kind when he asked, 'Did you suspect your mother of having a hand in your grandmother's death?'

Lia felt her hand tremble slightly and lifted the mug to drink from it, then gave up the pretence. 'The thought occurred to me, but I'm now confident that she didn't.'

'Doctor Thompson,' said the sergeant and flipped back the pages of his notebook, deliberately making a noise, or so it seemed to Lia. 'How exactly did your brother die? Was it an accident or was he helped?'

'My brother?' Lia was shocked that they'd got this far in their investigation. After all, it was something that had happened a very long time ago. How on earth had they found out? Had Connie told them? 'He was helped,' she said in a dead voice. Tears ran down her cheeks, but she gave up hiding them. They'd been shut away inside for too long. 'By my grandmother. I saw it.'

They waited for her to compose herself, and then without a word Lizard Eyes pulled a packet of tissues out of his pocket and handed it to her. She accepted it, and for a brief moment had an insane urge to laugh. Gone were all her theories of Good Cop, Bad Cop. She couldn't work these two out. They didn't fit the mould, but the mould was probably only for the benefit of television audiences anyway. A myth. Dutifully she wiped her eyes and blew her nose.

'Did your mother know what your grandmother did?' asked the DCI.

Lia shook her head. 'Of course not,' she lied. 'I never told her. She knew what my grandmother thought of Eddie, though. A freak of nature. Not a real human being. Should've been put down at birth, et cetera. She made that quite clear.' Lia shrugged. 'Not that I remember myself, I was far too young to understand any of it.'

'Do you think your mother capable of poisoning your grandmother?'

It took all the willpower she possessed to look the DCI in the face without flinching. 'No.'

The knowing smile which almost didn't cross his face told her he wasn't fooled. Let them think what they like, she thought. She wouldn't say anything which might land her mother in trouble, and they couldn't prove that Connie knew what her grandmother had done. Only Lia had been there that day.

They would have to look elsewhere for their evidence.

Sensing perhaps that she'd nothing more to tell them, they rose and thanked her. Lizard Eyes' hand was warm and not clammy and cold as she'd expected. He didn't really have lizard eyes either, now she looked at him more closely, just sharp and slightly off-centre as if to give him a wider field of vision.

'Thank you, Doctor Thompson,' said the DCI. 'If you think of anything else, please do give us a call.'

'Of course.' Lia took the business card he handed her. 'There is one thing. It's probably nothing, but I think there may be a prowler or burglar in the area. A few weeks ago I nearly ran a stranger over in the road. Didn't really see his face, but he was wearing some old camouflage gear or something. And I think someone might have been in my house a couple of times.'

'Right, we'll look into it,' Sommersby said, but Lia could tell that he didn't really take her seriously. Perhaps he thought it was a diversionary tactic on her part, but either way, he wasn't going to do anything any time soon.

He was far more interested in pinning her grand-mother's murder on her mother.

CHAPTER 25

Aidan spent an uncomfortable evening reflecting on the encounter with Mrs Larwood. It seemed too much of a coincidence for her to have been there, by his habitual parking spot, at the exact moment they returned to the car, and he came to the conclusion that his initial suspicions were right. The old bat had been waiting for them.

Or perhaps just for him.

Hazel Larwood had had something on her mind for a while now, and he knew what it was, so why didn't she just turn up at the farm and spit it out? At least it would give him a chance to justify his actions. He'd known her all his life – she'd be far more receptive to his explanations than Lia's grandmother had been.

Instead she fixed on a time when he was likely to be with Lia, confusing Lia with her oblique references and himself with her impenetrable motivations. It was almost as if she wanted to show him that she had the power to turn Lia against him if she chose to.

Afterwards he'd brooded in his studio for an hour,

cleaning brushes, and emerged later to discover Lia's note. He couldn't blame her for leaving him to be antisocial on his own, but still he was disappointed to find her gone.

Staring out on to the slowly melting snow with the cat purring in his arms, he felt the net closing in around him. If only he had a little more time, time to see the task he had set himself through to its conclusion. To make them take notice.

Then they could do with him what they wanted.

He waited until after dark, then slung on a jacket and headed for the smaller barn. The second of the two sheep suffering from acidosis had recovered and was back in the main barn with the rest of the herd, so the smaller building echoed eerily. The door creaked on its hinges, and the strip lighting came on with an audible plink. Even his footsteps boomed.

Pulling the door shut behind him, he shivered. At the far end of the space he pulled a tarpaulin partly aside, uncovering a carpenter's bench. On the bench lay a small black plastic box the size of a computer mouse with an On/Off toggle at the centre and two alligator clips attached to one side. The box wasn't quite shut, so he glimpsed the different coloured wires nestling inside. Next to it on the bench was a battery pack containing four AA batteries and an electrical resistivity Nichrome wire ending in a jack designed to plug into the black box.

Aidan removed four batteries from his jacket pocket and swapped them for the ones in the battery pack.

'That should do the trick,' he muttered.

All the while, he tried not to look at the wires. Red, green, white, they taunted him with memories of the past that threatened to swamp him. He took a deep breath and gritted his teeth, pushing his hands into his pockets to stop them from picking up a small cutting tool from a nearby tool box. The conditioning ran deep – check carefully, weigh the options, cut, retreat.

But not this time.

Pulling the tarpaulin back into place, he walked away, closing the barn door. He checked that the tricky latch was firmly in place, then fetched his car keys and mobile, and drove to the beach. After he'd made the necessary phone call, he stood back against the car, arms crossed, and waited.

As always the shadows grew denser and more watchful when he sensed her nearness, and he caught the soft tread of Hazel Larwood's sensible shoes approaching in the dark. The time had come to have it out between them.

Clearing his throat, he said, 'We need to talk.'

Feeling mellow from the time spent with Aidan yesterday, Lia decided to extend an olive branch to Susannah, but it was Zoe who opened the door.

'Mum's out, but you can come in and wait for her if you like. I don't think she'll be long.'

Lia was unsure whether this was the right thing to do, but Zoe hadn't waited for an answer and was already walking back into the house, so it seemed easier to follow.

'You once said you'd look at my drawings,' Zoe said abruptly, almost defiantly, as if she was challenging Lia to keep her word. 'Shall I get them now?'

'Yes, sure, good idea.' Lia had forgotten their conversation, blotted out by everything else during the last few weeks.

Zoe disappeared, but came back quickly with something under her arm.

'These are my newest ones.'

She opened an A3 sized portfolio with individual plastic pockets and let Lia browse her illustrations. They were mainly in ink and pencil, although there were a number of watercolours among them too, all naïve and charming on the one hand but also stunningly professional.

The absurdly long models had pointed feet in the shape of a 'V', and most of them rested a long wrist on non-existent hips while the other arm hung down at the side, following the contours of the model's body. The drawings were faceless and the few hands that were visible tapered into a point with no definable end.

'I'm not very good at doing hands,' said Zoe as if she thought Lia was going to comment on this deficiency.

Lia smiled. 'I don't suppose that matters, since it's the clothes that are important.' Flicking from sketch to sketch she thought how ironic it was that she who'd never cared much about art, let alone thought about it, had already been presented with the works of two very different artists after only having been here, at the back of beyond, for a short while. 'I think they're fantastic. You should show them to Aidan.'

'You think so?'

'You have real talent. *I* can see that, and I'm not even an artist. But he is.' Lia studied one of the captions. *Cashmere, leather with mercerised cotton edging.* 'But tell me, how do you know which materials go together?'

'Oh, that's dead easy.' Zoe opened the box she'd brought with her, a medium-sized plastic tool box, the sort a carpenter or joiner might use to store the smaller of his tools. At the bottom of the box, below a pull-out shelf stuffed to the brim with art materials, lay a stack of fabric swatches and a folded cardboard template with the cut-out contours of a woman in a dress.

Zoe took it out of the box and placed two fabric swatches underneath the template in order to simulate a two-piece outfit.

'Like this you get a feel for the fabrics that go with each other, and you do it, like, to avoid putting stuff together where one kind of material is much thicker and heavier than the other.'

She replaced the swatches with two different ones, a fake fur sample and a gauzy chiffon. 'See, this won't work because the fur at the top is far too heavy compared with the thin material below.' She shifted them around, so the outfit demonstrated became a chiffon dress with a narrow fur trim. 'But this here works.'

Lia looked at the fabric tester in fascination, then tried a couple of combinations herself. 'This is brilliant. What an excellent idea.'

'It wasn't mine, really. It was Mum's. She made me one of these when I was smaller.'

Lia experienced a pang of jealousy. Had Connie ever done as much for her? Yes, she had, Lia was being unfair. Her mother had meticulously cut out paper dolls from board, and Lia used to have a whole collection of them in a shoebox. She wondered what had happened to them and decided to ask her mum about it sometime. She had to stop being selective with her memories from her childhood; Connie had been a good mother.

With a frown, Zoe was studying the fabric combinations Lia had been making. 'Stop right there,' she said and took the swatches to one side. 'These are really cool. I've got to write this down before I forget.'

She retrieved a girlie pink notebook from her jeans jacket and pulled out a pen, which had been pushed through the spiral binding to keep it in place. A small roll of silver foil fell out of her pocket as she did so and rolled across the kitchen floor.

Jack, who had come in with Lia and who'd been slumbering nearby, jumped to his feet and skidded across the floor to investigate before Zoe could stop him. He grabbed the foil packet between his teeth and began to chew, then spat it out with a disgusted look on his face and looked around for some water to drink.

Lia picked up the teeth-marked packet, which had been chewed sufficiently for the foil to come apart. Inside was a mud-coloured substance the size of a rabbit pellet. She sniffed it, then arched an eyebrow at Zoe.

'Is this what I think it is?'

Zoe's eyes were wary, withdrawn almost. 'Are you going to tell Mum?'

Her question put Lia on the spot. She ought to, really, but who as a teenager hadn't done something they'd rather their parents didn't hear about?

Lia hadn't lived in Norfolk for nearly twenty years, but it had struck her when she returned that she'd entered a time warp. Back then there hadn't been much for teenagers to do, except get drunk and smoke dope. Clearly nothing had changed, except perhaps the availability of the various substances. What worried her was that Zoe, who seemed almost bordering on innocent compared to kids the same age, was mixing with dope heads. Drugs were big business, and dealers guarded their territory fiercely.

On the other hand, this was Norfolk and not Philadelphia, and Zoe's stash was probably grown by some local, peace-loving hippie. Patronising her would likely destroy their rapport and the trust she'd sensed earlier between them, and where, then, would Zoe turn if she got in trouble? She'd already said she didn't confide much in her mother.

Handing back the foil packet, Lia said, 'Not unless you want me to. I don't think it's my place to tell tales. I expect you know what you're doing. But I wouldn't mind knowing where you got it from.'

The colour on Zoe's face went from a greenish pale to the prickly pink of relief. 'Promise you won't tell?' she whispered.

'I've already said I won't.'

Zoe hesitated as if she thought the walls had ears. 'Aidan gave it to me.'

Lia raised her eyebrows, pretending to be only mildly surprised, but she was a little shocked. 'I see. Well, Aidan goes his own way and has his own reasons for doing things. Has he talked to you about the potential dangers and consequences?'

Zoe shook her head, and Lia cursed him silently. I'm going to have a word with him, she thought.

'We did the drugs talk at school,' said Zoe. 'I know all about it.'

'Right.'

'You don't believe me.' Zoe's voice was belligerent, spoiling for a fight.

Lia didn't give her one. She shrugged. 'I expect you know more about it that I did at your age. The trouble is, cannabis is a lot stronger now than it was back then. Some of the home-grown stuff's really potent.' And Aidan knows that, she thought and fumed quietly. 'So have you talked to anyone else about it?'

'Well, there's this really cool teacher who's more like a friend to some of us. She never moralises the way some of the other teachers do. As long as we do our work, she doesn't come down like a tonne of bricks about other stuff.'

'She sounds nice.'

'Yeah. We've been talking a lot, about drugs and stuff, and she said something about having an addictive personality, like, if you have that sort of personality you're more likely to become addicted.' She looked up and down at Lia as if sizing her up. 'You're a doctor, I guess you know about such things. Is it true?'

'It sounds like a reasonable view.' Lia's tone was measured. Who was this woman Zoe referred to, with this kind of insight? Did she have first-hand knowledge of drugs?

She shuddered at the thought of her friend's fifteen-year-old daughter picking up the tricks of the trade from a habitual drug user, but then she realised she was letting her imagination run away with her. Anyone employed as a teacher must be clean. Perhaps she'd worked with drugs-related issues; that sounded much more likely.

It always came to this in the end: if you were a doctor people expected you to have all the answers. She wished she didn't have to reply to this question. It seemed too much depended on it.

'But is it true?' persisted Zoe.

'Possibly,' she began in the hope that Zoe wouldn't perceive her insecurities. 'It's not really my area of expertise – I patch people up who've been hurt, I don't deal with what they've inhaled. If you want a scientific explanation, I think it's to do with a neuro-transmitter called dopamine, which is released by certain substances. This leads to a feeling of pleasure. It's only a problem if a person becomes dependent. They're not all dangerous; some of them are mild, like coffee and chocolate, but the principle is the same, though, of course, the intensity is different.'

Zoe sniggered.

'What's so funny?'

'My friend Mel is a chocoholic.'

'Well, there you have it. What's happening in your friend's brain is a craving for a substance which will give her pleasure.'

'Cool!' said Zoe. 'She's gonna love that.'

'Where the really addictive personality comes in,' Lia continued, warming to the subject and surprised at her own ability to recall stuff from way back at medical school, 'is when a person has less dopamine in his brain than the rest of us—'

'Then he'll, like, need more of whatever he's taking to feel good, right?'

'Something like that, yes.'

'That's really neat.'

Not exactly the words I'd have chosen, thought Lia. 'Some even say that our natural dopamine levels are genetically determined.'

'So, people are, like, born to be drug addicts.'

'You could say that,' she said, 'but I personally think it's more complicated. Why do people take drugs in the first place? Are they unhappy? Bored? Is it peer pressure? Are drugs easy to get hold of

411

where they live? Pure science doesn't explain everything. People aren't lab rats.'

'So you don't agree with it?'

Lia laughed. 'Why do I get this feeling you're trying to put me on the spot?'

'I'm not! Honestly. I'm interested, that's all.'

'I'm not sure,' said Lia. 'As I said, research isn't one of my strengths, but I don't like the idea that we do things only because of genetics. We're responsible for our own actions.'

Zoe went silent and began to put her fabric swatches away. Then she said, 'I wish I could have this kind of conversation with Mum.'

'I'm sure you could if you tried. Talk to her some time.'

It was false, and she knew it. Who was she to tell a young person to talk to her mum when it was the last thing she'd ever have done? Her suggestion was based on what she supposed was the right thing to say in the circumstances, not on personal experience. Zoe didn't entirely buy it either, she could tell, because she pulled a face.

'She's always busy. I don't really want to anyway, because I know she's going to be all horrified and parent-ey.' She shrugged. 'You don't understand. It's, like, I just can't reach her, like she blanks me out, and then sometimes she just tries too hard, and it feels really weird. Sort of puts me off, you know.'

Youth was wasted on the young, they said. It seemed unfair that insight and confidence came when a person had less need of it. Lia felt like

412

reaching out to Zoe to share what little wisdom she herself had. As it was, she was still learning.

'You might not believe me, but I do understand,' she said.

When Susannah hadn't returned by five o'clock, Lia went home and slumped in front of the TV without watching anything in particular. It had felt good having that conversation with Zoe, and she was proud of herself for not lecturing the girl, no matter how tempting it was.

At the same time she was aware that Susannah would see it as Lia encroaching on her territory, as it were, if she ever found out about it. Whether Aidan's relationship with Zoe made Lia a sort of step-girlfriend-mum or whatever, Susannah would resent her interference, she was sure of it.

Everything had been a great deal easier with Brett. She may have felt like an outsider in his life, but here she found herself caught up in a web of complex relations, of secrets and lies. The more she struggled to extricate herself, the more entangled she became. In fact, she was well and truly caught.

To stop herself from brooding further, she settled on a TV mystery movie on Channel 5, but found it difficult to follow the plot, and was strangely relieved when the phone rang. It was Susannah.

'Have you seen Zoe?'

'I saw her earlier.' Lia checked her watch. 'I dropped by, looking for you, and we chatted for a bit. I left about an hour ago.'

'She's gone out and hasn't come back.'

Lia had a fleeting vision of Zoe's bicycle and broken body in a ditch followed by thoughts of white slave traders, then logic kicked in. 'Have you tried her friends?'

'Yes, all the ones I know of. She's not there.'

'I'm sure there's a perfectly good explanation.'

'That's easy for you to say,' Susannah snapped. 'You're not a mother, you don't know what it feels like to worry about your kids.'

'Oh, please, not that old chestnut again. I may not have children myself, but that doesn't mean I can't empathise.' It wasn't Lia's own childless state which hurt, but to be thought lacking in understanding really rankled. However, she let it pass. 'She can't have been gone for more than an hour. It's not that late, and she knows the area like the back of her hand. What could possibly happen?'

'I don't know.' Susannah sighed despairingly. 'It's just that I can't reach her at the moment. She's shutting me out.'

'Interestingly, she said the same thing about you.'

'Really? She told you that?'

Lia took a steadying breath and skirted around the thin ice in front of her. 'Sometimes it's easier to talk to a person who's on the outside. But I think she'd prefer it if the two of you could talk.'

Susannah was silent for a moment, then she emitted a low moan. Lia heard the receiver clatter to the floor.

'Are you okay?' she asked when Susannah picked it up again.

'Just the baby getting a little too active.'

'Listen, perhaps you ought to—'

'I'm fine,' said Susannah. 'I just want Zoe to come home. I don't feel comfortable with all these soldiers on the road all the time. It's like we're at war. I want life to go back to the way it was.'

Which includes me not being here, thought Lia. The notion wasn't as hurtful as she'd thought it would be, but perhaps she'd acquired some armour against Susannah's innuendos. A little devil popped into her head. 'Maybe she's gone to see Aidan.'

'Aidan?' Susannah sounded puzzled, which wasn't the reaction Lia had expected. 'What on earth for?'

'I suggested she show her drawings to him. He's a much better judge than I am. I can call and find out if she's there.'

'I have his number, thanks.' Susannah's voice was terse. Then she delivered her bombshell. 'I suppose you've heard the news.'

'What news?'

'About Hazel Larwood.'

'Mrs Larwood?' Lia repeated. 'I saw her yesterday. Is she all right?'

There was a long pause. 'No, she's not all right. They found her on the beach this morning. Drowned, apparently. And *she* an expert swimmer for her age.'

CHAPTER 26

Aidan saw the Land Rover drive into the farmyard and realised trouble had come earlier than he'd anticipated. Squaring his shoulders, he opened the front door just as two military police officers emerged from the vehicle. Monkeys, he thought, settling on one of the milder slang terms used in the military. It surprised him that they were in uniform. Normally SIB officers swanned about in civvies, but they were probably trying to put the fear of God into the locals. He couldn't imagine it having the desired effect – Norfolk was military country after all – it was more likely to cause irritation as it did with him.

He tried not to act defensively, but his body language, arms crossed and jaw locked tight, probably spoke for itself. Even after all this time, his loathing for the army surged through him with unexpected force.

'Morning, officers,' he said as they approached the house. 'What can I do for you?'

The warrant officer in charge, a senior NCO, introduced them as Sergeant Major O'Reilly and

Corporal Jones of the Royal Military Police Special Investigations Branch. Nodding non-committally, Aidan didn't give his own name. They had it already, he figured.

'We're investigating the recent bomb threats in the area,' said O'Reilly. 'May we come in?'

Aidan remained in the doorway and made no move to invite them inside even though he was letting all the heat out of the house standing like this.

O'Reilly ignored his rudeness and carried on. 'We understand you've spoken out quite forcefully against the military in recent months.'

'What of it? Last I heard we had freedom of speech in this country.'

'Freedom of speech, yes, but our actions are subject to the law. You were a naval bomb disposal expert some years ago. You know about bomb-making. Perhaps you've done something you shouldn't have.'

Aidan shrugged.

The corporal, who hadn't said anything up until now but had instead been casting his eyes over his surroundings, turned around. 'It's a nice set-up you have here, sir. Perhaps you wouldn't mind us taking a look around.'

'Do you have a search warrant?'

'We don't, but if you'd only co-operate—'

'In that case, I do mind. Come back with a warrant if you must, but until then, the answer is no.' They would too, he didn't doubt it, but they'd find nothing. 'Now, unless you want to talk to me about something else, I'd appreciate it if you could let me get on.'

'Perhaps you'd like to tell us about your brother, former Lance Corporal Gerald Morrell,' said O'Reilly.

'My brother?' Aidan blinked. 'My brother is dead.'

'We know that, but presumably you had common interests? Were you close? Enjoyed doing the same things.'

Aidan's mouth went dry, and his forehead suddenly prickled with sweat. He clenched his fists and dug his fingernails into his palms, as anger rose in him. 'I don't think I like what you're insinuating. I loved my brother, yes, and we were as close as most people are with their siblings. Nothing wrong with that. Now, if you have any specific accusations, why don't you come right out with them? Or even better, come back with some evidence that I've done something wrong, and I'll make sure my solicitor is present.'

'With all due respect, sir,' said O'Reilly, 'it would save us a lot of time if you'd only answer our questions truthfully now . . .'

'Yes, well, perhaps saving you time isn't very high on my agenda this morning. I'm rather busy myself. Goodbye.'

Dismissing them, he turned away and would have closed the door if it hadn't been for the figure who jogged into the yard at precisely that moment.

Talk about being saved by the bell . . .

Lia.

Her black ponytail bounced from side to side, her blue eyes sparkled, her cheeks were rosy-red from her run. She was wearing a pair of lycra leggings, which showed off her long legs and strong thighs, and her white top was stretched tight across her chest, which wasn't by any means large, but still consisted of two well-proportioned handfuls, firm and round like halved grapefruits. Friction had caused her nipples to stand out through the fabric of the sensible sports bra she always wore underneath when running, and she'd slung a dark hoodie over her shoulders, leaving her arms bare despite the freezing temperatures.

And this is a woman who's always cold, Aidan mused, as he battled with other baser thoughts. There was no way around it, though. Lia was striding towards them oozing self-confidence, independence, and . . . . sex.

Both MPs stared, and Corporal Jones was positively ogling her. Aidan wanted to plant his fist in the man's gob to wipe the leer off his face, but he controlled himself.

'Hi,' she said. 'What's going on?'

'Nothing. These men were just leaving.'

'Ma'am.' The corporal touched his red cap with an appraising look, and the officers returned to their car. O'Reilly sent Aidan a hard stare.

'What did they want?' Lia asked as they watched them driving out of the yard.

'They wanted to talk to me about my brother.'

Lia sent him a sideways look. 'Not Mrs Larwood?'

'Why would they want to talk about her?'

'You *have* heard, haven't you?'

He sighed. 'I have. It's awful. They say she got caught by the tide.'

'You believe that?'

'Of course I believe that. What are you trying to say?'

She shook her head. 'Nothing. So, what did you tell them about your brother?'

'Not much. I can't tell them anything they couldn't learn from their own records anyway.' Aidan closed the door to the house and turned towards the greenhouses.

'Don't do this Jekyll and Hyde shit to me again,' she protested and followed him. 'So what are they doing here? It's to do with the bomb scares, isn't it?'

'Very likely. They're searching the area.' He pushed open the sliding door to the nearest of the greenhouses. 'All the deserted barns and dilapidated buildings you find around here. It's the perfect place for hiding things.'

'But why you?'

He glanced at her over his shoulder. 'Because of my media campaign against the MoD, I suppose, and because they know I worked with explosives in the navy, although I'm sure I'm not the only one they're questioning.'

She followed him into the greenhouse, pushing

the sliding door firmly to behind her. Inside it was hot and dry like on an African plain, and although he was used to it, whenever he came through the door, it reminded him of his first visit to the cactus house in the Botanical Gardens. The only difference was that the plants which grew here enjoyed the benefit of the dark, fertile soil of Norfolk. He uncoiled the hose and began watering the flower beds.

He sensed that she wanted to talk to him about something important, because she didn't normally turn up on his doorstep in her running clothes, and although he'd been happy to see her, he wasn't really in the mood. The visit from the MPs had unsettled him more than he'd thought possible. The last thing he needed right now was their involvement.

Lia strode after him through the row of plants, not letting him get off that easily. 'What do you grow in here?' she asked.

'Utility plants. Well, my mother does. I just help her look after them.'

Several species of plants were housed in this particular greenhouse and in the others as well, some of which were small, others almost as tall as Lia. Aidan smiled to himself as she felt her way through the long aisles, crushing a leaf here and there to inhale the aroma, a curious habit of hers which he found rather endearing.

'A lot of our plants are medicinal,' he explained, 'for the pharmaceutical industry. We've got sesame and aloe vera, that sort of thing.' He stopped in front of a tree reaching almost to his shoulder, and densely covered with shiny oval and elliptical leaves, about five inches long. 'And this here is camphor,' he said and held up a small label attached to the stem, bearing the inscription *Cinnamomum Camphora.*

She walked behind him, quietly as if deep in thought, as he moved into the next greenhouse and uncoiled another hose. In front of a row of shrubs, he saw her pick up one of the fruits, twirling it in her hand before dropping it in the pocket of her hoodie. As long as she was preoccupied, so much the better. There was one part of the greenhouse he wanted to avoid her seeing.

He cursed to himself as she swung down the aisle he'd been avoiding and snatched off a leaf before storming back to him.

Bugger.

'I want to talk to you about this,' she snapped.

Aidan looked at the characteristic leaf shape in her hand and raised a sarcastic eyebrow. 'I hardly have to tell you what it is, do I?'

'No, you bloody don't. I know a cannabis plant when I see one. So do most teenagers in this country. What I want to know is – why are you supplying Zoe with drugs?'

'I'm not supplying her with drugs. She was begging and begging, so I gave her a bit of home-grown weed, that's all. It's a damn sight safer than having her roam the streets of Norwich in order to score.'

'And you don't think that's a teensy-weensy bit irresponsible? Domestic is usually very strong.'

'Not the small amount I gave her. I cut it with something.'

'You cut it?' Lia's voice was shrill. 'God! I don't know how many times I've seen a young person die because they took a drug which was cut with something dangerous. I can't *believe* what I'm hearing, and this from you, who I thought—'

'Relax. What Zoe has is mostly dried oregano.'

She gawped at him. 'Zoe's smoking oregano?'

'Not on its own. It contains enough cannabis to give her a buzz. If I hadn't put that in, she'd have sussed it out and gone somewhere else. I wanted to avoid that.' Aidan felt the laughter bubbling in his throat at her stupefied expression.

'And what about dependency? When she comes asking for more? What will you do then?'

'I'll cross that bridge when I come to it. Someone needs to have a serious talk with her one day. It might as well be me.'

There was something else on her mind, he could tell. He saw her swallowing hard as she debated with herself, before blurting out, 'Because you're her father.'

He put the hose down, yanked off his gardening gloves, then crossed the distance between them and planted a kiss on her lips before she could escape. She wriggled in protest and tried to push him away, but he held her tight.

'Is that what you thought? All this time you

suspected me of being her father, of getting Susannah pregnant, and then dumping her? What sort of person do you think I am? All you had to do was ask.'

'I'm asking you now.'

He shook his head. 'Zoe is not my daughter, but she *is* my niece.'

'Your niece?'

It all fell into place for her, and he sunned himself in the look of relief which spread across her features.

'Yes,' he said. 'I like to know she's all right, that Susannah is all right.'

'But Susannah isn't,' said Lia. 'She doesn't want Zoe to know who her father is. I understand your feelings for your brother, but if she's against it, that's her choice, not yours, isn't it? At the same time, secrets can be so destructive.'

'And I have always respected that, but it's too late now. Zoe found a photo recently, of Gerald, and although we're very much alike, she knew immediately it wasn't me. Since the cat was out of the bag, the best I could do for her was tell her what a wonderful brother he was. I think that was all she needed to hear.' Hands on her hips, he pulled her close. 'Did you really think that badly of me?'

'It didn't fit with what I knew of you, but, yes, I did. Sorry.'

'Apology accepted. Were you jealous?'

'Very.'

He kissed her again, felt her quivering with passion and need. This was his Lia, nothing could come between them, least of all a smarmy git like that corporal earlier.

When they drew apart, he said, 'House. Bed. Now.'

'You're the boss.'

They got no further than the living room, however. Braced against the door, they fumbled with each other's clothes, pulling and yanking, tugging, unzipping. He pulled her T-shirt over her head, tossed her bra aside and cupped her breast, bringing his tongue to the rounded fullness in his hand. Lia undid his belt.

'I'm all sweaty,' she moaned self-consciously, when she'd freed the part of him she was after.

'It doesn't matter.' He eased down her knickers and without preamble brought his finger inside her, enjoying the way she gasped from shock and pleasure.

'I want you,' she whimpered when he teased her to near-climax.

He took her on the sofa, and before he lost himself in her completely, he made sure she forgot everything except the here and now.

Lia showered while Aidan cooked brunch, and later when he was going into the village on an errand, he dropped her off at the house. As they drove past the shop, Lia saw Susannah in the window and waved, but Susannah didn't wave back.

'Don't forget this afternoon,' he said when she

climbed out of his car still wearing her lycra leggings, although Aidan had lent her a clean top, which hung loosely on her underneath her hoodie.

'What's happening this afternoon?'

He rolled his eyes. 'You don't remember? Our first group dive? Hel-lo.'

'Sorry, but that had gone completely out of my head,' she said although it was far more likely she'd suppressed it from sheer terror because she wasn't sure she was ready to dive with anyone other than Aidan yet. 'Are you sure that's safe?'

'Don't be a spoilsport. You were fine last time, just the two of us. Trust me, it'll be fun.'

She spent the rest of the morning wandering around the house like a caged animal. She wasn't looking forward to the dive. It was one thing to go alone with Aidan and expose to him the fears she still felt and probably always would feel when it came to the water. Exposing herself, and her insecurities, to a whole group was a totally different matter.

Jack seemed to sense her mood, for he sat on the hearthrug in front of the cold fireplace and watched her toing and froing with his alert little eyes. Or maybe he was just sulking because she hadn't taken him with her on her run this morning.

She sat down beside him and stroked his head.

'What do you think I should do? Shall I go with them, even though I'm scared, or can I be a chicken and cry off?'

At the word 'chicken' Jack snorted and nudged

her with his nose. She grinned and gave him a hug, but he kept nudging her and sticking his nose near the pocket of her hoodie. Digging her hand in the pocket, she fished out the strange fruit she'd found in the greenhouse and looked at it more closely. It had soft prickles like an unripe lychee or a chestnut as she'd thought earlier, and it was quite pretty in an unremarkable sort of way. However, she still didn't know what it was.

She tossed it in the air in order to catch it, but Jack was faster and caught it in his mouth with a low growl. Shrugging, she rose. The dog could play with it if he liked. She wandered into the kitchen and put the kettle on, not because she wanted tea, but it was something to do. Anything to take her mind off the dive later.

Jack trotted after her and placed the chestnut-like fruit by her feet.

'You want to play catch, is that it?' She picked it up and tossed it again, but instead of jumping high to catch his prize, Jack waited for the fruit to fall to the floor, then he picked it up and placed it by her feet.

Lia didn't know much about dogs, and this particular one was a mystery to her half the time, but she'd always thought they'd be all eagerness if they wanted to play catch, barking and racing around with their tongues out, and generally being a nuisance. Jack seemed almost solemn by comparison.

She repeated the exercise, and Jack behaved in

exactly the same way. A shiver ran down her spine at his odd behaviour, almost as if he was trying to tell her something. She picked up the spiky fruit and examined it, then took it back to the living room where she kept a small collection of Ivy's gardening books and books on horticulture which hadn't gone to charity. Perhaps one of these tomes could tell her what this fruit really was.

But there was no reference in any of the books to a fruit matching the description. Mind you, most of the plants in Aidan's greenhouse were exotics, not native to Britain, and Ivy had favoured traditional garden plants, so maybe it wasn't surprising that she couldn't find it. She'd have to go in to Wells if she wanted to look it up on the internet. She could have just asked Aidan, but she wanted a distraction and always liked a challenge. It was bugging her now, and besides, it would take her mind off the dive. She might as well go the library, where she could look for an image that matched it on a larger screen, rather than using her smartphone. And if she couldn't find it online, they'd have books she could look it up in, too.

Quickly she changed into town clothes, bundled Jack in the car because she couldn't bear to leave him alone again, and entertained the vain hope that the library would allow well-behaved dogs to enter. Otherwise he'd have to wait outside, but she knew now that he was trained well enough to do what he was told. Some of the time, anyway.

She parked her car in the car park near the quay,

and walked down Staithe Street towards the public library. She was in luck. They weren't due to close for lunch for another hour, but Jack had to wait by the door. He whined as she tied his lead to a handle, and she took a bag of dried dog treats out of her coat pocket and put a handful down on the ground in front of him.

'There's more if you behave yourself.'

He seemed to understand and settled down.

Inside the library she headed straight for the line of computers, but soon had to give up because she didn't know the name of the plant she was looking for. Instead she sought out the Horticultural section and brought a number of promising-looking volumes back to a desk, but after an hour's search, and after several trips to check on Jack, she still hadn't found an answer. Frustrated, she slammed the last book shut.

The librarian, who'd been glaring at her suspiciously the whole time – it seemed that even in Wells strangers looked like strangers – sidled up to her desk and tapped her wristwatch.

'I'm sorry but we're closing at one today,' she said in a librarian's whisper, though there was no one else in the reference section to disturb.

Lia nodded. 'Are these all the books you have on plants?'

The librarian glanced at the pile of books teetering precariously on the desk. 'Yes, I'm afraid so. I saw you using the computer earlier. Did you not find what you were looking for?'

Sighing, Lia rose. 'The thing is, I don't *know* what I'm looking for.' It didn't really matter anyway what this fruit was, she told herself. It had been something to do, that was all, something to take her mind off things and give her a sense of purpose.

The librarian looked at the spiky pod Lia had left lying next to the books. 'Oh, you're trying to find out what that is. I know, let me think . . . oh, yes, my mother has a plant like that in her conservatory. It's quite beautiful. I can't think of the name, though, but you're supposed to open the seed pod.'

She pulled a dinky Swiss Army knife out of her pocket, which was attached by a chain to a belt loop of her trousers. An odd thing for a librarian to be carrying in her pocket, Lia thought, but this was Norfolk. Expect the unexpected.

'Here, like this.' The librarian made a cut through the centre of the fruit and twisted the two halves apart. Inside was a chunky bean, mottled and shiny like a rare beetle. 'I remember now. It's from a castor plant. They use the beans for making oils. Just don't eat them.' She ran her finger across her throat and made a strangled sound.

Lia found herself outside the library in a daze, head swimming, and there was a buzzing noise in her ears. Gulping for air like a fish, she leaned against the cold wall for support.

Aidan was growing castor plants in his greenhouse. Ivy had died from suspected ricin poisoning.

430

Aidan loved spicy food, Ivy might have eaten a curry a couple of days before she died. It didn't take a genius to work out that a connection had been staring Lia in the face the whole time. Technically it was possible that Aidan had served her grandmother food poisoned with ricin. If this was true, it explained the 'how' but not the 'why'.

Why would Aidan kill Lia's grandmother? And what about herself, now that she had worked out what had happened?

No. Aidan wasn't a killer. She refused to believe it. There must be another explanation. A completely logical explanation, which would push this whole situation firmly back into the realm of fantasy where it belonged. Something to laugh about one day with their children.

Now where did that come from? Lia shut her eyes to squeeze out the intrusive images. She had to stay focused, and right now that focus should be on the restaurant which might have provided the curry.

She discovered The Goa easily enough, tucked away in a little alleyway off the Quay. Unsure how to play it, she pushed open the door and was assailed by the most wonderful, exotic and spicy smells. Suddenly ravenous, she asked for a table.

'Sorry, no dogs,' the waiter said in heavily accented English, and Jack was again relegated to sitting just inside the door. Sighing, he lay down and stared at Lia with a doleful expression, but cheered up when she handed him a chewy stick.

She ordered both a chicken and a vegetable dish, with basmati rice and naan bread, as well as lime pickles and poppadoms for starters. This detective lark is hungry work, she thought wryly, then checked herself. This wasn't a joke. The toxin in the castor bean was seven times more deadly than cobra venom. And her grandmother had died a very painful death.

Whoever gave Ivy the poison – and she still refused to believe Aidan was guilty of it – would be a very cold-hearted and ruthless individual. Or simply mad.

When settling the bill and after praising the food, she saw an opportunity to ask a few questions. 'Do you do much takeaway trade?'

The proprietor, a small, rotund man with jet black hair and pock marks pitting his cheeks, took his time before answering. 'The majority of our customers enjoy coming to our restaurant to eat. Not much need for Indian takeaway in a town with fish and chips.' He cleared her plate and brushed down the tablecloth with practised elegance.

'So you'd be able to remember if someone bought a takeaway not so long ago, say, er . . .' she rattled off a date two days prior to the day Ivy was found dead. 'It would probably have been vegetarian food.'

'Why do you want to know?' he asked her, suddenly suspicious. 'Are you VAT? Environmental Inspector? Police?'

'No, nothing like that,' she said, but his question gave her an idea. 'But I am investigating a crime, of a sort. Someone attacked my grandmother, and we think it might be the same person who took a takeaway curry to her house.'

Mention of family and grandmothers seemed to win him over.

'We keep records,' he said. 'I will check for you, yes.'

She thanked him and watched him disappear through the double swing doors to the kitchen. Seconds later he was back at her table with a well-thumbed order book in his hand, held together by an elastic band.

'Let me see . . .' He licked his thumb and rifled through the book. 'Yes, here it is. It was a Wednesday. Only one takeaway order. Sag aloo, bhajee, vegetable biryani, chapatis, plain rice, and lamb vindaloo.'

'Lamb?' Lia asked. 'Are you sure? What about the day before, or the day after?'

He shook his head and said almost apologetically, 'No takeaway orders.'

'Is there a name?'

He sent her a searching look, but didn't question her further. 'Yes,' he said and tightened the elastic band around the order book again with a snap. 'The name was Morrell.'

CHAPTER 27

Heading back to the village, Lia was in two minds what to do. She still had the business card DCI Sommersby had given her. All she had to do was call. She thought of the way Ivy had died, on the kitchen floor with an open telephone directory by her bloodied head. There seemed to be a certain parallel between Ivy's situation then and Lia's own now, except Lia wasn't a phone call away from death. Or was she? She cast an involuntary glance over her shoulder, then told herself not to be so silly.

It was clear now that Ivy hadn't ordered a takeaway herself. Aidan had brought the curry, a lamb vindaloo, one of the hottest curries around – on the British Isles anyway – and perfect for disguising the bitter taste of the castor beans used to kill her grandmother. The right thing to do would be to call the police and tell them what she'd discovered. Wasn't it?

Perhaps sensing her inner turmoil, Jack barked sharply as Lia took the road towards the farm instead of the lane leading to her house. She had to speak to him. It was probably foolish, if he was a murderer – in fact, it was downright crazy – but not knowing why was even worse. In books and TV crime dramas it always came down to motive, and Aidan had no motive she could think of. She had to give him the benefit of the doubt. She just couldn't make herself believe he'd be that cold-blooded.

The farm was deserted when she got there, with only the cat slinking across the yard. Determined to get his own back against his arch enemy, Jack flew out of the car before Lia could stop him. In a flurry of fur and teeth the two animals wriggled under a sheet of corrugated steel, which had come loose at one corner, and into the barn where Aidan kept his sick sheep.

'Oh, shit,' she muttered under her breath. Following the sounds of mayhem, she opened the door and slipped inside, hoping to extricate Jack before Aidan came and caught them in the barn.

Snarling and barking like a mad thing, Jack stood with his front paws on the first rung of the ladder leading up to what appeared to be the hay loft. Lia couldn't see the cat, but guessed that he'd hightailed it up there to get away from Jack and was hiding in the hay. There were no sheep in here as she'd expected, but maybe they'd recovered from their illness.

Lia tried to scoop Jack up, but he wriggled out of her arms and ran to the far end of the barn, barking.

'Come here, you! We've had enough cat chasing

for now,' she said and grabbed him again, this time more firmly.

Turning to head back to the door, she almost tripped over a large blue plastic tarpaulin. As she struggled to maintain her balance, Jack slipped out of her arms. He dropped to the ground, ironically almost catlike on his feet, and immediately disappeared under the tarpaulin.

Lia's patience was wearing thin. She yanked the tarpaulin away to retrieve her dog and stopped short, her insides turning to stone in an instant.

On a workbench lay an electronic device which looked for all the world like a timed detonator, and beside the workbench, stacked against the back wall, was about half a tonne of fertiliser. Staring at her find she swallowed hard several times as the last piece of the puzzle fell into place.

She could no longer give Aidan the benefit of the doubt or dither in the face of all the obvious clues which had been thrown in her path. She'd studiously ignored them due to wilful blindness, because she'd fancied herself in love.

This she couldn't ignore, though.

Apart from feeding plants, ammonium nitrate fertiliser could also be used for making bombs. All you needed to do was to pour a bit of diesel into each bag of fertiliser, attach a detonating device, place the makeshift bomb where you wanted it, and set the timer. Lia had once read that the Oklahoma bomb had been fertiliser-based. Making one was as easy as pie, even a child could do it.

And Aidan was, of course, an expert. Who better to make a bomb than someone trained to defuse them?

Forcing her now shaking limbs to function, Lia scooped up Jack and ran out of the barn, slamming the door behind her.

Exceeding the speed limit as she drove home, Lia cursed herself over and over for being so stupid. It was so obvious now she thought about it. The un-detonated bombs found on military premises, Aidan's implacable hatred of anything to do with the army. Mrs Larwood had provided a subtle hint, but Lia had been completely blind.

What was it Brett had said about Aidan's painting?

Up close you don't see it.

She couldn't remember the exact words, but it was something to that effect, and it summed the situation up neatly. She'd been too obsessed with Aidan to see him for what he really was, to notice how he was playing with her.

Ivy must have found out, that's why Aidan had silenced her. Her grandmother was always sticking her nose in other people's business, and she'd paid dearly, with her life, as had Mrs Larwood.

Screeching to a halt outside the house, she banged her fists against the steering wheel in impotent rage. 'You bastard!'

Maybe Ivy deserved to die for what she'd done to Eddie, but not the way she had, alone and suffering excruciating pains. And maybe Lia could be excused for falling in love, for seeking someone to fill the void inside her, left behind by Eddie's death.

But the betrayal . . . Aidan had poisoned her grandmother and then calmly gone about distracting Lia, conning his way into her affections as well as her knickers with that lost cause act of his. How could he? How could *she*?

'You bastard!' she shouted again as shame burned her face.

She'd been the perfect foil, she could see that now, unwittingly throwing the army's investigators off the scent with her innocent presence in Aidan's life. All the times he'd been gentle, had helped her overcome her fear of the water and her insecurities and doubts, he'd had an ulterior motive: to hide behind her facade of normality.

Except he was far from normal. Angry tears stung her eyes from just thinking about it.

And yet, and yet . . .

It was mid-afternoon when Aidan drove back into the yard. He'd tried reaching Lia on her mobile several times earlier, wanting to remind her of their arrangements for later, but she'd either switched it off or was out of range.

It was only after he'd finished unloading his supermarket shopping bags that he noticed the door to the smaller barn was gaping wide open.

Odd, he thought. He was certain he'd secured

the latch last time he went in there, and anyone else connected to the farm, including his mother, knew that it needed an extra push to stay in place. The door couldn't have blown open, either, because there was no wind.

He entered the barn, full of misgivings. Had the SIB officers been back with a warrant and searched the place without bothering to present him with it? No, they couldn't have. The officers had only been here this morning; it took longer than that to obtain one.

He'd thought of moving the device earlier, but Lia had been with him then, and he hadn't wanted to risk her finding out.

At first glance nothing appeared to have been disturbed, but on closer inspection he noticed that the tarpaulin he'd covered the workbench with was slightly askew. A feeling of dread settled in his stomach. If the officers hadn't disturbed the tarpaulin, who had? Pulling it aside, he had his answer. In the dust under the workbench was a set of doggy footprints, small like those of a Jack Russell. Lia must have been in here, having returned later while he was out. The question was, when?

Since the police weren't waiting for him, it either meant that she hadn't told anyone yet, or that she had, but only recently, and they could be swooping down on him any minute now.

His next actions would boil down to what he knew of her. She was loyal, no doubt about that. He only had to consider the way she stuck by

Susannah even though he could imagine Susannah giving her all kinds of crap. She had a strong sense of what was right and wrong, but her morals weren't dictated by the law. She was attracted to him, cared about him, possibly even understood what he was trying to do, and why.

But was that enough for her to keep her mouth shut?

He decided he couldn't risk it. Scooping up the detonator and any traces of its manufacture, he closed and locked the barn, and went back to the house. He headed straight for the scullery where he stored the diving gear and slipped it inside a pocket of his BCD. Later it would disappear in the sea, and no one would be able to prove anything. This time around. In future he'd have to be more careful.

In the studio he pulled down the folder from the top shelf with all the drawings of Lia, poured himself a large whisky, and brought the glass to his lips. Then he stopped. There was only one way to solve this problem, and it required a clear head.

Stroking her face in one of the drawings, he traced the curve of her cheek, her nose, her blue eyes, colourless in the pencil drawing, and felt a tightness in his chest.

'I wish to God you hadn't found that,' he murmured.

The car which drove into the yard an hour later, however, wasn't an armed response unit, breaking down his door and throwing him to the ground, but John's people carrier, which they'd agreed to travel in together for the beach. Aidan picked up his gear as well as Lia's which he'd left ready in the hall.

'I'll sit at the back with Bella,' said Rachel, 'because you need to stash your gear at the front. No room in the boot.' She scrambled in, leaving Aidan to fit in two air cylinders at the foot well of the car. It was a squeeze with his legs, but he managed it.

'I have a bone to pick with you,' he said to John as John swung into the lane leading to the main road.

'Why? What have I done now?'

'You took my best drysuit.'

John frowned. 'Eh? What are you talking about?'

'You borrowed one of mine, remember? Yours was too tight, you said.'

'Oh, that.' John turned into the main road and headed in the direction of the village. 'I didn't in the end, as it happens. Turned out I got a decent Christmas bonus this year, so I was able to buy a new one. Latest model. Really dapper.' He went on describing his new suit, but Aidan wasn't listening.

If John didn't take it, where was it? Had he mislaid it? Left it behind after a dive by mistake?

Rachel interrupted his train of thought. 'Is Lia coming? Or is she chickening out?'

'I wouldn't let her,' Aidan replied and tightened

441

his fingers around his diver's bag. 'But you'd better talk to her when we get there. We're not on the best of terms at the moment.'

'Lovers' tiff?' asked Finn.

'Something like that.'

Turning away, Aidan stared straight ahead, at the road. No, she wasn't wriggling out of it.

Not this time.

For a while Lia dithered; then she called DCI Sommersby, but was connected to a voicemail. She left a message explaining that she'd uncovered an important fact – she couldn't quite bring herself to say the words out loud to an impersonal answering service, face-to-face seemed more appropriate, somehow – and asked him to contact her as soon as possible. Then she secured the house one more time, just to be on the safe side, and spent another hour pacing the floor.

When the doorbell rang, she almost jumped out of her skin and ran out to open the door. But it wasn't the inspector. It was Aidan and his motley diving crew, already kitted out for diving.

'Oh, no, I'd completely forgotten about the dive,' she said. 'I'm sorry, but I've got such a headache and—'

It was no use. Rachel shook her head. 'You're not getting out of this. No way. Aidan's told us what fantastic progress you've made. Come on, you'll love it.' She and Anthony almost manhandled Lia out of the door, shutting Jack inside.

She caught Aidan's eye when Rachel unceremoniously bundled her in next to Bella on the back seat and squeezed in after her. In the next row were Peter, Finn and Anthony. Aidan sat at the front with John.

'All right,' he said with a bright smile, and it seemed almost inconceivable that such a good-natured expression could hide such malice.

Lia mumbled something unintelligible and thought about the situation logically. Aidan didn't know what she'd learned at the library, wasn't aware she'd been inside the barn, and therefore didn't know that she'd discovered what he was up to. One more day wouldn't make any difference, as long as she pretended everything was normal.

And besides, she wasn't alone with him. There were six other people in addition to herself and Aidan. She reckoned she'd be quite safe.

She began to relax a little, even listened half-heartedly to Rachel's incessant chatter. In reality she had no direct proof of Aidan's involvement in the bombings and the two murders. Her conclusions were based only on guesswork and assumptions, plus her own paranoia that nothing was what it seemed. Rachel and Bella struck her as being completely normal. So did the blokes. No hidden agendas there.

She envied the easy friendship between the divers. It must be nice to feel part of a group like that, to know that each and every one of them would do everything in their power to keep the others safe. She stared out of the window and wished she belonged.

Would she ever have that? She had thought so with Aidan, but that had been blown out of the water. Almost literally.

The pale sun was low in the sky, casting a pink glow over the surf as they drew nearer to the beach. There had been talks of a night dive, but because Lia and some of the others in the group weren't qualified for that, Aidan and John had vetoed the suggestion. It made her feel slightly safer for some reason; complete darkness held far too many terrors at the moment.

The others waited for her to get suited up, and then the group set off for the softly whispering surf.

'Here, walk with us.' Lia found herself sandwiched between Rachel and Anthony. Several times Aidan tried to get close enough to talk to her, but each time she found a pretext to speak to one of the others, and he gave up.

She wished she'd never found the evidence against him. Only hours ago it had been a scene of simple domesticity between them, and now . . . What had happened to them? She was tempted to just confront him, because with people on all sides of her she'd be quite safe.

An innate reluctance to air their dirty laundry in public stopped her. And steeling herself, she honed in on what really lay behind it all. The force which had destroyed their tentative relationship, had reached out its tentacles to poison and choke out everything wonderful between them, was Ivy, pure and simple. If *she* hadn't drowned Eddie in the bath, Lia would have been a different person today, fundamentally happier. If *she* hadn't stuck her nose in everything or just turned a blind eye, she wouldn't have got in the way of Aidan's efforts to achieve justice on behalf of his brother, even if the manner in which he did it was wrong.

The Ivy Factor was all-powerful, and now Lia was going to dive in the sea, which she still feared, with a man who possibly loved her and certainly filled her with terror.

As bad situations went, it couldn't get any worse.

The divers lined up in the water. 'Okay, we go in two by two,' Aidan ordered. 'Bella, you can partner Lia, all right?'

Bella nodded, and they went through the usual buddy checks. When Aidan was satisfied the whole group had completed them down to the last detail, he gave the signal for them to dive one pair at a time. Lia and Bella were the last to go under the gently lapping waves.

The last thing Lia saw before she sank beneath the surface was the faint outline of the Point and the recognisable torpedo shapes of the seals, dark wraiths against the lighter coloured sandbank.

Then she entered a different world, a fantastical other dimension, and forgot all about her troubles. Suddenly none of that mattered. It was as if she was washed clean of all the cares that had weighted down her shoulders for weeks now. Carefree as the seals, her mind was filled with the wonder of the underwater world, and the sensation of weightlessness only added to her sense of freedom.

Bringing up the rear with her diving partner only three yards away from her on the left, she followed the rest of the group along one of Aidan's typical diving routes, a triangular path which used a number of orientation points for navigation. Despite the clear afternoon, visibility was low in the inky water, and she could just about make out the fins of the two divers in front of her.

Out of the corner of her eyes she caught a slight movement to her right. Her heart made a painful somersault, and for a moment she lost the ability to stay in the horizontal position and trod water wildly, but it was only an inquisitive seal which had come to investigate. A little laugh escaped her, and a cloud of shiny bubbles discharged from her mask and drifted upwards.

Realising that the others were ahead of her and almost out of sight, she fought to regain the horizontal stance and pushed forward to catch up with Bella.

Something clamped down on her ankle, and the sheer shock of it made her lose her mouthpiece. Instinctively she kicked out and freed herself.

Aidan had double-backed on the group and stolen up behind her. A vain hope that he'd come to help sprang up inside her, but this was immediately shattered when he grabbed her lead belt this time.

Lia felt as if her lungs were about to explode. She kicked and writhed against Aidan's superior strength, but managed to unhook the octopus from her jacket.

Invigorated by the precious air, a renewed strength flowed through her, and she struck him in the chest with as much force as she could muster. His hold loosened, and even through the distortion of the mask she saw the surprise in his face. Their eyes met, and she almost fainted with shock.

His gaze was cold and brutal, almost dead, but the person behind the mask wasn't Aidan. He looked like Aidan, was built like Aidan with the same broad shoulders and slim hips, but it wasn't him.

It was Gerald.

CHAPTER 28

Her fright must have registered with him. He advanced on her again, and a grim smile played behind the mask as he produced a lethal-looking knife from his belt. A long, curved blade swung towards Lia, but she was prepared and pushed out of the way. Even as she fought, she recognised the knife.

Her grandfather's kukri. She hadn't even noticed that it had disappeared.

He came at her again, this time with the blade angled to slice her air hose. Frantically she dived to the side, kicking out with her fins. The blade caught on her air cylinder with a hideous grinding metallic noise and fell from his hand, then disappeared into the depths.

A sudden kick forward, and he caught her around the middle, the impact sending bubbles rising from her regulator. Guessing that he wanted to yank her mouthpiece out of her mouth, she covered it with both her hands to stop him, then had no means of defending herself.

But she mistook his intentions. He wasn't going for her air supply, he was using his superior body mass to push her further into the deep, deeper than she'd ever been. Petrified in his grip, with her hands over her precious mouthpiece, her heart drumming in her chest and blood rushing in her ears as the atmospheric pressure grew around them, she saw only the gaping jaws of darkness opening up below.

An image of Aidan's jewel-green eyes contorted with pain entered her panic-stricken mind. She pictured him never knowing why she died, how he'd live the rest of his life with this on his conscience. She couldn't let that happen.

Gerald's grip loosened on her when he realised she wasn't fighting back, and she brought her elbow back, colliding with his mask. Bubbles exploded from his air supply, and with a muffled sound he let go of her. She pushed away from him. The temptation to swim to the surface, to fresh air, was strong, but not only would she risk getting the bends, she'd also be defenceless against him coming from below.

Daring a glance over her shoulder to see if he was going after her, she saw that he hadn't moved at all, but instead the sparse light showed him suspended in the water a little above her, his arms floating away from his body, as if he was suddenly tired. She hesitated, recalling that Gerald, whom she'd thought was dead, was ill, very ill. Sick in spirit and body. How else had she managed to overpower him?

Without rationalising it, she reached out to him. Her gesture seemed to pull him out of a trance, and before she could prevent it, he kicked hard for the surface.

No!

Frantic bubbles blew out from Lia's mask.

Too fast.

He's sick, he needs help, was her only thought. She rose as quickly as she could without risking getting the bends, in step with even the smallest bubbles breaking out of her regulator.

She found him floating on the surface, his lifeless face behind the mask staring up at a kaleidoscopic sunset, his air hoses dangling impotently. Grabbing the strap of his jacket, she inflated his BCD and began to swim towards the shore. In the water he weighed nothing, but as she got closer to the beach, his body became heavier and heavier, and she fell to her knees in the swell.

'Help!' she yelled at the top of her voice. 'Help!'

Aidan completed his usual triangular circuit and stopped at the point on the route where they'd set off, by a large rock covered in red algae. He waited for Finn, who was his diving partner today, to catch up with him. When he could just about make out Rachel and Anthony behind him, hand in hand as always, he signalled 'up'. Finn okayed back, and they began the slow ascent from their depth of about twelve metres.

At the surface he checked his air supply. There was plenty left, and they could have stayed under longer, but they'd agreed to cut the dive short for Lia's sake. It was still very new to her. He'd been in two minds whether to partner her himself or pair her with Bella. In contrast to Rachel and Anthony, he and John both felt as instructors that divers needed to be independent in the water regardless of their relationship on land, and of the other divers Bella was by far the most qualified.

You had to be when you taught sixth-formers, Aidan thought wryly.

Finn appeared beside him and removed his mouthpiece. 'Did you see that shoal of herrings?'

'I did. There was a blue shark as well.'

'Damn! I missed that. Must have been behind them when I passed.'

The next team emerged and Finn and Aidan began to swim towards the shallows, leisurely to make sure each pair had the team following them in their sights.

'Next time, eh?' said Aidan.

'You bet.'

Suddenly he heard a voice, and he swung his head in the direction it had come from. Ahead of them, where the waves were breaking, he could make out a dark shape. Pushing up his mask, he saw that it was Lia, tugging at something heavy in the water. As always the sight of her warmed him, but the feeling was quickly replaced by a feeling of dread. She should have been behind him, not in front of him. And what was she dragging? A body, another diver by the looks of it.

'Fuck!' he shouted. 'Bella!'

But it wasn't Bella Lia was holding. Hurrying closer, he recognised the suit as the one he'd mislaid.

So who was in it?

Then he knew, with the certainty of somebody progressing from one horror to the next. The body was that of his brother.

Dark figures came rushing forward, seven of them. Lia's heart gave a lurch when she saw Aidan's face among them.

'He's got the bends!' she cried. 'Call an ambulance!'

Strong hands relieved her of the dead weight, while others half-dragged, half-lifted her out of the water. John and Finn pulled Gerald away from the water's edge, as Aidan fell to his knees and began mouth-to-mouth resuscitation. Rachel ran as fast as her long legs could carry her up towards the dunes and the car beyond.

Exhausted, Lia sank down on to the sand, yanking off her mask and unstrapping her BCD. Her heart was pounding wildly, hot blood was rushing to her ice-cold cheeks and threatening to get the better of her, but even in her near-fainting state she could tell that Aidan, very obviously in shock, was doing it all wrong, even though normally he could probably do it in his sleep.

She crawled across the sand to him. 'Here, let me do it.'

'But he's my brother!' His voice broke halfway through his violent protest.

'That's why you should let me do it.'

She pushed him aside and felt for Gerald's pulse.

Her fingers shook, from terror and cold, as she placed them against his clammy skin, and she had to mentally pinch herself in order to concentrate.

This is what you trained for, she thought. *So just get on with it.*

Finding no pulse, she gently tilted Gerald's head back with his chin up, pinched his nostrils closed, and blew air in through his mouth until his chest rose, then followed with a second breath. When she still didn't find a pulse, she placed her overlapping hands on the centre of his sternum and began chest compressions. *One, two, three, four, five.* Count to thirty. Breathe in air. Press and count again. More air, feel for pulse.

No pulse.

She tried again. *One, two, three, four, five.* Up to thirty. One more time she breathed air into his mouth, then fumbled to feel his pulse. Was it there?

Nothing.

'Come on, breathe. Don't give up.' She pumped Gerald's chest again, breathed in more air, pumped the chest. Repeated the procedure. Checked again. One more time. Repeat, check. Repeat, check. And again, until she nearly collapsed with fatigue.

With a sudden clarity she knew if there was no pulse this time, that would be the end. She had no more strength left in her. With trembling fingers she sought out the vein on Gerald's white neck, her own heart thumping so loudly she thought the whole world would be able to hear it.

There, beneath the pale skin was the unmistakable

feel of blood pumping round in his body. With immense relief she sank down on the sand beside him. Whatever Gerald had done, whatever crimes he'd committed, she couldn't bear the thought of somehow being culpable in his death. Not even if he'd involved Aidan in all sorts of bad stuff, which she realised must be true because Aidan had shown no surprise that his brother was alive.

Saving his life was the only thing that mattered. Slowly she became aware of the others, gathered round in a circle, mute witnesses to her actions.

'Will he be okay?' Anthony asked, his voice a hoarse whisper.

'I don't know, but he's breathing.' In her exhausted state she couldn't remember the symptoms of the bends and whether or not the damage was reversible.

'You were great, you did all you could.' Bella sat down and put her arm around her. Lia clung to her, never wanting to let go.

'I'm so sorry I lost sight of you,' Bella whispered. 'I came back for you, but you weren't there so I thought you must be in front of me. I'm really, really sorry.'

This is where I'm supposed to cry, Lia thought, but the tears didn't come. The last few months of living in fear of something she didn't understand and the emotional impact of her recovered memories had left her stunned. The relief that no one had died at her hand wasn't enough to make it go away. It would, in time, but right now she was simply exhausted.

They sat like this until the ambulance arrived. On the cold sand Gerald lay wrapped in towels, while Aidan stroked his hair, and the only sound was Gerald's rasping breath and the wet sand which creaked whenever one of them moved. No one said anything because there wasn't anything to say, and Lia could only guess at everyone's thoughts about the sudden resurrection of a dead brother.

When the paramedics finally arrived, Aidan went with his brother. John and the others followed, running almost every single red light in Norwich, chasing the ambulance, and eventually left Lia to stay with Aidan as he settled down to a long wait.

Neither of them had the energy to say a lot, but holding hands provided the assurance they both needed, and for the time being it was enough.

Aidan knew it was bad news the moment the duty doctor appeared in the waiting room. Fresh-faced, he was wearing a white coat over green scrubs, and seemed far too young to be the harbinger of death.

Aidan rose, clutching Lia's hand. She hadn't said much about what happened in the water, only that Gerald had attacked her, and she'd defended herself. Aidan didn't blame her for the outcome, instead his relief that she was unharmed had left him at a loss for words. All he could do was squeeze her hand from time to time, grateful that she was alive and that she hadn't left him to hold his vigil alone, after what his brother had tried to do to her.

'Are you the next of kin?' the doctor asked.

Aidan swallowed, and he felt Lia stiffen. This was probably the first time she was on the receiving end of a doctor's news instead of giving it. 'I'm his brother,' he said.

'Well, he's alive, but the prognosis isn't good. Your brother has suffered potential brain damage from the diver's paralysis, but we also found a large amount of barbiturates in his blood stream. It's too early to tell if he'll make it.'

'May I see him?'

'He'll be transferred to Intensive Care in a short while.' The doctor smiled in a way which was meant to be encouraging. 'I'm sorry I can't give you better news.'

The doctor left them, and Aidan felt Lia slide her arm around him. She didn't say anything, and he was grateful for that – he couldn't have borne it if she'd tried to reassure him with hollow promises.

When they were allowed in the ICU, Aidan sat down next to Gerald's bed, and Lia pulled up another chair beside him. Again, their hands sought each other.

'So, that's what happened to my sleeping tablets,' she mumbled.

'Had you lost them?'

'Not lost. Someone took them. It must've been Gerald, at the same time he took the kukri. I just didn't know it then.'

'Do you think he wanted to die?' Aidan glanced at his brother. Tubes were coming out of his arms and nose, monitoring devices attached to his chest. Aidan searched inside himself for the grief he was supposed to be feeling in the circumstances, but found that he'd used up most of it the first time he'd thought Gerald dead. Now he felt only numb.

'I think so,' she replied. 'No one takes half a bottle of sleeping pills before diving unless they want to cause themselves serious harm.'

'He nearly took you with him. Why did you save him?'

The question seemed to surprise her, and she looked up at him. He realised then that it was a stupid question. Lia would save a child-killer if put in that situation. It was what she did.

'It was pity, I think,' she said after a while. 'I couldn't bear not to. Although I suppose I'm lucky to be alive because he could easily have overpowered me.' She paused, frowning, as if she was trying to remember a half-forgotten detail. 'In the water, when I hit him with my elbow, it was like he just gave up, like he'd been defeated too many times. I can see now that it was probably the drugs kicking in, but that look . . . he seemed so sad.'

She put her head on his shoulder. 'Why didn't you tell me?'

'I tried, a couple of times, but it just never seemed to be the right time.'

'You told me he was dead.'

'He was, for a while. In fact, I was convinced of

it. I hadn't seen him in years, no word, no sign that he was alive. Then last summer he turned up out of the blue. God only knows what roads he'd travelled. He was nothing but flesh and bones, filthy, rambling, utterly incoherent. Anyway, I took him in. There was no question about it. He's my brother, and there was so much I wanted to say to him. Not all of it pretty . . .'

He paused and rubbed his eyes while he composed himself. 'But first, I needed to sort him out. I wanted to tell my mother, but he wouldn't hear of it. He wanted to lie low, keep it quiet, because "they" were after him, and he mustn't endanger his "mission".'

'They? Which mission?'

Aidan shrugged. 'Your guess is as good as mine. He'd lost the plot. Completely. I tried to persuade him to see a professional, but whenever I did, he'd pull this disappearing act. He'd be gone for days, running around in some old combat gear he had, and each time he came back, we were back to square one.'

'The tramp,' Lia said.

'Probably. I thought maybe I could help him. If I played along for a while and then slowly tried to bring him back, it might work. Except I hadn't reckoned with his plans. They involved bombs, lots of them. Every single army base in Norfolk, with a roaring crescendo at the buildings of the MoD.'

'That's why you had fertiliser, and that . . . thing in your barn.'

'Mmm, I realised you'd been in there. I wanted to explain, but I couldn't get close to you. We do use fertiliser for other things, you know,' he added. 'And before you say anything, yes, I know it was a dangerous game to play, but I made sure I sabotaged every single one of his bombs. They were never going to explode.'

'How?'

'I switched the batteries for the detonator with dead ones. Not only that, but his "gelignite" which I'd got him, was just plasticine. He didn't know the difference, and he was too lost in his own world to work it out. They never reported this in the news, but any bomb disposal team would've known the bomb was a dud.'

'But you harboured a criminal,' she insisted. 'You let him run loose in the neighbourhood where he was spotted, not by one nosy old lady, but two. Despite your resemblance, and despite their age, they were nobody's fool. Now they're both dead, and I don't think Mrs Larwood's death was an accident.'

'I know, and I can't tell you how awful that makes me feel.'

Lia looked at their entwined hands. 'You know, at the beach before the dive I felt Ivy had got between us somehow, that maybe she always had. I realise it was an overreaction, but I'd still like to know what happened between you and my grandmother. Did you poison her?'

Taken aback, he said, 'But I thought you said

459

the police must've made a mistake. That she died of a heart attack.'

'She did. She died from a heart attack which was very likely brought on by ricin poisoning, disguised in a hot curry. You bought a lamb vindaloo at The Goa. And you grow castor oil plants in your greenhouse.'

'What? Come on, those are for industrial use. The oil is used in paints and varnishes, and stuff like that. Soap even. My mother's been growing the plants for years. Shit, I never imagined . . .' He raked his fingers through his hair. 'Look, I didn't put anything in your grandmother's food. I have no idea how it got there. You have to believe me.'

'Relax, I do, but obviously Gerald wasn't as crazy as you thought. He knew what they could do.'

Aidan glanced at the unconscious form in the hospital bed. Gerald had been on at him for weeks about Hazel Larwood, claiming she was spying on him, that she was working for 'them'. When she'd drowned, he'd thought perhaps Gerald had had a hand in it, but the police had regarded it as an accident, and he left it at that. Now it would seem that Gerald had more than one death on his conscience.

For a moment he was almost overcome by the hideousness of his own terrible judgement. Although he'd been fully aware of his brother's mental condition, he'd been so focused on helping Gerald *his* way that he hadn't appreciated the risk he might pose to others. He had, as Lia put it, let a murderer run around unchecked. He should have had him forcibly committed, not tried to persuade him out of his madness.

Clearing his throat, he said, 'All I can tell you is that your grandmother called, wanting to talk about the bomb threats. She knew Gerald was back, and had put two and two together. Said maybe we could work something out. So I suggested we should meet up, said I'd bring some food and wine. She agreed and I went to pick up a curry from The Goa, but then I realised I'd forgotten the wine. Susannah's was closed so I headed back to the farm to get some from the wine rack. I can't have been indoors more than a few minutes . . .'

He covered his face with his hands. 'I guess that's when he slipped something into the food. Maybe he'd overheard the phone call. But he didn't know I was coming back to the farm, did he? That was pure chance. Hell, he could've killed me as well! You think he meant to?'

Gerald still hadn't moved, and Lia wondered if he could hear them talking, through his coma, although he showed no signs of it.

Would he have wanted to harm his own brother? She doubted it. Aidan was the only person who'd listened to his rantings. Then she understood.

'Aidan, he knew you were a vegetarian,' she said, 'and wouldn't have eaten the lamb, so to his mind you were safe. He probably had several ideas of how he was going to prevent my grandmother from talking, and one of them was poison. I suspect slipping the beans in was part plan, part opportunity. Then, when he saw me come haring out of your barn after my discovery, he wanted to silence me too. That's why he went after me in the water.'

She shuddered to think what would have happened if he'd caught her in the barn. 'Did you teach him to dive?' she asked.

'A long time ago. I thought he'd forgotten how.'

'I saw him once, on the beach. I waved because I thought it was you, and got annoyed when he walked off. Jack was growling. I should've worked it out, but of course I didn't. You don't expect a dead person to suddenly not be dead.'

Aidan shook his head, his green eyes bloodshot and troubled, and something else. Something she couldn't read.

A last question still niggled. 'Did you tell Susannah he was back?'

'Of course. He's Zoe's father, and I wanted her to be prepared for a confrontation in case he sought her out. It took her a long time to get over the way he treated her. I thought a reconciliation might help them both.'

He sighed. 'You know, I once offered to shoulder the responsibility, but she wouldn't hear of it, didn't want me to ruin my life, et cetera. I expect in reality I'm a rather pale copy in comparison.'

'Not to me.'

He sent her a wan smile but didn't appear to be entirely convinced.

'I suppose he knows about Zoe,' she said.

'He's always known, but now he saw his daughter as something "they" could use to get at him. He had to either protect her by whisking her out of "their" reach, or simply eliminate the threat.'

Lia's scalp prickled with icy fingers at his words.

'Susannah's been living in terror these past few months,' he continued, 'partly because Zoe wanted to find out about her father and probably would've gone with him if he'd approached her, and partly because she feared for the rest of her family. I tried to keep Gerald occupied, but it hasn't been easy.'

'That must've been dreadful.' Lia felt a wave of sympathy engulf her. No wonder Susannah had been acting strangely. 'What happens now?' she asked.

Extricating himself from her, he rose and stood by the window, framed by the beginnings of a grey day. When he glanced back at her, she caught that look again. She hadn't liked it much the first time and liked it even less now.

'I'll be questioned, no doubt,' he said. 'You too, I imagine. What you choose to say is up to you. I don't expect you to lie for me.'

'It's my party, and I'll lie if I want to.'

He smiled, but it was tinged with sadness. A dead weight settled in her stomach.

'I think you'd better stay away from me, Lia,' he said. 'It's for the best.'

CHAPTER 29

'Why don't you let me be the judge of that?' Lia said and started towards him, but stopped when he held up his hand.

'Lia, I'm serious. There'll be reprisals. Gerald will be sent to a mental institution, and I expect I'll go to prison. Let's not forget the world is fighting a war on terror. That includes rooting out bomb-makers in deepest, darkest Norfolk. Not to mention it now looks like I'm guilty of hiding a murderer, even if he was out of his mind.' He turned to stare out the window. 'What we have – had – is special. I don't want it to be tainted by that.'

'But *prison*?' she queried. 'It's not really fair, is it? You were only trying to help him. Couldn't you pretend you didn't know what he was up to? With the bombs, I mean.'

He banged his fist against the window frame so hard the glass rattled. 'For fuck's sake, Lia, you were nearly killed because I'd lost track of him! I couldn't bear it if something else happened to you because of me. I made a monumental mistake, and now I need to face up to it.' Shoving his hands deep in his pockets, he turned his back on her again. 'There's nothing more to say.'

Oh, yes, she thought, plenty more, but perhaps now wasn't the time. They were both tired, and the strain of what had happened was beginning to take its toll. They needed to sleep on it, deal with it in the morning.

Not trusting herself to speak, she left without saying anything else.

In the hospital foyer she ran into Susannah's husband. Literally. He was carrying Ethan, who was asleep, collapsed against his shoulder. Fortunately the little boy didn't wake when they collided.

'Sorry, I didn't see you,' she said. 'I was miles away.'

'No problem. What are you doing here?'

Lia debated with herself whether to tell him or not. She had no idea how much he knew about Gerald's return and thought it best to give Aidan some time before all the questions. It would be all over the village soon enough.

'One of our divers had an accident last night.'

Nigel hoisted Ethan further up. 'Gosh! Is he or she okay?'

'It's not looking good.'

'Gosh!' he said again.

Changing the subject, Lia asked, 'What are *you* doing here? Is Ethan all right?'

'Oh, this little fella here is fine, just worn out.' He smiled suddenly, beaming from ear to ear.

'Susannah had a little girl last night. Don't worry, everything's okay,' he added when he caught Lia's expression. It was three weeks too early. 'Zoe's sleeping over with a friend, and my parents are away, so there was no one to take him. I had to bring him, but would you believe it, he just slept through it all.'

He smoothed a lock of hair away from Ethan's face. 'Good as gold, he is.'

'And Susannah?'

'They did an emergency Caesarian, but she and the baby are up on the ward now. I can take you to see her, if you'd like, unless . . .' He looked at her with concern, no doubt taking in her crumpled clothes and sleep-deprived face. 'Unless you'd rather be off.'

'I'd love to see her.'

He took her back to the postnatal ward. Susannah was sitting up in bed, struggling to get the baby to latch on, but the little girl wasn't co-operating and was waving her tiny fists and mewling like a kitten. Susannah was pale and had dark circles under her eyes, but smiled when she saw Lia, almost serenely.

'I've forgotten how to do this. Guess it'll come back to me.'

Lia sat down on the edge of the bed as the baby caught the nipple at last and attempted to suckle, still not effectively, but perhaps it was more for comfort and security than genuine hunger.

'I'll leave you to it,' said Nigel. 'I'll be back

466

later on. Is there anything you'd like me to get you from home, apart from what you've already asked for?'

Susannah looked at her husband holding their son, then down at her left hand which wasn't cradling the baby, then back at Nigel. 'My wedding ring,' she said. 'It's on the dressing table.'

'I do love a woman who's got her priorities right.' Nigel winked at Lia, then left them.

'I had to take it off while I was pregnant,' Susannah explained. 'Because of the swelling.'

Lia nodded. They sat in silence for a while just watching the baby's tiny mouth moving rhythmically, instinctively.

'Gerald's in hospital,' said Lia.

Susannah's eyes flew to her face. 'What happened?' she asked. Lia noticed she didn't say, *I thought he was dead.*

Lia told her, leaving nothing out of what she knew, and Susannah was able to fill in the details on her part. Then she cried, making no attempt at stopping the tears which rolled down her cheeks and into the baby's downy auburn hair.

Not so tough now, are you? Lia thought but without rancour. She couldn't pretend to understand exactly what Susannah had been going through.

The baby started fretting again, and Susannah dried her tears. 'I'm glad you're here. I wanted to ask you about names. When I was expecting her, I had a whole list of them, but now none of

467

them seem to fit.' She met Lia's eyes, for the first time giving her a genuinely friendly look. 'I'd be happy for you to choose one. And don't say Geraldine, please.'

'I wasn't going to.' Lia smiled and looked down at the prune-faced baby, dressed in a white baby-grow. She had red hair and a determined look about her, and although three weeks early, she seemed strong and healthy, so obviously a survivor. Mentally Lia ticked off the names associated with 'red' or 'strength' that she could remember, but then her thoughts took her in a completely different direction. Perhaps this baby was the person to bring everyone together.

'Erm, Wendy?' she suggested. 'I think it means "friend" or something.'

'Like from *Peter Pan*?'

'I was just thinking of the Lost Boys and all that. Silly really.'

'No, I like it.' Susannah smiled. 'Wendy it is. Thank you.'

Lia left mother and baby to rest and stepped out into the morning light just as the city was waking up to a new day. Meeting tiny Wendy had been a life-affirming moment, and despite Aidan's rebuff she was feeling more positive than she had in years, ready to embrace the future.

She wanted him, loved him now she gave herself time to truly examine her feelings, but she didn't *need* him to complete her. That was as it should be. Once she'd needed Brett, or so she'd thought, but that was because he'd anchored her, in a sense, even if she didn't belong in his world. Now, she'd found her own place, partly because of Aidan, but mostly because she'd stopped running.

She'd make him come around, but she'd give him time. And if they had to conduct their relationship from the confines of a prison cell, so what? She didn't want to think about that right now.

Gerald's heart lasted ten days and then gave out. The funeral was a quiet affair with only the closest family present; Aidan, his sister, his mother and her new husband, Derek, and Lia. Susannah came too, with little Wendy in a pram. Also, discreetly, at the back of the chapel, DCI Sommersby and DS Cromer.

As the coffin slid behind the curtain and into the crematorium, Lia caught Aidan's eyes across the aisle. She smiled in a way she hoped was encouraging, and he smiled back, but then he turned away as his mother needed him. Eileen had put on a brave face throughout the ceremony, but towards the end, having lost her son not once but twice, she could no longer contain her grief. Hiccoughing sobs echoed off the stone walls, and Lia felt tears well up in her own eyes at the terrible waste.

Susannah squeezed her hand. 'Pub?' she whispered.

'You bet.'

They went to the Crown Hotel and found an upholstered bench in a quiet corner. Susannah settled Wendy while Lia fetched drinks.

'I found Ivy's camera by the way,' Lia said when she sat down. 'On top of the fridge of all places. As you said, it had pictures on it of your shop and other places in the village. And of Gerald. That's why you wanted it, wasn't it? And why you were going through the drawers of Ivy's dresser. You were looking for pictures of him because you were afraid I was going to put two and two together. Am I right?'

Susannah gave a brief nod.

'It's okay, I'm not angry with you. I understand.' She took a sip of her drink. 'Question is, do you still want the pictures? I don't need them.'

Susannah was silent for a moment. 'It might be nice for Zoe. You know, one day.' She sighed, visibly relieved, then she smiled. 'Have you heard the latest about the investigation?'

'No, I wanted to give Aidan some space, so I've stayed away. What's happening?'

'Well, it turns out that just before that fatal dive, Gerald wrote an open letter to the CO of every single army base in Norfolk, and the MoD. Apparently it's some ranting manifesto where he explains the reasons for his bombing campaign. One thing he says is that his brother – and I quote – "is blameless of any wrongdoing". Not that Aidan ever did anything wrong. They were going to charge him with failure to disclose information pertaining to an act of terrorism, I think; but it looks like they've decided to drop the case.'

'That's a relief,' said Lia. 'I wonder what he'll do now?'

Susannah shrugged. 'Who knows? Seems to me he can do anything he likes.'

Anything he likes, thought Lia, and wondered if that involved her. He wasn't going to prison as he'd feared. He was no longer caring for a sick brother. He knew how Lia felt about him.

So what was he waiting for?

There was still no sign of him, and though she ached to see him, Lia threw all her efforts into selling Ivy's house. Eventually she found a buyer who was ready to exchange contracts by the end of March.

Then it was time to face her demons. She hadn't dived since that awful afternoon, had thought she could never bring herself to do it again, but she hadn't reckoned with the pull of the water.

On a clear morning, she drove to the usual beach in her new car, a chilli-red Mini Cooper with a white roof. Jack jumped out, ran up the bank and barked at the surf. Lia strapped on her rented BCD and picked up her mask and fins.

'Come on, you need to stay in the car.'

Jack barked in protest.

'Fine, you can wait on the beach. I'm sure there's something disgusting for you to chew.'

Her words were harsh, but she didn't mean them. Jack had been glued to her side since she'd returned from Gerald's hospital bed and kept her company each time the old dreams resurfaced, fortunately with decreasing regularity. In the end she'd exorcised the images completely.

Crossing the sand, she held up her hand to shield her eyes against the sun and looked towards the Point where the seals were sunning themselves. It seemed a lifetime since she'd last seen this sight.

Telling Jack firmly to stay put, she was just heading for the sea when she caught sight of another diver walking along the beach towards her. She felt a stab of irritation. Now that she'd finally come this far, she didn't want any interruptions.

Squinting against the glare, she kept her eyes on the intruder. There was something familiar about the way he walked – she was sure it was a he – slightly unevenly, perhaps because of the weight of his equipment.

Her heart lurched all of a sudden. It wasn't . . . it couldn't be Aidan, surely? This guy had short hair.

Jack jumped up, disobeying her orders, and flew across the sand barking and yapping, doing a strange little dance around the man's legs. The man scooped him up in one arm, and she saw then that it was Aidan after all. She felt a rush of emotion, but managed to stop herself from running towards him and throwing her arms around his neck. He might be here by chance, and she didn't want to make a fool of herself.

She watched him come towards her, his eyes not leaving her face, and he was grinning. She hadn't seen him in ages, and here he was, *grinning* like the cat that got the cream. It should have annoyed her, but instead she had to swallow back a lump in her throat.

'I was wondering if you were in the business for a diving buddy,' he said when he was close enough.

'Maybe. I've heard it's best to be two.'

'As your instructor I ought to take you to task for being here on your own in the first place.'

'Well, what are you waiting for?'

Aidan set his gear on the ground and put his hands on her hips. She slipped her arms around his neck. Their kiss was gentle at first as they each tested the other's sincerity, but soon the weeks of separation had them touching, exploring, burning for more.

Damned neoprene suits.

'And do you think,' he said after a while, slightly breathless, 'you might consider being my diving buddy, for better for worse, to love and to cherish till death do us part?'

'You call that a proposal? Tch.' Lia crossed her arms and tried her best to look stern.

He smiled. 'It's the best I've got. Lia, I've loved you since I was sixteen. You're more real to me now, but a lot has happened to me since then. I'm older, wiser hopefully, but I do come with a lot of baggage. There'll always be this . . . other me inside. Mr Hyde, you called him once. Is that something you can live with?'

'I think so,' she replied.

'You *think* so?'

'I know so, but why don't you kiss me again so I can be sure?'

'If you insist,' he said and gave her more than

she'd bargained for. They came up for air to a scornful snort from Jack who sat on the sand beside them.

'And you, matey,' said Aidan, 'had better get used to it.'